·K·A·N·D·I·D·E·
THE MASKS OF DECEPTION

BY

DIANA S. ZIMMERMAN

BOOK THREE OF THE CALABIYAU CHRONICLES

Braveship
BOOKS

NOESIS PUBLISHING

LOS ANGELES, CALIFORNIA

First Edition

ISBN-13: 978-1-939398-91-8
ISBN-10: 1-939398-91-6

Text copyright © 2017 by Diana S. Zimmerman.
Illustrations © 2017 Noesis Publishing.

Kandide: The Secret of the Mists
Kandide: The Lady's Revenge
Kandide: The Masks of Deception
Kandide's Coloring Book
All logos trademark Diana S. Zimmerman
All rights reserved.

12 11 10 9 8 7 6 5 4 3 2 1   10 11 12 13 14 15/0

Published by Braveship Books in association with Noesis Publishing, a division of Noesis Communications International, Inc.
Los Angeles, CA - kandide@kandide.com

www.kandide.com

www.braveshipbooks.com - www.noesispublishing.com

Printed in the U.S.A.

Kandide: The Masks of Deception is dedicated to:

The hundreds of thousands of fans around the world who have read the Kandide Series. With special thanks to the students, principal, and faculty at Sandy Searles Miller Elementary School in Las Vegas, Nevada who inspired Teren and Adriana's visit to the human realm.

As well as each of the individuals who inspired and helped with Book Three: Sherry Bennett, Jim Bunkelman, Jeanie Cunningham, Barbara Daust, Patricia Fry, Ishan Goel, Carol Ivy, Collins Key, Devan Key, Kathleen Longspaugh, Bruce Merrin, Ninon Pope, Paul Sponaugle, Brooks Wachtel, Lori West, Lee Wills, Nada Wright, Robert Zraick, Cynthia Unninayar, who inspired my faery collection; Alice Shultz, who read the first faery story to me; and Stan Shultz, who believed.

And to each of the Junior Editors of Book Three:
Blake, Elizabeth, Hailey, Isabelle, Kevin, Monica, and Vivian Irene.

Games

Music

More Stories

Contests

Teachers' Guides

Downloadable Artwork

Talk to Diana

And so much more...

WWW.KANDIDE.COM

At times, we each wear masks of deception.
Some are for good. Some are for evil.
But where vengeance grows, no kindness flows.
Cunning and spite consume delight,
devouring all within its sight.

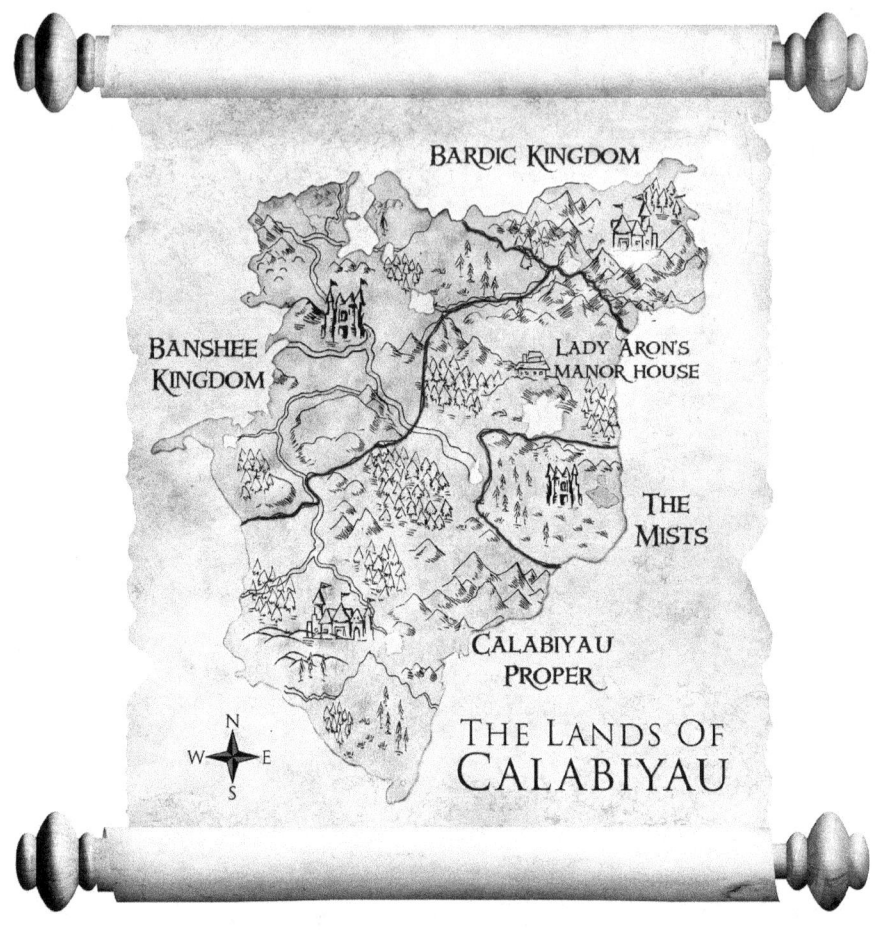

BARDIC KINGDOM

BANSHEE
KINGDOM

LADY ARON'S
MANOR HOUSE

THE
MISTS

CALABIYAU
PROPER

THE LANDS OF
CALABIYAU

MAP OF CALABIYAU

THE FOUR KINGDOMS

Within the elemental dimension lies a world that exists in parallel with our own. It's called Calabiyau. In the language of the ancients, "Cala" (pronounced like "calla" lily) means land. And "Bi-yau" (pronounced like "by" and "yow" that rhymes with "how") is the surname of the original conquering monarch. Four separatist Kingdoms maintain control.

CALABIYAU PROPER - THE KINGDOM OF THE FEE

The largest of the Kingdoms, Calabiyau Proper has been ruled since the beginning of ancient time by Kandide's relatives, the Biyau family. Today, it is governed by a reigning monarch, along with the High Council consisting of representatives from each of the twelve primary Fée Clans.

CALABIYAU WEST - THE BANSHEE KINGDOM

When precious gems were discovered in the Year of the Fée 88 BT, (Beginning of Time) the Banshee Clans split off from the other Fée. Since that time, hundreds of different monarchs have ruled this separatist Kingdom, mostly women. Crown Princess Cyndara is next in line.

CALABIYAU EAST - THE CHATEAU IN THE MISTS

Founded in the Year of the Fée 26,851 BT, the Château is presided over by Selena and Jake as an independently governed territory. Its walled Castle and seven villages are surrounded by the dead-land known as the Mists. The land is home to most Imperfects—those who aren't physically perfect—as well as all remaining griffins.

CALABIYAU NORTH - THE BARDIC KINGDOM

Founded in 20,247 BT and presided over by High Priestess Viviana, this secretive land is home to wizards and bards. It lies in the northeastern part of Calabiyau. Merin spent his last days at the Bardic Temple.

PROLOGUE

The sun's rays streaked across the sky, shining as brightly as ever. The woodland birds sang just as sweetly. And Princess Tara was free from the spell that trapped her in the block of ice. So why was the mood of Kandide's subjects so dark? Lady Aron had not been seen in months, and yet her sinister magic continued to permeate villages throughout the Kingdom. Kandide's popularity continued to decline. She was, however, more determined than ever to change the destiny of her reign and win the favor of her detractors. If only the fates would cooperate. Some days being Queen just isn't all it's cracked up to be.\

All this beauty, and only sadness consumed Kandide's thoughts.

ONE

Turmoil cast its relentless destruction across the land. Evil inflamed every village. The only place that seemed to invite calm was the Meadows.

Now this...

Kandide stared at Teren's left hand. "You know how I hate the sight of blood."

"It's only a drop." Her brother pressed the bramble thorn deeper into his finger and squeezed the wound to make it bleed.

"It's still blood. Are you sure you want to do this?" Calabiyau's teen-queen wasn't at all sure that what her brother wanted to do was a good idea.

Teren was not yet fifteen (in human years) and his journey to the Bardic Temple, a little more than three months earlier, had almost cost him his life—now he was determined to go back.

"Please think it through," she pleaded. "You know I—"

"I have thought it through, Kandide. And I know how dangerous it is. Something inside me says I have to go—like it's calling to me. I can't explain it. You read the letter Viviana gave me when I left her Kingdom."

Teren handed his sister a brown envelope then squeezed his finger again to keep the purple-red blood flowing.

She opened it and re-read the High Priestess's words:

My Dearest Prince Teren,

I have given you this letter because you passed yet another test—that of duty over desire. I know you will not consider returning to the Bardic Temple until the spell that entraps your sister, Princess Tara, is broken. Once she is free, it will be time for you to finally embark upon your own destiny. A fingerprint in your blood will bind your fate. Tarry not, as you have much to accomplish.

High Priestess Viviana

It was an invitation Kandide knew her brother could not refuse. Tara was, indeed, free from the block of ice that had entrapped her. She also knew that even if Teren made it to the Bardic Temple— home to the most powerful of mages—his life would be extremely difficult. He was, after all, born a prince, and as such enjoyed the protection of the court, along with its many fineries… *and comforts,* she thought. Living under Viviana's tutelage would be devoid of any such luxuries. *Besides, Teren's powerful magic—untrained as it is—often comes in handy right here in Calabiyau. And with the dark magic that seems to be lurking everywhere, I need him even more.*

Kandide's golden hair shimmered in the bright afternoon sunlight. Her purple-blue eyes gazed out across the vast carpet of green moss that covered most of the Meadows. It was fall and yet every plant was still in bloom. Bright red zinnias; blue cockleshells; pink, white, and yellow daisies; along with pansies in every color created prismatic tapestries that stretched to the base of the mountains that stood guard over this tranquil valley. In another month, the Meadow's forest of pomegranate trees would be ripe with juicy red fruit. It was, perhaps, the only peaceful place left in her Kingdom.

All this beauty, and yet only sadness consumed her thoughts. Kandide loved the Meadows and all its animals as much as Teren did. By being there, she hoped she might talk some sense into him about staying.

Noticing a brown beetle that had flipped on its back and was struggling to turn over, she reached down to help it. "There you go, little one." The beetle quickly flew away. Was she helping her brother do the same? "Perhaps you should wait until spring," she argued. "Maybe the raids on the villages will have stopped by then. It's really not safe to travel right now."

"You sound like Mother, always worrying. I survived one journey there."

"Barely. You were almost killed—twice." Kandide would not relent.

"But I wasn't!"

"Can't you think about anyone but yourself?"

Teren looked up at his sister. "That's pretty funny coming from you, Kandide."

"Well, what about me? What about what I want?"

"This isn't about you—for once." He snatched the letter from her and quickly pressed his finger against it. His fate was bound with his own blood.

Kandide's heart sank. At that very moment, her brother, who was nearly as headstrong as she was, had defined his destiny.

They both stared at his fingerprint on the letter. Viviana's message melted away, replaced by a glowing three-dimensional image of the High Priestess. She looked exactly the way Teren remembered her, with long black hair, large brown eyes, and olive skin. Her white robe was spun from the finest linen with threads of pure silver woven through it. A glowing crescent moon, suspended by a diamond studded crown, rested on her forehead.

Viviana turned to speak to Kandide. She offered only the slightest nod of respect. "Your brother has made his choice, Your Majesty. He belongs to the elders now, until such time as he learns to control his magic and has earned his rite of passage. How long that takes, only the fates can tell. Come, Teren, this is no longer your home."

"I will, Viviana, but first I have to pack my things and say goodbye to my mother and sister."

"That option is no longer yours. You belong to the Bardic Council now. We are your only family." A bolt of silvery light streaked from Viviana's hand.

"Teren!" Kandide shrieked. Her words, however, merely served to scatter a gaggle of black spotted geese that had been floating on the nearby river. The tousle-haired prince became translucent. Then he was gone. The letter, with its words once again intact, drifted to the ground.

"What have you done, my little brother?" *Mother will never forgive me,* she thought, angrier more with herself for not stopping him, than at Teren. *How could I have let him go? But then, how could I have stopped him? I may be Calabiyau's Queen, but I can't force him to not pursue his dream of becoming a powerful magi.* She knew his remarkable powers were the reason Viviana wanted him.

Everyone was aware of Teren's exceptional Talent—the gift of magic so strong that, even as a small child, he could create most spells by merely reading about them. Some didn't quite work the way they were intended, but nevertheless... *If only you hadn't wasted so much of your time creating silly pranks,* she thought, remembering how he delighted in causing mischief. Like the time he spelled all of the mirrors in the Castle to make her look really old. Fortunately, it only lasted for a day, but it was enough to make Kandide double the amount of night cream she used for the next few months. Another time he spelled the mirrors so she sneezed every time she looked at her own reflection. It took the royal healers nearly two weeks to figure out that Teren's magic, not a cold, was the culprit.

From what he had told her about the Bardic Council and Viviana, pranks would not be tolerated. *At least that's good,* she thought.

Kandide slid her hand into the pocket of her flowing blue satin trousers. She quickly pulled it out. The silver spiral around the quill of the white feather she always carried nearly burned her fingers. Her father, the late King Toeyad, gave her the feather upon his deathbed, not quite a year ago. "Keep this always near," he told her. "It will serve you well."

And so it has, as both a warning and a source of power in time of danger. She could tell by the spiral's intense heat that something was wrong, very wrong—something far more threatening than Teren's departure. *I must go,* she thought. In a shimmer of sparks, she vanished.

Reappearing inside her mother's chamber, Kandide found Tiyana sitting at her writing desk. Her sister, Princess Tara, was seated on the velvet swing near one of the room's many arched windows. Twisted vines of purple morning glories suspended it from the ceiling. It was Tara's favorite place to sit and chat with her mother.

Except for their manner of dressing and the color of their eyes—Tiyana's were purple-blue like Kandide's and Tara's were green—they looked very much alike. Both had auburn hair and pale green skin, unlike Kandide who favored her father, the late King Toeyad, and was fair. As always, Tara was dressed in britches and boots. She preferred to spend her time healing injured animals in the forest, such as the rare blue-eyed winged mother lynx she had just saved.

Kandide was thrilled to hear about Tara's success, especially that there was a new cub. "That's so wonderful, Tara. You are truly amazing. But I have some bad news. Teren... he's... he's gone."

"What do you mean Teren's gone, Kandide?" Tiyana stood up, straightening her dark green skirt.

Tara stopped the back-and-forth motion of the swing. "Gone where?"

Explaining what had just happened, Kandide added, "It was all so fast. I couldn't change his mind."

Tara heals a rare
Blue-Eyed Winged Lynx

Tiyana's brow creased with resignation. "No, I don't suppose you could. Your bother has always been far too impulsive for his own good. May the earthly spirits protect him."

Tara walked over to her mother. "At least Viviana could have let him say goodbye and pack a few of his things."

"From what he told me about how simply they live," Kandide replied, "I don't think he'll need much." She still couldn't imagine Teren exchanging the luxuries of the Castle for a tiny sleeping chamber. Living like that—for anyone, especially powerful mages—seemed utterly ridiculous to her. "I'm sure he'll tire of it soon and come home."

"If they allow him to leave." Tiyana sounded unconvinced.

"I'm sure they'll let us visit him," Tara said. "Now that Jake and Lord Salitar know the way and where the dangers are, we could travel there in a little over a week."

"And that we shall certainly do, but not right now." Tiyana surprised both Tara and Kandide with her response. "With so many riots against Imperfects going on, I don't think any of us should leave. Kandide, you need all the support we can give you—which is what makes Teren's departure so unfortunate at this time. From General Mintz's last report, seven of the twelve clans have experienced major protests against your rule."

"And the newest uprisings have been even more violent than before," Tara added. "I've healed at least three dozen Fée who have been brought here from various clans. Lars and the other healers have healed even more. From what they've all told me, the riots are not just about granting Imperfects equality. Many Fée suffered terribly from your having deployed the Frost to bring about winter in the middle of summer."

Tara's words were all too familiar to Kandide. The High Council, Calabiyau's ruling body, had warned of the consequences and, with so many clans having lost their summer crops due to the cold freeze, her popularity was at an all-time low.

"I deployed the Frost to save your life, Tara," she insisted. "Without it, the ice that entombed you would have melted in the summer heat and you would have died. We now know that's exactly what Lady Aron wanted. We also know that she created the spell that entrapped you, and I'm convinced she's behind all these protests. As far as Imperfects having equal rights, all Fée, even those who aren't physically perfect, deserve equality. No one agrees with that more than you and Mother. So, even if it means losing the Crown, I would do both of them again, given the same circumstance."

"Losing the Crown is not what I fear, my daughter. It's losing your life that worries me. You must take these death threats seriously. Even going to the Meadows like that with Teren was a risk. Perhaps you should also consider postponing your marriage to Jake for a while. Having an Imperfect rule by your side may not be the best idea right now."

"What? Mother, what are you saying?" Kandide's brow furled in stunned silence. "How could you even think such a thing?" Tiyana loved Jake like a son—his parents were her best friends. "Jake lost his feet in the Clan Wars saving the lives of his troops. He may not be physically perfect, but he's far more perfect than those who disparage him. Imperfect or not, our wedding goes as planned—in early December, one month after I deploy the Frost and winter settles in. My radiance will have fully returned, and I shall look my most beautiful. Oh, dear, I do hope Viviana will let Teren come back for the wedding."

"Mother only meant..."

"I know what Mother meant, Tara." Kandide glared, first at her sister then at Tiyana. "She's worried about what my subjects will think. When it comes to marrying Jake, I don't care. And now if you will both excuse me, I have a kingdom to run. In spite of the dangers, I am still Queen—at least for now!"

With a flick of her wrist, Kandide vanished.

TWO

Spirals of black smoke eclipsed the horizon. Kandide's lungs were heavy with the soot that filled the air. She reined her white mare to an abrupt stop. Reflections of the fiery-orange sky danced off the horse's silver armor. General Mintz insisted that she wear protective clothing when traveling away from the Castle. Kandide agreed only as far as her beloved horse was concerned.

"I won't have my subjects see me dressed for battle," she insisted. "I don't care how dangerous you think it is. We are not at war."

Normally being outdoors relaxed the tensions of her day. Not on this journey. Sliding out of her saddle, she led her horse down a cobblestone path and looked around. What she saw, gripped her stomach.

How could anyone...?

Smoldering ash was all that remained of what was once a thriving thatched-roof Bavarian-style village. *These were the homes of a Farming Clan,* she thought, *mothers, fathers, children—and now all their possessions are gone.* Chairs, beds, tables, everything they owned had been reduced to burning embers. *Why?*

The nearby fields lay dead with crops that had suffered from the summer snowstorms. Kandide couldn't blame her subjects for being angry. But to burn a village—that was beyond all reason. She had, after all, sent emergency food supplies to each clan.

Her eyes glimpsed a bright pink shape amid the rubble. She

knelt down to pick up a half-charred doll. It was the only thing left from the family's cottage. *I had one just like this as child,* she thought, blinking back a tear. *Of course, mine was prettier, but nearly the same.* No matter how many other toys her parents gave her, that little black-haired doll with its brightly colored dress and wings was always Kandide's favorite. Every night Tiyana had to tuck it into bed with her or she would refuse to go to sleep.

Kandide carefully placed the doll next to a nearby tree then turned to speak to General Mintz. He and four guards had accompanied her to this southernmost township. "From the amount of heat that consumed the village," she said, looking at the still-smoldering logs, "it could well be the work of Lady Aron. None of the plants or flowers are even scorched, and yet every house has been incinerated."

"It took some powerful magic, that's for sure," the silver-haired general replied. "It seems as though there's no limit to the amount of evil that Fire Fée is willing to conjure." His ears caught the sudden sound of cracking twigs. "We should be going, Your Majesty. This area is not secure." Mintz motioned to the four guards. "Surround Her Majesty. I'm going to see who that is."

Kandide's scream overshadowed his order. A razor sharp arrow had ripped through her left arm.

Racing to her side, Mintz shouted to the guards, "Seize him! He's in the corn stalks. And keep your eyes open, there could be others."

Two of the soldiers flew after the perpetrator, while the other two closed in around the General and Kandide.

"I'm alright," she said, more stunned from the attack than the wound. "I think it's only superficial."

Nevertheless, General Mintz ripped open the sleeve of her bright red jacket. "My apologies, Your Majesty, but I must stop the bleeding." He quickly tied his pocket-handkerchief just above the gash. "This should help. You're lucky he wasn't a better aim."

"At least I'm not wearing white," she said, watching the bleeding

KANDIDE IN THE BURNED VILLAGE

begin to subside. *I really do hate the sight of blood,* she thought. *Especially my own.* Glancing up, Kandide saw a bedraggled farm boy being pulled out from the corn stalks. *He's no more than Teren's age. Could he be the perpetrator?* The defiant look on his face told her all she needed to know—he had shot the arrow with the intent of killing her. "What's your name?" she asked as they drew him near.

Struggling to break free, the lad replied without the slightest bit of respect, "What does it matter? Neither my name nor my family holds any importance to your kind. First, you let Imperfects live as equals, then you destroy our crops to save your sister. I just regret that my arrow missed its mark—your heart."

"Take him away." General Mintz motioned to the guard.

"No," Kandide ordered. "Take his bow and arrows then set him free."

"But, Your Majesty," Mintz protested, "he just tried to kill you."

"Please, General, release him. And make sure he gets enough gold to rebuild his village and buy food for his clan." Seeing Mintz hesitate, Kandide continued, "That's an order."

Mintz turned to the farm boy. "You fool of a child, had you killed Her Majesty, you would have destroyed our world. She's the keeper of the Gift of the Frost. Without her, all of us will perish, yourself included." He grudgingly motioned for the two guards to let the lad go.

Though free, the boy did not run away, nor did his words soften. He glared straight at Kandide. "What do I care? You've already destroyed my world. That doll you were holding—it belonged to my sister." His eyes filled with tears. "She was just three. My brother was only five. After the other houses caught fire, my mother and father ran from the fields into our house to save them, when it exploded. I was in the next village or I would be dead, too. My world is gone. There is nothing left for me. Your gold won't change that."

The sudden surge of pain in Kandide's arm was nothing compared to the pain she felt listening to his words. Her stomach climbed to her throat. It was good she had not eaten breakfast. A year ago, she thought being Queen would be about parties and holding court. How could things have changed so much?

For the first time, Kandide truly understood the very real suffering of her subjects. She fought back her own tears. "I'm very sorry. So very sorry." Her mind flashed back to when she thought Tara had been killed. "I can't even imagine the pain you must feel. And you're right; there is no amount of gold that will replace your family. Deploying the Frost and losing your crops was my doing. But destroying your home and this village was not. I swear to you, on my honor as your Queen, when I find out who did it—and I will—they'll be punished."

The fury in the farm boy's brown eyes told Kandide that her promise, like her title, meant nothing to him. "My family and my village aren't the only ones destroyed under your rule. Your father was a great King. You're terrible. You'd best tell your guards to kill me now, because I'll make another bow and, given the chance, my arrow won't miss."

"Then I shall have to make sure you don't have that chance," she said, struggling to remain standing. Her vision was beginning to blur. In spite of the growing pain in her arm, she forced a regal stance. *I am, after all, his Queen.* "Put a sleeping spell on him, General—a mild one that will wear off shortly after we depart. Then make sure he's given enough gold from my personal treasury to rebuild his village. Anyone who has suffered so much deserves nothing less."

She turned back to the lad. It took all her strength to keep from collapsing. "There is nothing more I can say except that I will do everything I can to see you get justice. In time, I hope you can build a new life." Her eyes could no longer focus. Something was wrong, very wrong. "General, spell him. We need to be going."

Mintz did as Kandide ordered. With a few mumbled words, the dark-haired lad instantly slumped to the ground. Denan, one of the guards, placed him under the oak tree where Kandide had put his sister's doll.

"He'll wake up in about a half an hour," General Mintz explained. "But I still think we should lock him up."

"Perhaps…" Kandide dropped to her knees. *Could he have poisoned the arrow?* It was the last thought she had before her mind froze in blackness.

"Bring the horses," Mintz shouted to Denan. With Kandide in his arms, he instantly transported to her private chamber inside the Castle. After ordering her personal guards to fetch Tara and Tiyana, he gently placed the lifeless Queen on her bed. Her skin was bright red, and her breathing was beginning to slow. General Mintz tightened the tourniquet on her arm.

Tara, followed by Tiyana, raced into the room. She immediately poured a generous amount of a dark brown liquid onto her sister's wound. "This should counter the poison." She loosened the tourniquet on Kandide's arm so the ointment could begin to flow into her blood stream.

Minutes seemed like hours as all stood silent watching and waiting. Slowly, Kandide's color began to normalize. Her breathing also returned to normal.

Only when Tiyana was certain that her daughter was out of danger, did she ask General Mintz, "What happened?"

He explained about the village and the farm boy, adding, "As her mother, Your Highness, I don't suppose that you would have any better luck convincing our fearless young Queen to not venture out to the villages? Every time she hears about any kind of incident, she insists upon going to see what happened."

"I've certainly tried." Tiyana wiped the perspiration from Kandide's brow. "Perhaps nearly being killed will convince her to stay home."

Kandide's eyes fluttered open. Her vision was still blurred and her shoulder ached. Attempting to sit up, she spoke in a strained voice. "What good is a Queen if she hides in her Castle?"

"What good is a Queen if she's dead?" Tiyana scolded. "You're just lucky Tara was able to stop the poison from reaching your heart."

"Actually," Tara told her sister, "it was the quick thinking of General Mintz in tying that tourniquet around your arm to slow the blood flow that probably saved your life. Now lie still, I need to heal your wound."

She passed her hand over Kandide's arm. Silver pulses of light emerged from her fingertips. As they touched her sister's skin, it began to knit back together, leaving only a thin red line where the gash had been. "Here, drink this." Tara removed a small vial of golden liquid from her vest pocket and handed it to Kandide. "It will counter any lingering effects of the poison."

Kandide took a sip. Coughing, she practically choked trying to get it down. "What did you give me? If I didn't know better, I'd think *you* were trying to poison me."

"Is your vision clearing?"

Kandide looked up at her sister then around the room. "It is much better."

"Good, then stop complaining and drink the rest of it."

"Do as Tara says," Tiyana ordered. "And I want you to promise me that you won't venture out again as long as the riots continue. Next time, you may not be so lucky. If you can't think of yourself, think of the Gift."

Kandide placed the empty vial on her nightstand. Her mouth puckered from the liquid's bitter taste, yet in just those few seconds her vision had completely cleared and she was feeling much stronger. "I can't promise, Mother. I thank you all for saving my life, but my subjects must know that their Queen is there to help alleviate their suffering."

"Your subjects must also know that our world will not end because you get yourself killed," Tiyana scolded. "And that their Queen doesn't risk their fate on foolish choices." She picked up a scroll that lay on a side dresser near her daughter's bed. "Perhaps, you will at least forego the invitation by Crown Princess Cyndara to attend the Games."

Kandide stood up. She was still a bit wobbly, but determined to take the control back of her body. "The Games are starting? When?" Taking the scroll, she unrolled it and scanned the invite. "Cyndara's challenge—it begins tomorrow. Has it been forty-five days since King Nastae's passing?"

"It has," General Mintz replied. "The reverence honoring his rule as King is complete. The Banshee Crown Princess must now battle Lord Mywerk for the right to be crowned."

"We can only hope she wins." Kandide heaved a deep sigh. She was certain that Mywerk was somehow connected to Lady Aron and the failed attempt to attack the Château in the dead-lands known as the Mists only a couple months earlier. A sudden thought crossed her mind. "Lord Mywerk is a member of the Bardic Council and a powerful magi. Cyndara said he's the great-great-grandson of Merlin."

The color drained from Tiyana's face. "You don't suppose that's the reason Viviana was so anxious to get Teren there, do you?"

"That's exactly what I'm wondering," Kandide replied. "Though Teren's magic is undisciplined, with the proper instruction, I'm sure his Talent could be equal in strength to Lord Mywerk. Once he's trained, the two of them together would be unstoppable."

"And having him at the Bardic Temple," Tara added, "where he's under Viviana's control, certainly limits our ability to help Cyndara—or us, for that matter. Maybe we should go visit Teren and persuade him to return home."

"We should, but not just yet." Kandide looked down at the scroll. "Cyndara's invitation says she'll announce the battle game they are to play in the morning, and the challenge will begin tomorrow afternoon. The journey to the Bardic Temple, even if we had transport coordinates, which we don't, would take twice that amount of time—and without them, almost a week. No, Tara, I think the best thing we can do is to be at those Games."

"Please, Your Majesty," General Mintz objected, "if what you say is true about Lord Mywerk and Lady Aron working together, and he wins the Game, you won't be safe."

"Then let's hope Cyndara wins," she insisted. "Send a reply to the Crown Princess. Tell her that four of us will be attending."

Lines of concern creased Mintz's face. "Four? But, Your Majesty, I respectfully insist that you take at least twice that many guards."

"I don't intend to take any guards."

TEREN IN HIS TINY ROOM AT THE BARDIC TEMPLE

THREE

Teren woke with a throbbing headache. The zap Viviana gave him still pounded in his head. His back ached as well—and no wonder, the wooden bed where he had been sleeping was nothing more than a board covered by a thin blanket and a brown-and-orange patchwork quilt. A small dresser-desk, chair, and wall-mounted bookshelf were the only other pieces of furniture.

This isn't going to work, he thought, scrutinizing the tiny room. He stretched his shoulder muscles and rotated his wings. Teren felt the uneven wooden boards under his bare feet. *At least they could have put a rug on the floor. I am, after all, a prince and this is a castle... well, sort of, anyway.* He fully intended to speak to Viviana about his accommodations, as well as that bolt of light she knocked him out with. *I'm at the Bardic Temple to study magic, not be tortured.*

The simple white cotton robe he found himself dressed in—well, that wouldn't do either. He'd need his own clothes back and, since he didn't have time to pack, order additional trousers, shirts, and jackets from their court seamstress.

A knock on Teren's door interrupted his thoughts. "Come in," he called, still twisting his shoulders and wings. A boyish grin replaced his annoyance. "Adriana!"

She looked even prettier than when he met her nearly two months earlier on his first trip to the Bardic Temple. Her long silky black hair was pulled back and tied with a pale blue ribbon. She was dressed in a white robe, similar to his, except for the silver chain at her waist. Her brown eyes sparkled with delight as she entered his room. Teren could only think that she was the most beautiful Fée he had ever seen—even if she was mostly wizard and didn't have wings. "It's really great to see you again," he said trying to conceal his overly eager tone.

"It's great to see you, as well, Prince Teren. Mother sends her apologies for zapping you so hard. She only meant to have you sleep during the hours it takes to transport from your land. From the size of that bump on your forehead, I'd say she overdid it quite a bit."

"It's okay. I'm just glad she wasn't mad or something."

Adriana chuckled. "That you don't want to see. In any case, we're going to be late for our lessons if we don't hurry. Come, I'll show you where the learning chambers are located."

"Can I get my clothes back first? I really don't want to go around in this." He gestured to the white robe he was wearing.

Adriana simply smiled. "It looks better with a belt." She handed him the silver chain that was wrapped around one of the wooden bedposts.

"Are you saying that I have to wear this robe?"

"Well, it's better than nothing," she teased. "But to answer your question, it's what we all wear."

Just one more thing to discuss with Viviana, he thought, not wanting to be difficult—especially to Adriana. "I am a Prince you know. That should count for something."

"Very little around here." Her smile broadened. "Shall we be going? There are penalties for being late, and you certainly don't want to have your privileges taken away,"

"Privileges?" He looked around. "Like what?"

"Like this chamber. Most new attendees sleep in the group halls. Viviana felt it better to give you a private room to start with. Now, shall we go before you lose the privilege of it?" She turned to leave.

"Sure." Teren shrugged. Looking down, he realized that he was also missing his boots. The only shoes in his room were a pair of rope sandals. Slipping them on, he hurried after her down the hallway that led away from his chamber. "Please tell Viviana that I want to speak to her. These clothes really aren't for me."

"I'll tell her—if I see her. It's rare that she speaks to any of us." Adriana motioned for him to enter an empty room. "Your first lesson is here. My class is farther down the hall."

Teren stepped inside. "So, where is everybody?" But Adriana had already left. Except for one chair and a large velum book sitting on a wooden pedestal, the room was empty, without even a window to let in the morning light. *One more thing I need to discuss with Viviana,* he thought, walking over to the book and opening its dark red cover. *Learning doesn't have to be so dreary. Even our Royal Library has a domed skylight.*

"You have not been given permission to touch that," a deep voice rang out.

Teren turned around. It was Lord Centrod, Adriana's father, the Supreme High Priest of the Bardic Council. He was also dressed in a long white robe.

"Why do you always enter like that?" Teren flashed back to when they had met on his first visit to the Temple. The white-haired wizard seemed to always appear and disappear without notice, and always from the opposite direction Teren was facing.

"Would you prefer I ring a bell before entering?" Centrod snapped his fingers. A silver school bell with a brown wooden handle material-ized at his fingertips. He gave it a jingle. "Does this work for you?"

"I wasn't meaning to be disrespectful." Eager to change the subject, Teren asked, "So, what's my first lesson?" He couldn't wait to learn a new spell.

"You just had your first lesson—that of patience. Now you need to learn it." Centrod snapped his finger again and vanished, leaving the bell floating in midair.

Well, that's just great, Teren thought. *My head and back hurt. I'm running around in this silly robe, and now Centrod's mad at me. Besides, what's patience got to do with anything? Viviana wasn't very patient about getting me here.* He gently touched the still aching lump on his head. *Okay, guess I'll have to do a little magic of my own.* With a gesture and spoken spell, his robe changed into a white cotton shirt, green satin vest, and brown trousers. Looking at his feet, he said, "Forgot my boots." With another gesture, the sandals changed, as well. "Much better. Now to find Viviana so I can get some real clothes made. This spell won't last for more than a day or two."

"You wish to see me?" The High Priestess stood in the doorway. Her voice, though firm, had a melodic tone. "Coming to the Bardic Temple, Prince Teren, was your decision. Whether you remain here or not is mine." With a snap of her fingers, his clothes changed back to the simple white robe.

She looks a lot like Adriana, Teren thought, *but she sure doesn't act like her.* He could tell by the annoyed expression on her face that this probably wasn't the best time to mention getting a softer bed. Glancing down at the floor, he noticed his boots. "Uh, you forgot the sandals."

"No, I did not. You'll need to earn those back. Your formal lessons for today are over. You're due in the kitchen immediately."

"Great!" *Finally some good news,* he thought. "I'm starving." He couldn't remember the last time he ate.

"Perfect. Then you shall be fully incentivized to hurry through your chores so that you may have breakfast. Come, I'll show you the way."

Kitchen? Chores? Teren could only remember being in the kitchen in his own Castle a few times, and that was almost always to play a joke on the head chef.

Like the time he spelled the blueberries. That little prank cost him a week in his chamber—*and well worth it,* he chuckled, remembering how befuddled the entire kitchen staff was as blueberries popped out of the muffin batter and landed everywhere. *It sure made a mess. Guess I better not try anything like that here,* he thought, following the High Priestess out the door and down the long hallway. *Though it would liven things up a bit. Everyone is so serious—especially Viviana. Anyway, at least there will be food. I can always talk to her about a new bed at dinner. Maybe she'll be less grumpy.*

"Here you are," she told him, after turning a corner to enter the large kitchen area. The two of them were the only ones in the room. Teren immediately spotted the towering stacks of unwashed dishes, pots, and pans sitting next to an oversized sink. "Once these are all clean," Viviana continued, "you may join the rest of the apprentices for your morning meal."

"You want me to wash the dishes?" he asked, thinking it must be a test of his magic.

"Yes," she said, "it will be your morning chore each day this week."

Teren thought for a minute. He had never cast a dishwashing spell before—that's what the kitchen staff was for—but it couldn't be much different than the one he used to clean his room the time his father punished him for playing a prank on his governess. Every time she hung up his clothes, they would disappear and go back to the pile in the middle of his room. "I can come up with a spell to do that," he told Viviana, starting to gesture.

She caught his arm. "Not by using magic. Your chore this week is to wash them the old-fashioned way."

"Why would I do that?" He looked at her in amazement. "I'm a Prince. I don't wash dishes." More than a touch of annoyance leaked through his voice.

"Then you're going to be very hungry, dear Prince. For you may only eat once you have earned your breakfast."

"With all due respect, Viviana, that is ridiculous. I came to the Bardic Temple to study magic, not be a slave." This time, Teren didn't bother trying to conceal his annoyance. "My back already hurts from that bed, and the bump on my head is bigger than a plum." He pulled back his sandy blond hair to show her the lump on his forehead.

"Your head, I apologize for. The bed is your choice. You may sleep on it, on the floor, or wherever you like. It's your chamber—at least for the time being." The expression on her face told Teren that she was not at all moved by his complaints. "Perhaps your lessons aren't over for the day," she continued. "Until you are free from relying on your magic, you cannot begin to control its power." Viviana motioned toward the stacks of dishes. "How quickly you learn is up to you." With a gesture she vanished, leaving him alone in the room.

Doesn't anybody just walk in and out of rooms around here, he thought, looking up at the towering stacks of plates. "There must be a couple hundred dishes, and at least half that many pots and pans," he mumbled. "How am I supposed to get all this done?" Looking around the room, Teren confirmed that he was alone. *Good, I am*, he thought, snapping his fingers. The faucet began filling the sink with hot water. With another snap, a jar of soap tipped upside down and blue liquid flowed into the rising water, causing it to fill with bubbles. *That's more like it*, he thought. *I'll be done in no time.*

He snapped his fingers again, to stop the water, but it wouldn't shut off. The faucet kept running, and the sink was soon overflowing. Soapy water poured onto the floor, going everywhere. Teren tried another spell, and another, but nothing he did stopped the water. It just seemed to flow faster, and the soap bubbles got thicker. His boots were getting soaked as well, inside and out. Furious, he finally reached over to the faucet and twisted the handle. Instantly, the water stopped.

Why didn't I think of that sooner? he scolded himself. *I should have known Viviana would put some reverse spell on this.*

Angry, Teren sat down on a nearby chair. He was not about to be treated like some sort of servant. He was, after all, a Prince.

"Would you like some help?" Teren turned to see Adriana walking toward him. "Mother thought you might," she added.

"What I'd like is to be treated with respect," he snapped. "Not like some... some peasant." Teren tried to pull off his water-soaked boots, but they wouldn't budge. "That's it. I'm done. I didn't come here to be amusement for your mother and father."

"Is that what you think?" Adriana's voice was calm, but her face reflected a great deal of concern. She walked over and sat next to Teren. "We all have many lessons to learn. Your lessons, like mine, are each carefully designed to help where you are lacking."

"That may be true." Teren's voice softened only slightly. He just couldn't bring himself to be upset with Adriana—she was so kind— and had, after all, been raised in this place. *She probably thinks doing chores is normal,* he thought. "Living like this may be alright for some, but washing dishes is not a skill I'm lacking—or one I need to learn."

"Are you sure?" Adriana smiled with a knowing grin. "Maybe learning to wash dishes is exactly what you need. After all, as you said, you are a Prince. Come, I'll show you how."

Teren just stared at her. If this was another of Viviana's silly tests— something to break his spirit—then he'd had just about enough of it—and the whole place. "Sorry, Adriana, I don't do dishes." He stood up and turned to leave.

"Then I shall have to do them for you," she responded without a trace of resentment. "You are, after all, my charge."

Teren stopped short, looking back at her. "Your what?"

"My charge. All new students have a Keeper to help guide them. Father assigned you to me. I hoped you'd be happy about it. Was I was wrong to think so?" Her large brown eyes displayed a sense of disap-pointment.

"No. I mean, Yes, I guess I'm... happy about that part, anyway."

"Good. Then grab one of those sea sponges and let's get started. I'm starving, and if we don't hurry, breakfast will be over, and we'll have to wash those dishes, too." She swooped up a handful of soapsuds and blew them at him.

Wiping them from the side of his face, Teren quickly retaliated. With a flick of his wrist, soapsuds spiraled up from the sink and coiled atop Adriana's head like a fluffy white crown.

"As you wish, fair Priestess."

"Hey, no magic, remember," she warned, wiping the ring of bubbles from her hair.

"That was only for washing the dishes," he retorted. "Not for defending myself. I am, after all, your lowly charge, and need all the protection I can get."

"Well, 'get' washing then," she ordered. "Or your Keeper will use her magic to really take charge." She tossed him a large oval-shaped sea sponge.

"Is that so?" He caught the tan colored ball. With another snap of his fingers, it began to grow arms and legs, then a head, transforming into what looked like a small sea elf. "Viviana said we couldn't use magic to wash the dishes, but she didn't say anything about using magic to get some help."

The spongy sea elf began washing the dirty plates so quickly that Adriana and Teren almost couldn't rinse and dry them fast enough.

"Who's in charge now?" he asked with a twinkle in his eye. No mere High Priestess was going to get the best of him—*even if she is the great, great, great granddaughter of the Fairy Viviane who used her cunning to entomb the greatest wizard of all, Merlin.* A sudden thought brought his actions to an abrupt stop. Several plates crashed to the floor. *Viviana wouldn't lock me away in a tree, would she?*

FOUR

"Welcome, Your Majesty." Crown Princess Cyndara bowed her head to Kandide out of respect, even if it was ever so slightly. "Thank you for accepting my invitation. I'm both pleased and honored that you are all here." She then greeted Lord Rössi, a distinguished-looking Fée with shoulder-length brown hair who was from the Wisdom Clan and served as the head of Calabiyau's High Council. Her golden eyes met his and her smile broadened. "It's wonderful to see you again."

"It's wonderful to see you, as well, Your Highness," he replied with an equally broad smile, his eyes not wanting to leave hers. "It's been far too long."

"That it has." Cyndara stood in the throne room of her Castle—a massive hall with dark green marble covering every inch of the chamber. Dozens of gold-framed life-size portraits of past Banshee rulers dominated three of the four walls. Kandide imagined that Cyndara's portrait would soon be one of them—at least she hoped that would be the case.

The hall was much more brightly lit than on their last visit. Floating globes of silvery light illuminated the room. Cyndara stood near the gold jewel-encrusted throne chair that her father, King Nastae, had occupied for nearly four hundred years—the same place she and Kandide first met barely three months prior.

Nastae's crest of arms still hung behind her, as was the tradition until a new ruler could be crowned.

"Your invitation was most kind," Kandide said, breaking the momentary silence. "Of course, you know my sister, Tara."

"Of course. Thank you for coming, Princess Tara."

"I wouldn't have missed it. Besides, it's important that we show our support for your rule."

"Which I very much appreciate. And this must be Jake." Cyndara turned toward him. "We meet at last. I've heard so much about you. And I see that, when it comes to looks, Kandide was not exaggerating. You are a most handsome Fée."

Jake was, indeed, a "most handsome Fée." He had dark brown hair and eyes so green they could make an emerald blush. He flashed a boyish smile, then acknowledged her compliment with one of his own: "Nor is it an exaggeration about your beauty, Your Highness. If I may be so bold, you are a most beautiful Banshee." He bowed humbly.

Next time, I won't say anything about either one of them, Kandide thought, a bit annoyed at both of them for repeating her words. *I am, after all much prettier than Cyndara. And I don't even remember telling her about Jake—except maybe in passing, of course.* Gaining back her queenly composure, Kandide continued, "Now that the introductions are out of the way, what is your plan, Cyndara?"

"Shortly, I will announce the battle game that I have selected to compete against Lord Mywerk for my Crown. As you know, Banshee law gives me—the one being challenged—the right to select the game."

She certainly doesn't look as though she's dressed for combat, Kandide thought to herself. Tall and slim, Cyndara's petite features, long blue-black hair, and large golden eyes, made her look more like a Fée from the Earthen Clan, than a Banshee. Deep blue satin trimmed her elegantly flowing sleeves, and an enormous emerald adorned the bodice of her floor-length gown. On her head, she wore a gold crown

CROWN PRINCESS CYNDARA

accented with more emeralds and sapphires.

The Banshee symbol of royalty was tattooed in ambers and blues on her chest. Her green-and-blue shimmering wings were graceful like those of a dragonfly. *No, she definitely isn't dressed for a battle game—which means she has something else up those sleeves,* Kandide thought, not at all surprised.

"We're eager to hear your selection," Lord Rössi remarked, still smiling. "And know that regardless of the outcome, you are a valued friend of Calabiyau and always welcome in our land."

"You helped save my life," Tara added. "For that, I'll be forever grateful."

"It was the very least I could do," Cyndara responded. "Kandide helped save my Crown from my brothers when my father was dying. Saving it this time, however, is up to me—and I don't intend to lose."

From the determination in Cyndara's voice, Kandide was even more convinced that the Crown Princess was up to something beyond the norm. Before she could ask, the bellowing sound of a long-horn trumpet commanded her attention.

"That's the call to assemblage," Cyndara explained. "My subjects will be gathering in the courtyard. I must go. General Slant will escort you to the viewing balcony." She pulled on the yellow velvet rope that hung near the throne chair. Within seconds, a soldier dressed in the standard Banshee military garb, brown-on-brown with a red cap, appeared.

"It's my honor to see you again, Your Majesty." Slant bowed to Kandide. "And you, as well, Lord Rössi, Princess Tara—and you must be Jake." Another bow relayed his respect for Kandide's future husband. "Shall we go?" He motioned toward the arched doorway at the end of the hall.

"When will the Games begin?" Kandide asked, as they walked up the spiral staircase that led to the same viewing balcony where, only moments after King Nastae had passed, she watched Lord Mywerk issue the first challenge to Cyndara. Banshee law requires every new ruler, before they can assume the throne, to ask his or her subjects if there are any challengers. The last person Kandide expected a challenge to come from was Cyndara's long-time friend and mentor, Lord Mywerk.

"The Games will start shortly after Her Royal Highness announces her selection," General Slant explained.

Kandide heard the concern in his voice. Knowing that he was loyal, beyond all else, to the Crown Princess, and her most trusted confidant she asked, "Do you know what game Cyndara decided upon?"

"She has not shared that with me." Slant motioned for them to take a seat. The viewing balcony was one floor up and just across the courtyard from where Cyndara would stand. "My apologies, Your Majesty, but I must leave you and join Her Highness. I fear for her safety, especially now that her brothers have returned."

"Prince Kilmonth and Prince Yandell are here?" Lord Rössi sounded more than a bit concerned. Slant, however, had already departed.

The long-horn trumpet bellowed once again. A deep voice introduced Cyndara's half-brothers. They strolled onto the balcony. Typical of a Banshee, they were emaciated looking, with stringy black hair, red, brown, and green clothing, and sporting more gold chains and jewels than a royal treasury.

"I wouldn't have thought they'd show their faces," Tara said, "especially after the rumors that they were responsible for the army that was poised to attack Calabiyau."

"For many Banshees, an attack on Calabiyau would make them heroes," Lord Rössi reminded her. "Most of Cyndara's subjects aren't nearly as fond of our Kingdom as she is."

Kandide had to agree. "We have very few friends here. And I'm certain that I, personally, have even fewer. Most Banshees don't accept equality for Imperfects anymore than many of my subjects do."

Jake took Kandide's hand in his. "I'm afraid you're right. It will certainly take many years for them to accept those of us who aren't physically perfect."

"You're perfect to me, Jake," Kandide retorted. She would not allow anyone to treat him with disrespect. "Besides, you walk perfectly, thanks to your wooden feet. Maybe someday Banshees will learn to respect all Fée, as I have."

"Maybe." Jake sounded none too sure. "But even in the village outside our own Castle we still get whispers when we're together."

"That's just because I'm so beautiful and you are, as Cyndara said, 'a most handsome Fée,'" she teased. "They whisper because they're in awe of what a perfect couple we make."

"Well, you certainly are the most beautiful Fée," Jake replied with a wink.

"It's about time you said so."

Tara rolled her eyes. "At least they aren't fighting," she whispered to Lord Rössi.

"The day's not over," he whispered back.

The long-horn trumpet blew again. This time it was with two lengthy blasts, focusing their attention on the balcony directly across from them. "All kneel for Her Highness, Crown Princess Cyndara," the booming voice called out. Below, in the courtyard, thousands of assembled Banshees—men, women, and children, alike, dropped to one knee. They began to chant, "Long Live Princess Cyndara. Long Live Princess Cyndara." Only her two brothers remained standing, as was protocol.

Cyndara's appearance was spectacular. *Albeit a bit over the top,* Kandide thought. She couldn't quite imagine herself making an appearance like that, but it was impressive. First, a ball of sparkling green light appeared, hovering in the air. It slowly transformed into a glowing amber, and finally Cyndara's form began to materialize. As the crowd went wild, she dissolved into view, looking as radiant and stunning as ever. Allowing the crowd to continue cheering, she stood before her subjects, not saying a word. It was clear to Kandide that Lord Mywerk's challenge had only served to increase her popularity.

After several minutes, Cyndara finally raised her hand to silence the assemblage, and began to speak: "I am honored and most humbled to stand before you today. Please, everyone rise. I'm not your Queen… yet." The crowd cheered even louder as they rose to their feet. Cyndara silenced them again. "Today, destiny walks among us. A member of the Banshee Ruling Council has challenged my right to the throne. Lord Mywerk, does your challenge still stand?"

From the balcony where her brothers stood, a tall Banshee dressed all in burgundy stepped forward. His eyes and shoulder-length hair were brown, and a star made of blood-red rubies fastened his cape.

"My challenge stands, Your Highness," he called with a humble bow. "What is your battle game?"

Kandide watched Cyndara, who stood as regal as any queen. "She's up to something," she whispered to Jake, who nodded in agreement.

Before speaking, the Crown Princess paused, staring straight at Lord Mywerk. The crowd, as well, held silent. Finally, she spoke: My choice of games is…Chessaé."

"Chessaé?" Prince Kilmonth shouted. "That's not a game of skill!"

"It sure isn't," Prince Yandell added, crossing his arms in defiance.

"Isn't it?" Cyndara fired back. "I believe Chessaé is a game that requires a great deal of skill. And that is all the challenge decrees. Perhaps we should let our subjects decide." Without hesitating, she motioned to the crowd.

"Chessaé!" "Chessaé!" "Chessaé!" The entire assemblage took up the chant. Only her brothers did not seem pleased, mumbling to one another in loud protests.

"Do you accept my challenge, Lord Mywerk?"

"I knew it," Kandide whispered. "I knew she was too smart to enter into physical combat. She's well-known as a Chessaé expert."

"So is Lord Mywerk," Lord Rössi cautioned. "He's the one who taught her the game." His attention, as well as that of the others, quickly turned to Lord Mywerk.

"As you have abided by the rules of the challenge, Your Royal Highness, I have no choice but to accept." Mywerk again bowed to the Crown Princess. Kandide caught the flash of amusement that crossed his face as he continued to speak, "Chessaé it will be. Ready the boards and the game shall immediately commence."

The crowd started cheering. Workers instantly began to assemble what looked like a giant four-tiered structure in the middle of the courtyard. Kandide marveled as the massive game boards floated into place, one atop another, suspended in the center by a single pillar of pure crystal.

"What exactly is Chessaé?" Tara asked, watching the curious structure being magically assembled. She had heard of the game, but knew very little about it, and mimicked Lord Mywerk's exact pronunciation: "chess" and followed by the letter "a" as in ate.

"It's an ancient form of chess," Lord Rössi explained, "that's played on four game boards, each representing the Banshee's concept of the various cycles of life—what they call the 'Four Levels of Being.' It's a favorite game among their clans. Matches can go on for days and occasionally get violent when fighting breaks out between the opposing sides."

"That doesn't sound very encouraging." Tara looked down at the massive crowd. "Cyndara certainly doesn't need any more trouble."

"And from what I've learned about Banshees," Kandide added, "it doesn't take much for them to start a fight."

"Especially if betting is going on," Lord Rössi continued, "which it always is when any sort of game is played."

"Did you say it's played on all four of those game boards?" Jake asked. "How?"

"Well, to start with, in official tournaments such as this, it uses live gaming pieces," Lord Rössi replied.

"Live gaming pieces?" Kandide and Tara asked at the same time.

"Yes, it's played with Pixies."

"Pixies?" Kandide couldn't remember the last time she'd seen the tiny faeries who stand barely two hands tall. They used to reside all throughout the forests around Calabiyau, but to her knowledge, none had lived there for decades. "I know many of the Pixie Clans migrated to Banshee territory—up in the mountains—but I have no idea why."

"Rumor has it," Lord Rössi said, "that because of their exceptional talent in Chessaé, King Nastae, who was quite a fan of the game, lured them to his land with the promise of gold and jewels."

"How is it played, Lord Rössi?" Tara asked.

"Chessaé is extremely difficult because the players have to keep track of gaming pieces on all four levels. And regardless of how much of an expert the player is, the Pixies can deny his or her move if they don't agree with it, preferring instead one of their own. Even if the two opponents are extremely well matched, a Pixie can cause one side or the other to win or lose. It's a rule that has altered the outcome of many a game."

"How do they keep the games honest?" Jake asked.

"Pixies take tremendous pride in winning in fair combat," Lord Rössi continued. "Winning teams are considered to be great heroes among both the Banshees and their own clans. Top players can practically name their price for future matches. Should any hint of cheating occur, they would be disgraced and never allowed to play again. The winning team for a game such as this will be legendary and surely be rewarded with many bags of gold and jewels—a portion of which they will share with the losing team."

"That's a lot different than Banshee behavior," Kandide said, "where losers are more likely to be fed to those horrible garglan beasts." She looked at the towering game boards. Construction was almost complete.

The structure stood nearly two stories high. The smaller top board

—only four squares across—was at eye level with the viewing balcony where they were seated. The crystal boards glistened in the bright sunlight, and the alternating frosted and clear squares cast intricate shadows on the green grass in the courtyard below.

"They do have a very different sense of honor," Lord Rössi agreed. "Pixies, however, unlike Banshees, consider every opponent worthy— win or lose. They are known for their good sportsmanship and have, on occasion, refused to continue games for Banshees who become unruly during play. For some reason, the Banshees abide by it."

"Let's hope they do the same with this game." The more Kandide heard, the more concerned she became. There were just too many things that could go wrong. Cyndara was a good player, but Lord Mywerk taught her the game. The Pixies were supposedly honorable, and yet they could refuse any move. "It's all quite complicated," she said.

"That it is." Lord Rössi nodded. "This should be most fascinating."

"It'll be fascinating, alright," Jake said as he watched each of the game boards being locked into place by a large golden wrench that floated effortlessly from level to level under the command of the chief builder—a gray-haired Banshee dressed all in green. "Especially if Cyndara loses."

"I think the game is ready to start." Tara motioned toward the trumpeter, who had lifted the golden horn to his lips. He stood poised and ready for Cyndara to give the official signal to begin the game—a game they each knew would determine the fate of both Kingdoms.

FIVE

The temporary bleachers that had been constructed in the court-yard were overflowing with thousands of Banshees and more continued to stream in. Kandide and Tara marveled at the colorful street-hawkers who were peddling everything from flags and seat cushions to cushla—the Banshee's favorite drink.

Lord Rössi explained that it was made from fermented apples, and then sweetened with honey and cloves. It could be served hot or cold, depending upon the weather. Most Banshees had their own crest-engraved cushla mug that they kept clipped to their belt. Bet-makers were also out in full force. It seemed like everyone was willing to stake a small fortune on the outcome.

As was the custom, Lord Mywerk had taken his position on the balcony overlooking the giant four-tiered gaming board that faced opposite Cyndara. With a formal sign of respect, he nodded to his royal opponent. Her two half-brothers stood on either side of him. Their acknowledgement of her, however, was far less reverent—merely a slight raise of their cushla steins in a half-hearted salute.

"Seeing the three of them together surprises me," General Slant whispered to Cyndara.

"It surprises me, as well. I do, however, find it hard to imagine Lord Mywerk actually aligning with them."

"I hope you're right."

"Hope, my dear General, is for fools."

"Respectfully, Your Highness, without it, many a fool would not have become a victor."

"Then let us 'hope' it is not so in this case." Cyndara turned her attention to her brothers. The boldness of their return was, indeed, cause for concern. She was convinced they had funded the army that her former military leader, General Kandour, had amassed to attack the Château a few months earlier. Fortunately, the attack never happened. *Could Lord Mywerk possibly be involved as well? And if so, why?* she wondered. *Surely, not just to become King.* In all the years she had known him, he never once seemed even slightly interested in power. Could she have been wrong about him?

The booming voice echoed from the balcony, just above where Cyndara and Slant were standing: "All rise for the parade of Pixies."

Again, the long-horn trumpet sounded, announcing the start of their procession. Kandide, Tara, Jake, and Lord Rossi watched in amazement as thirty-two Pixies proudly marched in—sixteen to a side. Their flamboyant costumes were fashioned to represent jewel-laden Pawns, Knights, Bishops, Kings, Queens, and Rooks—the game pieces each would portray.

Cyndara's Pixie gaming pieces were costumed in mostly white and blue, ornately trimmed with silver, sapphires, and diamonds. While the Pixies who made up Lord Mywerk's Chessaé pieces were dressed in forest green, lavishly trimmed with gold, peridot, and emeralds.

"The whole thing is incredible," Tara remarked, watching the spectacle.

"I've heard," Lord Rössi told her, "that the opening of the Game is always spectacular, with each player's team trying to outdo the other with his or her elaborate attire. But this is, indeed, incredible. I'm quite certain that because of the Game's significance, it's even more outrageous than most."

"I'd say outrageous is an understatement," Jake responded.

They watched as each Pixie was introduced by name. With a great deal of parading and posing, each fluttered up to assume his or her respective starting position on the second level of the game board, where the play was to begin.

"You'll notice," Lord Rössi said, "that the second level looks exactly like a normal chessboard containing sixty-four squares. It's my understanding that this level represents the here and now, the 'earthbound world' where life as we know it exists."

"What does the third level represent?" Jake asked.

Watching the rest of the Pixies take their places, Lord Rössi continued his explanation: "The third level contains only twenty-five squares. It represents the higher consciousness and is known as the level of 'Enlightenment.' According to the Banshees, they can only attain this level when they have lived an exemplary life."

"And we all know," Kandide added, "that the meaning of living 'an exemplary life' to a Banshee is very different than for most Fée. So, I assume, Lord Rössi, that the goal of Chessaé is to reach the fourth and uppermost level?"

"That it is. As you can see, the top level has only four squares with a center circle that intersects each of them. It's the level of 'Oneness.' In Chessaé, as with Banshee beliefs, anyone can reach this level, but not without a great deal of hard work and good deeds. Here, too, the Banshee definition of 'good deeds' is quite different from ours. Those who do, however, become 'One' with what they call the Universal Intelligence, and can control their destiny for all time."

"It's all quite fascinating," Kandide remarked. She was eager for the game to begin—and ultimately for it to be over so she could return home. Teren had been on her mind all morning. *I wonder if Mother's heard anything from him,* she thought. *In any case, the High Council won't be pleased if I stay away for more than a day. They're hopeless without me.* Attempting to stay focused on the Game, she said, "I assume they move up a level when they capture an opponent's piece."

"They can choose to do so, or stay where they are," Lord Rössi explained.

"When they get four pieces to the fourth level, do they win?" Tara asked.

"Not exactly. After arriving on the top level, any piece can choose to remain there or return to any of the other three levels. Part of the strategy in Chessaé, as with Banshee beliefs, is that when a playing piece reaches the highest level, it can go back for the purpose of helping another piece that has been captured—like a Queen, for instance—and return it to play. Chessaé is ultimately won when four pieces from the same side are on the top level, and the opposing King is check-mated. Once that happens, the King from the winning side is placed in the center circle on the fourth level as a symbolic sign of victory."

"Sounds complicated." Jake was still not sure he understood the game-play. "What's the bottom level for?"

Before Lord Rössi could answer, the booming voice from below called for silence. With each of the Pixies finally in place, the over-flowing crowd was impatient for the game to start. They had begun stomping their feet and banging their cushla steins. "I said silence!" the voice called again. "Let the game begin!" On his cue, the crowd was instantly quiet. "Crown Princess Cyndara, as the player of white, you shall make the first move." He bowed in her direction. "Your Royal Highness, if you please."

"Pawn on 2- e2 move to 2- e4," she called.

Delighted that he had been selected to open the game, the Pixie on that square proudly nodded his acceptance, moving to where he was instructed with a great deal of flamboyant arm-waving.

"What do the numbers mean?" Tara asked Lord Rössi.

"The first number she called refers to the board level. The letters and numbers that follow represent the spaces where the Pixies move from and then to."

"Pawn on 2- e7 move to 2- e5," Lord Mywerk requested. His

Pixie-Pawn also quickly nodded in agreement, moving to the requested space with an even more lavish flourish.

All watched intently as Cyndara made her second move. "Pawn on 2- f2 move to 2- f4."

It was accepted by the Pixie, a petite girl who wore a tight-fitting diamond-studded cap that sparkled each time she moved her head. The crowd broke out in applause when she performed an elaborate double summersault that landed her squarely on the intended space. Her iridescent wings shimmered like tiny rainbows in the bright sunlight.

Lord Rössi explained that Mywerk was most certainly aware of Cyndara's initial strategy. Though, from the determined look on her face, it was easy to see that this was one match she did not intend for him to use that knowledge to his advantage. All watched Lord Mywerk as he carefully considered his next move, calling out, "Bishop on 2- f8 move to 2- c5."

It, too, was completed only after the Pixie nodded his approval. His pointed headpiece was completely covered in emeralds and gold beads. It certainly weighed more than the Pixie. Not to be outdone by the prior move, he did three back flips, landing on the desired square.

How his headpiece stayed on as he tumbled through the air, Kandide had no idea. "The Pixies are incredible," she said. Knowing that this was a match that would ultimately decide the fate of the Banshees, she was equally impressed by the remarkable composure Cyndara displayed. "From the amount of pomp and circumstance each move is given, this game is going to take forever," she whispered.

"It well might," Lord Rössi agreed.

"So what *is* the bottom level for?" Jake asked, as they waited for Cyndara to decide her next move.

"Level one contains thirty-six squares," he answered. "It's considered to be the level of 'Relearning.' When a playing piece is captured on any of the upper three levels, it's not removed from the game. It's sent to the bottom level to symbolically be re-taught the lessons of life—a feat that is achieved when it's rescued by a piece from the fourth level. In Banshee philosophy, level one is where individuals who have committed serious crimes or have done terrible deeds go when they pass. They remain there until they can redeem themselves through the teachings of others."

"I had no idea that there was so much symbolism involved," Kandide remarked. "It's really quite beautiful."

Cyndara voiced her next move. The crowd let out a huge cheer as the Pixie, who was dressed as a white knight in shining silver armor, leapt over a Pawn to take his place on the square nearby. All eyes shifted to Lord Mywerk. After calling his counter play, the designated Pixie, who was dressed as a Rook, catapulted to her square with an equally impressive leap.

For nearly four more hours, the game continued. Kandide knew very little about the strategies in Chessaé. She could, however, tell that Cyndara and Lord Mywerk had both lost several important pieces.

"Knight to capture e6," Lord Mywerk requested after a nerve-racking pause between moves.

The Pixie-Knight, who was seated on a gold horse with emerald studded armor, moved into place. The crowd became deathly quiet. Cyndara's expression also changed.

"Hmmm," Lord Rössi whispered. "That's not good."

"Pawn captures your Knight," the Crown Princess stated with a sense of regal humility. Her golden eyes were fixed on Mywerk's next move.

He wasted no time. "Rook captures your Bishop."

Neither Tara, Kandide, Jake, nor Lord Rössi dared to breathe as they watched the Pixie-Rook send its captive Bishop to the bottom level. This move contained no ceremony. That would be self-righteous and not within the Pixie's sense of proper sportsmanship. Everyone held his or her breath knowing that Cyndara must sacrifice her Queen.

LORD MYWERK'S PIXIE KNIGHT

Graciously bowing, Lord Mywerk looked across the crystal board at her. His manner was genuinely humble. "I believe the loss of your Queen will result in checkmate, Your Royal Highness."

Cyndara stood silent. Her golden eyes were fixed on her Pixie Queen as it descended to the bottom board. Her thoughts were not on the game—only on the fate of her land. What would happen to it now—to the plans she had to free her subjects from the tyranny of her father? Would it all be lost? When she finally did speak, her voice concealed her defeat. "Checkmate it is."

The capturing Knight stood reverently, as Mywerk's King took its place in the center circle on the top board. It had been a long well-fought six-hour battle, made even more impressive by the fact that she and Lord Mywerk were as evenly matched opponents as had ever played. Twice throughout the game, it seemed hopeless for him. But ultimately his many years of playing against her proved to be the deciding factor.

Looking remarkably regal, in spite of her agonizing loss, Cyndara formally announced to her subjects: "Lord Mywerk has fought fairly and well. The throne and the Crown are his spoils." Her voice began to tighten. Saying no more, she slowly left the balcony. While she would retain her title of Royal Highness, her rule of the Banshee Kingdom was lost. Everything she had worked so hard to create was about to vanish.

"Let's go," Kandide told the others, hastily standing. "I want to speak to her." She quickly led the others down the winding staircase as the crowd began to chant, "Long live King Mywerk! Long live King Mywerk!"

Leading the cheers were Cyndara's two brothers. "You did it!" Prince Kilmonth toasted Lord Mywerk with his cushla stein.

"Yeah, we're in charge now," Prince Yandell gleefully responded. "I say we banish our half-breed sister to the Mists with the Imperfects."

Kilmonth slapped his brother on the back. "Now that's a good idea, little brother. What do you think, Lord Mywerk? Should we banish her… or feed her to the garglans?"

"What we're going to do," Mywerk insisted, "is to treat your sister with the respect she deserves. Now, I must speak to my subjects." He stepped forward to do so, and the cheering began to lessen.

"Your Highness," General Slant, who had escorted Cyndara from the balcony to the entry hall, cautioned, "perhaps you should return with Queen Kandide for a time. It could be dangerous for you to stay here. I'm quite sure she will welcome you."

"Of course, we will," Kandide responded, meeting them in the large hall. "You're welcome to return with us, Cyndara. I agree with Slant; staying here could be dangerous."

"Your concern is most appreciated—both of you. But I belong here, with my clans."

"Are you sure?" Jake looked toward the balcony. "Your brothers seem pretty friendly with Lord Mywerk."

"That they do," Cyndara readily agreed, as she watched the two princes celebrate his victory. "But this is my home. There's no telling what they'll do if I were to leave. I must remain here and at least attempt to instill some compassion into Lord Mywerk's rule. He'll not order my death. The Pixies would never allow it. They honor a strong contender almost as much as they do the winner."

"And that you surely are," Lord Rössi replied with a deep bow. "At one point, I was certain the game was yours."

"As was I. My victory, however, was not to be." She sighed, her face revealing that she was still trying to comprehend defeat. "Shall we listen to Lord Mywerk's acceptance speech?" Cyndara's focus shifted to the royal balcony, where only moments before she had stood. Lord Mywerk and her two brothers had already transported across to it. The crowd continued chanting as he stepped forward.

As Lord Mywerk raised his hand, the crowd went silent. "I have fought a difficult battle against a truly worthy opponent." Glancing down at Cyndara, who had stepped outside with the others to listen to what he was about to say, Lord Mywerk graciously acknowledged her. Humility, in the face of victory, is an important quality for a Banshee leader—even if it is not always genuine. He continued speaking. "Princess Cyndara is truly a worthy opponent. But she has been honorably defeated. I embrace my destiny to be your King. Unless there are any who would challenge me, so be it."

"I challenge you," a voice called out.

All eyes turned to see who spoke. Stepping forward, Cyndara repeated her words, "I challenge you, Lord Mywerk."

"You can't do that," her oldest brother, Prince Kilmonth, shouted. Cushla sprayed from his mouth. "You already lost!"

Making her way to the front of the crowd, Cyndara continued, "What law says I cannot?"

"It's never been done before," Prince Yandell hollered.

"That is because, my dear brother, in most games of skill for the throne, the fight is to the death. In Chessaé, it cannot be. Pixie honor forbids it. Therefore, as a loyal subject to the Crown, I am within my rights to challenge Lord Mywerk."

The crowd started madly cheering, many of them shouting, "Long live Princess Cyndara!" Others shouted for Lord Mywerk. Though mostly divided in favor of the Princess, all seemed ecstatic that there would be another game, which meant even more feasting, more drinking, and a lot more betting.

Kandide watched the fury grow in Cyndara's brothers' eyes. She wasn't sure whether they or the surprised expression on Mywerk's face was more amusing.

Raising his hand, Lord Mywerk called for silence. "Since I have been challenged, I have no choice but to accept." His tone sounded almost pleased. "This time, however, the selection of the game is mine."

Kilmonth leaned toward him, whispering in his ear, "Archery. Pick archery. You're sure to beat her."

"Yeah... yeah... archery," Yandell insisted. "That's the game. She's terrible at it, and when she loses, you can put an arrow right through her heart. And I get to watch you do it!"

"This is better than we thought!" Kilmonth was elated. "But I say, only wound her so we can feed her to the garglans. I can just see their glowing red eyes staring at her before their claws rip her apart."

"That's good! That's good!" Yandell chortled, jumping up and down. "Yeah, just wound her so we can feed her to the garglans."

"And I get to do it!" Kilmonth exclaimed.

"Awe, you get all the fun, big brother. I want to help."

"Okay, you can help, little brother."

"Thanks, big brother!"

Lord Rössi moved closer to Cyndara, whispering, "What are you going to do?"

"I will accept whatever game he chooses," she whispered back. "It's Banshee Honor."

"Banshee Honor," he replied. "This is no time to stand on principle. Return with us and we can sort this out later."

"I'm afraid I cannot do that." Looking up at Lord Mywerk, Cyndara was well aware of the various deadly games that he could select—archery being the least of them. Her father ascended to the throne by destroying his opponent in a fiery battle of flaming swords. His father before him in hand-to-hand combat with poison knives. She also knew that to live under Mywerk's rule might be an even worse fate. Though he would not kill her, life as his virtual prisoner was not something she could endure.

Standing tall, Cyndara asked, "What is your choice of games, Lord Mywerk?"

*"Only the passing, and that is what
I fear could happen."*

SIX

Sneering, Prince Kilmonth elbowed Lord Mywerk. "Go ahead, tell Cyndara the game you picked."

"Yeah, tell her," Yandell whispered loudly. "I can't wait to see the look on her face."

Lord Mywerk scanned the anxious crowd. He slowly turned and looked directly at the Princess. "Your Royal Highness, I hereby challenge you to the game of... Chessaé."

"What?" Kilmonth spit his cushla out, spraying it over his brother and Lord Mywerk. "We said archery! You're supposed to challenge her to archery!"

Yandell squinted at Lord Mywerk with a suspicious glare. "What are you up to? You double-crossing us?"

"Now, gentlemen," Lord Mywerk calmly responded, "I have a better plan."

"Well, it better be better!" Kilmonth threatened.

"Yeah, it sure better be better!" Yandell pulled his knife out and flashed the highly polished blade in the afternoon sunlight.

Ignoring them both, Mywerk continued, "Do you accept my challenge, Princess Cyndara?"

"I accept, Lord Mywerk."

"Then we begin play in three days, upon first light. That will give my subjects time to attend to their crops, shops, and family duties."

The crowd went wild. "Long live King Mywerk! Long live King Mywerk!" The shouting continued even after he and the two still-grumbling Princes left the balcony.

"Why did Mywerk do that?" Tara asked Cyndara as they stepped inside the hall. "He could have named a really deadly game."

"Think about it logically," she answered. "If Lord Mywerk had challenged me to a battle game that he knows I cannot win, he would have to kill me. To challenge an opponent to a game that you know he or she is not proficient in is considered dishonorable by Banshee standards. And while it would be perfectly within his rights to do so, our subjects would not respect him for it. He would lose the support he earned by defeating me fairly in Chessaé. Because he is a magi and a half-breed, Lord Mywerk is still viewed by many with suspicion. Support is something he cannot afford to waste."

"That's interesting," Lord Rössi said. "And it certainly explains why you took the risk."

"A calculated one, but nonetheless it was a risk, " Cyndara agreed. "Mywerk's ego is bolstered by his win. By challenging me to Chessaé, he may win again. If he does, the Pixies will not allow a third game, and Lord Mywerk, by declaring victory as the reigning monarch, will immediately be crowned King. If I win, however, it will be a tie—one game to one—and he can re-challenge me. His honor will remain intact."

"I must confess, Banshee Honor is as complex as are Banshee politics," Kandide said. "And as much as I would like to stay for the second game, I need to return home. I'm worried about Teren."

"Prince Teren?" Cyndara asked. "Is something wrong?"

"He accepted Viviana's invitation to study at the Bardic Temple," Jake explained.

The expression on Cyndara's face changed to a deep frown. "Are you saying that Viviana personally invited him to study there?"

"Yes, why?" Kandide felt an odd chill run up her spine. Her first instinct was not to let Teren go. Should she have heeded that warning? "You look concerned."

"I am. As you know, I studied there, myself—for nearly two years. During that entire time, I saw Viviana only twice—once when she welcomed me and once when I left. To my knowledge, she never interacts with any of the students. For her to take a personal interest in Teren is very interesting."

"Do you think he could be in danger?" Tara asked with an undertone of alarm.

"Not as long as he obeys her rules. Viviana is arguably the most powerful magi in the world. It's rumored that her daughter, Adriana, when fully trained will be even more powerful. If my assessment is correct, she likely views Teren and his exceptional Talent in one of two ways—as a threat to her daughter or as a life-partner for her. In either case, it is cause for concern."

The chill that ran up Kandide's spine transformed into a clenching feeling in her stomach. "You think Teren is a tool for Viviana's quest for more power?"

"He may well be," Cyndara answered. "Lord Mywerk has long maintained that Viviana's goal is to make the Bardic Council the unrivaled center of power that it once was. A child born of Teren and Adriana could easily be the most powerful magi our world has ever known—possibly more than Merlin, himself."

"Jake, Tara," Kandide looked from one to the other, "I think it's time to pay a visit to the Bardic Temple. Lord Rössi, can you stay here? Cyndara may also need our help."

"Of course," he replied. "It would be my pleasure."

"Thank you, Kandide, for offering Lord Rössi's support. And thank you, Lord Rössi. I would like nothing better. I think, however, you should join Kandide. Your knowledge of Bardic history may come in handy when dealing with Viviana."

"Are you certain you'll be safe?" he asked.

"Is anything certain in life?"

"Only the passing, and that is what I fear could happen if…"

Placing her hand on his, Cyndara smiled. "Worry not, my dear friend, I shall be okay—at least until the re-match is complete. It is, however, kind of you to be concerned about me."

Their eyes met and Kandide knew Cyndara had developed a special fondness toward him, and he for her.

"A strong alliance between our lands is essential," Lord Rössi said, his eyes still meeting hers, "if we are to end the senseless raids and killings that have been going on for so very long."

"And if destiny decrees that I win the second and third games, I shall do everything within my power to create a lasting peace. Travel safely, my dear friends, and keep me informed about Teren. His fate is as much of a concern to me, as is my own."

LORD RÖSSI IN HIS STUDY

"Should we help him?" Centrod asked.
"That's got to be painful."

SEVEN

On the fourth morning after his arrival at the Bardic Temple, Teren stood alone in the kitchen. Adriana wasn't able to help him wash dishes that morning because she had early lessons. He looked at the towering stacks of pots and pans. It seemed as though there were more each day.

Oh, well, he thought. *If doing a few dishes is the price for learning new spells—especially if they are as good as the one I learned yesterday, I guess I can do it for a week.*

He began thinking about how Centrod had taught him the secret of drawing upon Nature's forces to harness the earth's energy. He could almost feel the intense heat of the glowing ball of fire he was able to create. In the past, conjuring up glowing orbs to light a room or heat a cup of tea was the most he could do. But this spell was different, very different. He was able to generate immense amounts of power.

Centrod had stopped him before the ball had grown too large. *And good thing,* he thought, *I'm not so sure I would have been able to control it.* With practice, however, he knew he could. The blisters on his fingers reminded him of just how much practice he still needed. His hands stung as he rinsed a shiny copper pot under the hot water.

Centrod had refused to heal him, stating: "The blisters are a reminder that this type of magic is very dangerous. The small amount of pain you experience now will serve as a warning that you must not experiment on your own—not until you are fully trained to manage such forces. Power restrained is power gained."

Why do Centrod and Viviana always use pain as a way of training? he wondered, stretching his aching back and shoulder muscles. He really did need to do something about getting a more comfortable bed. *Guess I'd better get busy washing these pots or I'll miss breakfast…again.* His stomach growled. The food at the Bardic Temple was tasty, but there never seemed to be enough of it—quite a contrast from the feast that was served the first time he visited. *Of course, I wasn't a slave back then.*

Teren placed both hands in the sink, scooping up hot soapy water then letting it flow through his stinging fingers. It gave him an idea. *If heat can be drawn from the earth, can it also be drawn from other places, like this water?* He would need to find out. Centrod had warned him about experimenting on his own—*but that was with the earth's energy. He didn't say anything about water.*

Closing his eyes, Teren began to focus on a spell similar to the one he learned the day before. He imagined the warmth from the water being pulled into his hands toward the center of his palms. His attention was focused on drawing in its heat, as he thought to himself: *Heat of life, release your power, into my charge, so it may flower.*

The water began to swirl and take on a prismatic glow. Teren repeated the spell concentrating even harder. There it was—a tiny ball of heat began to form between his fingers, glowing from its own warmth. He forced his thoughts deeper into the heat of the water. The ball grew larger until it began to generate steam.

Suddenly, Teren realized that he couldn't pull his hands out of the sink. It was no longer filled with hot soapy water; it was ice. His hands were frozen in a solid block of ice. *Oh, great,* he thought. *I guess I transferred a little too much heat. Now what to do?* It would have been funny, if his hands weren't burning from the cold.

Viviana sat with Centrod in her anti-chamber enjoying a cup of jasmine tea. Though her private quarters were larger and more elaborate than Teren's tiny room, they were still remarkably humble by Castle standards—simple wooden furniture painted white with touches of pale blue in the upholstery. She and Centrod watched Teren's antics in the silver viewing-mirror that hung over her writing desk. "The boy's clever," she remarked, amused by his sudden plight.

"A little too clever," Centrod replied. "And from how quickly he adapted that spell, I'd say even more talented than we first thought."

They continued to watch as Teren tried to figure out what to do about the block of ice that filled the entire sink. His hands were turning blue from the cold, and starting to blister even more from the hot glowing sphere that still floated between them. No matter how hard he tried, the ice kept him from removing his hands.

"Should we help him?" Centrod asked. "That's got to be painful."

"In a minute," Viviana replied. "I want to see if he comes up with a solution."

They continued to view his image in the mirror as Teren struggled to free his hands. He mumbled several counter spells, but none of them worked. His palms and fingers were bleeding from the burns. Finally, in desperation, he jerked the block of ice out of the sink and slammed it against the counter. Frozen shards sprayed everywhere as the glowing ball of fire instantly dissipated.

"Brute force is certainly one way," Viviana said with a slight laugh.

"It worked." Centrod could not have been more amused. "And I think our young Prince just took another step forward in his learning."

"You mean because he realized that not every dilemma requires magic to solve?"

"That, and the fact that he needs to stop experimenting without proper training."

"Ah, my dearest Centrod, we can only hope that part of the lesson is learned. It's going to take a great deal more work than I thought to tame this rambunctious magi."

"I fear you're right, Viviana. At least Adriana seems to have an effect on him. Where authority may fail, feminine charm can often prevail—especially with a young woman as charming and clever as our daughter."

"As long as he doesn't weave a spell on her. Women aren't the only ones with special charms." She brushed her hand lovingly across his check.

"Why, Viviana, if I didn't know better, I'd say you're flirting with me."

"Never. Now go heal the lad. His hands must be writhing in pain."

"Are you sure? Pain can be a persuasive teacher."

EIGHT

Kandide, Jake, Lord Rössi, and Tara arrived back at the Castle in the early evening—only to be summoned to an emergency meeting of the High Council.

As was his duty, Lord Rössi called the session to order. "All rise for Her Majesty Queen Kandide," he told the other members as she entered the chamber. Kandide took her place on the elevated crystal throne chair that sat in front of the crescent-shaped Council table. Eleven members were present, each representing one of Calabiyau's twelve primary clans. Only Lady Aron, who represented the Fire Clan, was not there.

"Any word on the capture of our dear Lady Aron?" Lady Batony of the Creativity Clan asked. The guardian of music, she was known for her beautiful voice. "It's been nearly two months since Tara was freed from that terrible block of ice. Why, when I was a young girl..."

"I know," Kandide tried to force a smile, but she was in no mood for the Council or Lady Batony's rambling, "when you were a little girl, enemies of the state were found instantly."

"Actually, they weren't always," she responded with a bit of a huff. "But your father, the great King Toeyad, was always respectful!" Lady Batony crossed her arms and leaned back in her chair.

"May we start the meeting?" Lord Rössi asked. "Several members of the Council have called this emergency session, and I, for one, am eager to learn why."

Lord Socrat, a white-haired Fée from the Wisdom Clan spoke up. "We are anxious to know how Crown Princess Cyndara fared in the battle games, as well as to inform Her Majesty that since her departure, two more villages have been burned to the ground."

"Two more?" Kandide was visibly shaken by the news. Her mind flashed back to the farm boy and the little doll. "Which ones? Did everyone get out safely?"

"One was to the north, and the other in the foothills," Lord Socrat answered. "They were two of the villages that are more sympathetic to you, Your Highness. As far as we know, everyone survived. The villagers were given a warning this time, and then every house was set ablaze. No one could tell how it was done. The houses just erupted in fire."

"Lady Aron's doing, no doubt," Kandide said. "I'm sure of it."

"As much as I wouldn't put it past her to stir up trouble," Lady Karena of the Heart Clan stated, "it troubles me to think she would do something so vile."

"It's no worse than some of the other things she's accused of doing," Lord Revên insisted. Always the outspoken one, his clans were the keepers of the Sacred Sciences. "I wouldn't put it past Lady Aron, if for no other reason than to show that Kandide has lost control as Queen—respectfully speaking, of course, Your Majesty."

"Of course." Kandide nodded to him. *Perhaps I am losing control,* she thought, trying not to let her emotions show. *Things seem to be getting worse, not better.* She took a breath before speaking. *You're Queen, Kandide. Think like one,* she told herself. "Well, her little plan isn't going to work. I shall have General Mintz double the patrols. We will stop her senseless violence."

"He has over half our soldiers patrolling now," Lady Alicia, of the Animal Clan, reminded her. The guardian of reptiles, her words, carried a sharper bite than the creatures she protects.

"Then he shall put the other half on it, as well," Kandide snapped. "I will not have my subjects being terrorized like this."

"This is not like the Banshee raids," Lady Socrat of the Plant Clan warned. The guardian of the Forest, she hailed from a village not far from where Tiyana grew up. "Dark magic is at work here."

"If I may speak frankly, Your Majesty," Lord Standish, of the Air Clan, added. At nearly 400 years old, he was the eldest of the Council members and never failed to speak his mind. "A growing number of Fée do not believe you are able to effectively rule. Between your constant travels back and forth to the Château in the Mists, this past summer's deploying of the Frost, and, of course, there is still the issue of Imperfects being treated as equals—even your plans to marry one—you've made many enemies."

His words stabbed at Kandide like a henchman's dagger. *I've done everything I can to send food and gold to the clans to replace the crops that were lost when I deployed the Frost to save my sister,* she thought then took a breath and spoke with unwavering verve: "Those are old arguments. I need solutions, not more of the same rhetoric."

"Rhetoric or not," Lord Salitar, of the Healing Arts, countered, albeit more diplomatically, "your subjects' anger is very real. You'll not win back their loyalty until you've proven that they can trust you to do what is in their best interest. Not yours."

"I do what is in the best interest of all Fée, not just those who think they are superior." Kandide's momentary self-doubt shifted to anger. *How dare the Council speak to me like that?* she thought. *I am their Queen.* In her heart, however, she knew he was right—she needed to do more to earn their respect, much more. "So, Lord Salitar—and the rest of my illustrious High Council—what do you suggest?"

All were silent. She looked from one to another. "Well? Lady Corale, you haven't said anything, what do you suggest?"

"I suggest you heed Lord Salitar's words." From the Water Clan, Lady Corale was the guardian of the seas and wore her long black hair braided with shells and coral. "Capturing Lady Aron and bringing her to trial would certainly be a good start. There are a growing number of Fée who believe that she is being framed, and that it was actually the Banshees who entombed Tara in the ice, not her. Putting Firenza on trial may well change their thinking."

"Framed? By whom?" Kandide asked.

"By you." Lady Batony was not at all diplomatic, quickly adding, "Of course, I don't believe it. None of us do. But there are those who claim..."

"That's absurd!" Kandide slammed her fist down on the arm of her crystal throne chair. "I will hear no more of this."

"Consider their words carefully, Your Highness." Lord Aron of the Earthen Clan spoke with his normally soft tone. Though he was still married to Lady Aron, they were estranged and he had no love for her. "Firenza, as contemptible as she is," he continued, "has many who side with her. I don't doubt she's behind the village burnings. And I'm certain she's doing it to raise questions about your ability to rule, Kandide. Don't, however, underestimate her power nor her cunning. She will spend her dying day trying to destroy you and become Queen."

Kandide leaned forward on her throne. She could not deny the truth in his words. "Well, then we just need to make sure that Lady Aron's 'dying day' comes sooner rather than later. I will never allow her to be Queen. All of you have sources. I want you to return to your clans and put as much pressure on them as is needed. Someone knows where our dear Firenza is. Someone is helping her remain hidden. And someone knows someone who can give us that information. I don't care what it takes, just be back here in forty-eight hours—and this time I want answers!" Kandide stood up. "The meeting is adjourned." She swept out of the chamber so quickly the wall torches flickered.

"Well?" Lord Rossi said, looking at the speechless Council members. "Can you get Her Majesty some answers or not?"

• • • •

Jake met Kandide in her private garden. He was dressed in a loose white cotton shirt, brown pants, and knee high boots—a far cry from the formal attire of the court. "I take it things didn't go well with the High Council," he said, warmly greeting her. "You look pretty upset."

"I'm not sure how they could have gone worse." Kandide inhaled deeply then slowly let the air release from her lungs. The warm afternoon sunlight felt good after being indoors for what seemed like forever. "Let's go for a walk. I need some fresh air." She took Jake's arm. "The Council has absolutely no information on the whereabouts of Lady Aron, and now they're even questioning their own decision to allow Imperfects to live in Calabiyau as equals."

"Did they say that?" he asked.

"In so many words. They're accusing my subjects of saying it. I know some of them feel that way, but they're a small minority."

"Small, maybe, but also a very vocal minority. It's probably time to have Tara completely heal your wing so the tip is no longer bent."

Kandide stopped short. "Never! Just because my wing can be healed, doesn't mean that those who aren't as fortunate are of less value. No, I will not do that. It's my symbol that all Fée are equal—and I'm going to keep it that way."

"I know how strongly you feel, but your bent wing can also be perceived as favoring Imperfects."

"I don't favor them. I just treat them equally. Oh, Jake, why are we arguing about this?" She leaned her head on his shoulder.

"Because, Kandide, I love you." He tilted her chin up and looked into her purple-blue eyes. "And I don't want you to be hurt. Sometimes, however, we have to face facts—Imperfects are equal by law, but not everyone accepts us. To those who don't, your bent wing is construed as flaunting that fact. As, I'm afraid, is marrying me."

"Don't ever say that!" She lifted her head up, wishing with all her heart that his words weren't true. "There are some things I will never compromise on and one of them is marrying you. I just don't understand why some Fée need to feel superior to others."

"You mean like the way you felt before the lightening strike that crumpled your wing?"

"I... well... I was young and only saw life from my own point of view. But I've changed."

"Do you think that if you hadn't been injured you'd feel the way you do now?"

"Well, of course I wou—" Kandide stopped herself. *Why does Jake always make me see inside my head?* she thought before continuing. "No...No, I probably would not have. If my wing hadn't been injured, and Mother hadn't sent me away to Aunt Selena and the Château, I'd probably still feel that way."

Kandide looked out at the yellow, purple, and pink gladiolas that filled her garden. "I've changed quite a bit since that terrible day. I guess I expect everyone else to be as enlightened as I am. But you're right, many of my subjects haven't evolved at all since the Clan Wars."

"Which is why we need to face reality, Kandide. I am and always will be an Imperfect."

"The only reality I intend to face is that, Imperfect or not, you are the most perfect Fée I've ever met... except maybe for your temper." She flashed a flirtatious grin.

"Speaking of tempers..."

"Mine doesn't begin to compare with yours."

"Of course not, Your Majesty." He mimicked the same flirtatious smile.

"Anyway, I love you, Jake. That is all that matters."

"If only it were all that matters." He pulled her into his arms. "I love you too, Kandide. I'll never forget the first time I met you—in the Château with Selena. Your hair was a mess, your dress was torn, and you had smudges of dirt all over your face. It didn't matter. I still thought you were the most beautiful Fée I'd ever seen."

"You never told me that."

KANDIDE AND JAKE

"Well, I'm telling you now."

As their eyes met, so did their lips. And for that brief instance, being together was all that mattered.

"Please don't let this moment end," she whispered, her arms wrapped around his waist.

"If it were in my power, I would make it last forever." He brushed a silvery wisp of hair away from her eyes. "But you are Queen. Your calling, Kandide, is greater than either one of us. So we don't have that choice."

"We could run away," she teased, "to some deserted island and live happily ever after."

"That only happens in faery tales. Besides, I don't quite see you cooking."

"Well, of course not. That would be your job, Jake. Teren says you make wonderful cornbread."

"I do, but who's going to grow and harvest the corn?"

"You."

"And wash the dishes?"

"You, again." She coyly grinned.

"And what would your job be, Kandide?"

"Why, I'd be Queen, of course." She sat down on a nearby bench and pulled him next to her. "It's really the only thing I'm good at, except looking beautiful, of course. I just wish it wasn't so hard some-times—I mean being Queen. As you said, I'm always beautiful."

"And as your father used to say, 'If ruling a Kingdom was easy, anyone could do it.' But it's not. And you're not just anyone, Kandide."

"I suppose Father was right. I am rather exceptional, aren't I?"

"Now, that's the Kandide I know." He gave her a hug. "Come on, you have a Kingdom to get under control."

NINE

"Egan, slow down." Lord Aron flew even faster to catch up with his young son. He was nearly out of breath when he finally caught up with him. "For being five and having artificial wings you certainly learned how to fly fast. Let's land over there." He motioned to a small mossy area nearby.

"I practice a lot." Egan allowed his translucent wings to slow their fluttering. "Besides, I'm almost six—in just two weeks."

Both drifted to the emerald green moss-covered ground. It was a warm sunny day. Even the clouds had decided not to soften the bright blue of the sky.

"Where are you going?" Lord Aron asked. "You know it's not safe to be out here."

"I... um, I..."

"I, um, what?"

"I'm going to see my brother. And I'm already late. I would have transported, but Alin doesn't want there to be any way Mother—I mean Lady Aron—can detect magic. If she knew we were playing together, she would tell Grandmam to lock him in the house like she did last time. Please let me go, Father. Please." His big blue eyes shone brightly against his brown skin.

"I've told you before, I don't want you wandering off like this. It's just too dangerous."

"But, Father, Alin's my brother and I love him. Last time..." Egan caught himself. "I mean..."

"Last time, when?"

"Oh, a... a long time ago."

"A long time ago, like yesterday?" Lord Aron suddenly noticed a nearby bush moving. He reached for his bow and arrow. "Get behind me."

"Don't shoot, Father," a young voice called out. A mop of reddish brown hair emerged from behind the thicket, followed by a round face and two very blue eyes. "It's me, Alin."

"Alin! Come out from behind there," Lord Aron ordered.

The young boy flew toward his dad, nearly knocking him over as he landed in his arms. "I've missed you so much, Father. Please don't be mad at me or Egan."

"I've missed you, too, Alin. And I'm not mad at either one of you. Disappointed, maybe—since Egan's been told not to go off on his own. But not angry. In any case, you shouldn't go out by yourself, either." Lord Aron's attempt at being stern quickly dissolved into a joyful smile. "I really am glad to see you. However, it's just not safe to be out here alone."

"But I'm not alone. I'm here with Egan...and you." Alin slid from his father's arms to the ground. Other than their wings—his were fiery red and Egan's were silvery white—the two boys looked exactly alike—twins in every other way.

"Besides," Alin continued, "Prince Teren's not the only one with magic talent, you know. I can protect us." He squeezed his right hand into a fist. A second later, he tossed a red-hot fireball into the bush he had hid behind. "Mom says I have even more Talent than Teren."

Lord Aron and Egan watched as the shrub burst into flames, disintegrating into ashes. "You just might, Alin." Lord Aron's deep brown eyes found it difficult to not reveal how impressed he was. No five-year-old should be able to do that—even if he is almost six.

"In spite of your exceptional Talent, it might not be enough to stop an entire band of Banshees. Terrible things have been going on—some of them not far from here. Besides, your mother will be extremely upset if she finds out that you've gone out on your own."

"That's why I don't tell her," Alin insisted.

"Me either." Egan nodded. "We were just going to the volcano lake. It's nice and warm, and I'm teaching Alin to swim. He's my best student. He already swims faster than me."

Alin put his arm around his brother. That's 'cause you let me. But this time you promised to make it a fair race."

"It was almost fair before. And it was only your third lesson."

"Third lesson, huh?" Lord Aron looked from one boy to the other. "What am I going to do with you two?"

With a mischievous grin, Alin replied, "Race us to the lake?"

How could anyone refuse that face? he thought. "Alright, but on one condition, both of you promise you will not go out again without me."

Egan looked at Alin, who shrugged and quickly flew off toward the lake. Egan was right behind him.

"What am I going to do with those two?" Lord Aron flew after them. Through the treetops they soared. The sun was nearly straight overhead, and the forest was alive with animals of every kind. Deer were grazing on patches of sweet clover, squirrels busily gathered pine nuts for the long winter ahead, a family of skunks nibbled on the abundant blackberries, and several blue jays squawked loudly as they flew in formation behind the three Fée.

Everything seemed right with the world. Lord Aron, however, knew this momentary tranquility was merely a reprieve from the atrocities that were continually unfolding. *At least they can have a few minutes of fun,* he thought, landing on the lake's edge next to Egan and Alin. With a twist of his wrist, both boys were dressed in bathing suits.

"Wow!" Alin exclaimed. "Can you teach me that trick?"

"Me, too," Egan said, staring at his dark blue trunks. "It would be really good when I'm late for dinner and don't have time to change."

"That's another thing I want to talk to you about, Egan. Seems as though you're late for dinner quite a bit these days."

"Um, well... I... I have lots of school work now."

"School work, huh?"

Egan looked from his dad to his brother. "Bet I can beat you this time!" He dove into the crystal clear water.

"Bet you can't!" Alin jumped in after him. Laughing and giggling, the two boys started a water fight.

"You coming, Father?" Egan called. "It's nice and warm."

"I think I'd better stand guard. Only swim out to that big lava rock and back." He pointed to a large partially submerged boulder about thirty meters away.

"Okay," Alin replied before ducking underwater to avoid Egan's splash.

The two boys shot off like unleashed arrows. Egan, as the more experienced swimmer, quickly took the lead, slowing down only when he was several body lengths ahead. Beating his brother was one thing, but he would never embarrass him by getting too far in the lead. With a sudden burst of speed, Alin surged past him.

"Hey, what was all that about?" Egan asked after climbing onto the craggy black rock. "You beat me this time, for sure."

Alin's smile stretched from ear to ear. "I think I finally figured swimming out," he replied. "You just need to get your arms and legs working opposite."

"No more lessons for you," Egan joked. He was so proud of his brother. Born only two minutes apart, Egan was the oldest, but Alin was far more competitive. Winning was important to him. To Egan it didn't matter; he had a brother. If only he could figure out how to make his mother love him, then they could be a real family. In his heart, he knew she would probably never accept him because he was born without wings. But that didn't stop him from trying.

From a few meters away, hidden in the treetops, Lady Aron watched the two boys. She had dimmed the flames of her fiery wings so they wouldn't glow in the shadows of the trees.

This is perfect, she thought. *I'm going to relish every minute as I watch that freak of a child die, and even more so when his father is dead.* Her pulse was racing. It would be so easy to kill the two of them right now. *Soon, Firenza, soon,* she told herself. *As much as I would love to destroy them this very minute, I mustn't let Alin know the true reason I tolerate them playing together. How he could think I wouldn't know is beyond me. He's such a headstrong child.* Her amber eyes shone with delight. *Just like I was when I was his age.*

"Time to go, boys," Lord Aron called. "I suddenly have a bad feeling about this place."

"We'll be right there, Father," Egan called. "Bet I can beat you back," he told Alin.

"Bet you can't."

They dove off the rock. Standing near the sandy shore, Lord Aron felt a chilling sensation. *She's here,* he thought, scanning the trees. *And not very far away, either.* He notched an arrow. Firenza was brilliant with a bow. He was just as good, having taught her many a trick when they were first married. *Little did I know she would one day turn against me,* he thought. Lord Aron slowly kneeled. He carefully scooped up a bright green beetle. "Find her," he whispered.

The beetle spread its iridescent wings and headed straight toward a cluster of tall pines. It made a clicking sound and was immediately joined by several other beetles—each flying toward the same tree.

"I could have married anyone," Lady Aron murmured. "Why I picked a Fée from the Earthen Clan is beyond me. He and those annoying insects." She swatted at one of the bugs, and it instantly darted out of the way.

Firenza hastily gestured, but there was no bright scarlet flash, as was normally the case when she transported—only a dim grey mist.

Her fiery energy was pulled inward, so as to not be seen.

The beetle flew back and landed on Lord Aron's hand. He gently rubbed the top of the tiny creature's head. "Thank you. I saw her." The bug made a slight chirping sound before flying off to a nearby fallen tree.

Egan and Alin stood on the shore watching their father. "Who was there?" Egan asked.

"I'm... not sure. But we need to leave right now. Alin, I want you to transport directly home. And both of you remember, no more venturing out by yourselves."

"Yes, Father." Alin hugged Lord Aron and then Egan goodbye. "See you soon," he whispered.

"Okay." Egan's eyes sparkled as he hugged his brother. "We're even now, so we have to race again to break the tie."

"Maybe in a couple days?" Alin looked up, hopefully, at his father. "Please."

"We'll see. Now go straight home." *He may be able to control balls of fire,* Lord Aron thought, *but not that mischievous grin.* In spite of his warning, Lord Aron knew it would be impossible to keep the two boys from sneaking off to see each other. He watched Alin vanish then turned to Egan. "Let's also transport home. I heard a rumor that the chef made your favorite beet and potato soup for lunch and there may still be some left."

"Rosemary Swirl? Let's go."

TEN

"**A**driana, look," Teren called out. "Over there."

"I don't see anything." She scrutinized the perfectly mani-cured park-like gardens behind the Bardic Temple. The labyrinth that dominated its center looked like it always did—an intricate stone maze draped in ivy and boxwood.

"There it is again—that red glow." He pointed in the direction of the maze. "I think it's getting brighter."

"Oh, my gosh, what is it?" Adriana watched as an eerie glowing red ball hovered at the entrance of the labyrinth.

"I thought maybe you'd know." Teren stared at the strange object.

"I've never seen anything like it. We'd better go tell Father." She turned to leave.

"Wait a minute." He caught her hand. "Let's see what it does. Besides, it's probably another one of Centrod's tests to see if I'll break my promise to not try any more spells on my own."

"He did heal your hands based on your promise," Adriana asserted.

"I know, but I didn't create this. Come on, let's get a closer look."

"I don't think it's a good idea, Teren." She stood watching the ball's pulsing glow. "Though it does seem like it's trying to get us to follow it."

"You said you've been through the maze a hundred times. Let's go see what it does. Besides, by the time we find Centrod, it may be gone.

Come on." He moved a bit closer.

"Alright, but we need to be really careful." The two of them cautiously approached the entrance of the maze, just as the glowing ball darted inside.

"I think it does want us to follow it," Teren exclaimed.

"I think you're right. Look." The sphere paused a couple meters ahead, as though it was waiting for them to catch up. Only when they moved closer did it move into one of the passageways.

As they followed it deeper into the maze, Teren asked, "You do know how to get out of here, don't you?"

"Of course, Teren. Don't you know the secret of a labyrinth?"

"Well, no—not exactly."

"You put your hand along one wall, and never lose touch of the side. Eventually, you'll find your way out."

"Is that true?"

"It is." She looked in both directions at a crossroads in the path. "Where'd it go?"

"There it is." The two of them darted after it.

Adriana stopped abruptly. "That's strange," she said looking at the walls of the maze. "The ivy, it's... Teren, it's growing!" she shrieked.

The vines began wrapping themselves completely around the young Priestess. Before Teren could help her, they coiled around him, as well. "Adriana!" he shouted, struggling to break free. The ivy tightened around his chest. He could barely breathe, let alone free himself.

The last words Teren heard were Adriana calling to him. Then everything turned a bright scarlet red. He felt himself being pulled through space. Not as though he was transporting, but more like he was falling—tumbling head over heels. The red light swirled around him. A gut wrenching chill swept through his body as he remembered the time he was trapped in the tornado cave that nearly cost him and Jake their lives. All he could think of was, *Where's Adriana?*

• • • •

For the second game of Chessaé, the Pixies' costumes were even more resplendent, creating a spectacle beyond compare. It appeared as though every jewel that they owned was sewn onto their costumes. There was so much gold and silver, it was difficult to see how the tiny faeries could stand up under all the weight, let alone parade and prance around. The Knights were not only dressed like their namesakes, but had gilded armor that covered virtually every bit of the fabricated horses that had been fashioned to look as though the Pixies were riding on their backs. Their bridles and saddles were spun from woven strands of silver or gold and accented with pink, blue, and canary-yellow diamonds.

For most of the morning, the Pixies paraded and posed. Each of the thirty-two players, in turn, danced and whirled or simply strutted around, showing off their elaborate costuming.

Throughout it all, Lord Mywerk and Cyndara patiently stood on their respective sides of the giant game boards, awaiting the start of play. Slant stood with the Crown Princess, who was surrounded by several ladies-in-waiting. Only Lord Mywerk's favorite valet accompanied him. Cyndara's two brothers were nowhere to be seen.

Finally, the trumpets heralded, and the booming voice from the overhead balcony announced the start of the Game: "Lord Mywerk, for this match you are of the white team. The opening move goes to you."

After a respectful bow to Cyndara, he called for the Pawn on Level 2 to move from e2 to e4. It was the same move that Cyndara opened with in the first Game. She matched his move by requesting her Pawn on e7 to move to e5—again a duplicate move from the prior game. In both cases, the Pixies agreed with their requested moves and, in elaborate fashion, somersaulted and spun to the requested spaces. The second Pixie was even showier than the first.

And so Game Two began—a game that Cyndara knew could possibly end her chances to rule, once and for all. She could not challenge Lord Mywerk again. It would not be allowed. The Banshee Princess also knew that from all of the posturing and parading that was going on during each move, it would be a long match.

It wasn't long, however, before the Pixies began to tire from all the posing in their heavy costumes. After only a quarter of an hour of game play, they called a halt for lunch. Much booing and hissing ensued within the massive crowd of onlookers. Nevertheless, the Pixies bowed to the crowd, and then to Cyndara and Lord Mywerk before parading off the boards. When it came to food, Pixies never missed a meal—especially if the Royal Chefs prepared it.

Lord Mywerk shrugged and then hastily retreated to also have a bit of sustenance while awaiting the restart of the game. Turning to Slant, Cyndara asked about her brothers. The fact that they were not there bothered her a great deal.

"I have no idea where Prince Yandell and Prince Kilmonth have gone," Slant whispered to the Crown Princess as they left the playing arena. "Your brothers haven't been seen since just after the first Game."

"I want you to find them and do it discreetly. Take only your most trusted soldiers. My brothers must not know that you're looking for them. With so much at stake, it's odd that they would not be here." *Unless,* she thought, *they're working on some sort of an alternative plan in case I win.*

"I'll set off immediately," he said. "But there's something else you must know—and it may be related to your brothers. One of my scouts reported that he saw a large number of Fée traveling down from the mountains this morning. I didn't want to interrupt you with the news, as the Game was just starting when I learned of it."

"How large a number?"

"Several thousand."

"Several thousand?" Cyndara was taken aback. "Could they be coming to the Game?"

"Not likely, since they were headed east," Slant explained.

"East, you say? What is east of here?" she asked.

"Crop lands and an aban—"

"Abandoned training field!" Cyndara exclaimed. "You don't think they're raising an army to attack our Kingdom, do you?"

"Even they are not that dumb—at least I hope they're not," he replied. "Respectfully speaking, of course."

"Of course." She nodded with a knowing smile. Her brothers may be royalty, but it was hard for anyone to respect them. "I think you'd better find out just how 'dumb' my brothers really are. And please hurry. Interrupt me at any point in the Game when you have news."

"By your leave." With a gracious bow, Slant hastily departed.

"Is something wrong, Cyndara?" Lord Mywerk entered the common area where she and Slant had been talking. "You appear to be upset."

"With only eight moves having been made, what could possibly be wrong, my dear Lord Mywerk?" Though she smiled at him, her response was hardly genuine. Something was, indeed, very wrong, and her mentor and life-long friend may be at the heart of it. *How could Mywerk have betrayed me like this?* If only she knew why. Turning to leave, Cyndara looked back, saying, "Do excuse me. I should like to have some lunch."

She felt his piercing stare as she walked away.

"Can you control your garglans well enough to bring a few dozen of them with you during the attack?"

ELEVEN

In a blazing scarlet flash, Lady Aron materialized on the edge of the Banshee training field, a cleared area deep in the Kingdom's eastern most forest. This time, her fiery wings and flowing red-and-amber hair blazed in the wind. No one could miss this entrance. Impatient to begin the implementation of her latest plan, Firenza anxiously eyed what were, for the most part, motley-looking troops, as they attempted some bizarre semblance of marching maneuvers. "How many soldiers do you have now?" she asked the two Banshee Princes.

"Seven thousand, give or take," Prince Kilmonth replied. "The other seven thousand we're not so sure about!" The two brothers exploded in laughter.

"Get it? Get it?" Prince Yandell elbowed her. "You said 'soldiers.'"

She flinched from his jab. "You do have a way with words." Her amber eyes looked straight at him.

"Yeah, I sure do, don't I?" He slapped his knee.

Frowning, Lady Aron rephrased her question, "So, how many total troops do you have?"

"Exactly 14,249 and one-half," he replied.

"One-half?"

"Just a joke, My Lady," Kilmonth chortled.

"You gotta get a sense of humor," Yandell added.

"No, I do not. Not when it comes to battle plans." Moving to avoid another elbow in the ribs, she glared at him with a look that said battle plans were not the only thing that she didn't have a sense of humor about.

"Yeah, well," Yandell continued, "if you can't laugh, then what's the point? Right, big brother?"

"Right, little brother. Hey, did Yandell ever tell you about the time he won the joke tellin' contest?"

"No, but I'm certain he will. Might I, however, request that it wait until our victory celebration? That way you can tell your new subjects, as well."

A sadistic smirk enveloped Yandell's face. "You mean the ones that we're gonna feed to the garglans?"

"Those very ones." She nodded.

"Okay," Yandell said, "but it's a shame to waste such a good story on Imperfects."

"Yes, I'm sure it is. And as King, you can do whatever you like with them."

"King Yandell of the newly formed Kingdom of Yandell. It does sound good. Doesn't it, big brother?"

"Humph!" Kilmonth was clearly not impressed.

"You're just jealous," Yandell chided. "And anyway, I'm going to charge you plenty for my Imperfects! You're not gettin' free garglan food from me. Hey, maybe we can swap—one garglan for one Imperfect!"

"That's not fair!"

"Is too!"

"No, it's not! Garglans are worth way more."

"Is too!

"Is not!"

"Is!"

"Not!"

"Is!"

"Not!"

"Gentlemen. Gentlemen! Please, I'm sure that something can be negotiated."

Kilmonth looked at her. "Yeah, that's what we'll do, we'll negotiate. Right, little brother?"

"Yeah. Good thinking, big brother. We'll negotiate. That's what we'll do."

"Good." Lady Aron glared at each of them. "We don't want one of you killing the other, now do we? Especially before you go into battle."

"We might kill each other now," Kilmonth told her, "but you don't have to be worryin' your pretty head about us gettin' killed in battle."

"Nope, not us gettin' killed in battle," Yandell said.

"Oh? And why is that?" Lady Aron asked.

"Because we're not goin' anywhere near the front lines," he answered. "We got General Kandour for that."

"I thought Banshees were supposed to be brave?"

"Brave, maybe. But fools we're not!" Kilmonth retorted.

"Yes, well, I guess where ignorance is bliss…"

"Hey, who you're callin' ignorant?" Yandell glared at her.

"It's just an expression."

"Yeah, dummy, it's just an expression." Kilmonth smacked his brother. "It's from that Shakespeare fellow," he added with an overt sense of pride.

"Actually it was from the human poet, Thomas Gray," Lady Aron explained. "But I am impressed that you know Shakespeare, Prince Kilmonth."

"Not personally."

"I mean, you know about human playwrights." She was more than a bit surprised that he would have any knowledge of literature, let alone human literature.

"Was Shakespeare a human?"

"That is an interesting question," she responded. "I'm sure you are aware that some human scholars don't believe that a man named Shakespeare actually ever lived."

"Now that's what's dumb." Kilmonth shook his head. "Of course he lived. Otherwise who wrote all those plays?"

"You do have a point. I'll be sure to ask Lord Rössi."

"You mean Cyndara's new friend?" Yandell snickered.

"What do you mean, Cyndara's new friend?" Lady Aron was extremely curious about his emphasis on the word friend.

"They were gettin' pretty chummy, those two."

"Really? Do tell me more, Prince Yandell."

"Don't know much more—except Mywerk didn't seem very happy about it."

"Really? That's very interesting."

"Hey, there's somethin' I'd like to know."

"And what is that, Prince Kilmonth?"

"How come you don't want us to invade Queen Kandide's Kingdom for you? We could capture her and make you Queen."

"I appreciate your offer. My reasons, however, are my own. And don't forget the treaty you both signed that forbids you from attacking Calabiyau Proper."

"We didn't forget," Kilmonth replied. "But it doesn't make any sense."

"It doesn't have to. Now get those troops in order. We attack as soon as Kandide deploys the Frost to bring about winter, when the Veil that protects the Château is at its weakest. If she follows tradition, it will be two days after the ceremonies of Samhain."

"You mean on November second, two days after All Hallows' Eve? We can't do that," Kilmonth asserted.

"And pray tell, why not, Prince Kilmonth?"

"Because it's Yandell's birthday. We can't attack on his birthday. It's bad luck."

"My birthday's not bad luck."

"No, dim-wit." Kilmonth smacked his brother again. "Attacking on a birthday is what's bad luck."

"That's true. We can't attack on my birthday. It's bad luck to attack on a birthday."

"That's absurd," Lady Aron retorted. "Think about it, with over fourteen thousand troops, every day is someone's birthday. Does that mean we can never attack?"

Kilmonth rubbed his chin. "Hmmm... I need to contemplate that."

"Hey, I know what we can do," Yandell suggested. "We can attack on Kandide's birthday. That way, it'll be bad luck for her."

"Kandide's birthday isn't until December sixth, and I highly doubt she'll wait that long to deploy the Frost."

"Her waiting's not the problem," Kilmonth responded. "We can't afford to feed these troops that long!"

"Can't we make it even one day later?" Yandell asked. "I was gonna throw myself a party."

"That, gentlemen, depends upon Kandide," Lady Aron insisted. "Just be ready."

Yandell pointed his finger at her. "Okay, but if things go bad, don't say I didn't warn you."

"I consider myself warned. Now, let's go see General Kandour. I want to discuss our strategy."

"It's about time," Kilmonth told her as the three of them headed off to General Kandour's tent.

"So, I see you've decided to come out of hiding," the distinguished-looking general remarked, seeing Lady Aron. He was sitting behind his desk looking over some maps. "Planning on a November second attack?

"How'd you know that?" Yandell eyed the General suspiciously. "You got spies listening to us? Cause my brother and I won't be having you spying on us."

"Now, would I do that, Your Highness? You are, after all, in charge of this operation, are you not?"

"Yeah, and don't you forget it!" Kilmonth exclaimed.

"I assure you, I never do. It's the only day that makes sense—the day Kandide deploys the Frost and the Veil is at its weakest—assuming she does it then. Am I correct, Firenza?"

"You are exactly correct. And I see no reason why she would delay it this year. Let's talk about your attack strategy." Lady Aron moved to a three-dimensional war table—a miniature replica of the Mists that surrounded the Château.

After much discussion, she and Kandour, who made several extremely shrewd observations, agreed upon an approach.

Fortunately, the two brothers are at least smart enough to keep their mouths shut during these types of discussions, she thought. "The plan sounds perfect, General. Do you have any concerns?"

Yandell spoke up before Kandour could answer: "I do. A big one. How we gonna know when Kandide deploys the Frost?"

"We look up in the sky," Kilmonth told him. "If it's snowing, she did it."

"That's exactly right, Prince Kilmonth," Lady Aron said. *How do I put up with them?* "Now, there's something you can do for me."

"What's that?" Kilmonth asked.

"Can you control your garglans well enough to bring a few dozen of them with you during the attack?"

"Sure, if we keep 'em on chains," Yandell answered. "What do you want 'em for?"

"You'll learn soon enough. Just bring them."

"Okay, but you best to be tellin' us pretty soon. We are, after all, partners." He held his hand out to her. It looked as though he hadn't washed it in weeks.

Ignoring him, she continued speaking: "Of course. Now, I need a traitor."

"A what?" Kilmonth looked surprised by her request. "We don't

GENERAL KANDOUR

have any traitors—not yet anyway."

"Nope, we don't have any traitors—yet," Yandell agreed. "We feed 'em to the garglans when they do stuff like that."

"Not a real traitor, gentlemen." She looked at Kandour who merely shrugged. "Someone who can leak part of our plan."

Kilmonth scratched his head. "Why'd we wanna do that? I say we surprise 'em."

"Yep, I say we surprise 'em," his brother mimicked.

Kilmonth smacked Yandell on the shoulder. "Hey, that's what I said."

"Ouch!" He rubbed his arm. "You better not do that when I'm King."

"Why not?"

"'Cause if you do, I'll kill you, that's why."

"Unless I kill you first."

Don't they ever stop? Lady Aron could only think how wonderful it would be if they actually did kill each other. *Pity they need to stay alive to uphold the treaty I had them sign.* She knew that without them, General Kandour would never honor it, and order his army to capture Calabiyau Proper. "Gentlemen, please. Can you focus on the discussion at hand for just a few more minutes?"

"He hit me first!" Yandell pouted, crossing his arms.

"You hit me back!"

"Stop it!" General Kandour all but shouted above their carrying on. "Both of you, please stop…Your Highnesses."

"You heard him, stop it!" Kilmonth ordered his brother. "So, what about this traitor?"

"He is not a real traitor—sort of a double agent," Kandour patiently explained.

"Oh, I get it." Kilmonth grinned. "He just pretends to leak the plan, but we're really doin' something else."

"Very good, Kilmonth," Lady Aron told him.

"Thanks, Firenza. Say, you don't mind me callin' you Firenza, do you? Being that we're partners and all."

"That's fine."

"Firenza. That's a really nice name." Yandell reached for her hand. "Hey, you still married?"

Pulling it away, the words could not come out of her mouth fast enough. "Yes, I am."

"Too bad. I was thinking that now that we're working together and all, we could…well you know."

"Very married! Shall we continue?"

"That's what I meant." Yandell began to snicker.

"Hey! Don't you be making remarks like that to Firenza. She's a Lady. Beggin' your pardon, ma'am." Kilmonth bowed to her. "You apologize, little brother." The look on his face told Yandell that he should do as his brother said.

"Beggin' your pardon, Lady. I was just jokin' with you."

"Apology accepted. Now, may we please continue? General Kandour, here's what I would like our traitor to do…"

Teren was sure he'd learned to be more cautious.
Now Adriana's life was also in danger.

TWELVE

Teren landed with a thud, jarring him back to consciousness. The vines that had nearly squeezed all the air from his lungs were gone; the glowing red light had dissipated. But where he was, he had no idea. The sun was starting to shift to the western horizon. The grass and flowers seemed familiar, yet different. As he looked around, he realized that this was a world unlike any he had ever seen. An oak, an elm, and an ash surrounded him. They were similar to the three sacred trees of the Fée. But why would they be growing in this strange land?

Almost before Teren could grasp the situation, Adriana appeared nearby. She also landed with a thud. He rushed to her, extending his hand to help her up. "Are you okay?"

"I think so." She brushed off the fall-colored leaves that landed on her hair and shoulders when she appeared. "Where are we? What is this place?"

"I don't know. Look at those buildings. They're square and..."

"Made of red bricks," she said. Suddenly, a bell rang and school kids started pouring out of the buildings. Grabbing Teren's arm, she pulled him behind the oak tree. "Look!"

"Earthly spirits, they're... they're humans! Adriana, those kids are human!" Teren wasn't sure whether to be excited or scared. "Do you think a portal could have opened up and transported us to the human realm?"

"That's the only way I know we could have gotten here." She suddenly remembered something she had learned about mazes—they were often built to conceal entrances to other dimensions.

"This is incredible." Teren had always wanted to visit the human realm, but he certainly hadn't anticipated it happening without him knowing it. "The question is, how do we get back?"

"I was hoping you'd know that."

"Well, the portal has to be right near here." He scanned the grounds.

"Look up there." Adriana pointed to a dark circle in the sky just above them. It looked like a funnel-shaped rain cloud with a glowing red outline. As they watched, it began to shrink, and then it simply vanished. "Where'd it go?" she asked.

"I don't know, but from what I've read about portals, it should stay there as long as we are here. You don't think...? You don't think it closed somehow?" A hint of fear crossed his face.

"I'm not sure, Teren." Adriana looked back up at the sky. Only a few wispy clouds broke the vast expanse of blue. "From the little bit I know about portals, they never just vanish like that. Unless..."

"Unless it was spelled to close once we went through." *Why does my curiosity always get the best of me?* he thought, his shoulders slumping. After almost being killed on his first journey to the Bardic Temple, Teren was sure he'd learned to be more cautious. Now Adriana's life was also in danger. "I bet that red orb in the labyrinth was caused by whoever wanted us here."

"And maybe doesn't want us to come back. What are we going to do?" she asked.

"I'm not sure." He forced himself to stand up a little taller, trying to hide how worried he was. "But what I do know is that we can't stay here for more than a few days or we'll start to age really fast."

"How fast, Teren?"

"From what I've been told, it doesn't take long, then all of sudden you're dead."

"That doesn't sound very appealing. We need to figure out how to reopen the portal. Any thoughts?"

Teren had no idea, but he wasn't about to let Adriana know it. "I think the first thing we need to do is change our clothes, so we blend in." With a wave of his hand, their white robes transformed into jeans and shirts that mimicked the clothing they saw the students wearing.

Adriana looked at him and began to giggle. "You can change your clothes all you want, Prince Teren, but with those ears and wings, I don't think you're ever going to look like these kids. Maybe a jacket and cap will help." She snapped her fingers and they appeared. "That's better."

"Who... who are you?" a voice from behind called.

Teren and Adriana whirled around. Standing behind them was a young human girl—about ten or eleven, he guessed.

"I liked your other costumes better," she said. "You looked like some of the characters in a book I was just reading. Hi, my name is Ninon." The young Asian girl with long black hair held out her hand. "You can call me Ni."

"I'm Adriana." She shook Ninon's hand. "And this is Teren."

"Wow, you both look exactly like the pictures in my book. Is the author coming back to speak to us again? She was here about a month ago. Is that why you're here?" A river of questions flowed from Ninon's lips: "Are you the actors that are going to be in the movie? Could you get me a part? Do you think I could play one of the apprentices at the Bardic Temple? I won first place in my drama class and they gave me a really big trophy." She held up her hand to show that it was almost as tall as she was.

Teren could tell by the excitement in Ni's voice that she had no idea they were Fée—real Fée. Not wanting to give their actual identity away, he stammered: "Uh, yeah, that's it. That's why we're here. We're in a movie. Right, Adriana?"

"Uh, yeah. That's right—in a movie." Adriana glanced at Teren. "We're actors. Well, I'm an actress."

"How did you get your wings to look so good?" Ninon asked. "It's like they're real. Would you take off your jacket so I can see? Can you make them flap? You have to show me how you do it."

"Well, uh, okay." Teren slid off his jacket and flapped his wings. "It's really pretty easy. They're attached to a… a harness on my back." His demonstration was interrupted by another ringing of the bell.

"Gosh, I need to get to class," Ni said. "Ms. Lee doesn't like it when we're late. Hey, why don't you come with me? I know she'd really like to meet you. She loves both of the books. She even let us have a party for Ms. Zimmerman."

"Ms. who?" Teren asked.

"You know, Diana S. Zimmerman—the author of the Kandide trilogy." Ninon looked at him a bit askance. "You mean you don't know her?"

"No…I mean yes, of course we know her," Adriana quickly replied. "Teren was referring to Ms. Lee. Right, Teren?"

"Right."

"I wish Ms. Zimmerman would hurry up and get the next book out," Ninon said. "I can't wait to see what happens with Kandide and Jake. Thank goodness you—I mean the real Teren—figured out how to break Tara's spell when Lady Aron froze her in that terrible block of ice. That was so clever. He's my favorite character."

"I am? I mean, he is? You…you know about Tara?" Teren was dumbfounded. This was all so surreal. Maybe it was a dream. How could a human know about Calabiyau? She couldn't. No. That's impossible. None of this was making any sense. And what did she mean Kandide trilogy? No one's ever written a book about his sister—let alone three books. "Ninon… I mean Ni, do you have a copy of one of those books?"

"Of course. Everyone in the school has Book One, *The Secret of the*

Mists. But mine's at home. I have the second one here—we're reading it in class. Except I read ahead and already finished it. Listen, I have to get to my creative writing class. Hey, why don't you come with me?"

"Uh, well... alright." Teren looked at Adriana, who nodded in agreement.

"Great. You are so awesome—both of you. Can you tell me how you made your clothes change? Is it like some of Ms. Zimmerman's magic?"

"Ms. Zimmerman does magic?" Adriana asked.

"You didn't know that? She used to be the number one lady magician in the world. She was on TV all the time. She can pull coins out of the air and then turn them into dollar bills. It's really cool. You know what else would be cool?"

"What?" Teren asked, wondering why, if Ms. Zimmerman is such a powerful mage, would she bother pulling coins out of the air and turning them into dollars. Why wouldn't she just make whatever she wanted magically appear?

"Well, if you were to walk in dressed like Teren in the book—you know, in those old-fashioned clothes—that would be so cool. I don't suppose you can do that trick?"

"You mean like this?" Teren waved his hand and his jeans and shirt changed to courtly attire. With another wave, Adriana's changed, as well. She was dressed in her white robe with its blue belt.

Ninon took a step backwards. "Okay, how did you do that? I mean, I saw a quick-change artist one time in a show at the Wynn Hotel, but not like that." She eyed Teren from top to bottom. "And your wings... and your ears. Oh, my Gosh!" she shrieked, backing even farther away. Her brown eyes were as big as moons. "I must be dreaming."

Adriana tried to calm her fears. "No. It's, uh, just a really good magic trick, Ni. That's all. Like the one you saw in the show at that hotel. Isn't it, Teren?"

Ninon stood staring at him. He could tell she wasn't at all sure what to believe. "Really, it's just a clever trick," he assured her.

"I... I don't believe you," she finally managed to say. "I asked Ms. Zimmerman if Calabiyau is real and she said it's as real as I want it to be. But it is real, isn't it?" A blend of fear and curiosity crossed her face. "You are real."

Teren looked at Adriana. *Could they trust this young human girl? What would Ninon do if she knew the truth?* He could sense that Adriana was wondering the same thing. "Would you like us to be real?" he asked.

I... I think so. I... I wish I lived there. Then maybe the other kids wouldn't tease me all the time."

"Why do they tease you?" Adriana asked.

"Not so much the kids in my class. Ms. Lee won't allow it—just some of the other kids, 'cause I don't have expensive jeans and I walk with a limp because my foot is twisted. See, my dad died a couple years ago, and my mom's job doesn't pay very much. So my little brother, Felix, and I don't have expensive clothes. But my mother's going to college at night so she can get a better job." Ninon's eyes lit up with pride. "She's going to be a lawyer and defend battered women. Then we'll be able to afford insurance so I can get an operation to fix my foot. So I won't be an Imperfect—uh, not that that's bad. I mean... I just would rather have my foot normal." Curiosity was beginning to overcome her trepidation. "So, are you real Fée?"

Teren still wasn't sure if he should tell her the truth or not. "I'm sorry about your father."

"It's okay. Sometimes he could be really mean to my mom—like when he drank too much because of being in the war. Mom said he was never the same when he got back. But Felix and I still miss him. I think my mom does too—even if she doesn't say so. 'Cause most of the time he was really nice."

"I'm sure he was," Adriana said softly. "Ninon, Calabiyau is real. And Teren and I need your help. You see, we somehow got in this portal that opened up and brought us to your world. Now it seems to have completely closed and we have no idea how to get back home—or even where we are."

Ninon took another step back. "Are you telling me the truth?"

"She is," Teren assured her. "We aren't actors. We're really from Calabiyau."

For a moment, Ninon just stood there, not saying a word. She then started jumping up and down. "Oh, my gosh! Oh, my gosh! Oh, my gosh! I have to tell Ms. Lee. She won't believe it. I can't wait to tell her...and my two best friends, Ishan and Kathy. Come, on!" She started toward her classroom.

"Ni, wait," Teren called. "Maybe that's not such a good idea—at least, not right away."

"Why? Ms. Lee loves your books. She's, like, Ms. Zimmerman's biggest fan—next to me, of course. She even arranged for her to speak at lots of other schools here in Las Vegas."

"Is that where we are—Las Vegas?" Adriana asked—though she had no idea where Las Vegas actually was. "Since you speak English, I assumed we were in England."

"Or America," Teren said.

"Teren's right," Ninon said. "Las Vegas is in Nevada, which is in the United States, which is part of the North American continent. So, how come you speak English and not a Fée language or something?"

Teren had to chuckle. He had never thought of their language as Fée. But what she said did make sense. "We speak English because most of our ancestors came from the area humans call England. At one time, about 2000 BC, as you humans measure time, we had over twenty-five different languages. But my great-great-great-great-grandmother, who was Queen back then, made English the official language to unite the Clans."

"But they didn't unite, and that's why Jake had to fight in the Clan Wars," Ninon said. "I think it's awesome how he made wooden feet and used diamonds for the joints."

"You know about the Clan Wars and Jake's wooden feet?" Teren was amazed.

"I know lots of things. It's all in the Kandide books."

"We really do need to get a copy of those books," Adriana said, just before the bell rang again.

"Oh, no!" I've missed my class. Ms. Lee will be really mad at me. Come on! We have to go." She motioned for Teren and Adriana to follow. "Maybe since I'm with you, she won't give me detention. I mean, I do have a good excuse."

"So, uh, Ni, do you know how to contact Ms. Zimmerman?" Teren asked as they hurried toward the classroom. "Maybe one of her books will tell us how to get back."

"Maybe her next book," Ni said. "I can't wait to read it. Ms. Lee can send her an email. Ms. Zimmerman helped me with one of my stories. I love to write. I'm going to be an author like her when I grow up. But right now, we really need to hurry."

"Okay." Teren had no idea what Ninon meant by an email, but he certainly didn't want her to get detention because of him. *I sure hope Ms. Lee doesn't make her wash dishes,* he thought. *Anyway, I'm sure she's nicer than Viviana. I wonder if they torture students in human schools.*

THIRTEEN

Shortly after lunch, the second Chessaé game resumed play. Lord Mywerk called for the Pixie on level 2, e9 to go to c3 on the same level. This time, however, the Pixie refused his move. The crowd went quiet. All knew that these were the moments in Chessaé that would long be argued about, regardless of who won. Annoyed that his move had been denied, Mywerk requested to speak with the unaccommodating Pixie—a common occurrence when a desired move is challenged.

Fluttering over to him, the Pixie defended her decision, and they began debating the strategy and merits of her refusal. "I demand a trial," she finally insisted.

Mywerk had no choice but to allow it, though he knew it would be a mock trial in which he couldn't possibly prevail. Pixies loved "holding court" as they referred to it, since it reinforced who was in charge when it came to Chessaé.

Within seconds, a Pixie dressed in a white powdered wig and a long black gown flew down from a top balcony. Several others joined him. They were dressed as lawyers, court appointees, and other such official representatives of the court.

"Will the defendant known as Lord Mywerk please address the court," the judge ordered. "You are accused of disputing a Pixie move. How do you plead?"

Not wanting the trial to go on any longer than necessary, Lord

Mywerk stated, "Guilty, Your Honor. But let it go on record that I am not without reason."

"So noted." Slamming his gavel down on the miniature desk that floated in front of him, the judge proclaimed: "This court finds you guilty as charged. The move stands. Justice has prevailed."

Loud hisses and boos erupted from the audience. Banging his gavel several more times, the judge hollered, "Silence in the court or I shall have every seat emptied!"

The crowd grudgingly quieted down.

"Your sentence, Lord Mywerk, is to accept the move. Do you agree to this?"

"Since I have no choice, I do, Your Honor."

"Then it shall be!" He slammed his gavel down one final time. "There will be a five-minute recess while Lord Mywerk rethinks his strategy based on this new move, then the game will resume." As quickly as they appeared, the judge and his entourage disappeared—desk and all.

During the mock trial, Slant had returned. Motioning for Cyndara to step off to the side, he whispered, "I am afraid I have bad news. Your brothers have assembled fourteen thousand troops; maybe more."

"What?" Cyndara couldn't believe what she was hearing. "Fourteen thousand—that's… How's that possible?"

"I don't know. And I apologize for telling you during the Game, but you asked that I notify you as soon as I learned anything."

"Yes, yes—of course," she replied. "Are you quite sure of the number?"

"I saw them myself. Such an army I have not seen since your father waged war on the Benders."

Images of that battle flashed through Cyndara's mind—if you could call it a battle. Though quite young at the time, she remembered the siege led by General Kandour. It was a bloody massacre of this gentle Banshee tribe who got their name because they are always bending down to pick low growing crops such as strawberries and lettuce. As a result, they normally walk stooped over. Their only weapons were the rakes and hoes they used to farm with. Thousands were killed in just a few hours—simply because they wanted to keep more of the food they grew for their families.

"The troops are training on the same field that your father used to train that army," Slant continued. "And what they lack in experience is more than made up for in numbers."

Cyndara was nearly white from shock. "How could my brothers have gathered so many?"

"As we all know, with the Frost this summer, it's been a very tough year for nearly everyone. Rumor has it that Prince Kilmonth is dropping gold coins around like autumn leaves."

"Do you think it's Calabiyau Proper they're after this time?" A sudden thought flashed through her mind. "You don't think they'd attack here, do you?"

"I wondered about that, myself, Your Highness. With General Kandour leading them, anything's possible. Perhaps it's a dual attack on both fronts. That could be the reason he's training so many."

"I can't imagine as such, but do you think Lord Mywerk could possibly be involved?" she whispered.

"I don't know. While I was able to find out a few things, I felt it unwise to get too close."

"As soon as the Game breaks for the evening, meet me in my chamber." Cyndara was visibly upset from this newfound information. She knew her brothers were desperate to gain control, but this?

From the balcony, the booming voice was heard, "Lord Mywerk accepts the move. The recess is over. It is now your move, Your Highness. Your Highness…"

Looking up, she quickly moved to the front of her balcony, responding, "Yes. Yes, of course." With only a cursory review of the boards, she requested, "Level 3, c9 to f5."

From the crowd, more booing ensued. It was a move that was obviously incorrect. The Pixie on that square also refused her request, instead making his own suggestion.

"Of course, yes…you're right. I misspoke." Finding it difficult to focus on the Game, Cyndara made two more wrong moves. The Pixies challenged each of those, as well. Murmurs spread throughout the crowd. Everyone knew that something was wrong.

Finally, it was Lord Mywerk who called a halt to the Game. Feigning weariness, he requested that they start fresh in the morning. Frustrated at the way the Game was going, the Pixies happily agreed. Cyndara immediately left the balcony.

Mywerk caught up with her in the Great Hall. "What's wrong? Are feeling ill, Cyndara?"

"I am feeling a bit faint," she answered, not wanting him to know what was really troubling her. "Thank you for calling a halt to the Game."

"Get Her Highness some fresh cranberry juice," he ordered one of her ladies-in-waiting, who scurried off to do as he requested. "Please, sit down." He motioned to a nearby chair. "It's been a long day."

"I'll be fine." She forced a smile. "I probably just need a bit of water. The sun is quite strong today. Your concern, however, is most appreciated."

"Of course," he replied. "Let me escort you to your chamber."

"Thank you, but that won't be necessary. Slant is here."

"Are you sure you're alright?"

"Worry not, my dear Lord Mywerk, I'll be fine." Taking Slant's arm, Cyndara started toward her private chambers.

"Never mind," Mywerk told the lady-in-waiting who returned with the juice. "She doesn't need our help—at least not right now." He watched as the two of them disappeared down the long hallway.

"I would have thought," Cyndara told Slant as she spelled the door to her antechamber so no one could enter, "that after the failed attempt on the Château two months ago, General Kandour would have abandoned the idea of any further attacks."

"Not only is he still training soldiers," Slant replied, "if you could call what we saw training—or soldiers—but they appear to be extremely well-armed."

"Probably the weapons that vanished from the armory a few days after Father passed."

"More than likely." Slant nodded.

"And I have no doubt that he will whip those farm boys into shape—or kill them trying." Cyndara sat down on the silver-and-blue chair next to her writing desk. "I am, however, convinced that there is someone else involved beyond Kandour and my brothers."

"Someone with inside information," Slant added.

"You think it's Mywerk?"

"I know he was your teacher, Your Highness. But with all due respect, I beg you not to let that fact cloud your judgment."

"Of course, you are right. Which means, I may just have to ask him directly about it."

"Do you think that's a good idea? If your brothers find out that we know about their plan, it could be extremely dangerous."

"That's just it, we don't know what their plan is—and that is the most dangerous part of all this. Mywerk is no fool. He, like my brothers, knows that winning a war against Calabiyau Proper could be just the thing to sway public sentiment in their favor. He also knows that attacking our Kingdom would have just the opposite effect."

"So, you think it's Calabiyau they're after this time?"

Cyndara stood up and began pacing. "It's certainly possible, but I can't bring myself to believe that Lord Mywerk would sanction such a plan, or that he'd get involved with General Kandour. He can manipulate my brothers, but Kandour is another matter. Prior to Mywerk becoming my teacher, he used to divide his time between the

Bardic Council and Calabiyau Proper. He spoke of those days with a great deal of fondness and still has many friends in Calabiyau. I know he's more aligned with their way of thinking than ours."

"Please, Your Highness, don't assume that to still be true. The taste of power is a far greater aphrodisiac than nostalgia. Lord Mywerk knows that, as a half-breed, he will never truly be accepted unless he can prove his loyalty. Conquering Calabiyau would go a long way in doing just that."

"Do you think that I, being half Banshee and half Fée, have my subjects' loyalty?" she asked.

"I think you're the daughter of a powerful King, and have spent many years earning their loyalty and respect."

Smiling at him, she took his hand. "Your counsel is wise, my friend, very wise. I am fortunate to have your loyalty. Emotional decisions rarely triumph over those made from intelligence."

"And you have all three, Your Highness—intelligence, a wonderful heart, and my loyalty."

"As do you, my dear General. As do you. We must, however, warn Queen Kandide as soon as possible. I need you to transport one of your most trusted soldiers to her Castle with this message." She scribbled a note on a sheet of parchment from her writing desk, then sealed it with hot wax and pressed the royal seal on her ring into it. "Make sure he gives it directly to Queen Kandide, no one else. My brothers' plan was designed by someone much brighter than they are, and I have a feeling there are traitors in both our Kingdoms."

"Politics does, as they say, make strange bedfellows."

"And I intend to find out just how strange."

FOURTEEN

The young corporal saluted. "Permission to enter, Sir."

"What is it?" General Pell, who was seated with Kandide, Lord Rössi, and General Mintz in the war room, motioned for the soldier to be allowed in.

He saluted both Generals then bowed to Kandide. "Permission to speak."

"Of course," she replied, hearing the sense of urgency in his voice.

"Our scouts captured a Banshee soldier. He says he has news from Princess Cyndara and must speak to you, Your Majesty."

"A second messenger from Princess Cyndara? How interesting. Bring him in." Kandide motioned for him to do so.

General Pell removed the gag from the Banshee soldier's mouth. "What's your name, Lieutenant?"

"I am Randolf, Sir, first lieutenant in Her Royal Highness, Princess Cyndara's army." Seeing Kandide, he quickly added, with a deep bow, "Your Majesty."

"To whom do you report?" Lord Rössi asked.

"Captain Slant," the lieutenant replied.

"Captain Slant, you say?" Kandide scanned the soldier's face. He seemed sincere enough, and yet… "Then do tell us her message."

"Her Royal Highness sent me to warn you of an army of seven thousand troops that has been gathered to attack Calabiyau."

"Seven thousand troops…really? And why would she do that?" General Mintz asked.

"The Crown Princess gave Queen Kandide her word that she would uphold the Treaty between our two Kingdoms. She learned of a plot by Prince Yandell and Prince Kilmonth to attack Calabiyau Proper in response to Lord Mywerk's second challenge. Her Highness believes that her brothers are doing this because they aren't happy that he chose Chessaé instead of archery."

"How did she learn of this alleged plot against us?" General Pell asked.

"I don't know, Sir."

"Then I don't suppose you know when it is scheduled to take place?" Mintz pressed.

"No, Sir, I don't."

"Is General Kandour involved?" Pell asked.

"Gen—General Kandour?" Randolf suddenly looked uneasy. "I'm not sure. I… I really don't know, Sir," he stammered.

"Thank you, Lieutenant Randolf. That will be all. You're dismissed."

"I am? I mean…the Crown Princess is waiting for your reply, Sir."

General Pell studied his face. "I don't think so, because you weren't sent here from Cyndara, were you, Lieutenant?"

"Sir, begging your pardon, what I tell you is true."

"So you say. But if you actually reported to Slant, you'd know that he's now her top general." Pell motioned to the same guard who had shown him into the room. "See Lieutenant Randolf out."

"I… uh, meant General Slant, Sir. I…I just forgot." Randolf's voice filled with desperation. "Please, you must believe me." He'd seen firsthand what General Kandour does to messengers who fail in their tasks. It was essential that he return with some sort of response. He tried again. "Her Highness' brothers are planning an attack on your Kingdom."

Pell responded with a dismissive gesture. "Send him away."

"But, Sir..."

"And provide him with a hot meal," Kandide ordered the guard, "before he travels home—wherever that might be. I'm sure he must be hungry after such a long journey." Once Randolf had left the room, Kandide turned to General Pell. "Where do you think he'll go?"

"Certainly not back to General Kandour. My guess is that he'll go directly to Cyndara and tell her everything he knows about Kandour's plans—which won't be much."

"Why would he do that?" Kandide couldn't imagine. "She won't take kindly to him joining her brothers' army."

"No, but anything she does to him and his family will be better than returning to Kandour, knowing that he failed in his mission—to convince us of a pending attack."

"His family?"

"Yes. They shall also pay dearly for his decision to join Kandour's army, unless he's able to convince Cyndara to spare them in exchange for information." Mintz walked across the room to the war table. "We can only hope that, before she kills him, she utilizes what he tells her to convince her Ruling Council to help us. I realize it's a long shot."

"It's something, anyway." Kandide thought for a moment, then suggested, "I wonder if we should give Lieutenant Randolf asylum and allow to remain here."

"You'd have to keep him locked up," General Mintz replied. "And that would be a fate far worse for a Banshee than Cyndara's wrath."

"What do you think, Lord Rössi?" Kandide asked.

"I agree. He would probably kill himself before he'd allow that to happen. No, it's far better to let him accept the destiny he created. I do, however, find it curious that both Lieutenant Randolf and Cyndara's actual messenger arrived within an hour of each other."

"That it is." General Pell nodded. "It makes me wonder who is feeding information to whom."

"It's likely there are more traitors than we know." Kandide made a sweeping gesture across the war table. Rows of tiny wooden soldiers began lining up along the border of her Kingdom. "Sending Randolf here certainly makes me question Kandour's real target. The lieutenant told us there are seven thousand troops poised to attack Calabiyau Proper. Cyndara's messenger told us that Slant estimated the size of Kandour's army to be fourteen thousand. Which means there are another seven thousand troops to do what? I can't imagine that they'd attack their own Kingdom."

"You think their real target is, once again, the Château?" Lord Rössi asked.

"I do," Kandide replied. "After their last attempt failed, I'm sure Lady Aron convinced Kandour to use these months to better train his army, then attack right after the Frost is deployed and the Veil that protects it is weak again."

"Makes perfect sense." Lord Rössi scanned the configuration of the soldiers on the war table. "You can bet that General Kandour wasn't happy about having to retreat last time. And it also explains why he sent the messenger—he knows we don't have enough troops to defend both Kingdoms."

"We don't even have enough troops to adequately defend our own Kingdom against that size army," General Pell insisted.

"We won't have to," Kandide said. "If I'm right, he'll position the seven thousand troops along our border as a distraction, while the other seven thousand attack the Château." She gestured again and wooden soldiers began appearing inside the wall that surrounds the tiny Kingdom. "Lady Aron would never let him actually attack us."

"That may be true," General Mintz replied, "but knowing Kandour as I do, she may not be able to stop him. He'll agree to anything, but won't think twice about double-crossing her."

Kandide knew he spoke the truth. Could Lady Aron stop Kandour from waging an attack on Calabiyau Proper? That, she hadn't considered. And postponing the deploying of the Frost would only delay an attack, not stop it. After the disastrous loss of summer crops, Kandide knew the Frost could not be postponed for more than a week or two, in any case. The growing season was already severely out of balance. No, she would have to deploy the Frost in early November.

"Now that we know Kandour's real objective," she continued, "we need to devise a strategy that will take advantage of his double-dealing nature." *Though I have no idea what that strategy will be,* she thought.

"Kandide!" Jake and Tara rushed into the war room. "Viviana and Centrod are here," Tara exclaimed. "They need to speak to you immediately."

"Centrod and Viviana? Here? Has something happened to Teren?"

"Yes," Jake replied. "You need to come right away."

"Excuse me, gentlemen. We'll continue this discussion later." Kandide barely finished her sentence before she, Jake, and Tara transported to the Receiving Room of the Castle.

"If he's working with Lady Aron," Tara pointed out, "why would he help us?"

FIFTEEN

"What do you mean, Viviana, that Teren has disappeared?" Kandide stood next to Tiyana in the Receiving Room. Jake and Tara were on either side of them. "How could you let this happen?"

"Your brother and my daughter were last seen entering the labyrinth," the High Priestess explained. "They never came out."

"It contains a hidden portal to the human realm," Centrod added. "We are certain they went through it."

"You let them go in there?" Jake couldn't imagine that they would allow such a thing. "Why?"

"The portal has been sealed for many years," Centrod replied, "since it was discovered to be unstable. How it was opened we do not know."

"Are you absolutely certain that's what happened?" Tiyana looked back and forth between him and Viviana.

"More importantly, why haven't you brought them back?" Jake asked.

"I'm afraid it is spelled shut," Viviana explained. "We wouldn't be here if unlocking the spell was that simple."

Kandide was furious. "Well, simple or not, both of you are wizards—supposedly the most powerful wizards in the world. You must know a way to bring them back. There has to be other portals you can go through. Fée used to visit the human realm all the time."

"And occasionally still do," Centrod replied. "But many of the portals have been lost over the ages. And those that are known to exist can lead to any place on earth. Even if we do go to the human realm, we still won't know where Teren and Adriana are. This portal lets out somewhere in the western part of the American continent, but because it is unstable, no one knows exactly where. It could take months to find them."

"But we don't have months," Tara responded. "They'll start aging in a matter of a week or so."

"Yes, they will." Viviana nodded. "By month-end, Teren will be lost to us. Adriana, because she is only part Fée, won't age as fast. But even for her, two months will be fatal."

Kandide's thoughts swirled in a circle of emotions. *How can my life get any worse? Why are the fates so angry? I know I was vain and arrogant as a child, but that was in the past. I'm kind and generous now—to everyone. With everything that's happened, haven't I already paid for anything I might have done back then?* Her anger surged. "Then it seems, Viviana, that we must find a way to un-spell your portal." The expression on both Centrod and Viviana's faces told her that may not happen. "You say a glowing red orb was seen just before they entered the labyrinth?"

"Yes," Viviana said. "To my knowledge, it has never appeared before."

Tiyana looked at her daughter. "Are your thoughts going where mine are, Kandide?

"Yes. There's no question in my mind that Lady Aron did this."

"I know you believe her to be the source of many of the problems that have occurred in your land," Viviana said, "but the Bardic Temple is impossible to penetrate without knowledge of its secret codes—and even then…"

"Knowledge such as Lord Mywerk has?" Jake asked.

"Lord Mywerk, you say?" Viviana sounded surprised. "Interesting you should mention him. Mywerk has traveled through that portal many times in years gone by—always bringing back human books and trinkets for our students."

"Then it's all starting to make sense," Kandide said. "Lord Mywerk's challenge to his long-time student, Cyndara. The two brothers supporting him. Kandour's massive army. The villages being burned. And of course, Lady Aron—she has to be the one conducting this orchestra of atrocities." *It's not the fates doing this,* Kandide thought. *It's Firenza.* "I think we need to pay a visit to Lord Mywerk."

"If he's working with Lady Aron," Tara was quick to point out, "why would he help us?"

"He probably won't," Centrod responded, "unless you give him a compelling reason to do so."

"And what would that be?" Tiyana asked.

"Lord Mywerk is an Imperfect," Viviana explained. "He has a wooden leg."

"A what?" Kandide and Jake spoke at the same time. "Lord Mywerk—an Imperfect?" *Could it be true?* She couldn't believe this stroke of good fortune. Maybe the fates favor her after all.

"Yes," Centrod replied. "Mywerk was injured in an accident. Two of his students were experimenting with explosion spells. When the spell went wrong, he lost the lower part of his right leg while saving one of them. Eventually, just as you did, Jake, he was able to perfect a wooden leg and foot that function like real ones. Shortly after doing so, he met Cyndara's mother, who convinced King Nastae to hire him to tutor their daughter. Her gift for Glamour was apparent even as a child, and her mother wanted to make sure she would learn to control it. I'm certain none of them knew about his leg."

"That's incredible." Kandide's mind was whirling. "It looks like his reason for challenging Cyndara isn't his only secret."

"And now we know the other," Jake added.

"Indeed, you do," Centrod told him. "If their Ruling Council ever finds out, he'll be a tasty meal for their garglans."

"Do you think Cyndara knows?" Tiyana asked.

"Likely not," Viviana replied. "I can't imagine that she would have let him get away with challenging her for the Crown, if she did."

"Guess we're just going to have to pay Lord Mywerk a little visit." Jake looked from Viviana to Centrod. "Will you come with us?"

"Not this time," he answered. "Viviana thought of one other unlocking spell while we were transporting here. It probably won't open the portal, but it could weaken the seal enough for me to slip through. We're anxious to try it. As soon as you've met with Lord Mywerk, use these transport coordinates to come to us." He handed Jake a piece of parchment from his carry satchel. "They'll take you directly to the garden near the labyrinth. Transporting from the Banshee Castle to our temple will take you about six hours."

Jake showed the coordinates to Kandide and then carefully placed them in his side pocket. "We'll depart early tomorrow—if that works for you, Kandide."

"It does. Cyndara's messenger told us that the Game ended shortly before lunch. It's scheduled to start again mid-morning. If we leave by four am, we should arrive there by breakfast. We'll transport to the Bardic Temple as soon as we finish meeting with Lord Mywerk."

"Perhaps, Kandide, you can bring him with you," Viviana suggested.

"He may need to leave once this information is shared..."

SIXTEEN

"It's incredible, Ms. Lee," Ninon told her teacher as they stood in the empty classroom. "I can't believe Teren and Adriana are really here. I mean, for real." From the expression on Ms. Lee's face, neither could she.

Teren wasn't sure if the teacher actually believed Ninon or not. He took his jacket off to show her his wings. They certainly looked real enough.

"But it's impossible," Ms. Lee kept repeating. "Simply impossible. I mean, Fée don't really exist. They can't. No. No. It's impossible… Or is it?" The look in her brown eyes changed from disbelief to wonder. "Maybe the fairy I saw as a little girl was real. I never told anyone about it because they would have said I made it up. How extraordinary."

She glanced out the window of her classroom and noticed two of her other students watching them. They also looked stunned. Ms. Lee quickly motioned for the kids to come inside.

"Is it true?" A red-haired girl named Kathy, who was about Ninon's age, asked Teren. "Are you a real Fée?"

He looked at Ms. Lee for some sense of how he should answer. When she nodded, he responded, "I am. I mean we both are."

"That's so awesome!" Kathy replied. "I knew it! I said Calabiyau was a real place. Didn't I, Ni?"

"You did. We both thought maybe—"

"I knew you were real as soon as I saw your wings," the other student, a dark-haired boy named Ishan interrupted. "Let's see you fly. Can I fly with you? Can I, Ms. Lee?"

"Maybe later, Ishan. Right now, I need each of you to promise me you won't tell anyone about this."

"Why?" Kathy asked. "Everyone in the whole school loves Ms. Zimmerman's books. They'll be really excited about it."

"I know. But just imagine if word got out. The authorities might come to investigate and take Teren and Adriana away."

"She's right," Ninon said, looking at her two friends. "You have to promise you won't tell anyone—even your moms and dads. Think what could happen if people found out Fée are real."

"Some people believe they're real," Kathy said. "We went to Ireland last summer and almost everybody there believes in them."

"Yeah," Ishan said. "But not so much here. Oh, my gosh, they might even try to experiment on Teren and Adriana like they do those poor dogs in the laboratories. It's terrible what they do. Really terrible."

"It is terrible, but I don't think they would quite do that," Ms. Lee said. "They certainly would, however, take them away."

"To where?" Adriana asked. "We need to stay here because this is where the portal is."

"Portal?" Ishan became even more excited. "Is that how you got here—through a magic portal?"

"It is," Ninon answered before Adriana could reply. "And if they stay here very long, they'll get really old, really fast. Isn't that right, Teren?"

"That's right." He was baffled by how much Ninon knew about the Fée. *I really do need to get my hands on one of those books by Ms. Zimmerman,* he thought. *Maybe she knows the secret to the portal.* "Ninon, you said you have a copy of Book Two here, could Adriana and I see it?"

"Sure." She ran to get it from her desk. "Here it is." Ninon handed the book to him. "But it doesn't have anything in it about magic portals. Look, there's your picture." She pointed to an illustration of Teren.

"Wow! The drawing looks just like me."

"And Adriana, too." Ninon turned to a page with a picture of the young Priestess.

"Gosh, it does look like me. But how could Ms. Zimmerman…?"

"We'll have to ask her," Ms. Lee replied.

"I think she's been to Calabiyau," Kathy told them. "Otherwise how would she know what you look like?"

"Yeah, and if she's been there, then she had to go through a portal. So maybe Book Three will have one," Ishan suggested. "Ms. Lee, I could email Ms. Zimmerman and ask her."

"Thank you, Ishan, but I just did." She looked at her phone to check for incoming messages. "No answer back yet."

Teren's curiosity was getting the best of him. "What's email?"

Kathy was first to answer: "I guess you don't need email or cell phones in Calabiyau—you just transport everywhere."

"Here, let me show you." Ishan held out his phone. "When we want to send a message to someone, we just type in what we want to say, then hit the send button and it goes right to them. We mostly text though, 'cause it's even faster."

"And if we want to talk to someone," Ninon explained, "we just touch their name and the phone calls that person. Like this." She pointed to a name on her phone.

"I don't hear it calling," Adriana said, looking a bit perplexed.

"Not calling like calling out loud," Kathy chuckled. "The telephone dials their number. I'll show you." She pushed the number two on her phone, held it up to her ear, and waited a few seconds. "Hi, Mom. I'm still at school with Ms. Lee. Say hello to some new friends of mine. They're from Cala—I mean… California.

She handed Teren the phone. "Say hi to my mom."

He cautiously took it and mimicked Kathy by placing it to his ear. "Hello, this is Teren."

He could hear her mother as clear as if she was standing in the classroom with them. "Hi, Teren. Where in California are you from?"

"Um, oh…just a small village. You probably haven't heard of it. 'Bye." He quickly handed the phone back to Kathy.

"Teren's kinda shy," she told her mother. "See you later, Mom. 'Bye-bye."

"Where is your mother?" Teren asked.

"She's at home with my little brother. He's six and in the same class with Ni's brother, Felix. We live about five miles from here."

"That's 8.04672 kilometers," Ninon explained.

"That's amazing," Teren said.

"I'm just good at math."

"No, I meant the phone. But that was really good, too, Ni, being able to calculate that fast," he quickly added, not wanting her to feel like he wasn't impressed. "Can you call other people?"

"Sure. Anybody who has a phone," Kathy replied.

Teren was beyond intrigued. "I wonder if a phone would work in Calabiyau."

"Do you have electricity there?" Ishan asked. "Because you have to charge them. Otherwise the batteries go dead."

"Of course we do," Adriana replied. "But we don't use it very much. We use spells to heat and cool things, and for light we mostly use orbs." She rubbed her hands together and a small glowing blue ball appeared.

"That's so cool." Ishan held his hand over the orb. "It's not even hot."

"That's because it's a light orb. Only heating orbs get hot."

"Wow!" Ishan was mesmerized. "Can you teach me how to do that, Adriana?"

"Maybe." She blew on it. The orb floated to his hand then melted away.

"Maybe later," Ms. Lee told them. "I just got a reply from Ms. Zimmerman. She's in London and there's a citywide power outage due to a really bad storm, so no planes are flying. She's going to try and get back here as soon as possible. She said she hasn't finished Book Three, but so far there isn't a portal in it."

"There will be," Ninon insisted. "So, what are we going to do if the portal doesn't reopen?"

"We'll just have to figure out another way to get Teren and Adriana back home," Ms. Lee replied. "What are your thoughts, Teren?"

"I'm not sure. I've always wanted to visit the human realm, but this was, well, rather unexpected."

"Does your school have a library?" Adriana asked. "Maybe one of the books could tell us where there are other portals."

"I don't think we have any books like that," Ishan said. "At least I've never seen any. But I have a better idea. Let's look on the Internet."

"Internet?" Teren asked. "What's an Internet?"

The intruders quickly gagged them both, then bound their hands behind their backs.

SEVENTEEN

"Captain Asgart, what are you doing here at this late hour?" Lady Batony stood in her chamber doorway looking at the dark-haired soldier. Dressed in a yellow satin bathrobe, she was just about to retire for the evening.

"My apologies for disturbing you, My Lady." Asgart handed her an envelope. "This was left for me a few minutes ago. I thought it important that you see it immediately—before I do anything else for Lady Aron."

Opening it, she quickly read the contents. "How very interesting. So that is what Firenza is up to. You've done well to bring it to me."

"How would you like me to answer it?" he asked.

"I don't at the moment. I'll take care of it, myself." Lady Batony read the letter again. *This is perfect*, she thought. "Thank you, Captain. Your loyalty will be rewarded."

"That's not necessary. You saved my life on our journey to the Bardic Temple—when the falling stalactites nearly killed us. For that, and your kindness, I shall always be in your debt."

"This letter, my loyal friend, is exactly the break we need. Now be off. And as usual, say nothing to anyone. As far as Lady Aron goes, I don't think she'll be bothering you or your family any longer."

Shortly after Asgart departed, Lady Batony, having changed into more appropriate clothing, rushed out of her room. After a brief stop, she hurried up the stairs to Kandide's chamber. "I wish to see Her Majesty," she announced to the four soldiers who were standing guard that night. "It's of vital importance."

"We're sorry, Lady Batony," one of them stated, "we have strict orders that no one is allowed to visit Her Majesty once she's retired for the evening."

"Of course you do. However, I have time-critical information that could save Teren and Adriana's life. I insist that you inform her of my visit—unless, of course, you wish to be held accountable for something terrible happening to them."

"But, Lady Batony, it's past eleven. I'm sure Her Majesty is sleeping, as she has to be up at three a.m."

Lady Batony would not be denied. "Trust me, she'll want to wake up for this."

Hesitant, but knowing that it must be important or a member of the High Council would not be asking to see their Queen so late, the guard reluctantly knocked on her door. "My apologies for disturbing you, Mylea," he called. "It's Lady Batony. She has urgent news for Her Majesty about Prince Teren and says it cannot wait until the morning."

A lock creaked open, and the door to Kandide's antechamber followed suit. Mylea, Kandide's lady-in-waiting, appeared in the doorway. She was in her dressing gown. "Lady Batony, Her Majesty has retired for the evening. May I be of help to you?"

"I realize the hour is late, Mylea, but this news is most urgent or I certainly would not be disturbing her. I must speak to Kandide at once. It's about Teren and Adriana."

"I'll let Her Majesty know. Let me un-spell the doorway." With a simple phrase and a gesture, she did just that, and Lady Batony was able to enter. Turning to the anxious guard, Mylea reassured him, "It's alright. It is, after all, Lady Batony."

"Yes, My Lady." The guard's tone remained uncertain. His orders were precise: No one, absolutely no one is to enter Her Majesty's quarters once she has retired. There were just too many who would do her harm. As he turned back to speak to the other guards, they were mysteriously gone. A blade suddenly slashed through his throat and he dropped to the floor.

Looking down at the dying soldier was a Banshee known as Anile. A malevolent smile crossed his lips. "Next time, Lieutenant, follow your orders. Shame on you for letting Lady Batony in." He chuckled, casually slicing off one of the guard's ears and placing it in the plain black satchel that hung from his belt.

As Anile watched, the guard dissolved into nothingness, leaving only a small pool of blood behind. Two other Banshees stepped out from the shadows of the hallway. They were dressed, as was Anile, from head to toe, completely in black. "Follow me." He motioned to the others. Unlocked and un-spelled, Kandide's door opened easily.

With her back to the entranceway, Lady Batony barely had time to realize what was happening before Anile grabbed her by the throat. Placing pressure on a nerve near her shoulder, she instantly passed out. "Put her in that chair," he ordered in a voice so quiet, it was barely audible. One of the other Banshees did as he was ordered, propping her up so she looked as though she had simply dozed off. Fading into the shadows of the dimly lit room, they waited.

Fastening her pink night robe with a loosely tied belt, Kandide entered the antechamber. "Mylea says you wish to see me, Lady Bat—" Before she could finish her sentence, Anile had his hand on her throat, pressing on the same nerve that caused Lady Batony to collapse. She, too, instantly passed out. The intruders quickly gagged them both, then bound their hands behind their backs. In another instant, Anile made a broad, sweeping gesture and all five of them vanished.

"Would you and Lady Batony care for tea, Your Majesty? Your Majesty... Your Majesty?" Mylea entered Kandide's antechamber. It was empty. She quickly looked outside the door. There were no guards anywhere to be seen, only a pool of freshly spilled blood. As fear tore through her body, Mylea screamed. Grabbing the long velvet rope that tripped the Castle's alarm system, she frantically pulled on it. Within seconds, dozens of soldiers filled Kandide's antechamber.

"Her Majesty has been taken! Get General Mintz and Tiyana... and Jake, and call Tara—then alert as many Council members as you can find—and search the entire Castle," she ordered. "Check Lady Batony's room as well. Hurry!"

Guards scurried off in all directions, as the near-panicked Mylea noticed three more small pools of blood in the hallway. She could only assume they belonged to Kandide's other guards. Tears began streaming down her face as the potential horror of the situation began to flood her thoughts.

The entire Castle was awakened. In a matter of minutes, General Mintz, Tiyana, Tara, and Jake were at Mylea's side, drilling her with question upon question. "Did you see anyone? What did Lady Batony want? Did you hear anything? Anything at all that might provide us with a clue?"

Finally, after one more round of questioning, Tiyana insisted, "I think she has told us all she knows, General."

Overwhelmed and in tears, Mylea collapsed onto a chair, sobbing.

"Obviously whoever did this must keep Kandide alive." Jake tried to comfort both Mylea and Tiyana. "She's out there somewhere and we will find her."

"Whoever it was had to have an inside connection," General Mintz responded. "There is no way they could get inside the Castle otherwise."

"You mean an inside connection like Lady Aron?" Tara walked over to him.

"It's entirely possible."

"What do you think Lady Batony has to do with all this?" Jake asked.

"Probably just a pawn," Mintz replied. "Mylea said she was holding a letter, and that she had news of Prince Teren and Adriana. Someone delivered that letter to her."

"I did." Asgart stepped into the room. "It was left for me. I don't know by whom."

"What did it say?" Tara asked.

"It said that if Kandide wants to see her brother alive again, she should be in the Sacred Garden tonight at half past eleven. It wasn't signed."

"Why didn't you immediately bring this to me, Captain?" General Mintz sounded more than displeased.

"I felt it best to give it Lady Batony and let her decide what to do with it," Asgart replied. "She and I have been working together to uncover information about Lady Aron's whereabouts."

"Do you think Lady Aron has something to do with this?" Tiyana asked.

"I can't be sure," he replied. "But it wouldn't surprise me."

"That will be all, Captain." Mintz dismissed him. "Stay near, however, in case we have more questions. Turning to speak to one of his senior officers, General Mintz ordered, "Muster a thousand troops. I want a major search of the woods. I also want a dozen scouts to scour the area around Kandour's camp. I have a feeling that he, as well as Lady Aron, is involved in this. Get back to me with anything that seems out of the ordinary. And bring me my maps of that area. I want to see what's near his camp—mine shafts, tunnels, caves—anything. Now, be off. Time is of the essence."

"Yes, Sir!" The officer saluted, making a hasty departure.

Turning back to Tiyana and the others, Mintz added, "Remember, as long as Kandide holds the Gift of the Frost, not even a Banshee will kill her."

"True, but who knows what else they may do to her," Jake said. "What makes you think General Kandour is involved?"

"If, as Kandide believes, he and Lady Aron are working together to attack the Château, then it's logical that his henchmen are responsible. It's my guess that he sent an assassin named Anile to kidnap Her Majesty. This looks like his handy work. Especially those small drops of blood right near the larger ones in the hallway."

Tiyana wasn't sure what he meant. In her hurry to get there, she hadn't noticed the blood. "I'm afraid I don't understand."

"Anile has, well, let's just say an ear fetish. It's rumored that he has a collection of several thousand, all taken from the Fée he kills. I'd be willing to bet that those small drops of blood happened when he cut off the guards' ears. It's sort of a signature with him—sick as it may be."

"No!" Mylea gasped. "He wouldn't... Not Kandide!" She began sobbing again.

Mintz tried to ease her fears. "There's no sign of anyone having been harmed in here. Whoever kidnapped Kandide wants her in one piece."

"Why do you think Kandide will be taken to the area around General Kandour's camp?" Tara asked.

"Kandour won't go into battle without Anile. He considers him a good luck charm, and is the only one he trusts. Which means that he's going to want him nearby. Additionally, as we all know, Kandide's stand on Imperfects has not made her very popular among Banshees. Parading Her Majesty as a prisoner in front of his troops will go a long way toward cementing their loyalty to him, as well as generating enthusiasm for battle, not to mention his increased stature at having captured Calabiyau's Queen."

"This makes me even more convinced that Lady Aron is involved," Tiyana said.

"Ironically, the fact that she is involved may be good. Firenza won't let Kandour have Kandide until she acquires the Gift, and that fact could buy us precious time."

"There might be something else that's important here," Jake said. "On our original trip to the Bardic Temple, Viviana told Teren that there was more than one traitor among his traveling companions. We know about Asgart's past relationship with Firenza—so that's one."

"And Lord Salitar and Lord Socrat, who also went on the journey, are two of my closest friends," Tiyana added. "I trust them implicitly."

"Which leaves only Lady Batony," Jake said, "as difficult as it is to believe that she would be involved in something so heinous. Especially, since she never misses a chance to throw barbs at Lady Aron. It's common knowledge that they dislike each other."

"Or so they make it seem," Tiyana replied with a strong undertone of cynicism. "Though, you're right, Jake, it's hard to believe that Lady Batony would be involved."

"You might change your mind once you read this report," Lord Socrat interrupted, having just joined the group.

General Mintz turned to look at him. "What report, Lord Socrat?"

"Remember the investigation that you ordered—to find out who arranged for Asgart to join Jake and Teren on their trip to the Bardic Temple? Well, this report explains it. Sometime tonight, someone slid it under my door."

"Who was it?" General Mintz was quick to question. "I haven't even seen it myself."

"I have no idea. But it seems as though there's a lot more to our dear Lady Batony than meets the eye, and someone wanted me, specifically, to know about it."

General Mintz skimmed through the report. "It says here that the scheduling orders have my signature, and that they were stamped for distribution by a BK."

"Well, we know that you would not have authorized Asgart to go on that trip," Tiyana asserted. "So who is this BK?"

"That's the interesting part," Lord Socrat replied. "If I am not mistaken, Lady Batony's eldest son is called BK. It's short for Bekonauber, and he works in the processing department of the military."

"Do you mean Colonel Bekonauber?" General Mintz's expression reinforced his surprise. "Now that you mention it, I do remember that the two of them are related."

"It is my understanding that they haven't spoken in any number of decades," Tiyana said. "Something to do with BK, when he was young, taking the side of her former husband during their nasty divorce."

"Apparently they're both on the same side, now," Tara observed. "It's starting to make sense."

"Not entirely," Mintz responded. "Bekonauber's department does process most of the military's paperwork, which means that he certainly could have forged an order. But if he did, why would he stamp his own initials on it?"

"Good point." Tiyana hadn't thought of that. "Unless he didn't forge it, but was set up by his..."

"Mother," Tara finished her sentence. "It's a way to get even with him."

Lord Socrat shook his head. "I can't believe Lady Batony is that mean...or that clever. Though, she was a different person on our trip to the Bardic Temple—amazingly resourceful."

"She was also extremely agitated over Teren not telling us what he and Viviana discussed in their private meeting," Jake added.

"Why would Lady Batony want to harm Kandide?" Tara asked. "As you said, it's hard to believe that she's working with Lady Aron."

"That it is," Tiyana replied. "There is, however, something else to consider. It could be a set-up by Firenza to frame Lady Batony and make us think she's involved."

"It very well could be," General Mintz said. "The question then becomes, who let Anile into the Castle? It's double shielded, so someone had to have known how to release it."

"And I still want to know who left that report under my door," Lord Socrat said. "And why tonight? I don't think it was Lady Batony."

"I think," General Mintz replied, "if we find that out, we'll be well on our way to discovering who's behind Kandide's kidnapping."

"There is someone else who may have knowledge of all this," Jake said. "Kandide and I were headed off to see him in the morning."

"You think Lord Mywerk is somehow involved as well, Jake?" Tiyana asked.

"I don't know, but I'm going to find out. We know he's able to breach spells. His skills could have possibly given Anile access. As much as I want to join you on the search for Kandide, General Mintz, I think I'd better go see Lord Mywerk."

"I agree. Just be very careful, Jake. I don't need my army searching for you, as well."

*"Do you think General Kandour
would actually do that?"*

EIGHTEEN

Long before the sun had splashed its morning glow across the horizon, Jake was on his way to the Banshee Castle. A few hours later, he appeared outside its massive iron gate. An army of soldiers greeted him with poison-tipped arrows.

General Slant was summoned and quickly escorted Jake inside. "Her Highness will be in her private chambers," Slant explained. "Come with me." They walked up the spiral staircase to the third level and then down the mirrored hallway that led to her chamber.

Hearing Slant's special knock, Cyndara snapped her fingers and the door to her receiving room swung open. "Jake is here? Alone?"

"Yes, Your Highness," Slant replied. "It's urgent he speak to you."

"Of course. Send him in."

"He's just in the hall." Slant motioned for Jake to follow him into Cyndara's antechamber.

"Is everything okay, Jake?" she asked, walking to the door to greet him.

"I'm afraid not."

"Please, do come in. What's wrong?"

"A great deal has happened in the last twenty-four hours." He proceeded to tell her about Teren and Adriana's disappearance through the portal and then Kandide's kidnapping. "We think Lord Mywerk might somehow be involved in this. That's why I need to talk to him."

Cyndara listened carefully to his words, replying: "Lord Mywerk is many things, but I find it hard to believe that he would do anything to harm Teren, Adriana, or Kandide. He is, after all, Viviana's second cousin."

"When," Jake asked, "has being related ever stopped someone from committing a heinous act? Just look at your brothers."

"What you say is true," Slant said. "But I also find it difficult to believe. Her Highness is right; Lord Mywerk is many things. What you are telling us, however, goes beyond even what I think he would do. In point of fact, he actually appeared to be genuinely surprised when a lieutenant named Randolf, a defector from Kandour's army, showed up. Shall I go fetch Lord Mywerk, Your Highness?"

"Yes, please."

After watching Slant leave, Jake turned his attention back to Cyndara. "So Lieutenant Randolf did come here. General Mintz said he probably would."

"He arrived last night, pleading for mercy for his family in exchange for telling us all he knew about Kandour's plans—which wasn't much more than we had already learned."

"And will you show his family mercy?" Jake tried to sound supportive of the idea.

"I'm considering it. Though I doubt General Kandour will when he learns what happened. Randolf's testimony to our Ruling Council this morning went a long way toward convincing them of my brothers' true intentions. Especially when he revealed that he believes Kandour is planning to attack our Kingdom."

"Do you think General Kandour would actually do that?"

"No. But Randolf was clever enough to put forth that possibility. With his testimony and what Slant had to say about the size of the army Kandour and my brothers have raised, the Council was extremely concerned. Mywerk and I had a bit of a talk during the meeting. He agreed to postpone the Game until we can sort all this out."

"Is he still the acting King?"

"Yes, and that may be best for now. We don't want Kandour or my brothers to think he is in any way aligned with me."

"How do you know he isn't feeding them information?"

"I don't." Cyndara's face was etched with doubt. "Please, be seated." She motioned toward a blue chair with silver arms, and then sat across from him in a matching chair. "Would you care for tea?"

"Thank you. That would be great. I left rather early. Even the chefs weren't up."

"You must have left very early to be here at this hour." Cyndara snapped her fingers and a steaming cup of pomegranate tea appeared on the small table in front of him. Another snap produced a bowl of sugar and a pair of golden spoons. "It tastes better sweetened," she advised.

He added a spoonful of sugar to the tea and took a sip. "You're right. It is bitter, even sweetened."

"Have a cranberry biscuit." A flick of her wrist produced a tray of muffin-like treats. "They are a specialty of our chefs and go especially well with the tea."

"They look delicious." Jake took a bite of one. "And taste as good as they look." He placed his cup back on its bright green gold-trimmed saucer. "I understand what you say about Lord Mywerk, but I'm still not so sure. There are just too many things that don't add up."

She added a teaspoon of sugar to her own cup of tea. "Such as?"

Jake's answer was eclipsed by a knock on her door.

"You asked to see me, Cyndara?" Lord Mywerk entered her chamber. "Greetings, Jake. Did Her Highness tell you that the Game has been postponed?"

"She did. I'm not here for the Game."

"What then? You appear to be upset."

"Please, join us." Cyndara gestured to the chair next to her.

"I've come to ask for your help." Jake told him about Teren and

Adriana's disappearance through the portal in the labyrinth, as well as Kandide's mysterious kidnapping. As he spoke, his gaze tracked Mywerk's body language. *Either he really isn't involved or he's a far better actor than most,* Jake thought, seeing the concern on his face. "Will you help us?"

"I don't know if I can. With both Teren and Kandide out of the way, Lady Aron has certainly shifted the fates to her side."

"And we need you, Lord Mywerk, to help us shift them back," Jake insisted. "Viviana told us that you've traveled through that portal many times. We're hoping you might know where it lets out."

"Not really. Unlike many portals, this one isn't static. It's very old, and in the ancient times, sorcerers often spelled them to shift locations so those who used them couldn't be followed. Each time I went through it, I ended up in a different place in the western part of the North American continent."

Jake studied Mywerk's face. "Assuming that what you say is true, how did the sorcerers know where to find it when they wanted to return?"

"They used a complicated mathematical formula to track it."

"Do you know the formula?" Cyndara asked.

"At one time I did," Mywerk replied.

Jake could feel his temper beginning to flare. *Calm down,* he told himself before continuing: "I'm sure the formula hasn't changed—or is it that you want Teren and Adriana to stay there?"

"I hardly think Lord Mywerk would wish that fate on any Fée, let alone Teren and Adriana. It's a death far worse than from any garglan."

"Are you sure, Cyndara? I came here asking for help. Lord Mywerk admits that he frequently visited the human realm through that very portal. Now he can't remember the formula to return. With all due respect, that seems a bit odd, don't you think?"

"Do you, Cyndara," Lord Mywerk calmly shifted his gaze to her, "think it odd?"

"Actually, I do. It's unlike you to forget such a thing. Especially since you remember every Chessaé move that I've ever made, in every game we've ever played."

"I see." Mywerk looked from her to Jake. "Then if you will both excuse me, I have a pending war to attend to."

"I think not," Jake said. "I came asking for your help—and perhaps that accident you had at the Bardic Temple, when you helped those students whose spell went wrong, will convince you to give it."

"Accident?" Cyndara looked from Jake to Lord Mywerk. "What happened to the students?"

"Why don't you tell her what happened, Lord Mywerk? Or should I?"

Mywerk was silent. Jake almost felt sorry for him. He was trapped by truth—like a caged prisoner, knowing that there was no way out. No matter how he answered, his life would never be the same.

Cyndara finally broke the silence. "Students are injured all the time while attempting spells. One can hardly blame Lord Mywerk for their carelessness."

"It wasn't the students who were injured," Jake said.

"No, Cyndara, it wasn't. I was the one injured."

Again silence reigned. And again Cyndara broke it. "Well, you appear to be fine now, and that is all I care to know—at least for now. So, gentlemen, I strongly suggest that the three of us work together to find a solution to bring Teren and Adriana back, to rescue Kandide, and to defeat my brothers."

Mywerk's reply was without emotion. "I agree, Cyndara."

She turned to Jake. "I've learned a lot about true perfection—in both Banshees and Fée. Over these past months, I've met several whose 'imperfections' have caused me to change my thinking for the better—Kandide with her crumpled wing; the blind healer, Leanne, who helped with my father; and you, Jake. Now, we can sit here divided and destroy each other, or we can unite and destroy our real enemies. The only choice you need to make, Lord Mywerk, is which side you wish to serve."

"The same side I've always served." He bowed his head humbly toward her. "What I told you about the portal is true, Jake. The last time I went to the human realm, I almost didn't return. The portal had become unstable and none of the calculations worked. After weeks of searching for it, I almost died."

Jake was still not sure he believed Mywerk. "But you obviously didn't die. How did you eventually find it?"

"I decided to search in the complete opposite direction of where the calculations said it should be—it was my last hope. Had the fates not favored me, I would have never found it. That's why I spelled it shut, so no one would ever be lost in it again. How it was opened and then re-spelled shut again, I do not know."

"If what you say it is true," Jake said, "then even if we could re-open it, it's likely that we won't be let out in the same place as Teren and Adriana."

"I'm afraid that is also true," he replied. "There is, however, a slight chance that, based on where it was when I last returned, and using my theory of it moving in the opposite direction from what it normally does, that we could approximate where Teren and Adriana ended up."

"Would you be willing to go to the Bardic Temple to see if you can un-spell it?" Cyndara asked.

"More importantly, are you willing to go back through it with me?" Jake asked.

Mywerk paused before answering. "No. I will not go back through that portal with you, Jake. You're needed in this world. Kandide must be found and Kandour defeated. If it can be un-spelled, I shall go through it by myself. But first, I have an errand to attend to. I'll meet you at the Bardic Temple at first light tomorrow. If I am not there, give this note to Centrod." Mywerk walked over to Cyndara's writing desk and wrote several strange characters on a piece of parchment. "If the un-spelling works, send him through. Do not go yourself." He bid Jake and Cyndara farewell and quickly left her chamber.

"Where do you think he's going?" Jake asked.

"I don't know. But I am going to have Slant make another trip to Kandour's camp."

"Then you don't trust him either?"

"Where politics are concerned, trust is a fool's game. I'm also going to send a hundred of Slant's best scouts to search that area for Kandide."

"Thank you. And thank you for sending the messenger, yesterday."

"Of course. Our Kingdoms have been at war far too long. It's time we work together to end all this senseless bloodshed."

Jake could tell that Cyndara was, at the very least, sincere in her desire for peace. But he was still curious about something. "If I may say so, you handled the news about Mywerk being an Imperfect rather well."

"Information like that should always be handled… well. One never knows when it will become useful." A knowing smile crossed her lips.

Kandide struggled to free her bound wrists.
Her efforts, however, were to no avail.

NINETEEN

Lady Aron approached the abandoned mineshaft. *Good, it's not been disturbed,* she thought. *The spell I placed on it is functioning perfectly. General Mintz's scouts have not been able to see it.*

Though every mine, whether active or not, was designated on the military maps of the region, most in this area had long since been filled in. With Lady Aron's spell intact, this one also appeared to have been covered over. A circular wave of her hand interrupted the spell and revealed its opening.

As she floated down the nearly twenty-meter deep shaft, her fiery wings cast light so she could avoid its sharp jagged sides. The deeper she went into the earth, the more the air grew damp and stale. *I'll be at the bottom soon,* she thought, her feet finally touching its soggy surface.

Looking straight up, Lady Aron reset the spell: "Seal tight from Fée and light. Erase this mine from normal sight." Again her hand moved in a circular motion, this time above her head.

The entrance to the shaft instantly turned black. Not even the most tenacious streaks of sunlight could penetrate the veil of camouflage she conjured.

"Search away, dear General Mintz. You'll not see this mine, nor find your beloved Queen. Not today. Not ever," she mused. *Everything is finally in place. I will have the Gift. But first I must find my way through these tunnels.*

With a snap of her fingers, a fiery yellow cloud appeared floating over her right hand. *Perfect.* She floated it out ahead of her so she could see where the puddles of water were. Like most of the mines in this mountain, it was extremely wet. After several twists and turns, a large chamber revealed itself.

Lady Aron surveyed the underground cavern. A glowing orb provided the only light, casting beast-like shadows as it rhythmically flickered in the darkness. The cave was full of odd-shaped arches that towered over islands made of red and yellow shale. They were surrounded by flowing black streams. Luminous green flares danced on the dark water, emitting a faint sulpher-like smell that reminded her of the volcanic fumes from her mother's manor house. She inhaled deeply. It was a smell she loved.

What she saw, however, did not please her. Her eyes shifted to the Banshee named Anile. He and his companions were standing guard over two limp bodies. "You were told to bring Kandide and the soldier who let you into the Castle. Where is he and why did you bring Lady Batony?"

"Weren't no soldier," Anile replied, spitting on the floor of the cave. "Except the ones we did away with outside Her Majesty's room. This one was there, so we brought her instead. When do you want me to do away with her?" Anile passed the blade of his knife above Lady Batony's left ear.

"Later." Lady Aron approached her. "How long will she be unconscious?"

"For a while—or until I do this!" With the back of his hand, he slapped Lady Batony across her right cheek.

Jolted awake, she let out a loud groan. Though the mineshaft was dimly lit, she could easily see Anile's evil grin. Struggling to free her still-tied hands, she looked around. "Where am I, and why am I here?"

"Kandour's orders were to bring the one who let us in," Anile said, "and that's exactly what we did."

"You let them into the Castle, Lady Batony?" Lady Aron asked.

"As usual, Firenza, my dear loyal Captain Asgart reported your orders to me. I must say, your plan to have an urgent note delivered to Kandide by way of me was a clever way to get her room unshielded. But how did you know I'd do it?"

"It was really quite simple. I knew you must be the other person giving Asgart orders when you went on that trip to the Bardic Temple with Jake and Teren. I assume it was also your idea to have Asgart step on Kandide's cape. Very clever of you. And arranging for him to accompany you on the journey—even I couldn't have pulled that one off."

"No, you could not have. And as much as I dislike you, Firenza, we do make an extremely effective team."

"Well, I must admit, I am more than a little impressed, if not surprised. Though, I suppose I really shouldn't be, especially after you made that long journey with them. It certainly could not have been very comfortable. Which means that you must have had very strong reasons for wanting to go."

"My reasons are my own. Now, I insist you untie me, immediately."

"You, my dear Lady Batony, don't seem to be in a position to insist on anything. Now, I would like some answers. Why are you…"

Before Lady Aron could finish her question, Kandide suddenly woke up. Her eyes slowly focused. "La… Lady Batony? What… what happened? Where are we? How did we get…"

Lady Aron immediately shifted the conversation. "Yes, Lady Batony, why did you arrange for Her Majesty to be kidnapped? I insist you tell us why you had Kandide and me brought to this abandoned mine shaft."

Momentarily taken aback by her words, Lady Batony replied, "What are you saying, Firenza?"

"You obviously wanted us both here for some reason."

"That is ridiculous. Would I be tied up, if I had arranged all this?"

Trying to avoid a sharp rock, she twisted around to show Kandide that her wrists were tightly bound.

Lady Aron stared straight at Lady Batony. "Not unless you wanted it to look as though someone else was responsible for it. Someone such as me. I must admit, it was, indeed, a very clever ploy, my dear. Obviously, we have all seriously over estimated your presumed senility."

Realizing what she was up to, Lady Batony retorted, "Well then, Anile, I guess it's time for you to release me."

"Not so quick," Lady Aron countered. "Whatever she is paying you, Anile, I will double it to free Her Majesty and let us go."

Annoyed at both of them, the Banshee's patience had expired. "Look ladies, I ain't for sale to nobody. I already got a boss and he pays me real good. Lots of fringe benefits, too, if you know what I mean." A cruel sneer curled his upper lip as he patted the black pouch that hung from his belt. "Besides, I gotta get going. Kandour's waitin' for me. So, Lady, if you want my help convincing Her Majesty to give you what you want, you'd better be quick about it."

Kandide struggled to free her bound wrists. Her efforts, however, were to no avail. The ropes were spelled. The more she struggled, the more they cut into her skin. "I understand why Firenza is doing this, but why you, Lady Batony? Why are you involved?"

"Yes, Lady Batony, why are you involved? Don't tell me you're still holding that grudge from when Kandide was a child and insisted that King Toeyad replace you with a younger, and I believe she called it, 'more up-to-date' court singer? No, that was much too long ago for you to still be holding a grudge. Let me see, perhaps it's because Kandide exposed those trumped up charges that someone brought against your former husband. Is that why? Is that the reason you hate her so much? Or is it that she never takes your advice at Council meetings?"

Kandide looked from Lady Aron to Lady Batony. "Do you hate me, Lady Batony? Do you? Tell me that what Firenza says is not true."

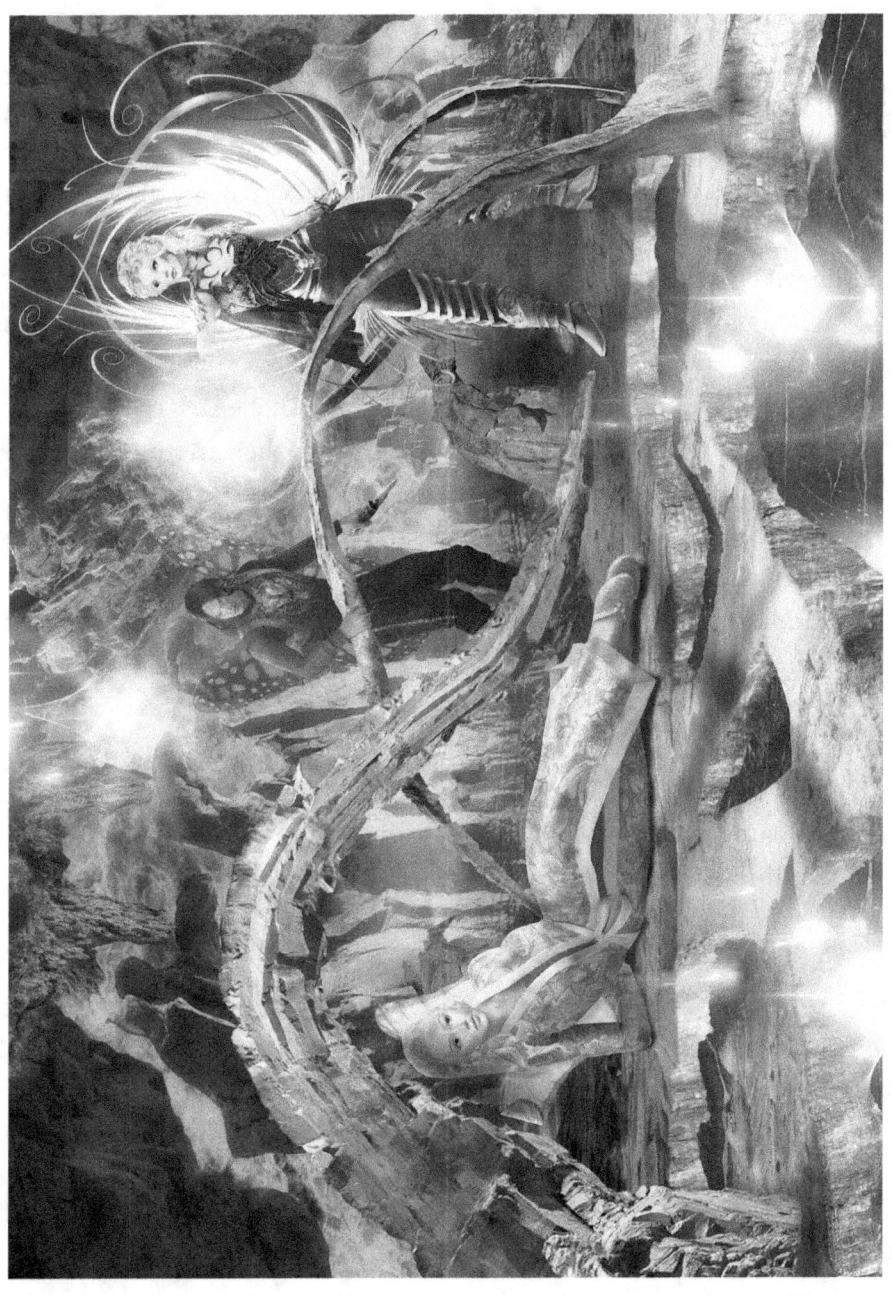

KANDIDE, LADY ARON, AND ANILE

"Tell her, Lady Batony. Tell Kandide that it's not true. That you put Asgart up to stepping on her cape just before her Crowning ceremony so all would see that she is an Imperfect. And that it was also you who arranged to have your dear loyal Captain Asgart go on the journey to the Bardic Temple. Perhaps, it was also you who froze our beloved Princess in that horrible block of ice. Was it? Go ahead, tell Her Majesty how much you dislike her."

"I had nothing to do with Tara being frozen and you know it, Firenza!"

"Really? Then explain why you helped a Banshee assassin get into Kandide's chamber tonight." Abruptly turning her attention back to Anile, Lady Aron continued: "My offer still stands. In fact, why don't you practice on Lady Batony right now? I'm sure that your two friends are perfectly capable of keeping an eye on Her Majesty and myself."

A look of sheer terror crossed Lady Batony's face. "You wouldn't, Firenza."

"Wouldn't I?"

"I… I can be of great help to you. Look what I've done so far."

"So, you admit it. You admit to springing this trap on our dear Queen. There's your proof, Your Majesty."

Kandide could only stare in disbelief. "Why, Lady Batony? Why? I've always thought of you as a friend."

"A friend?" she shrieked, driven by the thought of what Anile might do. "You ruined my life. You turned everyone against me—you, who think you're so much better than everyone else. Even in the Council meetings, you never listen to me. Yes, Kandide, I do hate you!"

With a gleeful smirk, Lady Aron responded, "Oh, and, Anile, make it quick."

"Nooooo!" Lady Batony's scream echoed throughout the mine-shaft. "You can't do this. I helped you! I can…"

"Please, Firenza, don't," Kandide implored. "Don't do this. The Council will deal with her. Even you can't be that cruel."

"Yes, Kandide, of course you are right. Anile, please take her into another area. I wouldn't want our dear Queen to have to watch her 'friend' die."

Anile dragged Lady Batony screaming into a connecting chamber. Seconds later, one more scream was heard, then only silence.

"Well, at least that's over—and mercifully fast, too." Lady Aron sat down on a rock near Kandide. "Now, Your Majesty, there's something you can do for me."

Kandide's insides felt like mush. No one deserves that—no matter what they've done. She needed to compose herself before speaking. "You're despicable, Firenza, and you can stop the act. I know it was you who instigated all of this. You'll never get away with it."

"No? It seems as though I already have. And Lady Batony is the perfect foil. She'll be blamed for everything, while I will become a heroine for attempting to rescue Calabiyau's Queen. Now all you have to do is transfer the Gift to me, and you have my word that Teren and Adriana will be brought back to our world. The Gift of the Frost for their lives; it seems like a fair trade to me."

"Centrod has already unlocked the portal." Though Kandide was bluffing, she would not let Lady Aron know he hadn't been able to break the spell.

"Even if he has, which I highly doubt, he won't find them. That portal is unstable. It never opens in the same place twice."

"Really, then how do you propose to find them?"

"I know exactly where it let out when I sent them. A place called Las Vegas in North America. Of course, even that is a very large area—impossible to search, unless one knows the exact coordinates. As I calculate it, Teren has about four more days before he starts aging. He'll be dead in a few weeks. Adriana, a little longer."

Kandide struggled to sit up. "Then I have an even better trade, Firenza. Their lives for your son, Alin's."

"I have no idea what you're talking about. No one knows where

Alin is except me."

"His brother, Egan, does. It seems that the two of them have been secretly sneaking away to play with one another." Kandide studied Firenza's face. A flicker of concern flashed across it. *I've definitely struck a nerve,* she thought.

"Alin would never disobey my orders. After their last little visit together, I forbade him to ever meet Egan again."

"Maybe so, but your son, like his mother, has a mind of his own. According to Lord Aron, they've met in secret at least three more times since you spied on them at the lake. It's my understanding that Alin has become quite a good swimmer. According to Egan, he's won four out of their five races to the big lava rock in the center of the lake near your mother's manor house."

Lady Aron's concern transformed into fury. "I swear, Kandide, if anything happens to Alin, I'll destroy your entire family."

"And if I'm not back by sunset," she calmly stated, "Centrod will send him through the same portal that you sent Teren and Adriana. Who knows were it will let out?"

"You would never do that. You have a fool's heart. You even pleaded for that dreadful Lady Batony's life."

"You're right, Firenza, I would never harm Alin. But you made a big mistake by sending Adriana through that portal. Viviana and Centrod will stop at nothing to get their daughter back—even if it means sacrificing your son."

"Sending Adriana through it was never my intent. Your annoying brother caused that to happen. Perhaps I should just let them die—and such an agonizing death, too."

"Perhaps you should really think about that. When Alin is trapped in the human realm, his death will be no less painful."

Lady Aron's amber eyes shone with ire. "I was hoping you'd be a little more cooperative—for Teren's sake. I guess Anile will, indeed, need to use a few of his persuasive techniques on you. I've heard they can be quite… disfiguring. But then, you do so love Imperfects, now don't you?" She flicked the bent tip of Kandide's wing with her fore-finger.

"Do what you will to me, Firenza. I will never transfer the Gift to you."

"Yes, my dear, you will. You know full well that if the Gift dies, all life will soon perish. You will never allow that to happen."

"Will you, Firenza? Allow that to happen? Has your need for power and vengeance flared to the degree that you will sacrifice your-self and your son?"

Lady Aron stood up. Turning to Anile, who had returned shortly after Lady Batony's final scream, she ordered: "Watch her. I have to leave for a few hours. But I'll be back as quickly as possible. And I don't want her touched, at least not until I return."

"Yeah, well I ain't makin' no promises. Besides, I have to get going. It's gettin' late and I have a war to help out with. Jab and Stif can stay." Motioning to his two sidekicks, Anile ordered them to remain and guard Kandide. "And try to do what the Lady says," he chuckled. "Don't be hurtin' Her Majesty. Unless she misbehaves."

"Unless, of course, Prince Kilmonth and Prince Yandell are tragically killed in battle."

TWENTY

"Feed him to the garglans," General Kandour ordered. His scouts had captured Lord Mywerk in a clearing in the pinewoods not far from the training camp. "They haven't had a decent meal in nearly a week. Not that a half-breed is what I would call decent."

"You can do that," Mywerk stated. "I'm not exactly in a position to argue." He had hoped to go there, find what he was looking for, and leave without being seen. His plan, however, hadn't quite worked the way he intended.

Mywerk's gaze tracked the dozen guards who encircled him. Their flaming arrows were pointed directly at his heart. He could easily take out four or five of them, but by being completely surrounded, escaping alive was unlikely. He felt the heat from the arrows on his neck as a breeze fanned their flames. *Time for a different approach,* he thought. "So, General Kandour, you must be at least a little curious as to why I'd risk coming here."

"Curiosity is not a weakness I indulge in."

"No, but strategy certainly is. It's one of your greatest strengths, and that is more in line with what I can bring you." Mywerk's voice held steady, though he wasn't quite sure how to reclaim the advantage. Kandour was not easily manipulated. "What harm can come from listening? After all, I came here alone and unarmed."

"Alone, perhaps. But you, Lord Mywerk, are never unarmed. You are, after all, half wizard."

"That could be a great help to you, as well."

"Or a great hindrance. I'd sooner trust a river snake."

"Then in lieu of trust you should consider a mutually beneficial alignment that can help both of us achieve our goals."

"I assure you, Lord Mywerk, your goals are very different than mine."

"Are they, General?"

"You're in love with Cyndara—another foolish emotion—and trying to protect her, just as you were with that ridiculous challenge to the throne."

"Perhaps or perhaps not. Cyndara knows my feelings for her. On that, I am counting. But whether I remain as King or not, she will never love me. Her heart belongs to another." It was the only time in the conversation that Mywerk's voice hinted of any emotion. "She will, however, be a constant thorn in my rule."

"You had your chance to eliminate her, once and for all, with the second challenge. She's no match for you in archery."

"Of that, you are correct. But think about it strategically." Mywerk knew what he said would challenge Kandour's pride. He selected his words carefully: "Cyndara has many loyal subjects. I have none. If I had killed her in a fight that all know to be one-sided, there would have been a backlash such as we've never seen."

"Even if what you say is true, it's a moot point. Cyndara's fate will be sealed when I return from having destroyed Calabiyau Proper. I will be the conquering hero, and she will be perceived as a cowardly half-breed." Kandour started to leave, turning back only to say, "Feed him to the garglans."

Lord Mywerk called after him, "It's not Calabiyau you're going to conquer. You cannot because of the treaty signed by her brothers— such talkative boys. We both know it's the Château."

"You're right—at least for now. Unless, of course, Prince Yandell and Prince Kilmonth are tragically killed in battle." Kandour let out a sinister laugh. Turning to the soldiers, he ordered: "Restrain Lord Mywerk and watch him very carefully, but do not feed him to the garglans—not yet, anyway. It has occurred to me that I may have another use for this arrogant wizard." Turning to Mywerk, he added, "Love will be your downfall. We'll see how quickly you trade your talents for Cyndara's life." On these words, General Kandour departed.

The soldiers bound Mywerk's hands and tied him to a nearby tree, spelling the ropes so he was unable to release them or gesture to transport. All twelve guards stood watch around him, each with their flaming arrows still pointed directly at his heart.

"May I have a drink of water," he requested of the soldier with the red cap. "It's Captain Delby, is it not?"

"Be quiet!" Delby snapped. Nevertheless, he motioned for one of the other soldiers to give Lord Mywerk a drink.

"I know your son, do I not, Captain?" Mywerk pressed.

"If you want that water, you best stop talking."

Staring directly into the red-capped soldier's eyes, Lord Mywerk continued speaking in a slow, metered fashion. "Let's see…that's right, his name is Kender. Nice boy. He must be about twelve now. Is he doing well in his classes? Did you know that it was I who convinced King Nastae to build that school for your Clan? Not that I expect any favors, you understand."

As Mywerk spoke, the Captain had not been able to break eye contact with him.

"Should I gag him, Sir?" One of the soldiers asked after giving him the water. "Sir…?"

"Introduce me to your friends, Captain Delby," Mywerk ordered. Without hesitation, he did as he was told. "Now order them to blow out their arrows and put them back in their quivers."

Again, the Captain did as he was instructed. Though the other guards objected, a sharp glance from Lord Mywerk caused each to do as ordered. "Excellent, gentleman. You obey like true soldiers. Now release the spell on my ropes."

Delby quickly obliged. He mumbled a few words and the knots untied themselves.

"Thank you." Once free, Mywerk placed a sleeping spell on each soldier. With a gesture, all twelve of them vanished. "Time for you boys to go back to your homes."

Now, to find what I came here for, he thought. He held out his hands, palms facing down and began walking in an ever-increasing spiral around a strangely twisted pine tree. As he paced, he could feel his hands start to be pulled toward the ground.

"Good, it's still here—weaker than before, but it's still active."

TWENTY-ONE

"Adriana, look at this." Teren pointed to the computer screen. Ishan was showing him how to navigate the Internet and he was fascinated by all it could do. "I think we found something."

"What is it?" she asked, hurrying over to look at it.

"Looks like a bunch of rocks," Ishan said, staring at the image.

Ms. Lee, Ninon, and Kathy also gathered around the screen. "Looks like rocks to me," Kathy said.

"Look closer." Teren zoomed into an area on the picture. "See those symbols?"

"Sure. They're petroglyphs," Ninon said. "They were made thousands of years ago by the native Indians."

"Can you interpret them, Teren?" Ms. Lee asked. "Even our leading archeologists don't have any idea what many of them mean."

"Not most of them. But see the one with the spirals? In the language of the ancients, that's the symbol for a portal."

"Really?" Ishan exclaimed. "Let's zoom out on Google maps to see where they're located."

"There's a bunch of them around a place called the Grand Canyon," Teren observed. "Have you ever heard of it?"

Adriana looked at Ms. Lee and shrugged. "It's only one of the most famous places on earth, Teren. Didn't you ever study geography?"

"Umm... I think I was studying spells that day."

"That day..." Adriana shrugged. "Spells are all you ever study."

"And ancient symbols. Anyway, is there a vortex near there?" Teren asked.

Ishan did a search for more spiral-shaped petroglyphs. "That whole area in Northern Arizona is loaded with them. But it looks like the closest vortex is about a hundred miles away in a town called Sedona."

"Okay, what's a vortex?" Kathy asked.

"It's where two ley lines connect," Ms. Lee explained. "At least that's the theory."

"Ley lines?" Kathy scrunched her brow.

"Ley lines are the naturally occurring electric currents that make up the earth's magnetic field," Ms. Lee continued.

"Remember in Book One," Ninon reminded her, "Kandide could only deploy the Frost at her Castle because she needed to do it where the ley lines crossed."

"Oh, yeah. That's right." Kathy's brow returned to normal. "They have vortexes in Sedona?"

"It says there are four vortexes in that area." Ishan pointed to the screen. "And take a look, there are a ton of those spiral petroglyphs all over the rocks around Sedona."

Teren watched as he clicked on one image after another, carefully examining each of them. "The Internet's really great. We need it in Calabiyau. Lord Rössi would go crazy on it. I wonder if it would work."

"It is pretty amazing," Adriana agreed, "but I don't think it would work. I'm not sure how you'd get it from one dimension to another."

"Unless we could find a stable portal," Ishan suggested. "Then we could maybe send the signal from here to there, right through it."

Kathy's face lit up. "That would be soooooo cool! Then we could email back and forth. How awesome would that be?"

"First we have to find a portal," Ms. Lee reminded them. "Teren, we can drive to Sedona in about five hours. But once we get there, how will you know where to look—if a portal even exists? As Ishan said, there are spiral petroglyphs all over that area."

"I'm not sure." Teren typed in the words portal and Sedona.

Dozens of articles came up. But none of them told him more than he already knew—vortexes are, in theory, connected to inter-dimensional travel. Some of the explanations of how they were supposed to work were down right silly. *Lord Rössi would definitely not like that*, he thought.

"So, what do we do now?" Kathy asked.

"I don't know," Ms. Lee replied. "But it's getting late, and the three of you need to start thinking about getting home. It's Friday, and remember, the gates lock early today."

"But, Ms. Lee," Ninon objected, "we have to help them."

"I have an idea," Ishan said. "Teren, can you sense a portal if you're near one?"

"Maybe. What about you, Adriana?"

"I did begin to feel the portal in the labyrinth as we got closer to it. What are you thinking, Ishan?"

"Well, there are only four vortexes in Sedona. Maybe if you go to each of them, you'll be able to tell which one has a portal attached."

"Perhaps," Ms. Lee replied. "But we don't even know if a portal exists in that area."

"Hey, look at this!" Ninon pointed to an odd looking set of petroglyphs that were carved on a red sandstone cliff. "I've never seen any like this before. It looks like three... no, four winged figures."

"They look like faeries. Make it bigger, Ishan," Kathy said.

"Okay." He clicked on it. "They really do look like faeries. See their wings? I wonder what those other two stick figures mean. One's standing upright and the other one's upside down, directly under it."

"They symbolize two worlds," Teren explained. "The one that we are in while we are alive and the one that the ancients believe we go to when we pass. See that long wavy line underneath them?"

"Yeah, it looks like a river." Ishan traced it with his finger.

"It is, sort of," Adriana told him. "In the beliefs of the ancients, a river is symbolic of the perpetual flow of all living things."

"Like when King Toeyad passed," Ms. Lee reminded them, "his essence returned to the eternal tributary of life."

Both Teren and Adriana looked at her quizzically.

"It's in Book One," she explained. "Do you think these symbols might mean that there's a portal nearby, Teren?"

"I think that's exactly what they mean. It's all there—the four winged Fée designating the four levels of being, the river flowing from one world to the next. Even the two figures, one standing upright and one upside down, indicating two dimensions."

"And there's a spiral right below the river," Ninon added. "It has to be near a portal entrance."

Adriana stared at the screen. Could it possibly be? "Are these petroglyphs in Sedona, as well, Ishan?"

"No, they're in a place called Zion National Park, in an area called Petroglyph Canyon."

"Zion? That's in Utah," Kathy said. "Is there a vortex there?"

"I don't know, but listen to this." Ishan clicked on an article that accompanied the petroglyphs. "It says here that those carvings were made by the Anasazi Indians over three thousand years ago. And look, it does say there's a vortex right in that canyon."

"That's really interesting," Ms. Lee said. "If I'm remembering correctly, the Anasazi were called the Star People and believed that Zion contained a doorway into another dimension."

"Which explains the drawings." Teren could hardly contain his excitement. "How far are we from there, Ms. Lee?"

"Only about two and a half hours. We could head out first thing in the morning."

"I want to go." "Me too." "So do I." Ninon, Kathy, and Ishan all chimed in at once. "Can we?" Ninon asked.

"I don't think so," Ms. Lee replied. "We don't even know if there

The Four Faeries of Zion

Petroglyph Canyon

ISHAN, KATHY, TEREN, ADRIANA, MS. LEE, AND NINON DISCUSS THE ZION PETROGLYPHS

actually is a portal there. Or if it's just a legend."

"Please," Ninon said. "The article says the petroglyphs are really hard to find, and I'm really good with maps."

"I know you are, Ni, but not this time. There is, however, something I want the three of you to do. From what Teren said, there's a chance the portal could reopen here at the school."

"It is possible." Teren nodded his head. "Though once they close like that one did, its energy just completely vanishes. So it's not likely."

"Well, just in case," Ms. Lee insisted, "we need to know about it if it does reappear. I want you three to keep an eye on the sky tomorrow. If you see anything that looks like a funnel cloud, call me immediately, and we'll come right back."

"I have band rehearsal tomorrow, anyway," Ishan said. "So I'll be out on the field in the morning."

"And I can come over, too," Kathy said.

"So can I," Ninon added.

"Good, then let's get the three of you home. Adriana and Teren will stay with me tonight."

"Teren, before we go, could we try flying?" Ishan asked.

"We can try. But we'll need to go somewhere with higher ceilings." He looked up at the acoustical ceiling tiles. "I don't think we will be able to fly very much with less than three meters of height."

"What about the auditorium?" Kathy suggested.

"That's a great idea," Ninon replied. "And if anyone sees us, they'll just think we're rehearsing for a play."

"Well, I do have the key." Ms. Lee reached in her purse and pulled it out. "I'm curious, about it, myself. First, though, text your parents to let them know you're with me, and that you'll be about a half hour late. Also, that I'll drive the three of you home."

TWENTY-TWO

Kandide looked up to see Lady Aron re-entering the cave. Firenza had only been away a few hours, but Kandide knew she had gone to check on Alin.

"So, Your Majesty, I see you behaved and Anile's guards haven't needed to use any of their persuasive techniques... yet."

Kandide refused to acknowledge her comment. She may be Lady Aron's prisoner, but she would never give her the satisfaction of showing any sign of fear. "And you, Firenza, what will General Kandour do to you if he takes control? Don't tell me you honestly believe that Kandour will keep someone as powerful as you around."

"I suppose that is my problem. You, however, seem to have a much bigger one. You see, both Alin and Egan are in my care now. It's amazing what a little 'sweetness' will do to lure that wretched little creature into my domain. He really should listen to his father and not venture out by himself."

Kandide had no idea what she meant, but it could not be good. "If you do anything to harm Egan, Lord Aron will destroy you."

"Harm him? Well, that's up to you. Egan is just one more reason for you to give me the Gift."

"Never!"

"Never say 'never,' my dear. You will give me the Gift, and beg me to take it once Anile's friends start... shall I say, persuading you."

"Your threats don't scare me, Firenza."

"No? Just the thought of what happened to Lady Batony scares me. Poor dear, what a misguided old fool. Insecurity and envy are such destructive emotions. I'm certainly glad I am not the type of Fée who seeks revenge for my inadequacies—not that I have any."

"Really? Then what do you seek?"

"Why power of course—the power to rid our land of Imperfects. To keep it strong for all future generations."

"It is strong, Firenza. It's strong because of diversity and acceptance. No one is favoring Imperfects. They must work to earn their place. They aren't being handed anything, but no one should deny them, either. It's Fée such as you who make our society weak. Do what you will to me, you will never have the Gift."

"Such strong words from someone in your situation. I wonder if you will still feel that way as you slowly become even more of an Imperfect. You know, Kandide, once I do have the Gift—and I will have it—my incentive to bring Teren and Adriana back will likely evaporate. So let me tell you about Egan. You were right. The two boys are still playing together. Of course I invited Egan to my mother's home. We had quite a lovely chat. Such a gullible little brat. Not at all like Alin." She sat down on the rock next to Kandide. "Did you know Egan loves gingerbread? Mother's recipe is truly wonderful. And its spicy flavor is perfect for concealing a deadly sleeping potion."

Kandide dug her nails into her hands. *I mustn't let her get to me*, she thought, trying to remain calm. *I don't even know if what she is saying about Egan is true.* "How can you be so incredibly heartless, Firenza?"

"I was just about to ask you that same thing. Let's see, you're willing to let both Teren and Adriana die a horrible death, and now Egan. Poor little Egan. At first he will merely fall asleep. But as the potion is slowly absorbed in his body, he will go deeper and deeper into a coma until his heart simply stops beating. That should happen in less than a week—plenty of time for you to agonize over your decision. I really don't see how you can be so uncaring as to let these horrible atrocities occur, especially when I'm offering you the ability to stop them."

Kandide's stomach was in knots. She had spent the last few hours trying to find a way out of all this, refusing to believe it was hopeless. *Surely Centrod and Viviana will be able to get Teren and Adriana back. They are, after all, the most powerful wizards in the world. But Egan's situation—that she hadn't counted on. Could she risk letting him die if it's true—if Firenza did poison him? And, yet, even if I do transfer the Gift,* Kandide thought, *Lady Aron will probably not release any of them.* The only words she could think to say were, "You truly are despicable, Firenza."

"It's interesting that you keep saying I'm despicable, Kandide, and yet you are the one refusing to save your own brother's life. You are the one who is willing to let Egan die. You are the one who is so selfish as to cling to the Gift, regardless of the cost. I, on the other hand, am perfectly willing to rescue Teren and Adriana. I'm also perfectly willing to administer an antidote to Egan so he simply wakes up from a good night's sleep, with only a slight tummy ache from having eaten too much gingerbread. Tell me, Kandide, who really is the despicable one?"

Kandide stared at the dark water flowing around her. *Life, like the rivers that run through this cave, is so transient and perplexing. Am I being selfish?* she wondered. *Am I behaving like I did before the accident and my wing was injured—only thinking of myself? I cannot let them die. Possessing the Gift isn't worth it.* Her head ached and her wrists were raw from trying to escape. *But that doesn't mean I give in without a fight. As Father used to tell me, "Self-doubt is your greatest enemy, Kandide. No matter how difficult the situation, do not let it rob you of your power." Father is right. I will not let Firenza's threats rob me of my power. What little I have…*

Though dirty, bruised, and dressed only in her night robe, she was still Queen—*and no one will deny me that.* She pushed herself up off the wet cave floor with a regal defiance. "When I have proof that

Teren, Adriana, and Egan are all free, then, and only then, will I discuss the Gift."

"Really? Well, I don't think you are in much of a position to bargain right now." Lady Aron flashed an evil smile. "First the Gift."

"How do I know that you'll keep your promise to free them?"

"I guess you don't. However, just to show you that my intentions are of the highest moral character, I will swear upon the name of my son, Alin, that each of them will be freed as soon as I possess the Gift."

"I'll need more than that. You must swear on Alin's life. Then you must set the curse." Not waiting for a reply, Kandide began to unfold the plan she had been developing since Lady Aron's departure. It wasn't much, but at least it was something. "Do you agree?"

With the Gift finally in her grasp, Lady Aron quickly answered, "As you wish."

"You'll have to untie me for the transfer to take place."

"Do you think me a fool?"

"A fool? Oh, Firenza, you are anything but a fool. That would be the last word that I would use to describe you. Cruel, vicious, heartless, and completely immoral, yes, but a fool? Never."

"You do say the nicest things. Now let's get started before I show you how 'heartless' I can actually be."

Kandide could see that Lady Aron was so eager to have the Gift that she was beginning to let her guard down. Perhaps her plan would work. "As we both know, I must transfer the Gift willingly. The process is precise and can be dangerous. It normally takes a great deal of preparedness. Father spent months readying me for it, and even then I thought I might pass before the transfer was over. Who knows, I may get lucky and you, my dear Firenza, may die during it."

"So nice of you to be concerned. That is a chance I shall just have to take." She motioned to one of the guards. "Untie her and keep your arrows aimed at her legs. Let me remind you, Kandide, that this mine is shielded. Any attempt to transport out of here will fail."

"The shielding may also cause the transfer to fail. It would be much safer if you release it."

"So you can transport out? I don't think so."

"You would do best to heed my warning, Firenza. We could both die, and the Gift would be lost forever."

Smiling at Kandide, Lady Aron was convinced that she was bluffing. After all, King Toeyad's chamber was more than likely shielded during the transfer to Kandide. In any case, she would know soon enough. With a flick of her wrists, both of the guard's arrow tips were set on fire. They were only centimeters from Kandide's knees. "Just a little extra precaution. I wouldn't want you to try anything funny."

Though she could feel the heat from the flames, Kandide did not flinch. She was completely focused on her plan. "Before we start, you must swear upon Alin that you will release Teren, Adriana, and Egan, and never do them harm again. Swear it and place the seven-year curse on Alin, Firenza. I must know that he will experience seven years of unimaginable horror, should you not keep any part of your promise."

Lady Aron hesitated only briefly. She was so close to having everything she wanted. "I swear upon my son, Alin, that I will free Prince Teren, Adriana, and Egan, for now and for all time. Should I fail to keep my pledge, may the seven-year curse befall my son, Alin."

"You must also swear that you will never harm any of them, ever again."

"You're starting to annoy me."

"Swear it!"

"If you insist. I, Lady Firenza Aron, also hereby swear upon my son, Alin, that I will never harm any of them. May the curse befall him, if I do not keep this pledge. Are you happy now?"

"Let's just get this over with." With her hands untied, Kandide instructed Lady Aron to be seated directly across from her and begin breathing deeply. "Let me warn you, Firenza, you will be in excruciating pain and will most certainly beg me to stop. But if these goons do anything to disrupt the transfer before it's over, we will remain joined forever. Do you understand?"

"Of course. Though I hardly doubt I'll beg you to stop."

"We'll see," Kandide replied. "I certainly begged Father to stop. The pain is, as I said, excruciating."

Lady Aron ordered the Banshee guards to not do anything to stop the transfer, regardless of what happened. "Do you understand my order?" she asked one then the other. "Do nothing to stop the transfer."

"Whatever you say, Lady." Jab replied.

Stif nodded. "Yeah, we won't do anything, Lady. No matter how hard you beg Queen Kandide to stop."

"Good. Make sure you don't." Kandide looked from one to the other, and then to Lady Aron. "We'll know soon enough if the shielding inhibits the transfer." Her tone was icy cold. "Place your hands, one finger at a time against mine, starting with the little finger."

Doing as she was instructed, Lady Aron could barely contain her excitement. Within minutes, she would realize her life-long dream of possessing the Gift. Each of her fingers, in turn, touched Kandide's.

"Do you, Lady Aron, willingly agree to accept the Gift of the Frost?"

"I do."

"Do you promise to guard it from all who would misuse it?"

"I do."

Do you promise to use it for…"

"I do. I do. I promise to do it all. Just get on with it!"

TWENTY-THREE

"**P**atience, Firenza." Kandide pressed each of her fingertips tightly against Lady Aron's. "The transfer must be done with precision. And remember, we cannot stop once it starts, no matter how painful."

"Yes. Yes. Just start." She tingled with excitement. The Gift would soon be hers.

"Keep your breathing in sync with mine," Kandide warned before beginning the process of transferring the Gift. In her mind, she visualized the transfer exactly the way her father had done it, nearly a year ago. She could feel the flow of energy begin to surface from deep inside her body. *I hope my plan works,* she thought. Emptiness began replacing the vibrancy she had become accustomed to feeling.

At first, Lady Aron felt only a slight tingle. As the transfer continued, however, it became stronger and stronger until the tingles transformed into sharp jolts of ever increasing pain. She felt as though megawatts of electricity were being shot through her hands, arms, and legs all at once. Just as Kandide warned, the pain quickly became unbearable. With all of her might, Lady Aron desperately tried to avoid screaming. Every fiber of her body was ravished by the terrible throbbing caused by the surges of current. A thousand needles stabbed the inside of her veins.

It took all of her focus to keep from passing out. Sweat poured down her brow and her breathing became extremely labored, when suddenly she was aware of a new sensation. The flow of energy seemed to be slowing. Could it be? Could she now possess the Gift? Elation replaced exhaustion. "It's mine," she gasped. "The Gift is mine."

Something, however, was wrong. She began to feel a different sensation. The flow, it was reversing. Her body shook uncontrollably and her breathing became even more difficult. "Noooo!" she screamed. Try as she would, Lady Aron could no more separate her hands from Kandide now, than when they first began the transfer. They were simply fused together as if by some powerful magnetic force.

"Noooo!" she screamed even louder, as the power continued to flow back into Kandide at an alarmingly fast rate. "Stop!" Not only was Kandide reversing the transfer of the Gift, she was draining Lady Aron of her own strength. "I said, stop! Listen to me, make her stop!"

Despite her pleas, the two Banshee guards, as per her orders, continued to do nothing but stare. Lady Aron gasped for what little air she could force into her lungs. "Stop her..." A dull gray tone consumed her skin. Her head felt like it would implode. Within seconds, she collapsed, her arm dangling in the black water that surrounded her.

Only then did Kandide release their hands. The force from having released the reverse energy flow catapulted her backwards. Two flaming arrows streaked through the air. She whirled around in an attempt to overcome the guards. One of the arrows had already come to her aid, impaling Stif in his chest.

"Very clever plan, Your Majesty," Jab said with a bemused smirk. "Not clever enough, though." He held her at bay with another arrow. "Guess I'll have the pleasure of handing you over to General Kandour, myself. Should fetch me a real nice reward."

"What about Lady Aron?" Kandide asked, hoping to momentarily distract him.

He, however, did not alter his focus. "Looks like you already took care of her. Too bad Anile isn't here. He'd sure like to have one of those ears. Gets mad if anyone else takes them. Says it's not honorable to accept an ear from someone else's doing. And you don't want to be makin' Anile mad. No, ma'am, you don't want to be makin' Anile mad."

"No… no, we certainly don't want to do that." Not daring to move, she knew that she must somehow divert his attention. Having absorbed so much power, she also knew that her body could possibly go into a sort of reverse shock. *I need a moment to rebalance my energy,* she thought. Curiously, the tip of her wing was no longer bent.

"Do you know how to un-shield this place so we can transport out of here?" the Banshee asked. "Otherwise I got to drag you up that shaft."

"I think so. But first I have to sit down for a minute and rest. May I? I'm feeling a bit faint."

With his arrow still drawn, he moved closer to her. "Okay, but don't take too long. And don't be trying anything funny, you hear?"

"I hear." Slumping over, she appeared to pass out.

"Well, that's just great!" Momentarily lowering his bow, the Banshee slapped her across the face. "I said be quick!"

Infused with power, Kandide grabbed him around the throat and placed him in a chokehold. She yanked the bow and arrow from his hand. "The old passing out trick. You really ought to know better." Squeezing a nerve on the side of his neck, Kandide watched as the Banshee dropped to the floor. "A little something I learned from your boss." She quickly bound his hands and feet with the same ropes that had constrained her. "I wonder what kind of reward you'll get when Anile finds out that I escaped."

Concerned that Lady Aron may be her only hope of saving Egan—if he actually was poisoned—Kandide reached down to feel her pulse. It was remarkably strong considering the ordeal she had just been through. "I told you the transfer could be dangerous, Firenza. You just never learn."

"Nor do you." Firenza grabbed Kandide by the arms. "The old passing out trick. You really ought to know better, Your Majesty."

Knowing that she didn't have nearly enough strength to keep Kandide restrained, Lady Aron shoved her across the cave. In that split second, she mumbled a phrase to un-shield the mineshaft. With a gesture, the Fire Fée dissolved into a gray film and vanished.

Kandide watched her disappear. *Now I need to get out of here*, she thought.

Transporting out of the cave, she scanned the horizon. Her eyes locked on the distant images of Kandour's training camp. *That means I must be near the easternmost border of Banshee territory.*

Her first impulse was to transport back to the Castle to find out about Egan. But that would take at least six hours. The Bardic Temple, however, was less than two hours transport from the Banshee border. *I'll go there first. Then immediately return home.*

TWENTY-FOUR

"Firenza? Goodness, child, what has happened to you?" Lady Maxella helped her daughter to a chair in the sitting room of her manor house.

The red and amber furnishings were brightly illuminated by Lady Maxella's fiery wings. Firenza's wings added no such illumination. They were dull, lifeless, and gray.

"I'll get you some hibiscus tea," her mother continued. She resembled her daughter in every way with flaming red-gold hair, and yellow eyes that contrasted sharply with their intensely blue pupils.

"I was kidnapped, Mother. It was terrible."

"Kidnapped? By whom?"

"By that awful Lady Batony." Barely able to sit up, Firenza's back rounded in the chair.

"Lady Batony? I'm not sure I understand."

"It turns out she is working with Kandide and her Banshee friends."

"What? I can't imagine such a thing. Lady Batony is working with Kandide and the Banshees? For what reason?"

"To make it look like the villages that are being destroyed are my doing."

Lady Maxella poured a cup of the tea, then held it tightly between her hands. It began to boil. "I still don't understand." She helped her daughter take a couple sips, then placed it on the side table next to her red chair. "Why would they want to blame that on you?"

"Because I oppose letting Imperfects live here. Think about it, Mother. You know both of them have always hated me. Who better to blame all this horrible killing and destruction on than someone who opposes Kandide's will?"

Deep lines etched Lady Maxella's otherwise smooth brow. "But why would they kidnap you?"

How many times do I have to explain things to her, Lady Aron thought, before speaking. Frustration leaked through her already weak voice. "The two of them arranged for it to look like they were the ones being kidnapped. Their plan was to blame it on me. They were going to kill me, while they allegedly were trying to escape. That way, there would be no need to bring formal charges against me for the village burnings—none of which they would ever be able to prove if I were alive."

"My poor, Firenza. I just can't believe Kandide would do something so vile. I know she doesn't like you, but… oh, dear, this is awful. Simply awful."

"It gets even worse, Mother. To make sure that Lady Batony would never reveal the truth, Kandide had her killed. It was terrible what those dreadful Banshees did to that poor woman—how they tortured her. Banshees can be so brutal. We were in this cave, deep underground, so no one could hear her screams. I begged Kandide not to do it—to spare her life. She laughed and said I was next. And that if I didn't want to be tortured first, I should sign a confession."

Lady Maxella shook her head. "I can't believe it."

"It's true, Mother. It's all true."

"How did you manage to escape?"

"After Kandide stole my power, she went into another chamber to discuss something with the head guard—a vicious scar-faced Banshee she called Anile. I could only hear a few words about what they were plotting—something to do with an attack. I don't know where."

"While Kandide was gone," Lady Aron continued, "I managed to free myself and, with my last remaining bit of strength, overcome the soldier they left to guard me. I then transported both of us to another mineshaft—where he is right now."

"Why did you transport him?"

"Why do you have to ask me so many questions? Do you doubt what I'm telling you?"

"No. No. I just need to understand. It's all so..."

Lady Aron took another sip of the tea. The heat helped her voice to strengthen. "Because he is the only one who can clear my name. I would take you to him, Mother, but I'm too weak. I almost didn't have enough strength to transport here."

"Yes, yes, of course. Lord Aron told me about Kandide's kidnapping, but I simply had no idea that you were also taken prisoner. I'm sure he doesn't know, either."

Lady Aron forced herself to sit up. "Lord Aron? When did you see him?"

"He arrived here not long after you left. He was looking for Egan. The boys are with him now."

"What?" She nearly collapsed again. "Alin is with Lord Aron? Where... where are they?"

"He's taken them to the Castle. I was about to go there myself, just before you arrived. I had a few chores to finish up first, and then pack. I told him I would join them in a few hours."

"Why in the name of the spirits would you have let him take them?"

"It's not safe to stay here, right now. A couple days ago, a village was destroyed less than five kilometers away. The bread maker's sister lost her home in the terrible fire. I only wanted..."

"You only wanted what?"

"I only wanted what's best for the boys. I thought you would agree—especially now that you've accepted Egan. I was hoping that you and Lord Aron would get back together. You did mention that possibility to Egan over lunch. The boy's such a sweet child. After you left, he shared his last two pieces of gingerbread with Alin."

"He did what?" Lady Aron's ashen-gray color turned white.

"He shared his last piece of gingerbread. I think they both ate a bit too much, however, as by the time I got Alin's overnight bag packed, they were falling asleep."

Sinking back into her chair, Lady Aron was shaking. *How could everything have gone so wrong?* she thought, trying to muster any last bit of strength. Her body, however, refused. Fire Fée burn tremendous amounts of energy. And with her system so drained, it would take weeks for her build up enough to function normally—much longer to create spells. She did, however, know exactly how to replenish it. "I must get Alin back. I… a… I overheard Kandide saying something about putting a sleeping spell on Alin, and then sending him to the Bardic Council so Centrod could retrain his mind not to remember me. That must be the real reason why Lord Aron came here."

"Lord Aron would never allow that. You don't understand. We had a lovely chat. He's eager to help you clear your name and wants to be a family again. When I told him that is what you told Egan, he was elated."

"It's you who don't understand, Mother." Seething with anger, Lady Aron clenched her fists. "He lied to you. Can't you see that? He's working with Kandide and would tell you anything knowing that I'd soon be dead. I can't believe you let him take my son. I just started trusting you again, after the last time you let Jake and Teren take Alin to the Castle. And this is how I'm repaid?"

"But, Firenza, things are different now."

"I don't believe it. I must get Alin back and quickly. Who knows what Lord Aron gave them to make them sleepy. Which means we don't have much time. I'm going to need your help."

"Of course, anything. I just…"

"I just hope I can trust you now. I'm exhausted and need you to infuse me with energy so I can regain some strength."

Lady Maxella took a step back. "How can you even ask that of me? You know how dangerous it is—especially at my age. It would be months before my strength returns—if I survive. I'll get Alin back. I'll go to the Castle right now and fetch him. You stay here and rest."

"I don't need rest, Mother. I need my power back. I won't take much from you—just enough so I can function. If you truly want to help me, and if you ever want to see Alin again, then you must do this for me. It's the only way. I cannot risk your failing me again."

"But what about the sleeping potion you say Lord Aron gave the boys? If I go there, I can have the healers give them an antidote."

"They don't have the antidote. I mean they... they may not know what to give him. Besides, if I'm correct, Lord Aron will only wake Egan. He won't want Alin to wake up until he knows that I am dead and the boy is at the Bardic Temple for retraining. I think I know what he gave them."

"Even so, I don't think it would be wise for you to go there right now. From what you told me, I'm sure Kandide will have every guard searching for you."

"Perhaps you're right. I'll send the antidote with you, Mother. Right after you transfer some energy to me. If there were any other way, I would never ask this of you."

Though still reluctant, Lady Maxella agreed to the transfer. "Only a small amount, though. You must promise me."

"Yes. Yes, of course." She placed both hands on her mother's temples. "Release the flow." It began to pulse through her body.

As soon as Lady Maxella felt herself start to weaken, she tried to pull away, but her daughter refused to stop. Her hands were fused to her mother's head. "Just a bit, more, Mother."

Forcing her hands even tighter against her mother's temples, Lady Aron continued to drain the life-giving forces from Lady Maxella.

Her entire body felt gloriously alive again—every cell refreshed and awake. Unlike the transfer of the Gift of the Frost, energy infusions provide a feeling of euphoria to the recipient. "I need more, Mother. More."

Struggling to breathe, Lady Maxella pleaded with her daughter to stop, until she had no more strength to resist. Ashen white and completely drained, she lapsed into unconsciousness.

"Nothing can stop me, Mother. Regardless of the cost, I will win." Holding Lady Maxella in her arms, she transported to her mother's bedchamber. "I will not let you pass, but neither can I trust you to go to the Castle. You've failed me twice. I can't risk a third time. Worry not, however, you will live to see me victorious. This sleeping spell will ensure you remain unconscious until your strength has regenerated." She spoke in a metered tone: "Night and day, sleep now, dear Fée, until your strength is no longer at bay."

After placing a blanket over her mother, Lady Aron closed the window shades. "And now I must prepare the antidote."

LADY ARON MIXES THE
SLEEPING ANTIDOTE

"Egan," Tara tried to explain, *"your father can't promise you that. It's not up to him."*

TWENTY-FIVE

"I thought the boys were just tired from so much excitement," Lord Aron explained to Tara. They were standing in his private quarters on the third floor of the Castle. "When I tried to wake Alin, he opened his eyes then fell right back to sleep. Egan won't even wake up. That's when I called you. My apologies for pulling you away from the meeting with General Mintz, but I felt it important."

"Of course. He was just updating me about Kandide."

"Is there any news?"

"Unfortunately, not." Tara placed her hand on the forehead of each boy. "They don't seem to have a fever, but there is definitely something strange going on. It could be some sort of a sleeping spell."

She hadn't been in Lord Aron's apartment since before Lady Aron moved out a few months earlier. It looked completely different. Gone were the red and yellow furnishings, replaced by a much more earthy color palette of rich greens and chocolate browns. It perfectly suited Lord Aron's refined nature.

"How were the boys when you picked them up?" she asked.

"Egan was a bit sleepy. They had gone swimming again—without my permission. I know how much they love to race, so I assumed they had just over extended themselves. Alin began yawning as we were leaving. I really didn't think much about it at the time."

"Do you know if they had anything to eat or drink before you left?"

"Actually, they did. Lady Maxella made gingerbread. The boys were sharing the last couple pieces when I got there. I must say, it smelled delicious."

"Did you eat any?" Tara felt Egan's pulse. It was much slower than normal sleep.

"No. I don't do well with ginger. Never have."

"And that's such a pity." Lady Aron materialized in the doorway that led to the boys' bedroom. "You and that pathetic excuse of a child could have both passed quietly in your sleep."

"What are you doing here?" Lord Aron reached for the yellow velvet chord that hung by Egan's bed. "One pull and the Castle guards will be here within seconds."

"I wouldn't do that if I were you." A streak of fire shot from Lady Aron's fingertips. "Unless, of course, you want to lose your arm in the process." He barely had time to pull his hand away before the chord burst into flames. With her second gesture, the flames disappeared. The charred chord dropped to the floor. "Now, my darling husband, shall we discuss the situation at hand?"

Lord Aron glared at her. "What have you done to Egan and Alin?"

"More importantly, what will you do to save their lives?" Lady Aron moved closer to Egan. "He looks so peaceful. And just think, in a few days, he'll be dead. Unless, of course, I give him this antidote." She held up a small bottle of red liquid.

"What do you want, Lady Aron?" Anger seeped through Tara's voice. She hadn't seen the Fire Fée since Firenza trapped her in the block of ice a few months earlier. "Obviously, you're not going to let Alin die."

"No, I'm not. Give my son to me and I'll give you the antidote for Egan."

"First," Lord Aron insisted, "give the antidote to both boys, then we can talk about Alin."

"Unfortunately, I only brought enough for one. And out of the goodness of my heart, I'm willing to give it to your son—after you agree to give me Alin. Oh, and you really should change the shielding codes on your chamber. One never knows who might drop in."

Tara stood firm. Her trust of Lady Aron was nonexistent. "How do we know your so-called antidote will work?"

"How dare you question my integrity." She released another stream of fire that incinerated a side dresser. Black ash drifted to the floor where the silver chest once stood.

"There's no reason for you to behave like that, Firenza," Lord Aron told her.

"Really? You, who lied to lure my son away from my mother, are telling me how to behave?" Another stream of fire destroyed the side table next to him. "Egan will die without the antidote. Give me Alin and you can have it."

"First, give it to Egan." Lord Aron was adamant. "Once he's awake, you can…you can take Alin. But I swear to you, Firenza, I will get him back."

"Not this time." She removed the wax seal from the bottle, tipped Egan's head back, and poured the red liquid into his mouth. "He should be fine in a few minutes."

Coughing, Egan slowly shook off the deep sleep he'd fallen into. His eyes brightened as he saw Lady Aron. "Mother, you're here."

Ignoring him, she turned to Lord Aron. "If I don't get Alin home right away, where I can administer the same antidote, he will die."

"What does she mean, Father, Alin will die? What's wrong with him?" Egan slid out of bed and gently shook his brother. "Alin, wake up. Wake up. Please."

"He needs the same medicine I gave you." Sweetness dripped from Lady Aron's voice. "Unfortunately, I didn't know both of you were sick, so I only brought enough for one. I need to take Alin home so I can get more for him. There isn't time for me to go there and come back."

"Maybe Tara has some." Egan looked up at her.

"This is a very special kind of medicine. Tara doesn't have it." She eyed the Princess. "Do you, Tara?"

"No, Egan. I'm afraid I don't."

"Then, Father, please, you have to let Mother take Alin back to Grandmam's house or he'll die."

"I know, Egan. I know." Lord Aron turned to his wife. "This isn't over, Firenza."

"No. It certainly is not." She lifted Alin into her arms.

"When will you be back?" Egan asked.

There was no reply. Lady Aron and Alin were gone.

"When will they be back, Father?"

Lord Aron sat down on the bed next to his son. "Egan, your Mother isn't coming back."

"Yes she is. She said we're going to be a family again. And that she was sorry for being mean to me. She said she wanted us to be together. She even had Grandmam make us gingerbread cookies."

"Egan, your mother is… well," Tara took a breath, "she's a very complicated person. Not everything she does is for the best. And not everything she says is true."

"I know, Princess Tara, but she's my mother." Tears filled his eyes. "I love her, even if she is mean sometimes. And Alin is my best friend. Please bring them back, Father, please. I know we can help her be nice again. I'll be good. I promise. Really, really good. And we won't have to sneak away anymore."

Lord Aron had no idea what to say. He knew it would never happen.

"Egan," Tara tried to explain, "your father can't promise you that. It's not up to him. Lady Aron is the only one who can decide to come back."

"I know. But I want it to be different. I want us to be together and be happy."

"I'm just happy that you're well again." Lord Aron hugged his son.

"Me too. Except my tummy kinda hurts. I hope Alin's okay."

"He'll be fine," Tara assured him. "Your mother will make him well. Now, I need to be going. I've got to get back to my meeting with General Mintz. I also want to let him know what just happened."

"Did he find Queen Kandide?" Egan asked.

"Not while I was there."

"Maybe Lady Alicia could ask the snakes to help. They know where all the caves are."

Tara thought for a minute. "Egan, you are so clever."

"Portals are powered by electromagnetic fields," Teren explained. *"Metal disrupts the field and causes it to collapse into itself."*

TWENTY-SIX

Teren and Adriana stared out the window of the car. Ms. Lee was driving down the Las Vegas Strip so they could see a little of the city before leaving. Though it was dawn, everything was still aglow with millions of light bulbs and dozens of massive flashing signs—some as tall as the buildings they stood in front of. Neither Adriana nor Teren had ever seen anything like it, certainly not in Calabiyau. They marveled at the towering hotels made of mirrored glass, roller coasters that streaked through the sky, jets of water that danced to music, a life-sized pirate ship, and even a massive pyramid topped with a beam of light that touched the sky. It was an unbelievable sight.

"I wish we had time to go inside some of the buildings," Teren said, trying to absorb it all. "It's incredible."

"It really is," Adriana agreed, her mind snapping mental pictures so she could tell the other apprentice priestesses every detail about what she saw. "Does every American city look like this?"

"Not at all." Ms. Lee had stopped at a red light. "Las Vegas is quite different from almost any other place in America—or the world, for that matter. And it's just this area; the rest of the city is really quite normal," she added as the light turned green and they headed away from the Strip. "Thank you again for letting us experience flying yesterday. It's an unbelievable feeling."

"I guess we don't really think about it," Adriana said. "Any more than you think about driving, which is also pretty amazing." She glanced around at the light gray upholstery and shiny chrome trim on Ms. Lee's SUV. "Just the control panel is, as Ni says, 'awesome.'"

"I've never thought about driving as being awesome. But you're right. If you've never been in a car, it probably is. We do take a lot of our technology for granted. Speaking of technology, can you watch for a text from Kathy or Ishan?" She handed Adriana her cell phone.

"Of course." Adriana reached out to take it. "I agree with Teren, cell phones would be great to have in Calabiyau."

"Yeah, I could talk to Tara and my mom anytime I want. Viviana wouldn't even know it."

"Don't be too sure about that, Teren," Ms. Lee said. "I always know when my students are texting."

"I guess you're right. Viviana seems to know everything I do."

"She knows everything everybody does," Adriana corrected.

Within minutes of leaving Las Vegas, they were sailing down the highway. The landscape had turned to desert. That, too, was something neither Adriana nor Teren had ever seen, asking question after question about the different types of plant and animal life. The cactus and shrub-like trees that grew out of the parched sandy soil fascinated both of them.

"Does it ever rain here?" Teren asked.

"On average about four or five inches a year," Ms. Lee explained.

"That's between 10.2 and 12.7 centimeters," Adriana told him.

Teren was sitting in the front passenger seat and turned around to look at her. "I didn't know you were good at math like Ni."

"I'm not. I looked it up on Ms. Lee's cell phone. You can find out anything on this thing."

"Yeah, well let's hope it helps us find that portal." He turned back around. "No matter what happens, Ms. Lee, Adriana and I really appreciate everything you're doing for us. Dinner last night was great. Neither one of us have ever had enchiladas or guacamole and chips.

And watching your television—that was so awesome." Teren loved the new expression he learned. "I can't wait to tell Tara about everything. Thank you so much."

"Thank *you*, Teren. You and Adriana have completely changed my understanding of our world. I keep thinking I must be dreaming and that I'll wake up and find out that none of this really happened. But even if I do, it's been…well, incredible." She changed lanes to pass a slow moving car. "Sunday drivers on a Saturday. I don't know why people insist on going fifty in a seventy mile-per-hour zone."

"Me neither." Teren marveled at how Ms. Lee maneuvered the car so effortlessly. "But I sure wish we did have cell phones in Calabiyau. I could keep all my spells on it so I don't have to remember them."

"We could also call Ms. Lee," Adriana said. "That would be wonderful."

"I'm due for a new phone pretty soon," Ms. Lee told her. "Would you like to take that one back with you? It's not likely that it will work. But you never know."

"I wish we could," Teren replied, "but it has metal in it, so it can't go through a portal."

"Why is that?" Ms. Lee asked.

"Portals are powered by electromagnetic fields," he explained. "Metal disrupts the field and causes it to collapse within itself."

"Any type of metal?" Ms. Lee was impressed by how much he knew about what she thought was human science.

"Well," Teren said, "ferrous metal like iron is the worst. It distorts the field lines. But even non-ferrous metals like copper have a negative effect. They'll actually cause the portal to reverse itself."

Adriana listened in amazement to Teren's explanation. She knew metal could not go through a portal, but had no idea why. She also had no idea that he would know why. "How do you know all that, Teren?"

He sat up a little straighter. The fact that he would know something that Adriana didn't know was, as Kathy would say, so cool.

"I always wondered why Fée didn't bring back more human technology, since so many of them used to travel back and forth. So, I did some research and discovered that metal can't be brought back. Explosive powders do the same thing."

"And that's probably a good thing," Ms. Lee said. "I'd hate to see some of our weapons in the hands of the Banshees."

"Can you imagine what would happen if General Kandour was able to use them?" Adriana said. "We'd all be killed."

"Yeah, spells are bad enough. At least we can usually counter most of them." Teren glanced down at the car's GPS. "Hey, it looks like we're about half way there already."

Ms. Lee nodded. "Just about."

Throughout the rest of the trip, Teren and Adriana continued to ask questions, as did Ms. Lee—each sharing as much as they could about the way they lived, their beliefs, and their homelands.

Slowly, the landscape began to change again. "Wow!" Teren exclaimed. "Zion is really beautiful." He looked up at the towering red and white sandstone cliffs. The sun was still fairly low in the eastern sky, bathing the rugged terrain in a golden glow. "We sure don't have anything like this in Calabiyau. We have red sandstone cliffs, but not nearly this high."

"Or this beautiful," Adriana added.

"I think Zion has to be one of the most beautiful places in the world," Ms. Lee said. "I only hope it's also magical and we find the portal." Her silver SUV had slowed to a crawl. "Looks like a lot of people are visiting this weekend. I've never seen traffic this bad."

"Is today one of your holidays?" Adriana asked. "Maybe that's why so many people are coming here."

"More than likely it's because of an accident," she replied. "People just go too fast on these winding roads."

"Your GPS says the entrance is only about another ten miles." Teren was enthralled by the way the device could navigate their route just by entering a destination. "Does it work like the internet?"

"Not exactly," Ms. Lee explained. "The GPS, which stands for Global Positioning System, gets a signal from the satellites that orbit the earth."

"Satellites?" Adriana asked. "What are they?"

Ms. Lee couldn't help but smile. "I guess you don't need satellites in Calabiyau. If you want to go somewhere, you just set the coordinates and transport there."

"Yeah, unless you have the wrong coordinates—then it's really easy to get lost," Teren chuckled.

"Sometime I get lost with the GPS, as well—even when I put in the right address. But they've gotten better over the years. This one is pretty good."

"So how does it know where we are?" Teren asked.

"GPS satellites are basically navigational transmitters that orbit the earth in a precise path. The commercial network—which is what GPS devices such as the one we're using are connected to—consists of twenty-four primary satellites, and I think a few back-ups. It doesn't matter where we are on the earth, at least four of them can track our location at any given time. They use high-frequency radio beams that travel at the speed of light, so tracking where we are, even as we move, is almost instantaneous."

"I assume the reason there are four," Adriana said, "is because they need to calculate our latitude, longitude, and altitude, and that requires signals from at least three different angles, plus one to overlap."

Teren looked at her. "How do you know that?"

"It's simple math, Teren. You really should get your head out of those spell books once in a while."

"Adriana's exactly right—at least about the three coordinates. Though learning math is also important."

"Now you sound like Centrod," he teased. "Only you're a lot nicer, Ms. Lee."

"Thank you…I think. Anyway, by knowing those three coordinates, the GPS can calculate our direction, speed, and how long it will take to get where we're going. It's pretty remarkable when you think about it."

"It sure is." Teren looked at the GPS and watched as it tracked the curves in the road. "In a way, it's kind of like transporting. To set coordinates, we need to know three different numbers. But I never thought about them being the latitude, longitude, and altitude."

"What did you think they were for?" Adriana asked.

"Like I said, I never really thought about it. Hey, now it says we're twenty minutes away. Before it said ten minutes?"

"That's because our speed is a lot slower." Ms. Lee glanced at the device. "Looks like the traffic is going to get even worse. I know a back way into the canyon. The turn-off is in about a half a mile."

"It really is pretty crowded on this road." Adriana leaned forward. "Ms. Lee, I hope you don't mind me asking. I couldn't help but notice that you seem to be in a lot of pain when you do much walking. Are you sure you're going to be okay to hike into the canyon? From what I can tell on the Google map, it's a long way to the petroglyphs."

"I don't mind at all, Adriana. Thank you for asking. The pain is in my lower back and hips. I'm supposed to have an operation, but I keep putting it off."

"Why's that?" Teren asked.

"Because the surgery is dangerous and it could leave me paralyzed."

"Surgery? Paralyzed?" Teren was shocked. "Why can't they just heal it?"

"Our doctors don't have the ability to heal like Tara or Leanne. I'm afraid, Teren, our methods are much less advanced."

"But you have technologies like the Internet, and cell phones, and GPS that are way more advanced than us. Why do your doctors still cut people open to heal them? That doesn't make any sense."

"I know. For all of its advances, in some ways, our medicine is still in the dark ages. Oh, good, here's the turn off." She steered the car onto a side road. Fortunately, it was wide open. "In any case, to answer your question, Adriana, I'll be fine. I'll take a couple pain pills, and I should be okay for a few hours."

"I wish Tara was here," Teren said. "I bet she could heal you in an instant. Hey, maybe…"

Adriana eyed him suspiciously. "Maybe what, Teren? I know that look, and it always gets you into trouble."

"Well, I was just thinking. When we find the portal, maybe Ms. Lee could come through it with us and Tara or even Leanne could heal her. Think it would work?"

Adriana thought for a minute. "I don't know. Humans do visit our world once in a while. But I'm not sure if they can be healed. Though, now that you mention it, I do remember Centrod talking about a human baby girl that was born with a twisted hand. Her mother stood in a fairy ring for days until Viviana's grandmother, who used to visit the human realm on a regular basis, took pity on her. She transported the baby to the Bardic Temple and the healers were able to fix her hand. But it's just a story and I don't even know if it's even true."

"But what if it is true?" Teren argued. "You could come with us, Ms. Lee. And maybe it would work."

"Can I come too?" a voice from the back of the SUV called out. Ms. Lee looked in the rearview mirror. "Ninon! How did… what are you doing here?"

"I snuck in the back and hid under the blankets. I guess I fell asleep." She yawned and stretched her arms.

"How could you do that? Your mother is going to be worried sick."

"No, she won't. I told her I was going to Kathy's and that we're going to Zion and would be back tomorrow night. We go on lots of trips together. Sometimes Kathy comes with Mom and me. And sometimes I go with her family. My mom's really busy with her classes. She has to study for her tests this weekend, so she said it was okay."

"Well, it's not okay." Ms. Lee insisted. "You can't just tell your mom a lie like that, Ni."

"It wasn't exactly a lie." Ninon crawled into the back seat with Adriana. "I mean, we are going to Zion. It's half true. And Kathy's going to cover for me if we're late getting back. So, can I come to Calabiyau with you? Can I, please? I know Tara or Leanne can heal my foot." Ni held up her leg. The special shoe she wore did little to conceal how badly twisted it was. "Once it's fixed, Mom won't have to worry about paying for the operation, and maybe the other kids will stop teasing me."

Ms. Lee shook her head. "Ninon, I don't think—"

"My apologies for interrupting, Ms. Lee. There's a text from Ishan." Adriana held up the cell phone.

"What does it say? Did he see the funnel cloud?"

TWENTY-SEVEN

"Is Lord Mywerk here?" Jake had arrived at the Bardic Temple just moments before. He, Centrod, and Viviana were standing in the garden near the labyrinth that had swallowed Teren and Adriana.

"We haven't seen him," Centrod replied.

"Have you been able to re-open the portal?" Jake asked.

"Unfortunately, not." Viviana sounded frustrated. "We've tried every unlocking spell possible. We're hoping Lord Mywerk will be able to provide some answers."

Jake could see that she was completely exhausted; not at all like the powerful Priestess he had first met. "Mywerk gave me this." He held out a piece of parchment. "Maybe it will help. He said if he's not here by mid-afternoon, Centrod should try it."

"I'll try it right now." The elder wizard took the paper and read the spell. His expression turned grave. "I'm afraid we've already tried this spell, Jake. It didn't work."

"But it has to. Are you sure you tried this exact one?"

"Yes." Centrod sighed. "We've tried every spell we know."

"We've scoured the library for answers," Viviana added, "even combining our powers to try forcing it open.

"But you're wizards—supposedly the most powerful wizards in the world. If you two don't know how to get Teren and Adriana back, who does?" Jake could feel his temper starting to flare. *Breathe,* he told himself. *Breathe. Getting mad won't do any good.* "There has to be a way."

"There is." Lord Mywerk appeared next to them in the garden. "My apologies for being late. I found another portal. It's even more ancient than this one. Unfortunately, it's also unstable."

"Can we go through it?" Jake asked.

"We, no. Me, possibly. I stopped by there on the way here. That's what took me so long. The vortex is still active—though the portal's energy is not as strong as I'd like. With some reinforcement, it may be able to support two trips."

"Two trips?" Jake wasn't sure what he meant.

"Going there and coming back," Viviana explained.

"There is one other problem," Mywerk continued. "It's is about fifty meters from General Kandour's camp. There are fourteen thousand heavily armed troops near it."

"How were you able to find it without being captured?" Centrod asked.

"I wasn't. As soon as I appeared, twelve of his archers surrounded me."

"How did you manage to get away?" Jake still wasn't convinced that Mywerk could be trusted.

"I almost didn't. Fortunately, Kandour's arrogance usurped his intelligence and he decided to keep me alive because he thinks I might trade my Talents for Cyndara's life."

"And would you?" Jake asked.

Mywerk's face revealed no sign of an answer. "Right now, saving Teren and Adriana is where my Talents are required. I've reverse-engineered where the portal they went through must have let out. If I'm correct, I can transport from where the Banshee portal lets out to that precise location. Hopefully, it won't collapse in the process."

"You don't sound very optimistic," Jake said. "There must be other portals to the human realm that are safer."

"There are—dozens all across Calabiyau. But I know of no others that originate in our world and let out in the western part of North America. It's a very long distance and requires a great deal of energy to sustain, which is one of the reasons most of them haven't survived. And probably why the North American continent took so long to be discovered."

"So what you're saying, Lord Mywerk, is that I'm standing here with three powerful wizards, and this unstable portal that's surrounded by Banshee troops is our only hope?"

"I'm saying it's our best hope. Unless you have a better solution."

"Then I'm going with you," Jake insisted.

"No, you will not." Mywerk's deep brown eyes told him that it was not subject to debate.

"High Priestess, Viviana." A young apprentice called, rushing up to her. "My apologies for interrupting. Her Majesty Queen Kandide just arrived. She's in the Receiving Room."

"Kandide is here?" Jake couldn't believe what he was hearing. He hurried inside to meet her. The others quickly followed. "Kandide! Thank the earthly spirits you're safe." Dismissing protocol, he threw his arms around her.

She happily reciprocated with only a slightly more Queen-like hug. "Thank the earthly spirits I remembered the coordinates Centrod gave us."

Jake took a step back. "You look a mess. What happened? And your wing, it's straight."

"Lady Aron doesn't exactly provide the best accommodations for those she arranges to have kidnapped. Though you might say that a sudden influx of her power did have an unexpected affect on my wing." Kandide glanced down at her torn and dirty pink dressing gown. "I really do look a mess. I'm surprised your young apprentice let me in."

"I can take care of that." Jake passed his hand in front of her. Instantly, she was wearing crisp new traveling trousers. "Blue okay?"

"Lovely. Thank you. You really must teach me that spell. Now, if you could do something with my hair." Kandide brushed a stray wisp away from her face.

"I still haven't learned how to do that. You look beautiful, anyway."

"Well, of course I do, Jake. Even Lady Aron can't change that—though for a while I thought Kandour's goons were going to try."

"I'm just glad you're safe. General Mintz has a thousand troops looking for you."

"Only a thousand?"

"Excuse me," Lord Mywerk interrupted. "While you two have a nice little homecoming, I have a portal to navigate through."

"Then you were able to unlock it?" It was just the news Kandide was hoping for. "Teren and Adriana—you know where they are?"

"Jake will explain everything, Your Majesty. I must go, now." A rare hint of a smile emerged on Mywerk's face. "It's good that you're safe." With a flick of his wrist, her hair swirled into a perfectly styled coif. Saying nothing more, he vanished as quickly as he had appeared.

Kandide turned to Jake. "The portal, is he…?"

"Please, be seated, Your Majesty." Centrod held a chair for her. "There is much you need to know."

Kandide listened carefully as Centrod told her about Mywerk and the Banshee portal. "Do you trust him?" she asked.

"I don't believe Lord Mywerk will let Adriana die. Remember, Kandide, she is of his blood. He, like Viviana and Adriana, is a descendant of Merlin."

"Then let's hope his blood flows stronger than his ambition." Kandide sounded none too sure. "Jake, there's something else you need to know. Lady Aron said she gave Egan a sleeping potion and without the antidote he will die in a few days. Her price for giving it to him, as well as for freeing Teren and Adriana, is the Gift, which, of course, she did not get."

Jake's face filled with concern. "Do you think she actually poisoned Egan or was just using it as a ploy to convince you to transfer the Gift?"

"I don't know. I wouldn't put anything past her—even poison. We need to get back to the Castle—just in case."

"I agree. Let's be off."

He picked up a leaf that had fallen to the ground and closed his hands around it. When he opened them, a yellow-breasted sparrow flew away.

TWENTY-EIGHT

"**E**xcuse me, young man, can you tell me the name of this place?" Ishan turned around to see who was speaking to him. He had arrived early for band practice in case the funnel cloud reappeared. "Oh, my gosh!" His jaw dropped. "You... you're Lord Mywerk!"

"You know my name?" Dressed in his usual burgundy and red Elizabethan-style attire, Mywerk looked more like a Shakespearian actor than a wizard. His flowing cape easily concealed his wings, and his shoulder-length brown hair covered his pointed ears. "How so?"

"Kathy!" Ishan called. "Hurry. Guess who's here."

She looked up from the drinking fountain near their classroom. "Oh, my gosh!" Grabbing her backpack, she raced over to them. "You're Lord Mywerk. Does that mean the portal is open?" Her eyes searched the sky. "I don't see the funnel cloud."

"Let's slow down a bit." Mywerk's imposing stature towered over them. "First, how do you know my name? And second, how do you know about the portal?"

"We..." They both spoke at once. Ishan nodded for Kathy to continue.

"We know about the portal," she explained, "because that's how Teren and Adriana got here."

"Teren and Adriana? Then they are here." Mywerk scanned the empty schoolyard. "Where?"

"They're not here anymore," Ishan said. "But they were here yesterday. They came through a portal and now it's closed so they can't go back home. Are you really half wizard?" he asked, squinting his eyes in semi-disbelief that he was actually talking to a real wizard. "Is that why you're here? To take them home?"

"Let's sit down." Mywerk motioned to a bench near the giant Elm tree where Teren and Adriana had first appeared. "Over there."

"Okay, but are you really half wizard? Can you do magic?" Ishan was full of questions. "Can you turn Kathy into a frog?"

"That's not very nice, Ishan. You better be careful or he'll turn you into a rat!"

Lord Mywerk sat down on the bench and gestured for Ishan and Kathy to do the same. "To answer your questions: Yes, I am half wizard. Yes, I can do magic. And no, I do not turn people into frogs. That only happens in human faery tales." He picked up a leaf that had fallen to the ground and closed his hands around it. When he opened them, a yellow-breasted sparrow flew away.

"No way! How did you do that?" Ishan stared at the bird as it landed on a nearby tree branch. "I thought you couldn't turn things into other things?"

"That I can do—just not charming young ladies into frogs." His expression told Ishan that magic was not to be used in that way. "Now that I've answered your questions, it's your turn to answer mine. You said Teren and Adriana were here, where are they now?"

Kathy looked at her phone to check the time. "They're probably just about arriving in Zion."

"Zion? You mean the National Park in Utah?"

"That's the one," Ishan answered.

"You know it?" Kathy asked, more than a bit surprised.

"I was there a few minutes ago."

"So there is a portal!" Ishan jumped up. "I knew it! I knew those petroglyphs were the right clue."

"You mean the one with the winged Fée?" Mywerk asked.

"That's the one." Ishan swiped his phone to reveal the picture.

"If you were just there, how did you get here so fast?" Kathy asked.

"I'm a wizard, remember? I can transport wherever I want, within reason, of course."

Kathy scrunched her face, the way she always did when she was confused. "Teren said transporting doesn't work in our world."

"For Fée, it doesn't. For those of us with wizard blood, it does. And while we can't transport across an entire ocean, a few hundred kilometers is easily achieved."

"Does it work for Adriana?" she asked. "She's part wizard."

"It may, though she probably doesn't know it."

"Mr. My…I mean, Lord Mywerk," Ishan sat down again, "can you go back to Zion right now and show them where the portal is? Ms. Lee, she's our teacher, is trying to help them find it. They don't have much time. Teren and Adriana will die if they don't get back to Calabiyau pretty soon."

"That is precisely what I'm going to do, thanks to the two of you. What did you say your names are?"

"We didn't. He's Ishan and I'm Kathy."

"It's a pleasure to meet you both."

"You, too." Kathy reached out to shake his hand. He quickly obliged.

"I'll text Ms. Lee and let her know that you're on your way. I bet they'll be really happy to know you're here." Ishan typed the message and hit send. "She can tell us where you should meet them."

Mywerk watched him with a great deal of interest. He knew about cell phones from his previous trips to the human realm. But he'd never actually watched anyone text. "Quite handy, those gadgets."

"Maybe you should take my phone with you," Kathy suggested. "That way when you get there you can call them. Zion is a really big place. Even when you know where to go, you can get lost."

"That's very thoughtful of you, Miss Kathy. Once I'm there, however, I won't be returning to Las Vegas."

"I know, but you can give it to Ms. Lee." She handed him the phone. "I'll get it back from her on Monday."

"Then you'll need to show me how it works. I'm afraid we don't have cell phones in Calabiyau."

"It's really easy. Ms. Lee's quick-dial number is four." She pointed to the keypad. "Just push the number four and the phone will automatically call her."

"That sounds simple enough. Are you quite sure you want me to take it?"

"I'm sure. Mom says I spend too much time on it, anyway."

"Ms. Lee just answered my text. They're going to meet you at the entrance to Petroglyph Canyon. They're almost there now, so you'd better hurry. Oh, and they're driving a silver SUV. How long will it take you to get there?"

"About ten minutes."

"Wow! That's awesome. Can we come with you?" Ishan asked.

"I'm afraid that's not possible. But I do have something for each of you." He reached into his cape pocket and brought out two spheres about the size of golf balls. They were perfectly round and seemed to glow from the inside. He handed one to Kathy and the other to Ishan.

She held it up to the sunlight. "What are they?"

"They're polished moonstones," Mywerk explained. "But these are not normal moonstones. They've been spelled to absorb problems and release answers."

"I don't understand." Ishan rotated the silvery-blue ball on the palm of his hand.

"When you have a problem or things aren't as you'd like, simply take out the sphere, place it between your hands and focus on what is wrong. Then allow your mind to refocus on the solution. Imagine what you want the outcome to be. See it in your mind."

Kathy placed the ball between her hands. "Does it really work?"

"It will, if you let it." He gently closed her hands around it. "Just as in life, however, you must stay focused on the solution. Not the problem. And now I must focus on helping Teren and Adriana return home. Thank you, my young friends."

"Thank you, Lord Mywerk, for such a cool present." Kathy was sure she felt the sphere emitting a gentle warmth.

"Yeah, and for helping Teren and Adriana." Ishan carefully placed the moonstone in his backpack. He looked across the schoolyard. His classmates were starting to assemble on the marching field. "I guess I better get going, too, or I'll be late for band practice. Want to come watch, Kathy?"

"Sure."

With a snap of his fingers, Lord Mywerk was gone, and Ishan and Kathy found themselves sitting on the bleachers in front of the assembled band members.

"What?" Teren took a step back.
"That's kind of important."

TWENTY-NINE

"What next?" Ms. Lee brought the SUV to a complete stop. "Another traffic jam. I wonder what the problem is now."

Teren stepped out of the car to see what was going on. "It looks like a bunch of people are all gathered around something. There's also some people in uniforms motioning for them to move away."

"Maybe someone was hurt in an accident," Adriana suggested.

A red-haired woman in a park ranger's uniform approached the left side of the car. Ms. Lee lowered her window. "What's going on, Officer?"

"The road is closed. We're not letting anyone through."

"How come?" Ninon asked the ranger.

"A sinkhole opened up—about thirty minutes ago. It's just a good thing no cars fell into it."

"A sinkhole?" Ms. Lee questioned. "I've never heard of a sinkhole in Zion."

"Me neither, and I've been a ranger here for almost twenty years. Craziest thing I've ever seen. It's really deep, too. One of the other rangers tossed a stone in it, and we never did hear the rock hit bottom. Could be it's full of water. Anyway, you can turn your car around over there, or park if you like." She pointed to a large open area full of cars. "As far as I know, all of the other entrances are open if you want to come into the park from another direction."

"Is there any way to drive around the sinkhole?" Ms. Lee asked. "We're supposed to meet someone at the entrance to Petroglyph Canyon and we're already running late."

"I'm afraid not. You'll have to go around or walk from here." The ranger left to speak to the people in the car behind Ms. Lee's.

"Of all things. What else is going to go wrong? First you show up, Ninon, and now a sinkhole." She drove to the open area and parked next to several other cars. "I guess we'll have to hike in."

"I'm really sorry, Ms. Lee. I didn't mean to make you mad. I just want to help Teren and Adriana find the portal. You know how good I am at finding things. Remember the time I found your keys when you left them in the library?"

"I remember you weren't supposed to be there, either. You skipped your French class to finish the first Kandide book."

"But I still got an A in French."

"You did. How, I'll never know. I'm not angry, Ninon, though I should be. I'm just feeling a little stressed right now, that's all. My back is killing me from sitting so long." Reaching into her purse, Ms. Lee removed a jar of pain pills. "Please hand me a bottle of water. I'll be fine as soon as I take a couple of these."

"Don't be stressed, Ms. Lee," Teren said. "I'm pretty sure we've found the portal."

"What do you mean?" She popped two pills into her mouth, then took a sip of the water.

"The sinkhole. Remember, Ishan said that Lord Mywerk arrived through the portal about thirty minutes ago? That's when the ranger said the sinkhole appeared."

"Teren's right," Adriana said. "Sinkholes often appear when portals reopen after being closed for a long time. Come on, let's go see." Adriana unfastened her seatbelt and slid out of the car.

Ninon was right behind her. She looked up at the sky. It was bright blue, without even a wisp of white. "How come there's no funnel cloud?"

"If it's a subterranean portal," Adriana explained, "there won't be a funnel cloud."

"Oh." Ninon hadn't thought of that. "Are you coming Ms. Lee?"

She opened her car door to get out. The pain was so bad she could barely stand. "I think I'd better wait here for a few minutes, until the pills kick in."

"I'll wait with you." Adriana helped her sit back down. "Lord Mywerk should be calling us pretty soon. Ishan said Kathy gave him her phone."

"She did, indeed." Lord Mywerk walked up to the car. "Here it is." He handed it to Ms. Lee. "She also said you'd be driving a silver SUV and this one seems to be the only one here. It's a pleasure to meet you, Ms. Lee. Thank you for helping Teren and Adriana."

"Thank you for coming."

"We're really glad to see you," Adriana said.

"We sure are," Teren echoed.

"And who might this young lady be?" Mywerk asked, looking at Ninon.

"I'm Ninon, but you can call me Ni, Lord Mywerk." She curtsied to him. "I've never met a real Lord before."

"Hey, you didn't curtsy when you met me and I'm a Prince," Teren teased.

Ninon flashed an impish grin. "My humble apologies, Prince Teren." With a flamboyant wave of her hand, she curtsied to him.

"Apologies accepted." He turned to Lord Mywerk. "Was the sink-hole caused by the portal opening?"

"It was, indeed. And there are a few things you both should know before we attempt to go back through it. The portal is unstable—not as bad as I thought it would be, but not completely solid either."

"Is it safe?" Adriana asked.

"With each of us providing energy stabilization along the way, I believe we can make it."

"What do we need to do?" Ninon asked, her voice full of excitement. "Ms. Lee and I are going with you so Leanne or Tara can heal her hips and my foot."

"Ninon, I did not say we are going. We discussed the possibility, but it was just a discussion, nothing more."

"But, Ms. Lee, you can barely walk. And I want my foot to be normal. Please?"

"You heard what he said, the portal isn't all that stable. What do you think, Lord Mywerk?"

"I'd be concerned about either of you going through it. And then, of course, we'd have to get you back. It is possible, just not a very good idea."

"But…" Ninon frowned.

"It's just too risky," Ms. Lee insisted.

"So is your operation. It can't be any more dangerous than that."

"I have an idea," Adriana told her. "Maybe we could bring Leanne here."

"But what if Viviana doesn't let you come back?"

The disappointment on Ninon's face tore at Teren's heart. "Ni, I promise—Adriana and I will do everything we can to bring Leanne or my sister back here."

"Okay." The corners of her mouth turned to a pout. "Anyway, how do you do the energy stabilization, Lord Mywerk?"

"It's really quite simple," he explained. "Teren, you and Adriana will go through first. I will be right behind you. If you feel the slightest bit of vibration, extend your hands, palms facing out and force energy directly toward it. Not too much, just until the vibrating stops. If it continues, I'll reinforce your efforts. That way the vibrations won't set off a chain reaction and make the portal collapse. Teren, you focus on the right side and Adriana, you stay close to him and focus on the left."

Teren stretched out his hands. "Like this?" Dirt and leaves began swirling up from the ground. He quickly released the energy flow and lowered his arms. The mini cyclone instantly stopped.

"That's exactly what I want you to do. But save it for the portal. We don't need a dust storm on top of everything else. We also have to get past the park rangers. I'll distract them while you jump into the sinkhole. At first you'll begin spiraling around. After the swirling stops, you'll float through the rest of the portal. Be alert and listen for vibrations, no matter how insignificant they may seem. If the fates favor us, we should be on the other side in about two hours."

"That sounds great." Adriana turned to Ms. Lee. "Thank you again for everything you've done. I just hope we can bring Leanne here really soon so she can heal you…and you too, Ni. Thank you both. We couldn't have better human friends."

"It's not worth risking your life, Adriana, by attempting to return." Ms. Lee took her hand. "Ninon and I will be fine. We're just grateful that you've opened our eyes to so much more of this world than we ever knew existed. That alone, is thank you enough. Now, let's get you home."

"There is one other thing, Teren and Adriana, that you must know," Mywerk said. "This portal lets out in Banshee territory, right near Kandour's camp."

"What?" Teren took a step back. "That's kind of important."

"Yes, it is. As soon as you land, put up a shield. As soon as I land, I'll do the same on the outside of yours. The instant you see me start to emerge from the portal, lower your shield and transport immediately out of there. You'll only have a second or two before mine will stop you."

"But if Teren and Adriana have to lower their shield to transport," Ninon asked, "how will you be able to get away, Lord Mywerk? What will protect you?"

"I'll have to be very fast. Now, do you understand everything?" Teren and Adriana nodded yes. "Good, then let's be on our way."

While Ninon, Teren, and Adriana ran ahead, Lord Mywerk walked to the sinkhole with Ms. Lee, helping to steady her. Bright yellow caution tape had been placed around it to keep onlookers from getting too close. Several park rangers reinforced the boundaries for those who tried to ignore the hastily constructed tape barricade.

Moving to the far side where there were fewer people, Mywerk motioned for Teren and Adriana to get ready. With a flick of his wrist, a burst of light streaked from his hand. The crowd gasped as it exploded over their heads. Golden sparks shimmered against the blue sky.

"Now!" he ordered.

They ducked under the caution tape and leapt into the sinkhole. The stunned crowd began yelling, "The kids! They jumped in!"

Ninon watched Teren and Adriana disappear down the abyss. To the onlookers' horror, she jumped in after them. "Another kid just went in!" someone shouted.

"Ninon, noooo!" Ms. Lee screamed. She pushed her way closer to the edge. "I can't let her go alone."

A burly-looking ranger held out his arm to stop her. "Stand back, lady. Do you know those kids?"

"I…" She started to answer, then thought better of it.

"They were in her car," the red-haired lady ranger told him. "We need to take her in for questioning." She looked at Lord Mywerk. "And Sir Lancelot with the fireworks, as well."

"Hold onto me," Mywerk whispered, "and be ready to jump." He put one arm around Ms. Lee's waist. His penetrating stare locked onto the female ranger's eyes. Her body stiffened. Mywerk slowly shifted his gaze to the burly ranger, who also became motionless. A few seconds later, both rangers turned and simply walked away. "They won't remember seeing you," he said.

With his free hand, Mywerk shot another burst of light into the air. As it exploded, he and Ms. Lee stepped off the edge and plunged into the sinkhole.

What have I done? she thought as she spiraled down what seemed like a giant corkscrew, drilling deeper and deeper into the earth. Darkness erased her vision, but not her overwhelming fear of small spaces.

There were no sounds other than Mywerk's voice. "Whatever you do," he told her, "do not let go of me."

"Believe me, I won't." She sensed the spiraling starting to slow. A tunnel of silvery-white light replaced the blackness. Her body began to feel as though she was floating inside a cloud drenched in moonlight. The air felt refreshing against her skin, not at all cold or damp. "What about Ninon?"

"She should be fine. She's between the four of us. Teren and Adriana will stabilize the portal in front of her and I'll keep the back steady. How are you feeling?"

"I'm okay...now. It's really quite pleasant. I can imagine Ninon must be terrified, however."

"From the little I know about her, she's probably more enthralled than scared. She's quite a handful."

"That she is. Always has been. I can just see the headlines now: 'Students led by Shakespearian actor commit suicide by jumping in sinkhole.' The local news stations will have a field day. With all the people taking pictures and video, who knows what they'll say."

"It certainly will be a story told for years to come by everyone who witnessed it. Don't worry, however, about there being pictures. I created a spell around each of us that will blur any of their images."

"You can do that?"

"Of course. I developed it on one of my trips to your world so I could not be photographed, in case someone should accidentally see my wings."

"That's amazing."

"It's effective. My hope now is that I can get you both back safely before your families begin to worry."

"It's Ninon that I'm..." She suddenly felt like she was in the middle of a bowl of jelly and a giant hand was shaking it. "The portal… it's vibrating."

He put his finger to her lips. "Shh… Don't speak for a moment. And don't let go of me." Mywerk held out his hands, sending pulses of energy into the portal.

The shaking got worse. She felt his muscles tense as he forced even more energy into it. *This has to be a dream,* she thought. *It can't be happening.* Her stomach told her otherwise.

Slowly, the shaking began to stop. "We should make the rest of the journey in silence," he said. "I need to listen for any warnings."

Ms. Lee answered by nodding. Her thoughts were on Ninon, as well as how she would keep her breakfast down if it happened again.

THIRTY

The journey home through the Banshee portal was very different from Teren's and Adriana's arrival experience where they were tossed around like leaves in a cyclone. Returning was, for the most part, smooth and effortless. The portal began vibrating only a couple more times. In each case, they were able to stop the shaking by infusing it with energy—something Ms. Lee was grateful for.

Having once been trapped in a rickety elevator, the thought of a portal collapsing around her was more than she would allow herself to think about. *Good thing I learned to meditate,* she thought, shifting her mind to a Zen-like state.

It wasn't long before streaks of sunlight began to penetrate the silver-grey mist that surrounded them. "I think we're nearly there," Teren whispered to Adriana. "I'll bring up the shield as soon as we land."

"Better do it now." She slid from the portal as though it were a playground slide.

Teren was right behind her. His hands immediately swept a large circle around them. "Shield's up." Blinking back the afternoon sun, he and Adriana found themselves standing next to a twisted pine tree in the center of a clearing in the forest. "I'd say that was perfect timing."

"And not a moment too soon." Adriana eyed the Banshee soldiers who began surrounding them. A dozen arrows were drawn and ready to fire. "Looks like we have a few visitors."

"The shield should hold them off until Lord Mywerk gets here." Teren sent more energy into it—just in case. Blue-green ripples distorted the air around them as his hands circled his body, once again. "I hope he gets here pretty soon."

"I hope your shield holds."

"Adriana, look!" Teren exclaimed. "It's Ni—she's here, outside the shield."

Rushing toward them, Ninon slammed into the protective veil. The force knocked her backward.

Momentarily releasing the shield, Teren shouted, "Grab my hand." He yanked her inside and instantly reset it.

A frightened scream reverberated through the trees. Adriana's legs buckled beneath her.

"No!" Teren dropped to his knees beside her. "Ni, Adriana's been shot!"

Standing frozen, Ninon stared at the arrow that penetrated completely through the calf of her left leg. Blood dripped from its metal tip. "It's all my fault. I'm sorry, Adriana" Tears began to stream down her face. "I'm so sorry. I didn't mean to do anything wrong. Really I didn't. Really. I was just…"

Flashes of Teren's own impulsive behavior swirled through his head. How many times had he almost gotten others killed? They wouldn't even be in this situation if he hadn't insisted on following that glowing red orb into the labyrinth. He couldn't be angry at Ninon, and yet his words found it hard to conceal how he really felt. "Stop apologizing, Ni, and help me."

"What…what do you want me to do?"

"Right now, just stop apologizing. It isn't going to help." He felt Adriana's pulse. It was beginning to slow. "There must be something on that arrow because she's already unconscious." Cradling her in his arms, he scanned the ever-increasing number of Banshees that surrounded them. "I sure hope Lord Mywerk gets here soon."

"I think he's here now… with Ms. Lee!"

Mywerk instantly created a circular shield around all five of them. A dozen arrows bounced off his protective veil, doing nothing more than sending a white-tailed hawk soaring into the sky. "Drop your shield, Teren."

Still holding Adriana in his arms, he released it. "She's been hit. We have to get her to the Château so Leanne can heal her."

Mywerk knelt down beside them. "First, we need to get the arrow out so I can stop the bleeding or she won't make it." Placing his hands on her temples, he spoke softly, in a metered fashion. "Sleep deeply, my child." Her head fell to one side and her breathing became less labored. "Teren, you hold her shoulders. Ms. Lee, help hold her leg for me."

"What about the Banshees?" Ninon watched as twenty more soldiers moved closer to the shield. One of them, a red-capped officer, placed his hand on it. He ordered the others to form a circle and do the same.

"They're going to try to release the shield by pulling the energy from it," Mywerk explained.

"Can they do that?" Ni asked.

"Not immediately. It should hold for a few more minutes—though probably not much longer than that." Mywerk reached down and broke the tip off the arrow. Holding the cock-feather on the opposite end, he carefully pulled the shaft back through her leg. Blood sprayed everywhere. "I think it hit an artery. I'll do my best to stop the bleeding, but I'm no healer."

He gently pressed his fingers against the wound, and then tied his neck scarf just above it. "That will have to do until we can get her to the Château. Teren, you carry Adriana. I'll bring Ni and Ms. Lee. Be ready. We'll only have a fraction of a second to transport out of here."

Teren lifted the young priestess into his arms. "I'm ready whenever you say." He held her tightly against his chest.

"Good. Now, I want you two ladies to stand as close to me as possible." Mywerk wrapped his cape around Ninon and Ms. Lee. "Keep your heads down and don't move." For the first time in Ninon's life, she didn't question what was said. Fear had invaded every cell in her body.

"Let's go." He lowered the shield and, with a gesture, they dissolved into a glowing red shimmer. A dozen perfectly aimed arrows sprayed between the surrounding circle of soldiers. Most simply impaled the twisted tree.

Ni felt her body becoming light, as though her spirit had been released to float freely in the clouds. And yet, it seemed like they must be moving faster than the speed of sound, since everything was so incredibly quiet. She tried to speak to Ms. Lee, but her words melted away before they could be heard. *I wonder why there wasn't a boom like when planes break the sound barrier?* she thought. *I'll have to ask Lord Mywerk. Anyway, it's a lot better than driving places, even if I can't talk to anyone.*

Though the scenery around her was a blur, she could tell that it was changing—becoming darker and more barren. *We must be coming to the Mists that surround the Château.* The smell of rotten eggs began to make her lungs sting. *Yep, we're definitely in the Mists,* she thought, remembering the description in Book One when Kandide first arrived in these dead-lands—how her lungs also stung from the acidic smell of the bubbling pools of black oily liquid that dotted the terrain. *I never could have imagined that I'd actually be here,* she thought. *It's like a dream—though I don't remember my dreams ever smelling this bad.*

Before long, her body started to feel heavy again and everything came back into focus. She, along with the others, had materialized in an open area a dozen meters from the massive golden gate that stood in front of the Château. The veil that protected it from unwanted intruders kept them from transporting inside the grounds.

Ninon stared at the majestic palace with its two golden towers and glistening purple, yellow, and teal-blue stained glass windows. It looked exactly the way she imagined it, only more beautiful.

"Selena!" Teren shouted as he hurried toward the gate. His aunt was standing on the other side talking to an outcast Banshee named Trace. They were assessing the endless stone wall that completely surrounded the Château and all of its villages, discussing a likely defense should they be attacked.

"May the earthly spirits help us!" Selena motioned to the tower guards to open the gate. "Teren? Lord Mywerk? And… and we have human guests? Oh, dear. What's going on, child? What's happened to Adriana?"

"It's her leg. She took an arrow." Teren rushed through the gate with the young priestess held tightly in his arms. "Get Leanne. I'll explain about the humans later."

"She's in the herb garden," Selena told Trace. "Bring her to Kandide's room."

"I'm on my way." Trace flew off to fetch her.

Selena quickly led them up the curved staircase and into the sleeping room where Kandide stays when she visits the Château. Pulling back the pale pink comforter, she helped Teren place Adriana on the bed.

"Is she going to be okay?" Ninon asked, following them into the neatly appointed chamber.

"She's very weak." Selena placed a pillow under Adriana's leg to elevate it. "Please, do be seated." She gestured toward two pink-and-green striped side chairs.

"Thank you." Ms. Lee motioned for Ninon to sit next to her. "We'll try to stay out of the way."

Trace escorted Leanne into the room. "An arrow went through Adriana's leg," Teren explained, guiding Leanne's hand to the wound.

"She's also lost a lot of blood." Though blind, all knew that Leanne could see better with her hands than most people see with their eyes.

"Trace, please have a fresh pitcher of water sent up."

"Right away." He quickly left to do so.

"Did you put the sleeping spell on her, Teren?" Leanne asked.

"No, Lord Mywerk did. How bad is she?"

"She's very weak." Leanne untied Mywerk's scarf then wrapped both hands around Adriana's leg. "There is some good news. None of her bones were shattered." Silver pulses of light began to emanate from the palms of her hands, penetrating Adriana's skin. Though still asleep, she let out a muffled groan.

"Is she in pain?" Teren asked.

"Not as much as if she was awake. Put your hand on her forehead and tell me when the fever breaks." Leanne gently rubbed a thick yellow-green salve onto the wounded area. Adriana's leg jerked. This time the moan wasn't muffled. "Does she still feel warm?"

"Yes," Teren replied. "Very warm."

"I don't sense any poison in her body. There must have been something else on that arrow that's causing the fever. Banshees often coat them with a combination of valerian root and elfwort. It renders their victims unconscious for short periods of time and can cause a fever, but it's not lethal. They use it when they want to take prisoners alive. I'm sure both you, Prince Teren, and Adriana would fetch a nice reward from General Kandour."

"That must be why she became unconscious so quickly." He felt her forehead again. The fever had still not broken.

"It's also very interesting," Ms. Lee said. "Humans use both those herbs as sleep aids. I guess they have an even stronger effect on Fée."

"That they do." Leanne reached into her apron pocket and pulled out an assortment of green plants. "Selena, I need you to boil up these herbs. They will help bring down her fever."

"Of course." She filled a cup from the pitcher of water that Trace had sent up. Placing the herbs in it, Selena held it between her hands. Within seconds the water was steaming.

"Bring it to a boil," Leanne told her, "while I finish healing the wound."

Teren watched as the silver pulses from Leanne's hands caused Adriana's skin to weave back together. Healing always amazed him—how quickly the body was able to repair itself. "It's almost perfect," he said. "You are incredible, Leanne."

"I'm afraid only the skin is healed. Puncture wounds, especially those as severe as this one, take a lot longer to fully heal on the inside. She'll be limping for a few days—and we still have to get that fever under control. See if you can wake her up, Lord Mywerk. I need her to drink the herb mixture."

Mywerk had been standing near the doorway, and walked over to the bed. Placing his hands on Adriana's temples, he spoke in the same soft tone that he used to place her into the deep sleep. "Come forth now, my child, and awaken."

She began to stir. Her eyes slowly focused on him. "Are we home?"

"We're at the Château," he replied. "You were injured. Leanne is working her wonders, and you'll be fine in a couple days."

"Are you able to drink some hot herb tea?" Leanne asked. "You still have a fever."

"I think so." She struggled to sit up. The pain in her leg reminded her of what had happened.

"Let me help you." Teren gently lifted her shoulders and slid several fluffy pink pillows behind her back. Taking the steaming cup of herbs from Selena, he held it for her to drink. "How's it taste?"

"Not bad." She took another sip.

"Ms. Lee," Ninon whispered, "Lord Mywerk...his cape is torn in the back by his shoulder."

Mywerk turned to look at her. "It's only a scratch. Nothing to worry about."

Ms. Lee walked over to him. "You were also shot, weren't you?" She reached up to feel his forehead. "And you've got a fever."

"It's nothing. I'll have Leanne look at it later."

"You'll do nothing of the sort," Selena scolded. "Leanne will take care of it right now. Sit down so she can heal you."

Mywerk didn't argue. The way his shoulder ached, he knew it was more than just a scratch. The arrow had ripped the skin away from his collarbone.

"This is going to hurt," Leanne warned, as she rubbed the green-and-yellow salve into the gaping wound and then forced his skin back together.

"It didn't hurt as much when the arrow went through it."

"You're just lucky that it didn't go through your neck or you probably would have bled to death by now." Leanne held the wound tightly closed with one hand, while placing her other hand above it. Once again, silver pulses of light began flowing from her palm. The skin quickly melded together. "Selena, you'd better boil up some more herbs." She handed her a few more plants from her apron pocket. "And you, Lord Mywerk, are to drink every last drop."

"Yes, ma'am." He glanced back at his shoulder. A faint red crease was all that remained of the open gash. "Thank you. That feels much better. Now, Leanne, if you could heal my cape, I'd be really impressed."

"You're the magi. I am but a mere healer." Turning back to Adriana, she asked, "How are you feeling?"

"Much better. Though I don't think I'll be doing any running for a while."

"You should be fine in two or three days." Leanne felt her forehead. "Good. The fever is down. And now, Teren, please introduce us to your friends. We've never had human visitors in the Château, and I think Selena and I are both eager to know why they made such a dangerous journey."

Ninon jumped up and hurried over to her. "I'm Ni and this is Ms. Lee. She's my teacher and is really amazing like you, Ms. Leanne. We're from Las Vegas. That's in North America. I think you're awesome."

"Why, thank you, Ni. That's very kind of you to say. And to what do we owe the pleasure of your visit?"

"Perhaps we should start at the beginning," Lord Mywerk said, taking the cup of boiled herbs from Selena. He took a sip. "This is quite refreshing."

"Shall we go downstairs?" Selena suggested. "You must all be quite hungry after such a long journey."

Teren hadn't thought about food, but... "Now that you mention it, something to eat sounds great."

"I think I'll stay here and rest," Adriana said. "I'll join you a little later. Just be sure to save some of Margay's shortbread for me. Teren says it's the best in the land."

Ninon walked over to her. "I'm really sorry, Adriana. I didn't mean to do anything that would get you hurt."

"I know, Ni." She reached out to take her hand. "It looks like I now have two very good friends who are both a little too impulsive for their own good." She looked up at Teren and winked.

"Who, me?"

"Yes, you. Now go get me some shortbread."

The dining hall was massive—big enough for several hundred Fée. Floating orbs of light illuminated the thirty tables and the twelve chairs that surrounded each of them. Selena showed her guests to a table near the front of the room. It overlooked the gardens that were still in full bloom.

Trays of food began appearing, including Margay's famous shortbread. Ninon and Ms. Lee had to agree, it was the best they had ever tasted.

"Try the mulberry crescents." Teren passed the tray to Ms. Lee. "They're really good, too."

"So is the pumpkin soup," Ni said, adding a dollop of whipped coconut cream to her bowl.

"Everything is delicious," Ms. Lee said. "And you're right, Teren, these mulberry crescents are amazing."

Dozens of other Fée joined them, including the oldest resident of the Château, a former general in Calabiyau's army named Matari. He, like Jake, had been injured in the Clan Wars and was sent to the Mists. Jake and Selena found him, just as they had all the other residents.

After explaining why they made the journey, Ninon and Ms. Lee answered question after question about where and how they lived, as well as what Las Vegas was like. With each answer, the gathering grew larger—so did the amount of food.

Several hours of eating, laughing, and storytelling flew by. The younger Fée sat spellbound listening to Teren tell them about the GPS and cell phones. They couldn't believe that humans can actually talk to one another anywhere in the world—or that the Internet was like having access to thousands of libraries.

"I wish I could visit your world," a young Fée named Petra told Ninon.

"Me, too!" another named Dalia exclaimed. "It's so magical."

"I wish all of you could come visit our world," Ninon said. "But phones and the Internet aren't really magic. They're just science."

"Centrod says the difference between science and magic," Teren explained, "is that magic always works. Science is still unfolding."

"That's certainly true with cell phones and computers," Ms. Lee said with laugh. "At least about them not always working."

"Speaking of working," Lord Mywerk glanced out the window, "it's getting late. And we still need to find out if Leanne's healing skills will work on our human friends. What do you think, Leanne, is it possible to heal Ninon's foot and Ms. Lee's hips?"

THIRTY-ONE

"Can you heal us, Ms. Leanne?" Ninon asked. "Can you?"

"Well, I've never attempted to heal a human before, but it would be my honor to try."

"Then we should probably get started." Lord Mywerk placed his napkin on his plate and stood up. "I need to take our human guests back through the portal tonight. We're less likely to be seen by Kandour's soldiers if we enter while it's dark."

"Then let's go to the clinic," Leanne suggested. "It's much easier for me to work there."

"That would be so awesome." Though Ninon didn't want to leave her newfound friends, she was excited about getting her foot healed.

Teren also stood up. "I'm going to check on Adriana. I'm sure she's ready for something a little more substantial than shortbread—as good as it is. I'll catch up with you later."

"Okay. We'll see you in a little bit." Ninon held Ms. Lee's arm and the four of them headed off.

Leanne's clinic was nothing like the doctors' offices they were used to. It was decorated in bright pinks and blues, with vases of giant gladiolas, and it smelled of fresh lavender. The room was lit by softly glowing pink orbs that floated overhead, giving it a soothing feel. The most curious feature was a long shelf of glass vials that contained liquids in almost every color.

"They're healing potions," Lord Mywerk explained, seeing Ninon studying them.

"The liquids kinda look like their alive. The way they shimmer and move in the bottles."

"They are alive, Ni," Leanne told her. "When I pick the herbs, I spell them so they don't die. That way, they maintain their full potency and are much more effective. In ancient times, in the human world—your world—healers, who were often referred to as witches, did the same thing. Sadly, as your medicine began to evolve in very different ways, it's an area of science that, from what I understand, has been all but forgotten by most doctors."

"You're right, Leanne. Though," Ms. Lee pointed out, "we have applied that same idea to vaccines with live cultures. And even supplements such as probiotics."

"Interesting. I'd like to learn more about that. Perhaps, however, right now we should get started healing the two of you. Would you like me to try you first, Ms. Lee? I treat a lot of patients with back and hip pain." Leanne motioned toward a padded table that looked as though it could be used for massages. "Let's see if the same techniques work on humans. Our anatomy is very similar to yours, except, of course, our bones are hollow like birds."

"That's fascinating," Ms. Lee said. "I had no idea that Fée bones are hollow."

"It's one of the reasons we can fly," Mywerk explained. "Having wings is, of course, the other."

"I wish I had wings," Ninon said. "It would be so cool to be able to fly."

"I'd just like to be able to walk without pain," Ms. Lee said, slowly making her way to the table. "How does healing work, Leanne?"

"It's actually quite simple. The silver pulses that you see coming from my hands infuse the cells with energy, stimulating them so they can repair themselves. I'm not doing anything that your own body isn't capable of doing. I'm just triggering it to happen—and at a much faster rate. If bone deterioration or muscle tissue is also involved, such as in your case, Ms. Lee, the energy pulses infuse those cells, causing them to re-grow and strengthen."

"That's incredible. Do you really think you can fix my back and hips?"

"We won't know until we try."

"Then let's try it."

Lord Mywerk lifted Ms. Lee onto the table. Her back, from sitting so long, hurt worse than ever. Even lying down was difficult.

Placing her hands on Ms. Lee's back near her hips, Leanne could feel the pain as it traveled through her own arms. "How have you managed?" she asked. "I know of very few Fée who could tolerate the amount of pain you're feeling right now."

"I don't manage very well. I live on pills most of the time."

Leanne pressed her fingers into the muscle tissue around Ms. Lee's hips causing her to flinch. "Tell me when you feel the most pressure."

"Right there."

"Just as I thought." She placed both hands on that area and pressed her fingers deeper into Ms. Lee's back. She flinched again. "I want you to focus on breathing and let me know when the throbbing starts to diminish."

A sudden warming sensation swept through Ms. Lee's lower back and waist. It quickly traveled up her spine and down her legs. At first, it felt as if her muscles were on fire—like they would explode. Just as quickly, the extreme heat transformed into a soothing coolness. "The pain...it's starting to go away."

"Good. Then what I'm doing is working." Leanne forced even more energy through her hands. The silver pulses became a solid stream, glowing with a prism of colors. Ms. Lee's skin around her hips and back also began to glow, as though it was radiating from its own source of power. It turned bright red before Leanne slowly stopped the flow.

"That's enough for now. We need to let your cells absorb the energy that I've given them and start the repair process. Ni, tell me when the redness starts to fade."

Ninon watched in awe as slowly it began to diminish. "It's almost gone, Leanne. Her skin is turning pink again."

"That is a very good sign. It means the energy is being absorbed into the deep muscle tissue and bone fibers. How are you feeling, Ms. Lee?"

"It's amazing. The pain—it's completely gone." She turned onto her back. Then lifted her right leg above her head. "I haven't been able to do that in years."

"Don't do too much right now. Your bones are still soft. They need a few more minutes to completely regenerate. And your muscles still need more strengthening. Some of which I can do, and some of which you'll need to do on a regular basis. I want you to try walking, but do it slowly."

Lord Mywerk reached out to help her. Ms. Lee took his hand and slid off the table. "I don't believe it. I can stand without feeling any pain." She cautiously took a couple steps. "I can even walk without limping. How can I ever thank you, Leanne?"

"Knowing that healing works on humans is thanks enough. I do want to give you one more treatment, but right now, shall we see if we can heal your foot, Ni?"

Ninon wasted no time hopping up on the table. "I'm ready."

Leanne felt her ankle and the bones in her foot. It was worse that she had expected. "Were you born this way?"

"Yes. My mom never had the money for an operation to fix it."

"Well, hopefully, you won't need one after today. I am afraid, however, that this is going to hurt quite a bit. Your ankle is badly twisted, and I need to pull it back in place before I can strengthen it. I'll be as gentle as I can."

"I don't care if it hurts. I just want it fixed."

"Can you hold her leg still, Lord Mywerk? She's going to jerk it away, but try to keep it steady. Maybe you should also help, Ms. Lee."

"Certainly." He stood on one side of Ninon and Ms. Lee stood on the other, each steadying her leg.

"Are you ready, Ni?" Leanne gripped her ankle.

"Ye…" She let out a loud scream. A sharp pain shot through her foot and up her leg.

"Breathe," Leanne told her. "Keep breathing. The worst is over. Just one more small adjustment."

Ninon shrieked again, trying to gulp for air. She looked down at her ankle. It was bathed in the same prismatic-like glow that had engulfed Ms. Lee's skin. "My foot, Leanne, you made it straight! Ms. Lee, my foot is straight." Though still reeling from the pain, she was smiling from ear-to-ear. "I don't believe it, my foot… it's normal." She threw her arms around Leanne. "It's all healed."

"Not quite. The muscle tissue, though stretched, is still weak. You need to stay off it for a minute or two so the bone and muscle cells can fully stabilize." She placed her hand above Ni's ankle and infused it with a bit more strengthening energy. Ninon started to rotate her foot. "Don't move it," Leanne gently scolded. "Keep your foot very still while I give Ms. Lee one more treatment."

"Okay." Ninon froze, not daring to moving a muscle. She couldn't stop staring at her foot. For the first time in her life, she was like other kids. She'd be able to run without limping and maybe even be on the girls' soccer team. Maybe she could learn to ice skate with Kathy or march in the band with Ishan. Maybe the other kids would even stop teasing her. "It's like a miracle, Ms. Lee."

"I agree." Without any help, she lifted herself up on the table and sat next to Ninon.

"It's not a miracle," Mywerk clarified. "It's a real-life faery tale with a happy ending. And like all faery tales, most humans won't believe what has happened to be true. Perhaps that is good. We have enough problems in our land without it being overrun by those from your world seeking cures. Present company excepted, of course."

"Of course." Ms. Lee nodded. "Besides, it would put all our doctors out of work."

Leanne gave her another infusion of energy, then a strong lecture on the importance of starting an on-going exercise program. "Ever since transporting was discovered, Fée don't fly any more. They just don't get out and exercise like they should, and that is causing many more back problems than we used to have. I'm sure humans with their cars are the same way. You're healed now, Ms. Lee, but if you don't keep strengthening those muscles, in a few years, you'll be right back where you were."

"You can come with my mom and me to the YMCA," Ninon suggested. "We take a Pilates class three times a week. Our instructor, Ms. Pope, is really good. Her husband, Mark, even comes to class."

"I might just do that, Ni—now that I can finally move. For the first time in nearly five years, I'm not in pain. I don't know how to thank you, Leanne. It's... It's amazing."

"You just did. And Ni, you should be okay to stand and even walk now. Just don't overdo it to start with."

Ninon slid off the table. At first her foot was a bit wobbly. She cautiously took a step, then another, and another. Slowly, she got her balance back. "You made me perfect, Leanne. Thank you soooo much."

"You're very welcome, Ni. Now, for fear of being impolite, I have several other patients who also need my attention. And I want to check on Adriana, as well. Lord Mywerk, why don't you ask Selena to show our guests around the Château before they have to leave?"

"Excellent idea. Let's go ask her, Ladies."

The gardens were their first stop. Never had they seen anything so beautiful. Late blooming cockleshells, meter-high gladiolas, and trailing peonies combined with exotic botanicals of every color and size.

"I've never seen such a variety of plants," Ms. Lee said. "What is this one with all the different colored flowers?"

"That's a rainbow bush," Selena replied. "On any given plant you'll see flowers that range from bright yellow to orange, dark red, pink, and purple-blue. The flowers are very tasty on salads."

"You can eat them?" Ninon asked.

"Yes, and they're also quite good for you. Very high in vitamin C. The yellow taste like sweet lemons, the orange like tangerines, the red like raspberries, the blue like blueberries, and the pink like wintergreen. What flavor would you like, Ni?"

"I've never tasted wintergreen, may I try that one?"

Selena picked one of the pink flowers and handed it to her. "Here you are. Would you like to taste one, Ms. Lee?"

"Maybe yellow."

"Try this." She handed her a yellow flower.

"Gosh, they're really good. May I try a red one?" Ninon started to reach for it.

"You may, but be very careful picking them," Mywerk warned. "The thorns are quite sharp. And if you get pricked, you'll break out in a terrible rash."

"Maybe you should let Selena pick it," Ms. Lee suggested. "We don't want to have to trouble Leanne again."

Selena picked two more flowers—a red one for Ni and a blue one for Ms. Lee. "It's a very curious plant," she explained, "because as soon as you pick a flower, a new bud opens up right next to it."

Ninon watched as two new buds appeared near the flowers Selena had just picked. "That's so cool." She popped the red flower in her mouth. "Mmm. It does taste just like a raspberry."

"Shall we continue the tour?" Lord Mywerk asked.

"Do you think we could see a griffin?" Ninon's eyes lit up. "Maybe even Courage? I bet he's really grown since Kandide rescued him from the garglans."

"He has, indeed," Selena replied. "Lord Mywerk, do you think you might bring a copy of those books Ninon told us about back with you? I'm amazed at how much Ni knows about our world."

"I didn't know about rainbow bushes. And probably lots of other things."

"I have a few copies of both Book One and Book Two in my car, Selena. I'll give them to Lord Mywerk after we get back through the portal."

"That would be lovely. Thank you. Now, about seeing the griffins—they should be coming down to the lake to drink very shortly—when the sun sets. Do we have time to go there, Lord Mywerk?"

"If we hurry and don't go to the hot springs with the waterfall that runs up hill. Which would you rather do, Ni?"

She turned to Ms. Lee. "Which would you rather do?"

"Well, I've never seen a waterfall that runs up hill, but I do have to say, seeing a griffin would be even more amazing."

"Then it's settled, we'll fly out to see the griffins, Lord Mywerk said.

"You three go ahead. I'll get some papayas."

"Papayas?" Ms. Lee asked.

"It's their favorite treat," Lord Mywerk explained. "Come, ladies, let's be off." He put one arm around Ms. Lee's waist and the other around Ninon's. They soared above the treetops, across the orchards, and over a tiny village.

"Is that the lake where the griffins drink?" Ninon asked, marveling at the fact that they were flying above the trees.

"That, it is." Mywerk nodded.

Selena caught up with them, flying alongside Ninon. "Here they come, Ni. See that one? That's Courage. His mother, Gertie, is just behind of him."

Lord Mywerk landed with Ni and Ms. Lee a few meters from the edge of the lake. The griffins began landing as well. There were at least twenty of them, including a newborn cub."

"Looks like we have another new member of the pride," Selena said, her eyes dancing with delight. "And it's a little girl, too. She's going to need a name, Ni. Would you like to do the honors?"

"Me? Really?"

"Really. You did, after all, help save Teren and Adriana's life."

Ninon thought for a minute. "I think we should call her Adri, Ms. Selena, in honor of Adriana. It's the least I can do after what happened to her because of me."

"That's a lovely name. Adri it will be."

Spotting Selena, Courage flew toward her. His powerful wings caused a sudden rush of air that blew Ninon's long black hair across her face. The nearly full-grown half lion, half eagle nuzzled Selena's hand. "I want you to meet some new friends," she told him.

Courage's golden eyes sparkled in the late afternoon sunlight. He cocked his head to one side and sniffed the air, uncertain of their strange smell.

"It's alright. They're human friends."

"May I give him the treat?" Ninon asked, cautiously taking a step closer.

Courage raised his body to its full height. His sharp beak and even sharper talons were no match for anyone who dared to challenge him, let alone a ten-year-old human.

"What do you think, Courage?" Selena asked. "She brought you a papaya."

The magnificent creature eyed Ninon's outstretched hand, seeing the juicy yellow fruit. His sharp beak gently plucked it from her hand, then pushed his white-feathered head under her hand as he swallowed the papaya.

"He likes you," Mywerk said. "That's very unusual. Griffins are not the most social of creatures." Courage looked up at him and growled. "I meant nothing personal by that."

"I think you're beautiful." Ninon rubbed his neck feathers. "The most beautiful creature I've ever seen."

An approving purr came from deep within Courage's throat.

Ms. Lee nodded in agreement. "He really is magnificent. If I only had my phone, we could take a picture."

"I don't think that would be wise," Selena said. "We don't want anyone knowing they're here. Many millennia ago, humans hunted and killed most of the griffins that lived in your world. Kandide's great, great, great, great—I don't know how many generations back—great grandmother, who was Queen at that time, transported the remaining ones to our world. I'm afraid the Banshees weren't much kinder to them. Though they revered them, they also hunted them for sport—if you can call using a high-powered cross-bow against these remarkable creatures sport."

"Sadly, it's still not much different in our world." Ms. Lee shook her head. "Many humans call hunting a sport, as well."

"That's why King Toeyad brought the remaining griffins to the Château," Ninon chimed in. "To protect them from the Banshees."

"You know that, as well?" Selena was, once again, amazed. "I really must read those books Teren told us about."

"As soon as we return home," Ms. Lee assured her, "you'll have your very own copy of each—complete with pictures. I must say, Selena, you are even more beautiful in person than your likeness in the books."

"My picture is in the books?"

"Yours and Tiyana's," Ninon said. "So is Lord Mywerk's. He's better looking in person, too."

Mywerk sidestepped her compliment. "It's getting late and I need to get the two of you home."

"Do we have time to stop and say goodbye to Teren and Adriana before we leave?" Ms. Lee asked.

"They would be disappointed if you didn't," Selena replied.

Ninon hugged Courage's neck. "Goodbye. I love you."

He let out another soft purr then flew back to his pride. The

NINON GIVES COURAGE A PAPAYA

sudden gust of wind from his more than two-meter wingspan almost knocked her over.

Fours hours later, after saying goodbye to Teren and Adriana, the trio arrived back at Ms. Lee's car. The full moon cast a luminous sheen on the steep red cliffs.

Other than a brown and white spotted owl hooting their arrival, it was eerily quiet. The area where she had parked was still full of cars, but no people. More than likely, they were all camping in the park. Red lights flashed relentlessly, warning of the danger should someone decide to cross the yellow caution tape that surrounded the bottomless sinkhole.

"That was quite a journey," Ms. Lee told Lord Mywerk, happy to be on solid ground.

"It sure was," Ninon agreed. "I've been on roller coasters that didn't shake as much." She was still a little shaky from all the vibrations they had encountered.

Mywerk held Ninon's arm lest she should fall. "I'm afraid the portal is becoming less stable."

"Will you be okay to go back through it?" Ms. Lee asked.

"I don't have a choice." He sounded confident, but his expression told her he was extremely concerned.

"Be really careful. And thank you so much for everything." Ninon glanced down at her foot. It was still just as perfect as when Leanne had fixed it.

"What will you tell your mother about how it was healed?" Mywerk asked.

"The truth. She probably won't believe me, no matter what I say. So why not tell her the truth?"

"Good point." He escorted them to the car. "How are your back and hips, Ms. Lee?"

"I still say it's a miracle. There is absolutely no pain. Though I don't think I'll be telling my doctors the truth. They'd probably have me committed," she chuckled. Opening the back of her SUV, Ms. Lee handed him a bag with the books. "There are three copies of each. One set for Selena, one set for the Royal Library, and one set for you."

Mywerk bowed slightly. "That's most kind of you. Now, it's time for you to head back to Las Vegas. It's already Sunday night and, if I'm not mistaken, you teach school tomorrow."

"Sunday?" Ni looked at him with a confused frown. "How can it be Sunday? We left on Saturday and we didn't spend the night in the Château."

"Time passes differently in Calabiyau. Which means that I also must leave if I'm to return before the sun rises. I'll close the portal as soon as I'm through it. Drive safely, my new friends. Perhaps we can meet again someday." His dark brown eyes punctuated the sincerity of his words.

"I really hope so." Ninon gave him a hug. "Can I ask you one last question before you leave?"

"If you'd like."

"When we were transporting, I tried to say something to Ms. Lee, but I couldn't even hear my own words. Were we traveling faster than the speed of sound, and if we were, why was there no bang like when planes break the sound barrier?"

Mywerk had to laugh. "You are a remarkable young lady, Ni. We actually can talk while transporting. We just need to speak in double time so our words stay up with us."

"So, we weren't going faster than sound?"

"Goodness no, child. The sonic boom would shatter our eardrums. And now I really must be going. May the earthly spirits protect you on your drive home."

Ninon and Ms. Lee watched as Lord Mywerk vanished into the sinkhole. It also disappeared—as though it had never existed. Only the flashing red lights and yellow caution tape remained, standing in the middle of the road as if for no apparent reason.

Off in the distance, they heard the owl hooting again. This time he sounded forlorn.

Ninon looked up at the star-filled sky. "Ms. Lee, are we dreaming? Because if we are, I don't ever want to wake up."

"Neither do I. Let's go home and see what Monday brings." She opened the car door, slid in and picked up her phone. "Look, Ni, a text from Ms. Zimmerman. They finally got the power back on in London."

"What did she say?"

"She says she's standing-by for a flight."

"Is she coming to Las Vegas?"

"Let's give her a call when we get on the road and find out."

THIRTY-TWO

Following their meeting with Viviana and Centrod, Kandide and Jake transported back to the Castle. Though they hadn't yet learned the fate of Adriana and Teren, they were eager to find out about Egan. Moments after they arrived, the entire Castle was abuzz with the news—their Queen was safe.

"I'm just happy Egan's okay," Kandide said after hearing about the gingerbread.

"And that you also weren't hurt." Tiyana hugged her daughter a second time.

"Thank you, Mother. Right now, however, Jake and I need to meet with General Mintz to see how the plans are going to defend both the Château and our land. With Lady Aron having lost her chance to possess the Gift, she may order General Kandour to actually attack us."

"Would he do that?" Tara asked.

"He would," Jake replied, "if Firenza works out a deal with him to give her the Castle in exchange for his returning home, not just with a victory at the Château, but here, as well."

"Those two victories," Kandide added, "would almost certainly enable him to take the throne away from Cyndara—or Lord Mywerk, for that matter. Which is why we need to immediately let General Mintz know about this possible new development."

Kandide and Jake headed straight to a meeting with her two top generals in the war room—a large chamber on the uppermost floor of the Castle's highest turret. Piled with maps, the octagonal room had floor-to-ceiling beveled glass windows that provided a 360-degree view of her kingdom. For the moment, at least, all was quiet. There hadn't been a raid on any of the villages since Kandide's kidnapping.

The stress of her abduction, along with General Mintz's inability to find her, weighed heavily on his normally commanding stance. Seeing her safe reinstated much of it. He and General Pell listened intently to how Kandide had outwitted Lady Aron.

"That was brilliant, Your Majesty," Mintz told her. "And a masterful escape strategy on your part, if I may say so."

"Thank you." Pride shone on her face. "It's definitely not a situation I want to be in again."

"We'll be tripling your guards," Pell assured her. Like General Mintz, he too was relieved to see his Queen safe. "I am, however, sorry to hear about Lady Batony. We grew up in the same village and, as terrible as what she did was, it's a tragic way to end a life."

"And so unnecessary." Kandide wasn't sure how she felt. Lady Batony had betrayed her. And yet she couldn't help feeling somewhat responsible. *Perhaps if I had been a bit more considerate of her feelings,* she thought. *Maybe a little more tolerant of her endless stories…* Her purple-blue eyes drifted off into the distance. "It's sad that she hated me so much that she would destroy her own life. Very sad."

"Revenge is the most corrosive of all emotions." Mintz sounded more like her father than her top military general. "It destroys logic and ultimately the one who indulges it. As Lord Rössi says, 'Where vengeance grows, no kindness flows.' Lady Batony made the choice to hate and that is what destroyed her, not you, Your Majesty. You mustn't blame yourself."

Jake could see how conflicted she felt. "General Mintz is right, Kandide. Just look at the monster Lady Aron has become. She's never gotten over the fact that King Toeyad married Tiyana instead of her, and she's letting spite destroy everything she touches—even her own sons."

Kandide sighed. "I know both of you are right. Thank you for your support." She did know they were right, but it didn't make her feel any better about Lady Batony. Only time would heal that wound. "Do you know where Lady Aron or Alin might be, General Pell? Tara told us about the gingerbread and her visit to Lord Aron. I'm just grateful that Egan is alright."

"Our intelligence says she has Alin hidden with his cousins somewhere down south. But no one has been able to find them. And right now, we can't afford to send more than a handful of soldiers to search for him. I imagine, however, that Firenza is with Kandour."

"More than likely." Kandide walked over to the war table, where each of the four Kingdoms in Calabiyau was displayed on its three-dimensional surface. "General Mintz, can you take us through your plan to defend the Château, as well as our own Castle? I'm beginning to be concerned that his attack on us might be more that just a diversionary tactic."

"Interesting you should say that," Mintz replied. "I'm beginning to think that, as well. Let's look at what we do know. Kandour will attack the Château shortly after you deploy the Frost—when the Veil that protects it is weak."

"That's in three days from now." Kandide studied the miniature soldiers situated on the war table. "Are you certain you're ready?"

"We're far too outnumbered for my liking," Pell said. "While we were searching for you, our scouts confirmed that Kandour does, indeed, have over fourteen thousand troops. We have no more than five thousand. Those aren't exactly the best odds. And now with your new theory…"

"What General Pell says is true," Mintz countered. "But it's not going to change our numbers. So, we need to out strategize him."

Jake joined Kandide at the war table. "When I was with Cyndara, she committed her army to help us. Has General Slant contacted you?"

"Yes. He and I met yesterday. He'll be sending two thousand troops. I'm convinced that he's completely loyal to Her Highness."

"I'm convinced he's loyal to her, as well," Kandide agreed. "Though I think, being Banshees, they'll be more likely to want to help defend Calabiyau Proper than the Château."

"And that's exactly where I intend to use them," Mintz said. "If for no other reason than seeing their own kind standing with us may dissuade some of Kandour's troops from attacking. Especially since they are mostly farm boys and not experienced soldiers like General Slant's army."

"Let's hope you're right." Kandide looked down at the war table. The Castle, though shielded, was still vulnerable, as were the many small villages that surrounded it.

"In any case," Mintz continued, "I intend to have the Castle as heavily fortified as possible, both from the front and from the rear." He passed his hands over the table and his army split into two legions—one in front of the Castle, and the other hidden behind the rolling hillside to the rear of where Kandour's army would need to be in order to stage an attack.

"That's probably the best strategy, considering everything," Kandide agreed. "What's your plan for the Château?"

"Under the command of General Pell, we'll move two thousand troops inside the Veil." Mintz, again, waved his hand and miniature soldiers appeared on the war table inside the wall that surrounded the tiny Kingdom.

"How will you do it without being seen?" Jake asked.

"It's all about timing," Mintz explained. "We'll take advantage of the fact that the moment Her Majesty triggers the Frost we'll be able to transport directly inside the wall. My estimate is that we have a window of about thirty minutes before winter spreads that far north and Kandour realizes that the Frost has been deployed. It will take General Pell most of that to get all two thousand of his soldiers inside. From the time Kandour sees the first snowflake, until he can transport a couple thousand of his own troops inside, will be at least thirty minutes more."

"That's cutting it pretty close." Jake watched as miniature Banshee soldiers also began appearing behind the protective wall.

"It is," Mintz admitted. "But remember, sometimes a weakness can also be a strength."

"In what way?" Kandide asked.

"Transporting that many Fée has to be done in groups—probably not more than fifty to a hundred at a time. We're testing it now. Like our soldiers, Kandour's army can't arrive all at once. By the time they do start appearing, Pell's troops will be in place and ready for them."

Kandide was still concerned. His plan was good, but… "Why don't we just move our soldiers in there now?"

"With the Veil strong," Pell explained, "they would have to transport outside the wall. Kandour has scouts placed in the Mists all around it. If they see us moving troops in, we lose the element of surprise. Trace and Selena are the only ones who know the plan right now and I'm told they are in complete agreement."

"They are." Teren walked into the war room.

"Teren!" Kandide rushed over to him. "You're back!"

"Looks like we both are. I just saw Mother and Tara. They told me about your kidnapping. Very clever how you tricked Lady Aron."

"Thanks. I thought it was. Where's Adriana?"

"She went to the Bardic Temple to let Centrod and Viviana know that we made it back. After hearing about General Mintz's plan from Selena, we decided that I should come directly here. There is one other thing you should know, however. When I was leaving, I heard strange hissing sounds. So I decided to investigate."

"What was it?" Jake asked.

"About a hundred garglans."

"A hundred garglans?" Jake gulped, remembering the problem they had trying to stop the thirteen that Teren and Tara encountered when they first transported to the Mists.

"They're in groups of ten scattered about a half a kilometer apart in the Mists outside the wall. My guess is they plan to release them when Kandour attacks."

"Ari and his pack are in the Mists." Jake looked at Kandide. "I need to get them inside the wall. They won't stand a chance against that many garglans."

"I'll go with you, Jake," Teren said. "Ari and the other wolves helped save Tara and me when we went there to find Kandide."

Kandide knew she would not be able to talk her brother or Jake out of going—and she wouldn't, even if she could. Ari helped save her life, as well, when she first arrived in the Mists. "Please be careful, both of you. Jake, I know that once you've found Ari, you're going to want to stay at the Château and help General Pell defend it. But, Teren, I would greatly appreciate it if you would come back here. I could use your help. I'm sure Viviana and Centrod will understand."

"Whether they do or not, I'll be back as soon as I know Ari is safe. I'd like to be back for Samhain, anyway."

"That reminds me, should we cancel the celebration tomorrow night?" Kandide looked from General Pell to General Mintz.

"No. I think it's important to proceed with it," Mintz replied.

"As do I." Pell nodded. "We want Kandour to think we don't know his real plans."

"I wish we knew them better." Kandide studied the soldiers' positions on the war table. "With seven thousand troops poised to attack the Château and another seven thousand poised and ready to attack our border, my desire to hold a massive party is not very high right now. Who knows what deception will be behind all those masks?

THIRTY-THREE

"I think we've looked just about everywhere." Teren shook his head in frustration. He and Jake had spent the entire next day searching the Mists for Ari and his pack. They flew as close to Kandour's scouts as they dared, but the gnarled and tangled forest was shrouded in heavy black fog making it even more difficult to see below the dense canopy of branches. Several times they were forced to land and walk, barely escaping detection.

Avoiding the oily puddles of black goo was also difficult, even though the sun's most persistent rays still afforded some light. Soon darkness would set in making it impossible to navigate. The Mists were not a place either of them wanted to be after the sun set. "Maybe the wolves have already made it back to the Château."

"Maybe, but there's still one more area I'd like to search." Jake motioned for Teren to follow. They flew above the treetops in a northerly direction. Along the way, they passed two more open areas, each with a dozen garglans chained to the trees. They also counted four more scout camps.

Finally, Jake spotted something. "Teren, look over there." Swooping closer, he not only saw the wolves, but a large herd of white-tailed deer.

"What are they doing in the Mists?" Teren couldn't imagine why deer would be this far away from the lush green forest they called home. "There's nothing out here for them to eat."

"The Banshees probably brought them here as garglan food." Jake cautiously landed in a thicket of tangled trees.

Teren landed beside him, barely missing a large puddle of the thick black goo. "It looks like Ari's trying to free them."

"I think you're right. How many guards do you see?"

"Five. Though one of them looks like he's asleep under that dead tree."

"Think you can spell five guards?"

"Twenty, I might have trouble with. Five. That's easy." With a wave of Teren's hand and a few chanted phrases, each of the soldiers instantly froze. "How long do you want them to sleep?"

"A couple hours ought to do it. Come on." After making their way through the thick underbrush to the frozen Banshees, Jake checked each one to ensure that he was, indeed, immobilized. "What do you think about transporting them far away from here?"

"I can try," Teren said. "I've never done it before with someone frozen. But, hey, you have to test new spells on someone."

"Better on them than Kandide."

"Oh, so she told you about my prank on the aercaen field when I was first learning this spell?"

"Yeah. Unfortunately, I thought it was funny." Jake couldn't help but chuckle as he remembered the story.

"So that's why she was mad at both of us for a while. My sister just doesn't have a sense of humor."

"She's getting better."

"If you say so. Speaking of better, we'd 'better' get going. Where do you want to send these guys?"

Jake thought for a second then said, "Try these coordinates: 17, 15, 28. They should be perfect."

"17, 15, 28? Isn't that the volcanic lake by Lady Aron's manor house? Egan used to transport near there to meet Alin. I went with him once, just before I went to the Bardic Temple."

"Could well be," Jake smirked. "I was never good at geography."

"Maybe not, but you haven't lost your sense of humor." One at a time, as Teren gestured, the five soldiers vanished. "Sure hope they know how to swim."

"Since they're frozen, they'll probably float like logs of ice. Come on, let's get Ari and move those deer out of here. Something tells me we're being watched."

The sudden cracking of twigs confirmed Jake's suspicion. He whirled around to see another soldier. Just as the redcap was about to release an arrow, Ari leapt on his back and he tumbled to the ground. Snarling, the magnificent silver-grey wolf grabbed the Banshee's neck in his jaws.

"It's okay, boy." Jake rushed over to them. "Freeze Ari's new friend, Teren. And from the looks of him, he could also use a bath."

"And I know just the lake." Teren instantly froze the soldier, who, the moment Ari released him, vanished.

"Good boy." Jake patted his four-legged friend on the head. "Thank you. There are over a hundred garglans out here. We need to get you and the other wolves inside the wall where you'll be safe."

With a bark of concurrence and a few guttural howls, twenty-some members of Ari's pack emerged from the trees. He scanned them to make sure they were all accounted for, then barked again.

"What should we do about the deer?" Teren pointed to the herd that numbered in the hundreds. They were corralled inside a large makeshift pen. "There are way too many to transport all at once."

"I know. And I'd like to be out of here before it gets so dark we can't see. And I'm sure there are other scouts lurking around."

"If not, there will be once they know the deer are missing. So what's the plan?"

"By my calculations," Jake guessed, "we're about a fifteen-minute walk from the northern wall of the Château. We can move them there."

"I thought you weren't good at geography."

"That's not geography. It's survival. Let's go."

Jake and Teren opened the pen, and with the help of the wolves begin moving the deer. Ari spread his pack around them to keep any from straying. The Mists were marshy, wet, and getting darker by the minute. They didn't dare move too quickly, lest a deer slip and fall. As the sun began to drop beneath the horizon, seeing even a few steps in front of them became difficult. Nevertheless, they pushed ahead. Several times they spotted Banshee scouts. In each case, however, Teren was able to freeze the soldier and transport him to the lake.

The unlikely entourage finally reached the wall that surrounded the Château and its villages. The sun had long since slipped behind the steep mountains on the northwest side of the misty dead-lands. Even the moon seemed reluctant to show its face, hiding behind a thick layer of clouds.

"I know there's a gate around here." Jake created a softly glowing orb so he could see in the starless night. "It's probably not been opened since it was built, but it's here somewhere." His fingers searched around each block that formed the wall. "Found it." He pushed on the trigger-stone and a heavy door creaked open.

"What the…!" Leaping back, Jake tumbled to the ground. An arrow landed inches from his right boot.

"What's going on?" Teren rushed over to him.

"They're attacking us."

A loud voice rang out, "Hold your fire! It's Teren and Jake—and a whole bunch of… deer?" Landing on the ground near the two of them, Benji held up a lighted torch and began laughing. "Well, well, what do we have here?"

"You tell me!" Jake snapped at his long-time friend. Standing up, he brushed himself off. "Somehow, I miss the humor of nearly being killed."

"Sorry. We thought you were one of Kandour's scouts. Let's get you inside. It won't be very funny if they find you and your friends out here." He held the torch up, penetrating the darkness. Deer and wolves were scattered as far back as he could see.

Jake motioned for Ari to guide the herd through the gate. "So, you've seen Kandour's scouts?"

"Several times. Though never with white-tailed deer," Benji said with a slight chuckle.

"They were intended as garglan food," Jake explained.

"Then you'd really better get a move on." Benji motioned for the other guards to help move the herd. "Something tells me they aren't going to be very happy when they find them missing."

"I'm sure they won't." Using Benji's torch, Jake scanned the surrounding area as the deer passed through the gate. It seemed quiet enough, but Banshees were known for their stealth movements and he sensed they were probably lurking nearby. When the last deer was safely inside, he told Ari: "Take them down to the lake. I'm sure they could use a drink and there's still plenty of fresh grass to nibble on. Then come back to the Château so you and the other wolves can also have dinner." Ari barked and he and his pack, once again, began moving the deer.

Jake turned to Benji. "How are preparations going for the attack?"

"About as good as can be expected. The nets are ready, and Trace has been developing a crazy contraption that might just work. I'll tell you about it over dinner. I'm sure you and Teren could use some food, as well."

"Actually, as much as I like Margay's cooking," Teren said, "I'm going to say hello to Selena then head back to the Castle. I promised Kandide I'd return as soon as Ari and the other wolves are safe."

"Respectfully, Prince Teren, this is our home. We built it, and I, for one, will not leave…ever."

THIRTY-FOUR

Inside the wall, the grounds surrounding the Château were teaming with activity. Temporary accommodations had been set up in virtually every home and spare room that could possibly house one or more of the nearly two thousand troops Pell would be transporting in.

Trace quickly finalized orders to his own recruits—any and all of the Imperfects from the Château and its surrounding villages who were able to fight—then sent them off to continue preparations. From making arrows to weaving nets, everyone was helping.

A large hospital had been set up inside the Great Room of the Château to care for the injured. When the Veil was strong, no one ever worried about an attack from the outside; and while there was plenty of food, the Château's emergency care facilities were limited and needed to be greatly expanded. Leanne was busily overseeing the activities, making sure there was enough salve and herbs to help heal those who became injured.

Trace joined Selena, Jake, Benji, and Teren in the large gathering hall. "We're glad you're back, Jake. You, too, Prince Teren. Any word on Kandide?"

"She's home." Jake told them the story of her remarkable escape.

"Thank the earthly spirits she's safe." Selena was truly relieved. "Does that mean you'll be staying with us during the attack?"

"It does. Teren, however, promised Kandide he'd return in time for the Samhain celebration."

"Goodness, I'm surprised General Mintz wants her to hold it— what with everyone dressed up in masks and all, who knows who will be lurking around. We certainly canceled ours."

"Kandide wanted to cancel the party at the Castle," Teren explained. "But General Mintz feels that doing so will cause panic throughout the villages. People are already scared enough with all the rumors floating around."

"And so they should be," Selena insisted. "If Kandour takes the Château, they'll be no stopping him."

"We're not going to let him," Jake assured her. "We have at least two strategic advantages."

"Two?" Teren asked. "I know Pell's troops transporting in at the last minute is one of them. But what's the other?"

"Trace." Looking over at the Banshee, Jake smiled. "He briefly served under General Kandour."

"I didn't know that. So, what do you think he'll do, Trace?" Teren asked.

"We all know that Kandour will attack as soon as he knows the Veil is weak. He'll use darkness to maneuver his troops into place and be ready to transfer them as soon as he sees the first signs of winter. His front lines will move forward in metered batches to make the first strikes. While they are creating a distraction, his major fire power will be transporting in for an attack from the rear."

"Is that possible?" Teren asked. "There are mountain cliffs behind us."

"Normally, not," Trace said. "But remember, with the Veil weak, he can transport troops anywhere. They're likely to start appearing ten to fifteen minutes after the first soldiers enter from the front."

Jake looked at the hastily built war table. It showed the entire area and how vulnerable they actually were without the protection of the Veil. If what Trace said was true, the situation was even worse than he anticipated. "So you think the rear battalions will be his main line of attack, and his front troops are primarily for diversion? Does General Pell know this?"

"He does." Trace nodded. "We discussed it when he was here. Though, don't underestimate Kandour's diversionary tactics. The frontal attack will be just as deadly. You also need to know that strategically, there is one thing Kandour is consistent about and that is not being consistent. Which means that what I'm saying is probable, but it's still just a guess—an educated one, but a guess."

"Now, you see why I'm so concerned, Jake," Selena said.

"I do."

"We both do," Teren concurred.

"You can also bet that Kandour will have heavy back-up support on the left and right flanks." Trace pointed to two areas on the war table. "On this side of the wall and on that side. And there's more. Kandour is known to change his strategy in a heartbeat. He has battle communication down to a science. What you may think of as just another Banshee war scream is more than likely him issuing new orders. Plus, he'll keep changing the signals so no one, not even his top officers, know everything he has planned."

Jake, Teren, and Selena had never heard Trace talk so much at one time. Unfortunately, they became more concerned with each word he spoke. They also knew that Pell's army was out-numbered by over three to one, and that virtually all of the troops Trace had mustered had very little actual battle experience.

"Maybe, Selena," Teren suggested, "we should transport everyone back to the Castle and let the Banshees have the Château. There's still time and it could save a lot of lives."

"It's something I've been considering."

"Never!" Trace banged his fist on the table. It was also the first time anyone had ever heard him raise his voice. "Respectfully, Prince Teren, this is our home. We built it, and I, for one, will not leave... ever.

I would rather die than turn the Château over to that maniacal traitor. And what about the griffins, Selena? They'll never leave here."

Knowing that what he said was probably true, her apprehension grew stronger. She had experienced first-hand the terror of a Banshee attack. As a young girl, several of her friends were brutalized by Kandour's troops during a raid. Even after the peace treaty was signed, he continued raiding villages near the borders. "Many will die if we stay and fight, Trace, and we may not win. Leaving now, while there's time, is an option we should seriously reconsider. I think we can convince the griffins to follow."

"This isn't like you, Selena." Trace placed his hand on her shoulder. "You've always been the one to stand strong. I've seen you confront horrible danger head on and never back off."

"It's not for me that I fear. My life has been about helping others. The thought of sending so many Fée to their death is not a decision I can easily endorse."

Benji, who sat quietly listening to everything that was being discussed, finally spoke up: "Do you honestly think, Selena, that once the Banshees have taken the Château, Kandour will stop here? From what I understand, his goal is to ultimately conquer all of Calabiyau."

"What do you think, Jake?" Selena asked.

"I think Benji is right. The only thing that's stopping General Kandour from attacking the Castle is Cyndara. If he conquers us, he'll return home as a hero, and be one step closer to overthrowing her rule. Then he won't stop until every Fée in Calabiyau is killed or enslaved. And it won't just be our clans that will be devastated. Banshees will be catapulted back to the darkest days of their past. I don't think they could have a worse King."

"Or one that is more cruel," Trace added. "Lady Aron has enabled a monster far greater than she knows."

"Then if we must fight, we must win." Selena spoke with a resolve that resembled more of her former self. "I only ask that anyone who wishes to leave, be allowed to do so."

"That's fair." Benji nodded his head in agreement.

"They can come with me tonight, or anytime tomorrow." Teren explained that he had promised Kandide he would return as soon as he knew Ari was safely inside the wall.

"So far, Prince Teren," Benji told him, "no one wants to leave. Even Matari has been readying his bow and arrows."

Noticing Teren's quizzical expression, Selena explained, "Matari is over five-hundred years old. He was quite the war hero in his day."

"You don't mean General Matari?" Teren asked. "Father used to tell me stories about him. He said he was a great general—maybe the greatest ever. I thought he was killed during the Clan Wars."

"That was the official story. But I assure you, he is very much alive," Selena said.

"Shouldn't he be in here helping us?" Teren asked. "We could use someone with his skills."

Selena shook her head. "He never fully recovered from his years of being a Banshee prisoner. You've actually met him, Teren. He's the white-haired gentleman who plays the fiddle and tells stories to the children."

"That's General Matari?" Teren was amazed. "I guess I never connected the name. You're right, though, he probably can't be much help."

"I don't know," Jake said. "Maybe we should speak to him anyway. If he's having a good day, there might be something we can learn."

"I'll go fetch him." Benji headed off.

"Thank you." Jake turned back to Selena. "We're not only fighting this battle for our freedom, but for Fée like General Matari who have given so much so that each of us may live in peace."

"Including you, Jake," Trace said. "We may be out-numbered, but we won't be out-smarted. I've got a few tricks left up my sleeve. The Château is where we draw the line. The Château is where we stand. And the Château is where we will win!"

Jake could not have been prouder of his Banshee friend. Little did he know when he found Trace half dead in the Mists that they would become so close. "And win, we will. Here's Matari now."

"General Matari, it's great to see you again." Teren warmly greeted the frail Fée who looked as though he could easily be a thousand years old. His hair was pure white and his face was deeply creased. He bore a scar that ran from the top of his forehead, across his permanently closed left eye, and down to his upper lip. He was also missing an ear. Nevertheless, he hobbled into the room with a sense of dignity that only someone who was once a great leader could command.

Matari eyed Teren ever so closely. "Do I know you, young man?" His voice was almost as frail as his body.

"I'm Prince Teren. You served under my father, King Toeyad."

"King Toeyad, you say. I was his top general once upon a time. Fought in the Clan Wars, we did. We won, too, you know. Did I tell you that I was once a general? Looking closely at the emblem on Teren's jacket, he bowed. "Pleasure to see you again, Prince Teren. Did you know that I was once a general? Fought with your father, I did."

"Yes, and Father said you were a great one, Sir."

"What'd you say? I was a late one? Never late—always on time, I was. It's important to be on time, you know. Always on time. Never late, I was."

"Of course not," Teren responded, realizing that Matari was merely a shell of his once great self.

"You here to help fight the war?" Matari asked. "General Kandour's coming, you know. Causing more trouble. That Banshee's a mean one, he is. If there weren't ladies present, I'd use another word. Even for a Banshee, he's a bad one. But I've got a plan this time. Yes, sir, Prince Teren. I've got a really fine plan this time. No need for you or Selena to worry. I've got a plan."

"What is your plan, General?" Teren asked.

"Just about everywhere. Yep. Got a pain just about everywhere.

MATARI PLAYS HIS FIDDLE FOR PETRA,
LORI, LEANNE, SELENA, KATRINA, PONDA,
DALIA, ROSE, AND EGAN

Got to sit down now, with your permission that is, Prince Teren. I've got a plan you know."

"Please sit down, General." Teren helped him to a chair. "We'd all like to hear your plan."

"Going to take out General Kandour. That's my plan. Now, don't you worry, Selena, or you either, Jake. I won't fail. You have my word on it. It's all set up, it is. Been working on it for days. I just have to rest a bit first. Just need to rest. Just rest now. It's a real fine plan, Selena. I won't fail you. It's all set up…" Matari closed his eyes and drifted off to sleep, softly snoring.

Selena placed a soft blanket over him. "May the spirits bless him, he's just not capable of helping."

"What happened to him?" Teren whispered.

"He told us that the Banshees held him captive for years, and that his torture was overseen by General Kandour, personally. We don't know how he escaped. When Jake found him wandering in the Mists, his body was full of burns, his ear was missing—probably the work of the assassin, Anile—and his left eye was badly lacerated. It's only because of Leanne that he survived."

"He was a great general." Teren felt a surge of anger. He was beginning to understand how brutal life could be, especially for Imperfects. And why Kandide was so passionate about defending the Château. It provided a sanctuary for those who would have otherwise died tragically—for no other reason than they weren't physically perfect. "Father said there was no one better. After we defeat Kandour, I'm going to ask Kandide to award a special medal to him. It's the least we can do."

"That would be wonderful," Selena said. "He certainly deserves it. Are you sure you can't stay for dinner, Teren?"

"It's late and I really need to get back to the Castle." He hugged his aunt goodbye, hoping beyond belief that it would not be the last time. In all the world, Selena was one of the most remarkable people he had ever met. "Be safe. All of you."

THIRTY-FIVE

Geneal Kandour sat down on a dark brown upholstered chair. His tent was remarkably well appointed and comfortable for a Banshee training camp. Unlike his troops and the other officers, he was not short on comforts. Floating orbs illuminated every corner as though it was day. "So, Lady Aron, what are you saying?"

"I'm saying that I want you to actually attack the Castle."

"Are you crazy?"

"No more than you are, General. I want Kandide's entire family, as well as that despicable husband of mine and his freak son, killed."

"My, my, such hostility. You don't take defeat very well, do you? Especially when it's your own fault. Have some cushla, Firenza, it will calm you down." He handed her a cup of the steaming beverage. She ignored it.

For a Banshee, General Kandour was unusually good-looking. Unlike Prince Yandell, Prince Kilmonth, and most of the other military officers, his appearance was neat and well kept, with carefully groomed short black hair. Even his hands and nails were clean and perfectly manicured. The five star-shaped rubies on his collar indicated his rank and were the only gems he wore on his military uniform.

"I don't need calming down—especially when two of your best guards were so incompetent that they let Kandide escape. And I don't drink that vile beverage, either." Lady Aron's wings flared.

Flames scorched the ceiling of his tent. Though she'd never admit it, Kandour's words stung with truth. Had she not been so impatient to possess the Gift of the Frost, she would not have forced Kandide's hand until she had better control of the situation. "It won't happen again, I assure you."

Kandour glanced up at the blackened ceiling of the tent. "Please, try to control yourself. Strategy forged from emotion instead of intellect is always dangerous. We are about to engage in a war that will decide the future of my Kingdom… and yours. I'm not interested in your personal vendettas. Nor can I afford your impetuous desires."

"Impetuous or not, we have an agreement."

"No, Firenza. Let me remind you that you have an agreement with Cyndara's sniveling brothers. Not me. Once I take the Château and they lose their lives in battle, that treaty is meaningless. So, I suggest you start using your pretty head to think about an alliance with me." He took her by the arm. "Of course, if you make it worth my while…"

Slapping him across the face, Lady Aron jerked away. "Don't ever do that again!"

Kandour rubbed his cheek. "I've killed Fée for less than that." A cruel sneer crossed his lips. "Perhaps you will be part of the spoils. At least for as long as you behave."

"Never!" Her amber eyes were blazing.

"Never? You, my fireball, are hardly in a position to say 'never'. One word from me and fourteen thousand troops go marching home."

She momentarily glared at him. "That you won't do."

"No? What makes you so certain?"

"Because Cyndara is fully aware of your plan to overthrow her. And she has your entire Ruling Council on her side. You can no more return home without this victory, than I can."

"Then I guess that means we truly are in this together."

"We are in this, but we will never be together."

"There you go again saying 'never'. Wouldn't your time be better spent trying to figure out what you're going to do about Kandide?"

"I've told you, I want you to attack the Castle and kill her entire family. Then you are to take our dear Queen prisoner—again. This time, perhaps, your assassins won't let her escape. Once she has been captured, I will come forward and negotiate a treaty with you that will include your complete withdrawal. With the rumors I've already spread that Lady Batony and Kandide arranged their own kidnapping to frame me, and Kandide brutally killed Lady Batony to avoid anyone knowing about her plan, it won't be hard to convince her subjects to support me. Especially when they see seven thousand Banshee soldiers surrounding the Castle."

Kandour leaned back in his chair and crossed his arms. "It's not a bad strategy. But you still haven't offered me anything in return."

"Once I rule Calabiyau Proper, I'm sure Anile can convince Kandide to transfer the Gift. After that, you may have the pleasure of feeding her to your garglans."

"That's a start. Kandide has been quite a disruptive force in my land—all that nonsense about Imperfects being equal. What else do you have to offer, Firenza?"

"After you take over the Banshee Kingdom, we'll be able to solidify a treaty that will make both our Kingdoms strong again."

"That's all well and good, but I could also just conquer Calabiyau Proper, and then I don't need you. I'll simply keep Kandide imprisoned, allowing her out once a year to deploy the Gift."

"You could. But you will never win the loyalty of the Fée. They'll never stop fighting to overthrow you. With me as your ally, no one can defeat either of us."

"It seems as though you've finally started thinking with your head, Firenza. I accept your offer. Tell me, have you ever seen a garglan eat? It can be quite... amusing."

Lady Aron's expression revealed nothing short of contempt. "You disgust me."

"So you do have feelings for me. What, my dear, would *you* like for dinner while Kandide *is* dinner? Delicious thought, isn't it? The two of us dining together while Kandide is…"

"I'm afraid you'll be dining alone."

"We'll see. In any case, as much as I would like to continue this conversation, amusing as it is, it seems as though I have a new plan to put in place." He summoned a guard. "Lieutenant, fetch Anile. I have an assignment for him." Turning back to Lady Aron, he added, "Consider it done. The morrow after next, the Château will fall. Then it's on to Calabiyau Proper, the death of Kandide's family, and, of course, our victory celebration."

"Let's just hope your confidence turns into more than simple arrogance. And now, I also have a few arrangements to make."

"I suggest you be careful traveling about tonight. The Samhain celebrations have started, and who knows what evil might be lurking behind those masks. I'd hate to see you miss our dinner."

• • • •

By the time Teren returned to the Castle, the parties were well underway. Of all the celebrations, Samhain (pronounced sow' ween and often referred to as Calloween) is perhaps the most important celebration to the Fée, for it signals summer's end and winter's start.

The festivities began at sunset on the eve of October thirty-first and normally continued throughout the entire next day and into that night. As was tradition, the trees in every village and town were strung with brightly glowing orbs, and every Fée, young and old, was dressed in lavish costumes and fanciful masks. The Castle was no exception.

Teren quickly changed into his own Calloween costume, a star-studded medieval wizard's robe, pointed hat, and a blue and white mask. Holding a glowing staff with a large blue sapphire in its center crown, he floated down the Castle's central staircase and joined the festivities.

Kandide's purple-blue eyes tracked his path to the bottom of the steps. Dressed in a golden costume that resembled something the human Queen, Cleopatra, might have worn, she made her way through the crowd to meet him. The legendary Egyptian ruler had fascinated Kandide since she was a child and read a book in the Royal Library about her. It had been brought back from the human realm nearly a century before. Cleopatra quickly became one of Kandide's favorite heroines.

Teren stared at the beaded black wig that completely concealed his sister's silvery blonde hair. "Wow! I almost didn't recognize you. Great costume."

"Thank you." She lowered her ornately decorated mask. "Did you get Ari and his pack inside the wall?"

"We did, and a few hundred deer, too. They were meant as garglan food."

"How terrible. It's a good thing you and Jake both went. How are the battle preparations going?"

"Really well. I didn't see them, but Trace has some new contraptions that he came up with and he says they're really powerful."

"That's sounds like Trace. He's pretty clever. In any case, let's hope General Pell's plan works."

"It'll work." Teren's voice only slightly conveyed his concern. "It has to. How are things going here?"

"As good as can be expected. By late tomorrow afternoon, we'll have over five thousand troops in place. That includes our soldiers as well as Cyndara's."

"That's good. Where do you want me?"

"I'd like you by my side, on the front lines," Kandide replied. "Tara, of course, will be stationed in the Castle hospital with Lars and the other healers who aren't out with the troops. Mother will be with the village children and the elderly in the Castle's lower chambers."

Throughout their conversation, a masked Fée stood listening—*a little too intently*, Kandide thought. As soon as she told Teren where Tara and Tiyana would be, he merged back into the crowd. Kandide motioned for Captain Denan, her head of security, to follow him.

"One of Lady Aron's spies?" Teren whispered.

"Probably, and it looks like he got the information he came for."

"You are clever, Kandide. Very clever."

"I know. We'll discuss more at the briefing tomorrow. Right now, we should join the party."

Teren looked around the large hall. Almost no one was dancing. "It sure doesn't feel like much of a celebration, but I guess we probably should."

A couple thousand Fée were in attendance and, though the costumes and masks were as elaborate and colorful as Kandide had ever seen, no one was in a celebratory frame of mind. Lady Jennáe of the Music Clan had been selected as the featured singer, replacing Lady Batony's life-long role. As wonderful as her voice was, even she couldn't get the large crowd in a festive mood.

Virtually everyone was focused on the rumors that they would soon be at war. All knew that the Frost would be deployed in two days, enabling Nature to rest under a mask of white until the warmth of spring awakens a new burst of life. They also knew that the first signs of winter this year could lead, not just to the rebirth of Nature, but to the death of an entire Kingdom and its rebirth ruled by a brutal new King.

It was the first time since her Crowning nearly a year ago that Kandide was able to rally the majority of her subjects around her. She may not be perfect—certainly she was not her father, King Toeyad, the greatest King the Fée had ever known. But she was their Queen. And many had to admit that, over the past few months, her unwavering concern for the villagers' welfare was without question.

Word also spread of her courageous escape from the Banshee kidnappers. Many were convinced that Lady Batony had perpetrated it, while others steadfastly argued that Lady Aron plotted the heinous deed. Even Kandide's most ardent detractors agreed that her escape

KANDIDE, TEREN AND THE SPY

was that of a brave and heroic leader. It was exactly the message she needed to help unite her subjects.

Another rumor, however, was also beginning to percolate—Lady Batony was the victim of a plot by Kandide to frame Lady Aron. Throughout the evening, she answered question after question, hoping to squelch it. Again and again she explained what happened, then laid out the strategy she and General Mintz were embarking upon to defend the Kingdom—at least as much as she wanted Kandour to be aware of. Spies were everywhere. And the party was a good place to disseminate information that could help mislead him.

Supporters were encouraged by her plan. Others sharply criticized sending troops to protect the Château when their own army was so outnumbered. A few weren't sure what to believe. It was politics as usual at the Castle—but at a much more fervent pitch.

Kandide continued drifting through the crowd, trying to calm fears and win allies. She stopped to speak to Lord Socrat, who had been doing very much the same thing. "This new rumor is interesting," he said.

"Yes, and it's certainly an insight into Lady Aron's continuing strategy—attack from within and from without."

By the early morning hours, all had returned to their homes. Kandide and Tiyana sat alone in the empty great hall. "I can't believe anyone would actually believe that I arranged my own kidnapping."

Tiyana took Kandide's hand. "People will believe almost anything if it advances their purpose."

"But what purpose is there in thinking I would do something so awful?"

"Fear, insecurity, hatred, jealousy, anger, greed—it could be any or all of these things. You know that. Lady Aron has many loyal followers. You may never win over some of them. Those who want to believe her, will, and those who don't, won't."

"So it seems." Kandide sighed. "I just don't see why anyone is fooled by her."

Tiyana's answer reminded Kandide of her father: "Samhain isn't the only time we wear masks of deception, my young Queen. As you've learned from both Lady Aron and Lady Batony, a pretty face does not mean that the heart isn't evil. They both wore deceitful masks. You, on the other hand, also used a mask of deception to defeat Firenza and retain the Gift. We all put them on from time to time. Some, as with you, for good. Some, as with the two of them, for bad."

"I never thought of deception as ever being good. But I guess it can be. If I hadn't deceived Lady Aron into thinking she could have the Gift, I wouldn't be alive today. Though I'm not convinced that Lady Batony was evil. Her heart was simply devoured by spite. I wish I'd done more to change that."

"Wishing won't change the past. But it can be a guide to changing the future. As your father often said: 'Focus on what you are able to control. Not what you cannot.' And right now, you need to focus on getting some sleep. Much will happen in the next two days, and all of it will affect our future."

"As usual, Mother, you are right. Let's both get some sleep—if either of us can."

• • • •

On the second morning after the party, Kandide stood with Tara Tiyana, and Teren in the sacred garden. She spread her arms, opened her hands toward the sky, and deployed the Frost.

In an instant, tiny balls of fire erupted above the grounds like golden fireworks.

THIRTY-SIX

General Pell watched as the first snowflakes began to paint the grounds surrounding the Château with shimmering crystals of white. At any other time it would be a welcome site—Mother Nature beginning her journey toward slumber, and children donning mittens to build snowmen.

Not today, he thought. "Stand by for the attack." Pell's words were repeated throughout the villages that surrounded the Château. Pulses of fear alternated with a sense of brave determination as everyone embraced the inevitable—far too many would be lost on this day.

Within minutes, Banshees began appearing on the grounds inside the wall. Their piercing battle cries were enough to spread terror throughout. Their fierce looks evoked even more fear within this peaceful Kingdom.

"Hold steady," Pell ordered from his position in one of the guard towers atop the wall. A thousand of his troops lined the area in front of the Château. Motionless, they watched and waited.

"But, Sir..." Benji protested, seeing several of his clansmen, who happened to be standing in the gardens where the Banshees appeared, go down in hand-to-hand combat. They were no match for Kandour's well-trained front line troops.

"Part of General Kandour's strategy is to intimidate his opponents right from the start," Pell explained. "He'll send his lesser-trained soldiers in after the first skirmish."

Benji raised his wings to fly down and help his friends. "I must…"

Pell put his hand out to stop him. "You can't save them. And you'll be killed trying. We need to wait for the right moment."

Benji knew he was right, and yet his friends were down there. He watched as purple-red blood began staining the freshly fallen snow.

"War is ugly for everyone," Pell continued. "Those Banshees have fathers, mothers, and children just like we do. Most of them don't want to be here any more than we want them to be. It's the reason we must win. To stop these atrocities from ever happening again."

Lowering his wings, Benji unsheathed an arrow. "I know, General, but I…"

"Soon," Pell told him. "Soon." Two more groups of Banshees appeared in the courtyard, over a hundred in all. "Now!" he shouted.

Giant webs of rope snared the intruders, lifting them high into the air. The massive hoists that were mounted along the wall worked perfectly.

Angry shouts erupted as the dumbfounded Banshee soldiers struggled to break free. Their knives were of little use. The nets were spelled and even the sharp steel blades could not slice through them.

Jake stood next to Pell and Benji in the wall tower. He quickly voiced a spell, and the netted Banshees vanished. "These guys really should be held prisoner in their own land," he told Pell. "Not here."

"I agree. And so they shall be—in a couple hours when they reappear in Mywerk's holding pen." Pell couldn't help but smile. It was a crazy idea—to net the Banshees as they appeared and then transport them back home. But it was, at least for now, working quite well. He turned his attention back to the fighting on the ground and watched his army quickly capture the soldiers who escaped the nets.

Again and again, the process was repeated. Almost as fast as they appeared, the large nets hoisted the invaders into the sky. Jake transported each group to the far side of the Banshee Kingdom, near the abandoned mine where Tara had been held captive months earlier.

Lord Mywerk and Cyndara sat on their black steeds watching as the netted prisoners appeared in the holding area. The number of troops increased by the minute.

"Brilliant idea, Your Highness," Mywerk said, pleased as he watched the astonished soldiers try to penetrate his invisible shield, "to transport the troops home."

"And your idea of spelling this area so they can't escape was equally as brilliant," she said. "We'll release them only after they swear allegiance to my rule."

"Actually, it's to my rule," Mywerk reminded her. "Especially after I win the next game of Chessaé." He turned to one of the nearby guards. "See to it that they are given a meal. I have another errand to attend to." He reined his horse around and rode away.

The netting continued to work as planned, but General Pell could see that Jake was beginning to tire from having used so much energy to transport so many large groups. Nearly a thousand soldiers in all had disappeared almost as fast as they'd appeared. "You need a rest," he told Jake, just before pulling him out of the way to avoid a stray arrow that seemed to appear from nowhere.

"Thanks." Jake scanned the area to see where it had come from. But the perpetrator was already gone. "I'll be fine," he said.

"You'll be better with a short break," Pell insisted. "Besides, it's time for a new tactic. Explosives, fire round one!" he hollered.

In an instant, tiny balls of fire erupted above the grounds like golden fireworks. A shower of Banshees began dropping from the sky as the aerial bursts randomly caught them in mid-transport. "Perfect," Pell said, watching his own troops take them prisoner.

Aerial explosives were a relatively new military technique that had never been tested in battle. Judging from the number of hits, however, it seemed to be extremely effective against the large groups that were transporting over the wall. They also gave Jake that much-needed chance to regain his strength.

"Drink this." Benji handed him a canteen filled with a dark red liquid. "Leanne concocted it to help you keep up your energy."

Jake took a couple sips and made a face. "I'm sure it must work, because it tastes terrible."

"Think you can transport another group?" Pell asked, ordering a pause in the explosives. The sight of so many Banshees being injured from the aerial bursts was more than even he could bear. "Hoist the nets," he called.

Jake set the coordinates, voiced the transport spell, and a hundred more Banshees dissolved from their swinging cages into nothingness.

In spite of their efforts, the number of Banshees who escaped the netting or were not stopped by the explosives continued to grow. Swords clashed, engaging soldiers from both sides in a fierce ground battle. Pell's army was far better trained than Kandour's second round of troops, but the sheer number of Banshees that kept appearing, quickly replenished those who fell. He could see that his front line troops were beginning to fatigue from the relentless fighting.

"Fire the explosives!" Pell grudgingly called, knowing that it was the best way to slow down the onslaught.

Selena, Margay, and several others transported as many of the wounded as possible—both Banshee and Fée—into the temporary clinics. The fighting, however, was so intense, and there were so many casualties, that they could barely keep up.

Leanne worked feverishly to heal anyone and everyone who was hurt. But even her remarkable skills were no match for the endless rows of injured soldiers that lined the halls. With the attack having only just begun, she had no idea how she could help everyone, and stopped only long enough to take a sip of the same type of red liquid Benji had given Jake.

"I hope I made enough of this," she told Margay. Her strength returned and she immediately began healing more soldiers. "Bring me the most seriously injured first."

"That's almost everyone here," Margay replied as she helped a young Banshee solider, not more that seventeen in human years, take a drink of healing herbs.

His brown eyes were blank as he starred at his badly injured arm. "Why don't you let me die? I was trying to kill your kind."

"We value all life," Margay told him. "You're no more than a boy with a long life ahead of you."

He kept staring at his arm, unable to move it. "I'm an Imperfect now. I don't deserve to live."

"Leanne will heal your arm, and then Selena will transport you home, just as she's done with the others. Take this serum with you." Margay handed him a small vial of thick green liquid. "You may need more of it once you arrive back in your land."

"Thank you." He placed the bottle in his pocket. "I still don't understand why you're saving us."

"I know." She moved on to help another solider whose leg was bleeding. Childhood memories of losing her wings during a brutal Banshee raid on her village taunted her. *How well I know,* she thought, pushing the images away and quickly going back to helping others.

Scanning the fog-laden dead-lands that surround the Château, Pell saw another thousand troops ready to transport over the wall. He knew there were at least that many more hidden deeper in the Mists. Fortunately, it looked as though his army was gaining the advantage—at least with the ground fighting. According to Trace, however, this battle was going to be fought on multiple fronts, and he also knew that his help was needed elsewhere.

Calling to his commanding officer, Pell ordered: "Take over. I'm heading to the back to see how Trace is faring. Keep the nets going, and in two minutes fire another round of aerial explosives so Jake can rest again. From then on, continue netting and fire at will." He turned to Benji and Jake. "May the earthly spirits protect you."

"They will." Benji unleashed an arrow. His aim was perfect. A Banshee redcap fell backward, over a wounded companion.

"Good shot. Keep it up." With a gesture, Pell vanished. Less than a minute later, he reappeared next to Trace at the far end of the villages that surround the Château. "Any sign of them?"

"Not yet, but they're out there." Trace scanned the horizon from a camouflaged bungalow that was hidden among an orchard of apple trees. "How's it going up front?"

"Not as well as I'd like. It may be that Kandour thought us vulnerable enough to have all of his troops attack head-on this time. I could sure use a lot more of my army up there." Looking out at the empty field that bordered the wall, Pell added, "Still think he'll attack from the rear?"

"I'm betting my life on it."

"And quite a few thousand others, I'm afraid. Our casualties are already too high."

"You think that because I'm a Banshee, I'm on Kandour's side, don't you?"

"No. No, of course not, Trace. It's just that..."

"It's just that I'm a Banshee. Let me explain something to you. Like everyone here, I didn't have a home until I met Selena. And even with her support, it wasn't easy being accepted. With the other Imperfects who live here being... well, different and having experienced so much prejudice, you'd think they would have accepted me right away. But they didn't. It took years and a lot of hard work on my part to earn their trust and respect." As was normally the case, Trace's tone was matter-of-fact, and without emotion.

"They certainly respect and trust you now."

"But you don't." As he spoke, Trace's one good eye continued to search the mountain range behind them. He was blinded in his other eye by a mining accident years ago, which is why the Banshees sent him to the Mists.

"I…" Pell wasn't sure how to respond.

"My father used to tell a story about two villagers. One was a Banshee and the other was from the Fire Clan. They were neighbors along the neutral zone. After a lot of hard work, the Banshee finally completed a really nice house—much better than the Fire Fée's. Not long after he and his family had moved in, it burned to the ground. They lost everything. It was discovered that the Fire Fée had caused it. When he was brought up in front of your tribunal, his excuse was, 'If you aren't better than a Banshee, who are you better than?' I know prejudice, General. But right now we have a war to fight, and it's not with each other."

"You're right. I'm proud to fight alongside of you, Trace." Pell saluted him.

"Glad to hear it, because… here they come!"

No more than a couple hundred meters away, hundreds of Banshee troops dissolved into view. These weren't just soldiers armed with bows and arrows. Nearly half of them were holding chains that restrained hideous beasts. Snarling and hissing, the bat-winged creatures' beady red eyes darted back and forth. Their forked tongues dripped with a slimy drool. They were howling to be set free. This would surely be the feast of a lifetime for these menacing creatures that relished Fée above all else.

"Garglans!" Pell stood staring. He, of course, knew about the beasts, but had never actually encountered one. "I had no idea they were so big. They must be at least a meter and a half tall."

"They're a lot bigger than the ones we usually see around here. I'll bet Kandour's been breeding them just for this battle."

"Sir, what do we do?" one of Pell's officers asked. "We've never fought anything like these things before?"

"Fight them like any other creature," Trace replied. "They're mean, but an arrow will kill them, just as sure as it will a Banshee. Tell your archers to aim at their necks or undersides. It's where they're the most vulnerable. We'll take out as many as we can from back here."

"Do you really think your contraptions will work?" Pell sounded none too sure.

"I hope so. Are your firing teams ready, Tori?"

"Sure are—all three teams," Trace's second in command replied. "Just tell me when."

"Go ahead and adjust the diamonds, then aim the mirrors. We should be able to do some serious damage before they get much closer."

THIRTY-SEVEN

"I wish we'd had time to make more than three of these contraptions," Trace told General Pell as he helped Tori adjust one of the tangerine-size diamonds. He checked its alignment with the mirror positioned near it. "Perfect. Let's get this one fired up."

Tori and two other Fire Fée began breathing in sync with one another. They pointed their hands at the perfectly cut diamond lens. Streams of white-hot energy emerged from each of their fingertips, passing through the priceless gem and reflecting off the mirror.

Pell watched as a bright red laser-like beam streaked across the field. It incinerated everything in its path. Howls of rage filled the air as the powerful light beam scanned across the area, searing through a dozen garglans, causing them to drop faster than the flurries of snow that continued to fall.

"Let's get the other two ready," Trace told the remaining two teams of Fire Fée. They quickly focused their own white-hot energies onto their respective diamond lenses. Once again, red beams of laser-like light emerged, bouncing off the mirror and piercing through garglans and Banshee soldiers, alike. "Keep it going," Trace said, carefully adjusting one of the mirrors to better aim the beam at a large group of the beasts that was racing toward them. "It's working better than I expected."

"How'd you ever come up with the idea?" Pell asked, as Tori's team took out yet another bunch of garglans and their Banshee handlers.

"Ironically, from Lady Aron," Trace replied, while helping the third team focus their beam on a newly arrived band of the snarling beasts. "We can't get the same amount of power that she was able to generate when she destroyed the aracno-beast last summer after it spun its cocoon. But as you can see, it's working well enough to do this job."

"How long do you think Tori and his team can keep the beams going?" Pell was concerned that it was taking quite a bit of energy to generate even short blasts.

"Not long enough, I'm afraid. I'm just hoping we can at least make a substantial dent in the numbers, but I fear, as they begin to tire, it will become more of a defensive maneuver."

"Aim the mirrors over there," Tori hollered, as several dozen garglans were set free by their handlers. Trace quickly did so. While they were able to eliminate many of the beasts, it seemed as though as soon as a few went down another group appeared. The Banshee soldiers had begun unleashing the snarling creatures from their chains, and the garglans scattered in every direction. The beams were able to destroy fewer and fewer with each blast.

Pell's troops released a barrage of arrows. Many hit their mark. The garglans, however, were lightening fast, making them difficult to kill— even for his best marksmen. A few had already penetrated his first line of defense. The screams of Banshees and Fée blended together as the newly freed garglans attacked their prey—not caring who was master and who was foe.

"We need to ignite the fire wall," Pell said, referring to the line of tightly packed bales of oil-soaked grass that stretched completely across the open field in front of them. "They'll burn, even with the snow. Hopefully, those beasts won't cross the flames, and may turn back on their own troops."

TRACE AND SELENA LOOK AT THE DIAMOND FOR HIS CONTRAPTION

"We've got several hundred of our soldiers out there," Trace objected. "If they get trapped, they'll also be killed."

"We've got several thousand back here and at the Château that will die if we don't stop these creatures. If more of them break through our lines, even your light beams won't be able to eliminate them."

Knowing that Pell was right did very little to make Trace's decision any easier. Reluctantly agreeing to do so, he ordered the fires set. "Let's hope the wind doesn't turn and blow the flames back toward us."

"Once the grass bales start burning, there should be enough distraction to enable our soldiers to fly out of there," Pell tried to reassure him.

They could only watch and wait. Tori's team needed to rest. Trace called a temporary halt to the beams. Fortunately, the garglans did not cross the path of flames. Instead, they raced up the nearby fruit trees, hissing and howling in annoyance. Pell's troops flew above the fires, showering the creatures with arrows. Having nowhere to flee, the garglans were much easier targets.

From high above on a mountain cliff overlooking the Château, General Kandour and Anile watched the attack.

"They're playing right into our hands," Anile observed.

"That they are." With an odd sort of whistle, Kandour signaled the next legion of soldiers. Several hundred Banshees took flight, and while they weren't particularly good aerialists, the troops in this squadron were highly skilled archers. Their accuracy with a bow and arrow vastly outweighed their inability to fly great distances.

Trace, Tori, and the others tried desperately to pick them off with the light beams, but they were still not powerful enough to do much damage. Kandour's elite squad of soldiers managed to kill or set fleeing most of the Fée who were attacking the garglans. They watched in horror as something else, far more devastating began to happen. The Banshee's arrows were tipped with a substance that caused its victims to be instantly paralyzed.

BANSHEE SOLDIER WITH GARGLANS

Garglans began leaping from their perches in the treetops onto the helpless Fée.

General Kandour gleefully watched the carnage from the safety of the mountain cliff. "Now that's what I call good strategy, Anile."

"You are the best," he replied with an evil smirk.

"That I am. Delicious, isn't it? It's a pity that we'll have to destroy all those lovely beasts after they devour every last Imperfect in the Château."

"Sure is. You bred 'em really mean this time. Much too dangerous to keep around. When do you want me to take care of that other task?"

"Soon, Anile. Very soon. Once you've eliminated Kandide's family, and we have her under our control, Lady Aron and I will have that dinner with the garglans. What she doesn't know is that she will be their dessert. I detest that Fire Fée—even more than Queen Kandide."

"Okay, but not before I get one of her ears." Anile continued to watch the carnage below. "I have a feeling that this battle will end sooner than expected."

"I think you're right." Kandour snapped his fingers and two chairs appeared. "Might as well be comfortable."

Trace turned to General Pell. "We've got to get the rest of our troops out of there. Kandour's using arrows dipped in plaxiion. Sound the retreat!"

Pell did so immediately. What he had just witnessed was horrifying beyond belief. "What is plaxiion?"

"A poison that was banned nearly fifty years ago. It's so vile, even King Nastae wouldn't use it."

"It doesn't seem to affect the garglans," Pell observed.

"It's made from their saliva."

With the Banshees in rapid pursuit, the remaining troops began fleeing for their lives.

Trace continued using the light beams, rotating between each of Tori's three teams so they could rest. Though their power was still weaker than he wanted, for those they hit, it was lethal. For each Banshee who fell, however, two more took his place.

"It's not looking good," Pell said. "I'm going to set off the aerial explosives along the wall."

Trace's words did little to conceal his concern. "That will slow them down, but I'm not sure it will stop them. Besides, how are you going to get past that many Banshee soldiers to do it?"

"I'm going to transport to the guard tower, and hope for the best."

"Then be careful, my friend. Once we see you appear, we'll use every bit of fire power we have to cover your back."

"Thanks… my friend. We have to win, Trace. With any luck, we'll shift the fates to our side."

Momentarily taken aback, Kandide took a breath before responding.

THIRTY-EIGHT

ive thousand Banshee soldiers encircled the Castle and its surrounding village. With two thousand more troops hidden in the woods, the situation was dire. Thirty cannons were aimed directly at the Castle's exterior wall.

"General, look!" Kandide pointed to a lone rider who emerged from the row of cannons. She, Teren, and General Mintz, along with several guards, were standing atop the watchtower near the Castle's front gate. "May I have your looking glass?" Holding it up to her eye, she could not believe what she was seeing. "It's Lord Mywerk."

"Mywerk!" Mintz looked through the telescope, seeing for himself that it was, indeed, Lord Mywerk. "That traitor! Wait a minute…"

"What's he doing?" Teren was equally as confused. Mywerk had, after all, helped save his and Adriana's lives only days before. "Wait a minute is right. What *is* he doing?"

"He's turning his horse around to face his own troops," Kandide replied.

"I believe he's…" Mintz said.

"He did." A quizzical look crossed her face. "But how?"

Not only did Lord Mywerk order the cannons to be raised, but to swing back around so that they aimed directly at the Banshee army. Completely under his control, the cannoneers did precisely as they were ordered, taking aim at their own troops.

In a loud voice, Mywerk shouted, "I, Lord Mywerk, member of the Banshee Ruling Council and your acting King, order you to retreat! Those who remain loyal to General Kandour will be dealt with swiftly. Those who show their loyalty to my rule will be given great honors and rewards."

From amidst the troops, a flaming arrow streaked toward Mywerk. Raising his hand, he stopped it in mid-air. Astonished murmurs erupted from the soldiers as the half wizard, half Banshee forced the flaming projectile to reverse its course and fly back in the direction from whence it came. It landed just short of the Banshee front line.

"You can stop one arrow!" a voice yelled from the crowd. It was General Omire, Kandour's number two in command, "but your magic tricks can't stop them all. Neither can these traitors who man the cannons. In spite of your hypnotic spells, you are outnumbered, Mywerk."

In an instant, another arrow hurled through the air. General Omire keeled over as it embedded deeply into his left leg. All looked to see who could have possibly made such a shot. Kandide lowered her golden bow. "Next time, I won't be so compassionate!" she called out. "Teren, transport their wounded general to Tara so she can heal him."

Omire instantly vanished.

"Listen to Lord Mywerk," she continued. "Our Kingdoms have been at peace for nearly a hundred years. You have my pledge, it will continue as long as I rule Calabiyau Proper."

For a brief moment, all was silent. "She favors Imperfects!" General Strands, Kandour's third in command, finally shouted as he emerged from the rear flanks. Others joined in, repeating his words. Their jeers increased in volume until Mywerk ordered a cannon fired. The loud boom again silenced the massive army.

"In your Kingdom," Kandide continued, "any individual has the right to challenge the intended King or Queen for the throne. As Queen of Calabiyau Proper, I submit the same opportunity for any of you to challenge me. Should you win, you will assume my throne."

GENERAL MINTZ, KANDIDE, AND TEREN ATOP THE WATCHTOWER

"What are you doing, Kandide?" Teren gasped. "That's crazy."

"So is killing thousands of innocent Fée." There was no room for negotiation in his sister's tone. "Besides, remember, I select the game." She repeated her words to the Banshee army: "Who among you will represent your clan and prove your worth to rule my Kingdom by challenging me for that right? Or are you all cowards who can only fight behind General Kandour?"

"Kandide, no," Teren pleaded. "Don't do this."

"Listen to him," General Mintz warned. "This is absolutely not necessary."

Ignoring both of them, her eyes skimmed across the thousands of Banshee troops. Not a word could be heard. All were stunned by her offer.

Suddenly, a vivid scarlet flash appeared. "I will challenge you for that right, Queen Kandide." Lady Aron stood a few meters in front of the cannons. "Lord Mywerk, there's no need to do battle with your own kind."

Momentarily taken aback, Kandide took a breath before responding. "I am afraid, my dear, Firenza, my offer was to the Banshees. Unless, of course, you have now openly defected to their side."

"I heard nothing of any restrictions in your words. You clearly stated, 'Who among you will represent your clan and prove your worth to rule my Kingdom?' And I accept that offer."

Laughter broke out among the Banshees. While they loved a good fight, they also loved a good play on words, especially when it resulted in one-upmanship. Lady Aron had done just that. Riding forward, General Strands called, "Before we can sanction you representing our Kingdom, Lady Aron, we must know for whom do you fight?"

Dressed for battle, her fiery wings fluttered in the cold air. Though it was snowing, she threw back the hood of her bright red cape and spoke with rebellious conviction: "I fight for the supremacy of all those who uphold perfection, to keep Banshee and Fée, alike, free from the

the devastation Imperfects bring. I fight so that each of us may live in a society that is worthy, not weak—pure of body, not repulsive in form. I fight for the right of Banshees and Fée to be free of these hideous dregs that will destroy us all. I fight for lasting peace between our two Kingdoms. As the supreme ruler of Calabiyau Proper, I shall restore dignity to both Banshee and Fée."

Lady Aron paused only briefly, her eyes landing on Strands. "So, what say you, General? Do I fight for the supremacy of our Kingdoms, or do you succumb to the decadence of Kandide's purpose?"

Knowing that his troops had been sent there merely as a distraction while General Kandour conquered the Château, Strands was more amused by this new development than concerned with its outcome. He also saw it as an opportunity to humiliate Lord Mywerk, whom he despised. "I stand by you, My Lady. What say you, Mywerk? Do you stand for the 'supremacy of our clans or do you succumb to the decadence of Kandide's purpose?' Which side do you assume in this matter?"

Clutching the dangling Banshee, she soared into the sky where a large male griffin met her.

THIRTY-NINE

From the cliffs above, General Kandour and Anile watched the battle below. Hundreds of injured Banshees and Fée, alike, were strewn across the snow-laden fields. Those who were able, continued to fight. Others lay paralyzed from the plaxiion-tipped arrows.

"I must say, I haven't had this much fun in decades, Anile," Kandour chuckled. A perverse grin crossed his face. "Listen to their screams. It's like a medley of macabre."

"Hey, that's a good one. I like that, 'a medley of macabre.' You're good. Real good."

"That I am. We really must do this again when I conquer Kandide's Kingdom."

"Yeah, that'll be even more fun. When do you want me to eliminate Prince Kilmonth and Prince Yandell? A little of that plaxiion on my knife and they're history."

"All in good time, my friend. All in good time. Right now, we still need them to ride victoriously with us so they can force the Crown from Cyndara or Lord Mywerk—or whoever has it by now. Once that is done we can easily eliminate them."

"Good thing you have 'em hidden away back at the camp. They'd just be causin' trouble here, not that they would go anywhere near the fighting—sniveling cowards that they are."

"True. And I must say, I am pleased at how well things are going.

We should have the Château completely under our control before noon."

"Not by noon, Kandour. Not ever," a raspy voice called out. "Let's see how smart you are in a contest with me." On another ledge, a few meters away, Matari hobbled forward. Waving his walking staff, he added, "Remember me, General?"

"Not really, old Fée. But shouldn't you be down there with your Imperfect friends?"

"Or in some home for the nearly dead," Anile mocked, spitting on the ground. "Hey look, he's missing an ear."

"So he is. Pretty nasty scar on his face, too. Who are you?"

"Name's Matari."

"Not General Matari? I thought we fed you to the garglans years ago. Looks like you let another one slip away, Anile. I hope it's not becoming a habit."

"Yeah, well I guess I'll just have to take care of him right now." Anile hurled his knife toward the feeble Fée. But Matari was gone. The blade bounced off the boulder behind where he had been standing.

Kandour was not at all amused. "You really are getting sloppy. Do you think you can take care of him, or must I do everything?"

"Well?" Matari reappeared in exactly the same spot. Picking up the knife, he added, "Nice blade. Tell me, assassin, is it the same one that cut off my ear?"

"I think it was this one." In an instant, Anile was holding another knife. Before he could toss it, however, a deafening screech was heard. Directly above, two paws with razor sharp talons reached down and lifted him high into the air. The four-inch claws were attached to a female griffin. Her white neck feathers and golden fur shone brightly against the dark clouds overhead.

Clutching the dangling Banshee, she soared into the sky where a large male griffin met her. Anile's indignant shrieks overpowered the screams from the battle below. His attempt to escape, however, was to no avail. In an aerial tug-of-war, the two powerful griffins made short work of him.

The fighting below came to an abrupt halt. Even the garglans paused to watch as his lifeless body fell to the ground.

"Poetic justice, don't you think?" Matari called to General Kandour. He then looked skyward again.

Twenty more griffins began circling above. Their screeches filled the air with an eerie sound that, for most, had not been heard in over a century. Just the sight of these magnificent creatures brought a sense of awe to everyone. Having thought them extinct, the Banshee soldiers stared in amazement.

Griffins were considered a symbol of strength and courage to their clans. Many a ruler had incorporated their likeness into his or her royal crest. But to Kandour's troops, they were known only in Banshee legends. Watching them kill Anile, the most feared assassin in all their land, was not a good omen.

"That was Gertie and her son, Courage," Matari added. "Mighty powerful griffins, they are. Mighty powerful. Guess they thought they'd even up the odds a bit. It's just you and me now, General. How brave are you without your murdering bodyguard to protect you?"

Kandour's eyes bulged. His entire body seethed with anger. He had lost his trusted friend, tricked by a half-witted Imperfect. "It will be a delight to kill you, myself, you old fool!"

"Fooling? No, I'm not fooling. I plan to kill you all by myself. Come on up here, or are you incapable of a fair fight?" Matari's body was frail and weak, but he spoke with an inner strength that would not be denied.

"Take one last look at your miserable homeland, old Fée, for it will be your last." With a gesture, Kandour instantly transported to the ledge where Matari was standing. "Pity I'm in such a hurry. I would enjoy making you suff—"

Before Kandour could finish his sentence, Matari snapped his fingers. The dimly glowing yellow ball on the top of his walking staff burst into flames. He tossed it into the tiny cave behind them. The last thing Kandour heard was a loud cracking noise before the cliff they were standing on gave way. As it fell, the entire side of the mountain blew apart.

Massive boulders showered down on top of them. The heavy stones formed a granite tomb at the bottom of the mountain. A thousand Banshee soldiers who waiting to be transported into battle were buried as well.

"Matari!" Trace screamed, watching helplessly as his friend disappeared beneath the tons of falling rock. He stared at what was, only seconds ago, the side of the mountain. A tear rolled down his cheek.

Standing in the watchtower atop the wall, Pell knew the battle was over. It was a bittersweet victory. *As are all victories where so many die,* he thought, disabling the trigger mechanism for the aerial bursts in case the Banshee soldiers should try to use them against the griffins. He quickly transported back to Trace. His voice revealed the sorrow he felt. "As a young lieutenant, I idolized General Matari. A braver soldier there never was."

"You knew him?" Trace asked.

"Only by sight. I was in his battalion during the Clan Wars. I think everyone who served under him will agree, there is no greater hero. He's the kind legends are made of and bards write songs about. He will surely assume his place of honor in the history of Calabiyau."

Trace softly sighed. "I only wish he had been honored while he was alive."

"It's the destiny of most heroes. Death claims its prize and in return affords immortality. I've never been convinced, however, that it's a fair trade."

"It's not." Trace shook his head. "But it is the destiny Matari chose. He belongs to eternity now, and for that I am grateful."

Looking up, Pell and Trace saw the sky filled with griffins. They were plucking garglans from the trees and dropping them into the fires below. The stench was gagging, but no one—not Banshee nor Fée—seemed to mind. The fighting had ended.

Without Kandour to lead them, the Banshee soldiers began a hasty withdrawal. It was a bitter retreat, but their only other choice was to surrender, and that they would never do. Being held prisoner by the Fée would be a far worse humiliation than their defeat. As the Banshees retreated over the back wall, a trumpet blasted, signaling the remaining soldiers who were still fighting in the front of the Château to also withdraw.

"Tori, see to the wounded," Trace ordered. "I'm going up front to let Selena know what has happened."

"I'll come with you." General Pell ordered his commanding officer to help Tori, then transported with Trace back to the Château.

Injured soldiers, both Fée and Banshees, were in every hallway and room. More were being brought in by the minute. Exhausted, Leanne and Selena, along with the others were helping as many as they could, still unaware that the fighting had stopped.

Selena glanced up to see Pell and Trace enter the makeshift clinic. "Thank the earthly spirits you're both safe. We saw the fires."

"The battle is over," Trace announced. All stopped what they were doing to listen to his words. "We won." A loud cheer erupted. "Matari killed General Kandour. His army has retreated."

"Ma… Matari? How?" Jake asked, having raced into the clinic as soon as he heard the Banshee trumpeters sound the retreat.

"He actually did have a plan," Trace explained. "He tricked Kandour onto a cliff where he was standing, then caused it to explode. They were both buried under the falling rock."

"Matari is…?" Selena's eyes filled with tears.

"I'm so sorry." Pell knew how badly the news hurt. "He was a great general until the end. Are you okay, Selena?"

"I will be. Thank you for asking, General." She looked out across the gardens. Even the freshly fallen snow could not conceal the streaks of purple-red blood. So many had already lost their lives and now this terrible news. "Matari was more than a great general. He is proof that every life is valuable, no matter what phase he or she is in."

"No one personified that more than him," Jake said. "Though, even I thought he had become just a kindly old man with visions of bygone glories. I was so wrong. So very wrong."

"We all thought that, Jake." Selena dabbed her eyes with the only clean corner of her bloodstained apron. "And we were all wrong."

"Do you think Kandour's army will re-group and return?" Leanne asked as she healed a soldier with a badly cut leg.

"Not without their leader," Pell assured her. "My guess is that most of them are halfway home by now."

"What about the Castle?" Selena had been so busy she hadn't had time to think about what might be happening with Kandide. "Do you think any of them will join his other army?"

"I doubt it. Kandour's generals will kill them for retreating, and they all know that. More than likely, they'll return to their clans and try to blend back in as though they'd never left. Though I doubt their welcome will be a warm one."

"I think he's right, Selena." Jake nodded in agreement. "In any case, I'm going to transport back to the Castle. General Pell, as soon as you've secured the grounds around the Château, please send as many of your troops back there as you can. I'm sure General Mintz could use the extra support."

"Of course. I'll leave a few dozen here to help with the injured and the rest should be ready to leave as soon as they are assembled."

"Be careful transporting, Jake," Selena cautioned. "We don't know what's happening there." She turned to Pell. "And thank you, General, and your soldiers for everything you've done for us. Matari was not the only courageous leader in this battle."

"It is I who must thank you, Selena. I've learned a great deal from all of you. And made some wonderful new friends." He turned to Trace and extended his hand. "I'd be proud to serve by your side anytime. They don't come any more courageous or honorable than you, my friend."

"I feel the same way about you, General. We've both learned a great deal. But there's much more to do, and right now the injured from both armies need our help." Trace walked over to Leanne and lifted a wounded soldier onto a makeshift bed so she could treat him. Turning back to Pell, he saluted.

LORD MYWERK AT THE CASTLE

FORTY

Lord Mywerk turned his majestic black horse to confront General Strands. His imposing stature amplified his words: "As your acting King, I stand by the Banshee throne." He shifted his attention to the vast army of Banshee soldiers: "This is not your fight. You have been sent here as a diversionary tactic. Kandour's real goal is to conquer the Château in the Mists. He gets the spoils of that Kingdom, while you return home empty handed. Tell them, General Strands, why do you, and not General Kandour, command here if conquering Calabiyau Proper is your purpose? Reveal the deceitful plan that he and this Fire Fée traitor have devised to gain control of their respective thrones."

More murmurs erupted throughout the Banshee troops. They quickly transformed into hostile shouts:

"Where is General Kandour?"

"Why isn't he here?"

"What spoils do we get?"

"Silence! I say silence!" Strands ordered, eventually quieting the legions. "Tell us, Lady Aron, if we agree to your offer, what spoils will you give my troops?"

She wasted no time in answering: "The chance to return to your clans as the victors of a world that is free from Imperfects. Plus a plot of land along the neutral zone for each who support this most noble of causes."

Owning land was the life-long dream of most Banshees—something many could never hope to realize since the Crown owned most of the Banshee Kingdom. Lady Aron knew her proposal would win them over. And it did. Cheering broke out.

"We accept your representation, Lady Aron," General Strands shouted, knowing that if she wins, he would also benefit. And if she lost, he would simply retreat and wait until Kandour assumed the throne to strike again.

"So, Your Majesty," Lady Aron called to Kandide, "you've heard General Strands' reply. Do you stand by your offer?"

"Please," Teren pleaded, "you don't have to do this, Kandide."

"You're wrong, Teren. I do have to do this. We will never live in peace while she's alive."

"Then let my soldiers put an arrow through her chest right now," Mintz offered. "I have archers standing by."

"An arrow yes, but I must do it. And in a fair fight."

Impatient for an answer, Lady Aron called again, "What is your answer, Queen Kandide? Or is it that you have no courage or integrity when it comes to facing a real opponent in a real battle?"

"You dare speak of courage and integrity, Firenza? My sister, Tara, has revealed to all that it was you who spelled her in that block of ice. It was on your orders that I was taken captive, and it was you who ordered Lady Batony to be brutally murdered."

From both the Banshee and the Fée armies, angry shouts erupted once again.

"Silence!" Lady Aron ordered, sending a sheet of flames above their heads. "I have been falsely accused of these heinous crimes by my own Queen. And yet she presents no proof."

This time it was troops from Mintz's army who did the shouting. "Princess Tara told us what happened," someone hollered out.

"Yeah, she says it was you," another joined in.

"Again, I beseech you to let me speak. You have not heard my side."

Lady Aron was not about to back down. "Our very future is at stake." The shouting stopped, as all waited to hear what she had to say.

"Tara claims that it was I who entombed her. And yet, I ask you, who deceived her own subjects by bringing Cyndara to use a Glamour spell to make it look as though the Princess was set free? Was that not you, Kandide? Could it be that you and the Crown Princess used this same glamour to make Tara's real captor look like me? I contend it was you who perpetrated this horrible deed. All I know is that your true allegiance lies with the Château and those Imperfects you have chosen over your own subjects."

A swift undercurrent of questioning flowed throughout the troops.

"If what I say is false," Lady Aron continued, "then explain why you ordered nearly half of our army to defend Jake's Kingdom, instead of keeping them here where they are desperately needed? We all know that it was Lady Batony who came to your room to facilitate your alleged kidnapping. You then had her killed so she could not reveal the truth. No, Kandide, it is you who are the true villain. And yet, despite all of the treacherous deeds you have done, I openly stand here in accordance with your offer, ready to challenge you by proving my worthiness and loyalty to Calabiyau Proper."

"What say you, Your Majesty, about her accusations?" General Strands shouted.

Taking Kandide's arm, Teren, again, pleaded, "You've got to let General Mintz put an arrow in her heart and end this craziness. If you can't do that, let me transport her to some far off cave and seal it shut."

"No, Teren. Those who believe me will continue to do so. But there is nothing I can say right now to convince those who choose to believe her. Following through with my offer is the only way to prove that I am worthy to rule. I must openly defeat her, once and for all."

"Do you cower from an answer, Your Majesty?" Lady Aron chided. "Or are you only brave behind Cyndara's cloak of Glamour?"

Both armies stood in silence awaiting her response.

Ignoring Lady Aron's question, Kandide turned her focus to Strands: "General, since Lady Aron is now your designated contender, do you agree to obey by the Banshee rules for her challenge? Do you agree that the victor is the rightful Queen of Calabiyau Proper, and that you will withdraw your troops?"

"Of course, Your Majesty." He bowed in a manner that showed genuine respect for her courage.

"Banshee Honor?" General Mintz called in a loud voice.

"Banshee Honor," Strands pledged.

"Then your challenge to my Crown stands, Firenza." Kandide's words resounded with the nobility of a true leader. "According to Banshee law, I must select the game."

The snow began falling even harder. Lady Aron pulled the hood of her red cape over her head. "What is your choice, Kandide?"

FORTY-ONE

Neither Banshee nor Fée uttered a sound. Holding her golden bow with arrow poised, Kandide aimed it at Lady Aron. Releasing the projectile, it landed just inches from her feet.

Firenza didn't try to avoid the arrow nor divert it from its path. Instead, she reached down and pulled it from the snow-covered ground. "Archery it is." She placed it in her own quiver, warning, "You will meet this very arrow again, Your Majesty. Shall we say the gaming woods in an hour?"

Kandide's only response was a regal nod. Another cheer rang out. Within seconds, odds-makers began emerging from the Banshee troops. As was always the case with battle games, everyone was eager to get in on the action. Would Kandide win? Would Lady Aron win? This battle was turning out to be much different than anyone could have imagined—and far more interesting.

General Mintz escorted Kandide down the spiral stairs of the watchtower. "Why archery, Your Majesty? You could have easily beaten her at aercaen."

"I know that. You know that. And so does everyone else. It's no different than the rationale Lord Mywerk used in the second challenge with Cyndara. He could have easily beaten her in archery, like her brothers wanted. But he knew it was unfair, as her skills in that game are not equal to his. If I were to beat Firenza at a game that she's not particularly good at, my victory, like his, would be accepted, but not respected."

"At least it would be a victory!" Teren exclaimed, having followed them to the bottom of the tower steps.

"Not really. If we are ever to live in peace, I must prove my worth in a way that even the Banshees understand and respect. Archery is their expertise, as well as Lady Aron's. The Banshee's know of her exceptional skill with a bow and arrow. A win by me will ensure their respect."

Mintz was not at all in favor of what she was about to do. "I know you're right, Your Majesty, however…"

"Don't worry, General, I'll win. Besides, I have the bow father made for me. There is none more accurate."

"I could put a spell on her," Teren offered, "so she can't shoot straight."

"Not this time, little brother. I have to win this fight on my own." Looking at how grown-up he had become in just the past few months, Kandide quickly added, "I guess I shouldn't call you that any more. You're almost as tall as I am."

"You can call me anything you want, as long as you win. I can't even imagine what she would be like as Queen. We'd be sent back to the dark years."

"That Firenza would most assuredly do." Tiyana met them as they walked into the Castle. "You'll beat her, Kandide, I have no doubt. Your father's wisdom in having you play all those games in the forest with him will finally be put to good use."

"Father was smart in training me so well, Mother. Now, I need to change clothes. This battle armor will hardly do in the woods." Kandide transported to her bedchamber where Mylea had already laid out her clothes. There was nothing discreet about her selection with its golden crest emblazoned on the front for all to see. She would go to battle as a Queen and return as the undisputed leader.

"Perhaps you should listen to General Mintz," Mylea suggested as she helped Kandide dress. "You don't have to do this. That's why we have an army."

"I've listened to all my trusted advisors, Mylea. Their words are wise, but they don't change the facts: I made the choice to uphold the rights of Imperfects. I made the choice to save my sister and deploy the Frost that destroyed most of the summer harvest. I made the choice to send half of our army to defend the Château. None of those choices were popular with my subjects. And I would make each of them again, even if it meant losing the Crown."

Mylea fastened Kandide's protective vest. She had helped raise her since she was born. To see this once self-centered child become a passionate advocate of the very Fée she once disdained was worth all the tantrums she had endured while Kandide was growing up. "You also sent food and gold to every village," Mylea reminded her. "You set free the farm boy who tried to murder you. Strengthened the treaty between our Kingdom and Cyndara's. And, you outwitted Lady Aron when she had you kidnapped."

"And I'm going to outwit her again. Father taught me many things. But perhaps the most important is that no one should ever let anyone else determine another's self worth. I have great things to do for all my subjects. And I will do them."

Mylea handed Kandide her quiver and bow. "I'm so proud of you."

"I know you are. And soon you're going to be even prouder."

In Kandide's heart, she also knew that in an archery game based on skill alone, she could never out-shoot Lady Aron. She had watched Firenza compete in many tournaments, all of which she won.

This game, however, would take place in a ten-hectare gaming section of the forest not far from the Castle. It's an area that Kandide was very familiar with, having competed there many times with her father. Winning in this arena requires strategy, wit, and cunning, far more than skill.

And that I am exceptionally good at, she thought. This would not be an easy victory. Her confidence was high. Her determination even higher. *Only one of us will return from the woods as Calabiyau's Queen. And it's going to be me.*

FORTY-TWO

"Each of you will have your bow, twenty-six arrows, and a shield," announced General Mintz. He and General Strands were with Lady Aron and Kandide near the edge of the gaming woods. "The use of flaming tips is not allowed." Mintz directed his comment to Lady Aron. "Since this challenge cannot be a battle to the death, the winner will be declared when one of you has taken the bow, quiver, and shield from the other. You may injure, but not kill one another."

Lady Aron listened without emotion. Her entire focus was on winning this fight. Remaining calm was essential. She looked every bit a warrior. Dressed in a deep red gaming suit that appeared as though it had been crafted from the very flames she was forbidden to use, it was a sharp contrast to Kandide's white and gold attire. Both of their outfits were very different from the normal green and brown worn in most archery games. But then this was a very different type of battle.

"Other than these rules, and competing entirely on your own," General Strands added, "there is only one other rule. You may use any type of magic you like, except spells that inhibit the other from free will or free movement. The challenge is archery, not spell-weaving. Do you both agree?" They each nodded yes.

"Good. Then when one of you emerges from the woods with the other's shield, quiver, and bow the game will be over and the winner shall assume the throne. Do you each agree to this as well?"

"Of course," Lady Aron replied. "Do you agree, Your Majesty?"

Kandide answered by stating, "You may sound the starting horn, General Strands."

A military trumpet heralded the beginning of the game. The two Fée headed into the forest, moving in opposite directions from each other. The heavily wooded area was dense with ferns and fresh-smelling pine. The rugged landscape, steep trails, and a fast moving river that divided it down the middle, made the battle more about strategy than mere skill.

It was a terrain that Kandide knew well. Her first thought was to transport to the old water wheel—a place where she could be protected from an attack from the rear. Lady Aron would know this, however, and assume it to be Kandide's first strategic move. *Better to be the hunter, than the hunted*, she thought as she transported to the upper branch of a tall tree. From there she was able to search the woods for any sign of the Fire Fée.

It was also a strategy Lady Aron had anticipated. With her arrow notched, she ever so quietly drew back her bow. In an instant, the projectile was released, aimed directly at Kandide's left leg.

Reappearing behind Firenza, Kandide called: "You have twenty five left, so you'll need to do a lot better than that." She released an arrow of her own. It landed in the exact center of Lady Aron's shield.

"Now I have twenty six again," she retorted, vanishing; only to reappear not more than ten meters away near a large outcropping of stones. Before she could take aim, Kandide, once again, disappeared. At the back of the outcropping was a cave-like opening. Trapping Firenza inside would quickly end the game.

Shafts of light danced across Firenza's feet. Realizing that she may have placed herself in danger, she whirled around, just in time to block yet another arrow with her shield. "It appears the odds are in my favor, now," she said, once again removing the arrow from it. "You won't win this time, Kandide. That I promise." Her words, however, fell on

KANDIDE IN THE BATTLE
WITH LADY ARON

emptiness. Kandide was already gone.

For several more hours, the two played a game of cat and mouse. It was not uncommon when two opponents were so equally skilled, for the games to go on for days—until one or the other became tired and began making mistakes. This battle game would be no exception.

FORTY-THREE

"Are you saying, Jake, that General Kandour is dead?" Tiyana was stunned. She, along with Teren, Tara, and General Mintz met him in the war room. It was the best place to view the gaming field.

"Yes, Tiyana. The battle is over and we've won."

"That's great!" Teren was overjoyed. "But then…then Kandide's challenge is for nothing. We have to stop it, right now."

"I'm afraid we cannot do that," Mintz responded. "To stop it would undermine her power and authority."

"What challenge, General Mintz?" Jake asked.

"To avoid an all out war, Kandide offered to do battle, one-on-one, for the right to the throne. Lady Aron challenged her, and now they are in the gaming woods in a fight to be Queen.

Jake could not believe what he was hearing. He had expected to return, tell them about Kandour, and the fighting would be over. "How could you let her do that?"

"How could he stop her?" Tiyana asked. "General Mintz had no knowledge of her plan until she announced it in front of both armies."

Jake shook his head. "That sounds like Kandide."

"Does General Strands know that Kandour's dead?" Tara asked.

"If he doesn't by now," Jake replied, "I'm sure he will soon enough. Several thousand Banshees had already withdrawn by the time I left."

"General Mintz," Tiyana said, "there must be some way we can stop this senseless battle between Firenza and Kandide."

"Even if we tried, I don't think your daughter would allow it."

"Sir!" Captain Denan came rushing into the war room. I have a message from Lord Mywerk and General Strands. They must speak to you immediately."

"Sounds like they've heard the news. Let's go find out." Mintz motioned for the others to follow him.

General Strands and Lord Mywerk were standing just outside the Castle wall, not far from where Kandide and Lady Aron began the game.

Strands was the first to speak: "My scouts tell me that General Kandour has been killed and that his army has retreated."

Mintz nodded. "Jake just told us the same thing."

"Then with Kandour's disgrace, our allegiance to him ceases. My troops will withdraw immediately and return to their homes. Lord Mywerk, until the Chessaé games can be decided, we will serve you as our acting King." Saying no more, he saluted Mintz then departed, stopping only long enough to order the retreat of his army.

"What will happen to him?" Teren asked Mywerk.

"If he's lucky, one of his officers will kill him. It's a shame. Believe it or not—and though he dislikes me—of all Kandour's reporting generals, Strands was the most reasonable. I doubt, however, that Cyndara or General Slant will agree to let him live."

"What if he doesn't go home?" Tara asked.

"He'll go home or his family will pay the price. It's a question of Banshee Honor."

Tiyana shook her head, sighing, "I fear, Lord Mywerk... I mean King Mywerk, I will never accept many of your clans' ways."

"Do call me Lord Mywerk until I am formally crowned. In any case, Tiyana, nor will I ever accept many of my clans' ways. And I share their blood."

"Fortunately for us, you're not of their mind," General Mintz told him. "And thank you for all your help. It was a very dangerous and noble thing you did out there."

"It was the honorable thing to do. I only wish the news of Kandour's death had gotten to us sooner. Perhaps we could have avoided the challenge between Kandide and Lady Aron."

"Perhaps it is her destiny," Mintz replied. "She feels it necessary to prove her worth. We can only hope that the fates are on her side."

"Will you stay to see the outcome?" Jake asked Mywerk, looking toward the woods. If only he knew what was happening—if Kandide was okay.

"I can remain here if you so desire. Though I feel it is my duty to return home as quickly as possible, as I am sure Cyndara and General Slant will be anxious to know what has transpired—on all fronts. As you know, Slant stayed with her in case Kandour had a third attack planned. And there is, after all, still the matter of Cyndara's brothers to contend with. I assume that one of Kandour's officers has informed Prince Kilmonth and Prince Yandell by now of his death."

"I'll bet those two are trying to figure out what to do next," Teren said with a laugh. "I sure would have liked to have seen their faces when they heard the news."

"Yeah, but I sure would not want to be the one who told them," Tara added.

"Dealing with them swiftly will be important to maintaining stability," Mywerk said. "Cyndara will need my help with that, as well."

"Then please, Lord Mywerk, return home," Tiyana urged. "And I, too, cannot thank you enough for all you've done—both for our Kingdom and for Teren and Adriana."

"I hope it's the beginning of a true and lasting peace between our Kingdoms. May the earthly spirits now protect Her Majesty."

*"That is the problem with integrity,
Your Majesty. I don't play by that rule."*

FORTY-FOUR

Silence commandeered the forest. Only the occasional black crow could be heard cawing warnings. Other than that, all was quiet, very quiet. When battle games ensued, the woodland animals headed for the safety of their dens, caves, or nests.

Kandide listened for the slightest sound—leaves rustling, a twig breaking, branches bending—anything that would reveal Lady Aron's location. Her sense of hearing was heightened. Her concentration, however, abruptly ended when the sound of trumpets reverberated through the trees.

Not knowing why or what was happening, Kandide could only assume it was for the Banshee army to withdraw until she or Lady Aron emerged as the victor. *Soon they'll be heralding my victory,* she thought, *and Calabiyau will be safe for all Fée.*

The momentary halt in their fighting was as brief as the trumpets' call for retreat. From hunter to hunted, both Kandide and Lady Aron continued to use skill, strategy, and magic—creating noises where none existed, flashes of colors when no one was there, and firing arrows without an archer—yet neither seemed to be able to gain the advantage. If ever two warriors were equally matched, this battle was certainly seemed to be the case.

The hours lumbered on as the sun climbed directly overhead and then slowly descended into the western sky. Night shadows replaced streaks of sunlight and darkness began to diminish their ability to see. For Kandide, nightfall created a slight advantage, as all Fire Fée, even if they reduce their energy output, give off a faint glow that can be seen in the dark by a discerning eye. Albeit slight, it was an advantage that Kandide was eager to utilize. She also knew that she must conserve her energy. This would not be a short battle.

Suddenly, something happened that neither Fée anticipated. Nearly a dozen hissing garglans appeared in the trees that surrounded them. Their bat-like wings created a chilling flapping sound—a sound Kandide knew all too well. She whirled around just in time to see one of the vicious beasts leap toward Lady Aron, knocking her to the ground. With her arrow already notched, Kandide easily killed the creature. Covered in black slime, Firenza pushed the garglan away, only to see another fall dead near the first. Kandide's second arrow had also hit its mark.

"If either of us is to survive," she called to the Fire Fée, "we'll need to fight these things together." Kandide took aim at a third hissing beast. It dropped from the branch above, an arrow through its heart.

Standing up, Lady Aron moved close to Kandide. "I know why I must keep you alive," she said quickly taking out two more of the hideous creatures. "But tell me, Kandide, why didn't you let that beast kill me? The Crown would then be yours."

"Being devoured by a garglan is not a fate I would wish on anyone, not even you, Firenza. Besides, we both agreed to the rules—that this cannot be a fight to the death, and that I must and will defeat you myself." They each sent several more arrows flying, and several more of the beasts fell to the ground.

"How noble of you. I'm afraid, however, that your nobility will be your demise." Turning, she grabbed Kandide's arm, shoving her to the ground. Lady Aron released another arrow, killing a huge garglan as it leapt toward them. Its wings were almost two meters across and its claws were aimed at Kandide's throat.

They both stared at the carnage. Garglans littered the small clearing. The nauseating stench was enough to make their stomachs queasy. Kandide rose to her feet—standing back-to-back with Lady Aron. Splattered with black slime, they searched the trees for more of the vicious creatures.

"That seems to be all of them," Lady Aron finally said.

"I hope so." Kandide turned to face her. "Thank you. We're even now."

"No, Kandide, we are not." With her arrow inches away from Kandide's shoulder, Lady Aron continued, "What a pity, you seem to have dropped your shield. And don't even think of transporting. My arrow will pin you to that tree long before you can disappear. Once that happens, the Crown is mine."

Kandide felt the arrow's tip pressing into to her skin. "You're right, Firenza, I should have let that garglan kill you."

"That is the problem with integrity, Your Majesty. I don't play by that rule. Now, drop your bow."

"It doesn't appear that you play by any rules." Kandide tossed her bow aside. During that momentary distraction, she also threw her body sideways, barely escaping Lady Aron's arrow. A split-second later, she vanished, reappearing directly behind the Fire Fée. With a powerful blow to her neck, Lady Aron dropped to her knees. "Your problem, Firenza, is that you're so eager to claim your prize, you get careless."

Before Lady Aron knew what had happened, an arrow pierced her left shoulder. She collapsed, face down, on the ground.

Stunned, Kandide looked to see where it came from. Prince Yandell and Prince Kilmonth were standing a few meters behind her.

Kilmonth lowered his bow. "Thought you might need some help, Your Majesty."

"Yeah, we thought you might need some help," Yandell repeated.

"You fools!" Kandide shouted, bending down to see if they had killed her. "You simple-minded fools!"

Kilmonth walked toward her. "Now that's no way to talk to us, after we went and helped you like that."

His brother followed him. "Yeah, that's no way to talk to us, after we helped you. Besides, she's not dead... yet." He pulled out his knife. "I can take care of that."

"Put that thing away," Kandide ordered. "What are you doing here?"

"We told you, we came to help," Kilmonth told her.

"Yeah, we heard about the challenge," Yandell added, "and figured if we helped you win, you'd say good things about us to our sister, being that you're friends and all."

"Or maybe even let us stay in your Kingdom. Now that General Kandour is dead, we don't have any place to go right now."

"Kandour is... He's dead?" Kandide couldn't believe what she was hearing. "Then the Château... it's safe?"

"Yep," Yandell replied. Too bad, too. Now I won't get my own Kingdom. And King Yandell had a really good ring to it."

"That's why we don't have a place to go," Kilmonth explained. "So, how about it? We helped you, and if you help us, we'll tell everyone how the attack on the Château was all Lady Aron's idea. Even about the treaty she forced us to sign so we wouldn't attack your Castle."

"If Lady Aron is on your side, why didn't you shoot me?"

"Because you got the Gift." Yandell slid his knife into a sheath on his belt. "Besides, we don't trust her."

"That's right, Your Majesty, we don't trust her. Never did. She's got no integrity. Just look how she betrayed you just now—especially after you saved her from those garglans and all. It's not honorable to do that. Is it, little brother?"

"Nope, big brother, it's not honorable to betray someone who saves your life. And since we know the truth about her, we figure she'd for sure betray us."

"Besides," Kilmonth insisted, "we warned her about it being bad luck to attack on Yandell's birthday."

"Yeah, we warned her not to attack today. It's my birthday. She got what she deserved." He spit on the ground. "And I didn't even get a party. So, how about you giving me a birthday present in exchange for us tellin' everyone what she did?"

Though Kandide would never understand what Banshee's consider honorable, she also knew that since she was not the one who shot Lady Aron, she could not legitimately claim victory. If these two would, indeed, tell what they knew about Firenza's plot, Lady Aron would be forced to stand trial. "Banshee Honor you'll testify against her?"

"You'll let us stay in your Kingdom?" Kilmonth pressed.

Looking from one to the other, Kandide nodded. "You may live where you like. But protection from Cyndara's wrath, that I cannot promise."

"Deal!" Kilmonth hastily extended his hand.

She ignored it. "Swearing Banshee Honor is sufficient. Now swear it, both of you. I need to get Firenza back to the Castle or she will die."

"So?" Yandell shrugged.

"Just swear it," Kandide ordered. "Then help me get her back to the Castle."

"I swear to tell the truth about Lady Aron's plot with General Kandour," Kilmonth declared. "Banshee Honor." He elbowed Yandell to do the same.

"I swear, too—Banshee Honor."

"Happy Birthday, Yandell. You and your brother can remain in Calabiyau Proper. Now, lift her up and be gentle. Then let's transport out of here."

He did as she requested—though none too gently. In a gesture, the four of them vanished, reappearing moments later at the edge of the woods where the challenge first began. Cheers rang out as Kandide appeared. Seeing Lady Aron in the arms of Prince Yandell, however, prompted the excitement to transform into a rush of questions.

"Get Tara," Kandide ordered one of the soldiers. "Firenza won't last much longer.

"What happened?" General Mintz asked.

"More importantly, what are they doing here?" Jake motioned toward Kilmonth and Yandell. "Are you alright, Kandide?"

"I'll explain about them later." She wiped black slime from her face. "And yes, I'm fine, other than being a bit of a mess."

"Garglans." Teren knew that smell. "They were this far into the woods?"

"Yeah, a whole bunch of 'em," Kilmonth said. "We helped kill 'em. Lady Aron caught an arrow. Isn't that right, Your Majesty?"

"Yeah, isn't that right, Your Majesty?" Yandell reiterated as he placed Firenza on a nearby bench.

Kandide looked from one brother to the other. "We'll discuss it later." Spotting Tara, she asked, "Can you can save her?"

"Mother!" Egan screamed, pushing his way through the large crowd that had gathered around them. "Mother!" He reached for her lifeless hand.

Standing motionless, Tara stared at the Fée who had entrapped her in the ice, who tried to poison Egan, who sent Teren and Adriana into the human realm to die a terrible death, who burned villages with no remorse, and who kidnapped Kandide. Though her instinct was to save lives, at that moment she would rather save a garglan than Lady Aron. "I…I don't know…"

"Please, Princess Tara. Please," Egan begged. "Don't let her die. No matter what she's done, she's still my mother."

Tara hesitated. Seeing the anguish in Egan's eyes, she reluctantly kneeled down to examine Lady Aron. "Your mother's very weak. I… I'm not sure if I can do anything."

"Please try," Egan pleaded. "Please."

Tara looked at him. In her heart she knew she could never let anyone die, even Firenza. "I'll do my best." She placed her hands on

Lady Aron, infusing her with a small amount of energy. Without it, she would not survive the arrow being removed. Tara carefully pulled it from her back. "If it had been any closer, it would have pierced her heart." She placed her hands on the open wound. Slowly, the bleeding stopped and the skin began to knit back together. As it did, Lady Aron's color returned and she regained consciousness.

"Mother," Egan called.

"Alin," she whispered, her vision still blurred. "You're here?"

"It's Egan. Kandide brought you out of the woods and Princess Tara healed you."

Her eyes began to focus. Looking first at him, then Tara, and finally at Kandide, Lady Aron smiled. "You never learn, do you?"

In a muted flash, she slowly dissolved into nothingness.

"No one does vanity better than you, Kandide."

FORTY-FIVE

The testimony of Prince Kilmonth and Prince Yandell dispelled any doubt of Lady Aron's involvement with General Kandour and the Banshee attack on the Château. Though an intense search of the Kingdom failed to locate the Fire Fée, the High Council tried and convicted her of treason, issuing a proclamation for her arrest.

They also awarded Matari Calabiyau's highest honor for his bravery, as well as declared seven days of reverence in tribute to his life. General Mintz's entire army saluted him during the ceremonies that were presided over by Jake, Selena, Trace, Kandide, and General Pell. All five stood on the same balcony where Kandide's own subjects had booed her when they discovered she was an Imperfect.

On this day, however, her speech was greeted very differently. "General Matari will forever live as an example that *all* life is valuable," she stated. "We must never allow anyone to be treated with disrespect. Not the young. Not the old. Not the injured. Not anyone. Our Kingdom has taken a colossal step forward. It's time for old wounds to heal, arguments to be set aside, and a higher consciousness to reign. Just as Mother Nature has blanketed our world in snow so it can rest, we must put to rest our differences and allow the beauty of this great land to guide the way we treat others."

"We are Fée," she continued, "the most magical of all beings. We can use our special talents for good or evil. It's time to use them for good—to become the wisest and most caring of all beings. To shed masks of deceit and transform our land into a world where kindness is strength, and cruelty is weakness. As your Queen and the daughter of King Toeyad—the greatest King Calabiyau has ever known—I pledge this to you: I will never allow evil or treachery to rule. Each of you will control your own destiny, regardless of who you are. Each of you will be free to become all you can be, regardless of your age or physical condition. And I will give my life to ensure that each of you can live in peace, regardless of where you dwell. Hail, Calabiyau!"

"Hail, Calabiyau!" the crowd began chanting. Pride raced through the thousands who attended the ceremonies. "Long Live Queen Kandide." "Long Live Queen Kandide." The cheers continued long after she left the balcony.

No one was prouder of Kandide than Tiyana. "Age doth find wisdom," Toeyad had told her when she questioned their daughter's selfish behavior. *How Kandide has changed in just one year,* she thought. *How proud Toeyad would be of her. And how much like her father she has become. Yes, Calabiyau will be strong again, and Kandide will lead us to that victory.*

"That was an awesome speech," Teren told his sister as she walked into the Receiving Room.

"I know. I mean… uh, thank you, Teren. I'm glad you liked it."

"I liked your first answer better. Don't go changing too much. No one does vanity better than you, Kandide. Besides, if you get too nice, what will Jake and I have to complain about?"

"Jake complains about me being vain? Jake…" She waved him to come over. "Teren says you complain about me being vain."

He grinned. "Well, a…only when you are."

"Really? Well, let me tell you both something; it's not vanity when it's true."

Teren turned to Jake. "She's back."

"And as for you, Teren, when are you going to stop telling Kandide everything I say?" Jake playfully scolded.

"Oh, now it's my fault."

"It's always your fault, Teren." Kandide winked at him. "It always has been."

"I'm going back to the Bardic Council. At least when I get abused there, I learn a new spell."

"Not until my...I mean our wedding. We have a lot to do. Right, Jake? And I need your help, Teren, to weave the magic."

"I'll think about it. But right now, Tara and I are going ice skating." He snapped his fingers and two pairs of ice skates appeared, one white and one black. "Hey, Tara, ready to go?" he called.

She walked over to them. "Awesome speech, Kandide. Sure, let's go, before it snows again." The two of them ran off.

"What's with this word 'awesome?'" Kandide asked Jake.

"Teren learned it in the human realm. It seems like everyone is saying it now."

"Really? That's kind of... well, awesome," she said, mimicking her brother. "Want to go ice skating?"

"Right now?"

"Why not?"

"Yeah, why not?" Jake snapped his fingers and both of them were dressed in clothes much more appropriate for an afternoon on the ice than the formal attire they were previously wearing. He handed her the matching pair of skates that had also materialized. "What do you think?"

"I think I look perfect... and so do you."

"What about your wedding plans, Kandide?" Tiyana called, as they headed out of the room.

"I'll work on them later."

"That's my Kandide," Tiyana told Selena.

"That's *our* Kandide," Selena replied. "Some parts of her personality will never change. So, Tiyana, want to join them on the ice?"

Tiyana looked at her twin sister. "To quote Kandide, 'Why not?'"

The afternoon was cool, but sunny—the air fresh, invigorating, and the ice was perfect for skating. It wasn't long before the frozen lake near the Castle was overflowing with skaters. Egan started a snowball fight that got everyone involved, and then snuck away to build a winged snowman.

This is the only kind of fighting we should ever be doing in Calabiyau, Kandide thought, dodging Teren's carefully aimed snowball. "Oh, no you don't." She scooped up a ball of snow and hurled it toward him.

"Oh, yes I do." He vanished, reappeared behind her, and slipped a chunk of ice down her back.

"Hey, that's cheating." She untucked her blouse so the ice could fall out.

"Who's cheating?" Jake skated over to her.

"Me," Kandide grinned. This time Jake was the target as she stuffed a snowball down his shirt. Then quickly skated away.

"Are you sure you want to marry her?" Teren asked, watching him try to shake out the wet snow.

"Somebody has to. Don't worry, I'll get even." He skated after her.

• • • •

In the ensuing days, a sense of hope and enlightenment rippled throughout the Kingdom. Calabiyau was finally at peace. For the first time in almost a year, the raids on the villages stopped, as did the protests. Kandide was certain Lady Aron would reappear one day, but that didn't stop her from continuing to enjoy the winter weather… or planning her wedding to Jake.

As the arrangements got underway, so did Cyndara and Lord Mywerk's rematch of the second game of Chessaé. The four-tiered playing boards were put back in place, the bleachers installed, and the Pixies' costumes were more elaborate then ever.

Everyone who could cram into the courtyard attended—everyone except Cyndara's brothers. They disappeared shortly after testifying against Lady Aron. Kandide heard rumors that they were living in a small thatched-roof cottage near the neutral zone. But as she told Cyndara, they were only rumors and no one had actually seen them.

The Banshee Princess was far more interested in resettling the troops who had been transported back to her Kingdom during the battle at the Château. After swearing their allegiance to the Crown, they were sent home without penalty.

Now it was time to focus on Chessaé. Kandide, Jake, and Lord Rössi sat in the same balcony where they had watched the first Game. It was a long and competitive match with a great deal of fanfare and excitement, but Cyndara finally won. When her Pixie-king playing piece took his place in the center of the four spaces on the top gaming board, all cheered her victory. Copper mugs sloshed cushla as the onlookers toasted her success, and the bet-makers paid those who had wagered on the Crown Princess.

A broad smile crossed Lord Rössi's face. "It's wonderful that she won."

"Yes, it is." Kandide, as well, could not contain her joyful smile. "I must say, however, I've completely changed my opinion of Lord Mywerk, even though I still don't quite understand him."

"I don't think any of us do," Jake said above the raucous applause. "It'll be interesting to see what happens in the final game. And it looks like he's going to issue the challenge right now."

Standing on the balcony that was one floor below and across from them, Mywerk silenced the crowd. "I, Lord Mywerk, issue my final challenge for the right to the throne."

Cyndara calmly replied, "We are one-to-one in the Chessaé matches, Lord Mywerk. Your challenge is both proper and accepted. I now must select the final battle Game. Will you agree to my choice?"

"I will."

Cyndara's mind flashed back to all that had occurred. The fighting was over, but the battle for solidarity was yet to be won. It would take strength and accord to unite her Kingdom. She glanced across the courtyard at Lord Rössi, her expression frozen from the knowledge that to a Royal, duty over desire must always prevail. Cyndara scanned the large crowd before speaking: "Then I choose the most challenging and difficult game of all..."

Throughout the assemblage, no one breathed. Her choice would most certainly be Chessaé, and yet, what did she mean "the most challenging and difficult game of all?" All waited to hear what the Crown Princess would say.

"I, your acting Queen, Cyndara, challenge you, Lord Mywerk, contender to my Crown, to the most challenging game of all... marriage."

Her subjects sat in stunned silence. What had they just heard? Marriage?

Kandide broke out in laughter. "Marriage? I should have known Cyndara would have yet another clever trick up those flowing sleeves." She could tell that Lord Mywerk was also caught off guard. It was a reaction she had never seen from him.

Stepping forward, he graciously bowed. "I..." He paused. "I... accept your challenge, Your Highness."

Everyone began cheering and chanting: "Long live Queen Cyndara! Long Live King Mywerk!" Even the Pixies joined in, somersaulting and tumbling up and down the Chessaé boards. Colorful bursts of light exploded overhead. It was time for a celebration and Cyndara had arranged to kick this one off in style.

Banshees love games. But they love celebrations even more. And this one, which would culminate in both a wedding and the crowning of not only a Queen, but also a King, would be talked about for decades. Most agreed that they had been far too long without a formal ruler. Finally, their Kingdom would be stable again.

Kandide glanced at Lord Rössi, whose smile had faded. "Cyndara may marry Lord Mywerk," she whispered, "but her heart will always be with you."

"In the world of the royals," he replied, "heart rarely matters."

"Perhaps not with Banshees, Lord Rössi, but in Calabiyau Proper, my heart will always belong to Jake."

"Remember that the next time you think about putting snow down my shirt," Jake teased.

"I'll try. I do, however, have an idea, Jake."

"Am I going to like it?"

"I hope so—a double wedding in the neutral zone for all to see. It will show the unity between our two Kingdoms in a way nothing else can."

Jake nodded. "I think it's a great idea."

It was also an idea that both Lord Mywerk and Cyndara wholeheartedly embraced. "It will launch an entirely new chapter for both Kingdoms," Mywerk stated. "One of peace and prosperity."

"Perhaps even equality," Cyndara smlied at Kandide. "I think we have some planning to do."

"Not to mention dresses to design." Kandide's eyes sparkled. "And I already have a few ideas."

"Then why are we standing here?" Cyndara asked. It was the first time Kandide had ever seen her truly at ease.

• • • •

With the wedding day rapidly approaching, thousands of Banshees began to gather along their side of the neutral zone, as did thousands of Fée along their side. This was a celebration no one wanted to miss.

"That's the farm boy who tried to kill you," General Mintz whispered. "I'll have him arrested."

FORTY-SIX

Finally, the big day arrived. Kandide's wedding dress with its flowing train seemed to change color each time she moved. It looked like a shimmering rainbow of iridescent hues. Her crown was fashioned from more than a hundred perfectly matched diamonds. It rested lightly on her silver and gold curls and sparkled like a halo of heavenly stars.

Cyndara was dressed in a floor-length gown of vibrant blue and shimmering silver. A ring of blue sapphires and another of canary diamonds crowned her blue-black hair. Dangling strands of the vividly colored diamonds framed her face. Both brides looked more beautiful than anyone could have imagined.

Jake was dressed all in green, and his eyes sparkled even more than usual. Lord Mywerk traded his burgundy attire for deep blue. A large star sapphire replaced his ruby clasp.

Seated in two golden chariots that were drawn by the griffins, the betrothed couples sailed across the sky. Throughout both Kingdoms, parties and celebrations were already under way. Those who could not attend the main ceremony waved and cheered as they watched the synchronized fly-over of the two chariots. Millions of flower petals showered down like summer rain, released by the hundreds of morning doves that flew behind them.

When the golden chariots finally landed, both couples, led by

Courage and Gertie, walked through the enormous assemblage on a flower-laden path. Five bridesmaids—Tara, Leanne, Selena, Margay, and Mylea—followed Kandide and Jake. Five more bridesmaids followed Lord Mywerk and Cyndara—three were her ladies-in-waiting and two were members of her Ruling Council. General Slant stood as Lord Mywerk's best man, and Benji as Jake's.

Egan proudly walked behind them, carrying one royal purple and one royal blue satin pillow, each displaying sets of matching gold wedding rings. Cyndara's ring sparkled with a large emerald, and Kandide's with a deep purple-blue sapphire that perfectly matched her eyes. Glistening diamonds surrounded both center stones.

The Banshee royal gemsmiths, who were the best in all the land, made the four rings. Cyndara and Lord Mywerk presented them to Jake and Kandide as wedding gifts. In return, Kandide's royal seam-stresses, who were also considered the best in all the land, made their wedding attire.

Thousands watched in awe as the spectacular processional stepped onto a circular platform that had been constructed in the exact center of the neutral zone. It was adorned with peach gladiolas, blue and green hydrangeas, purple orchids, and sweet smelling white frilly jasmine. Mother Nature's gift of a spring-like day radiated with warmth, as four rainbows crisscrossed the sky, painting it with shimmering prisms of color. Overhead, a canopy of monarch butterflies shaded the couples from the afternoon sun.

Lord Socrat stepped onto the platform to pronounce their vows—a ceremony written by both couples. It concluded with the exchanging of rings and their first kiss as husband and wife. The assemblage erupted in cheers. Who would have thought that such harmony could prevail? Everyone's attention was quickly diverted to the butterflies overhead, who took flight to reveal a fireworks display that lit up each of the four Kingdoms in Calabiyau.

On a second platform, the delicate strains of a harpist soon replaced the booming fireworks. Lady Jennáe, of the Creativity Clan, had written a special song for the couples' first dance. Her amazing voice and incredible skills on the violin complimented the harp so beautifully that even the songbirds stopped to listen. Everyone begged her to perform it again so they also could dance to it.

Tara, who was Kandide's maid of honor, reluctantly agreed to wear a dress for the ceremonies. Much to Tiyana's chagrin, she quickly changed into trousers as soon as the partying began.

"But you looked so gorgeous," Tiyana argued.

"Looking gorgeous is Kandide's job, Mother. I did my duty, now it's time to be me again." She ran off to dance with Benji.

"When are they going to cut the cake?" Egan asked Lord Aron, eyeing the nearly two-meter tall ginger-spice wedding cake with its fluffy white frosting, purple flowers, and swirls of fresh raspberries, blackberries, and blueberries. Margay made it and he knew it would taste as wonderful as it looked.

"Soon," he replied, looking at his son's plate piled high with exotic food. "Are you still hungry? That's your second helping."

"I know, but everything's so good. I never had Banshee cooking before. It's really spicy, and I love it." He took another bite of curried sweet potato soufflé. "Did you try this? We need to get the chefs at the Castle to make it."

"So you like Banshee food? Trace asked, having joined them. "Try the spicy cranberry pumpkin bread. That's my favorite."

"Okay!" Egan hurried over to the massive buffet tables in search of this new treat.

Trace smiled. "You know, Lord Aron, I'm really happy Egan lives with you. But I have to say, I kind of miss him at the Château."

"We all miss him," Selena said, as she walked up to them. "How about a dance, Trace?"

"Uh... How about you dance with Lord Rössi. I, uh... have to help Egan find the cranberry pumpkin bread." He shot off in the direction of the buffet tables.

"I would love to dance with you, Selena." Lord Rössi took her arm and escorted her to the crowded dance floor. "I hope there's room."

Kandide and Jake hadn't sat down since their first dance. As he twirled her around, she spotted a boy Teren's age watching them. He was carrying a young girl, about three or four years old, she guessed. The little girl's arms were wrapped around a doll with a pink dress and charred wings.

Kandide stopped dancing. "Just a minute, Jake. There's someone I need to talk to."

General Mintz was immediately by her side. "That's the farm boy who tried to kill you," he whispered. "I'll have him arrested."

"No, please, General. I want to talk to him." Kandide approached the lad. "Hello. I'm glad you are well."

His eyes shifted to the floor, then back up to hers. He quickly bowed. "I... I came to apologize to you, Your Majesty, and give you this." The farm boy handed her a chain with a tiny gold replica of the doll suspended from it. "I made it from some of the gold you sent. You see, this is my sister. I found her in the next village."

"That's... that's so incredibly wonderful." Kandide's eyes sparkled with joy. "What's your name?" she asked the little girl.

"Kenna. When I grow up, I want to be just like you."

"Thank you, but you should be just like you, Kenna. A sweet wonderful young lady." Kandide looked back at the farm boy. "I'm so happy you were able to find her. And thank you so much for this beautiful gift. Seeing your sister here with you, however, is the best gift I could have. You didn't need to give me anything else."

"I wanted you to know that I'm really sorry for what I did. After I woke up from the sleeping spell, I went to our neighboring village and discovered she was still alive. Kenna told me that she saw a lady whose wings were made of fire making the houses explode, and that our parents were able to transport her to our friends who live in the next village, just before our house blew up. They stayed behind because they were trying to find our brother. They didn't make it out."

"I'm so sorry." The anguish Kandide felt the first time she met the boy resurged like a dagger being thrust into her heart. "So very sorry."

"Me too. I could have killed you—and everyone else in our world. Thank you for letting me go." With Kenna still in his arms, he turned and walked away.

"Wait a minute," Kandide called, rushing after them. But they had disappeared into the crowd. She looked at the tiny gold doll suspended on its matching chain, then at Jake and General Mintz, who had followed her. "This has to be the most wonderful wedding present I could ever imagine." Kandide handed the necklace to Jake to fasten around her neck. "I can't tell you how happy I am right now. It's as though the fates have blessed our entire world with love."

"They've certainly blessed me," Jake told her.

"And blessed me with both of you," General Mintz said.

"That they did," Kandide teased. "Come on, you two, let's find Cyndara and Lord Mywerk and cut the cake or Egan will never forgive me."

"Good idea." Jake, along with General Mintz hurried after her.

Following the cake cutting—that included a large slice for Egan, which he quickly devoured—he, Teren, and Adriana danced to almost every song the orchestra played—some with each other and some with their friends from the Château, as well as the apprentice wizards from the Bardic Temple.

Each member of the High Council from both Kingdoms was also there, and traded dances as though they had never been enemies. Even Viviana and Centrod waltzed around the pearl-white dance floor until both were exhausted.

Ari and his pack, along with many of the forest's other animals also joined in on the fun, bringing their own special gifts for the royal couples. Squirrels brought baskets of nuts. Deer presented them with rare purple mushrooms from deep within the forest, and the bees honored them with heart-shaped honeycombs. The entire world was at peace, simply enjoying these magical moments.

The feasting, fun, and dancing, the likes of which no one had ever seen, lasted until the first rays of sunlight blossomed through the towering pines.

Holding Kandide in his arms, Jake gazed into her purple-blue eyes and softly kissed her. "I love you, Kandide."

"I love you, too, Jake. I always have and I always will."

From a vantage point hidden among the trees, one Fée did not join in. "Enjoy this moment, dear Queen. My day will come." In a blaze of scarlet, Lady Aron was gone.

To be continued...

EPILOGUE

Ninon pulled the red cotton sweater over her head. She was already late for school on the Monday after she and Ms. Lee arrived back in Las Vegas, but couldn't stop listening to the early morning news reports. "Hey, Mom, come here," she called, switching channels on the TV in her bedroom. "Guess what they're saying now."

Each station featured a story about the Zion sinkhole. This particular report wasn't just talking about the mysterious disappearance of a "family of Shakespearian actors"—which made her laugh—it focused on how the sinkhole appeared and then vanished without a trace.

Since the hundreds of photos and videos that were taken were all completely blurred, no one had any physical proof that the incident ever happened. Many who weren't actually there to see it relegated the entire story to just another Zion legend, but the reporter on this particular news station had a completely different take.

"Can you believe what she's saying?" Ninon asked her mother. "That it was an invasion by aliens. And the flash of light everyone saw was a space ship swooping down and absconding with us."

"Well, Ni," her mother replied, "you have to admit, your story is just as unbelievable."

"Except she has proof." Ninon's brother, Felix, pointed to her foot.

"That she does." Their mother wasn't sure what to believe. A visit to Calabiyau was more than she could comprehend, but then Ni's foot was completely normal. A few days later, she took her daughter to the doctor to see if he had an explanation. He was equally as amazed. So were Ms. Lee's doctors who simply could not believe her remarkable healing. An "inexplicable miracle" was the best explanation anyone in the medical profession could come up with for either of them.

Four months later, Ninon was accepted on the girls' soccer team, and helped her school win the state championship. The following year, her mother passed the state bar examine and was hired by a high profile law firm where she embarked on her lifelong dream of providing legal aid to battered women.

Ninon decided she wanted to become a doctor and bring awareness of Leanne's approach to healing into modern day medicine. Ishan, while in high school, started his own successful marketing company. And Kathy went on to study physics, specializing in multi-dimensional research. They have remained good friends and are hopeful that, someday, they can find a way to return to Calabiyau.

Ms. Lee became the principle of her school, and in just two years elevated it to the highest rated elementary school in the U.S. She was also asked to serve on the President's Advisory Council for Education.

Ms. Lee, Ninon, Kathy, and Ishan also became close friends with Diana Zimmerman, who, with their input, began her fourth book in the *Calabiyau Chronicles* series. Other than what they told her, Diana still does not know where the facts about this magical land come from or how she knows the information. Fortunately, for her fans, however, the story continues...

After completing a business book on Branding, Diana began book four, *Kandide: The Mirrors of Betrayal*. It takes place ten years in the future. Kandide and Jake have two children—a son and a daughter, who is even more vain than Kandide was at her age. Egan reunites with Alin, only to discover that Lady Aron has turned his twin brother against him. Alin's magic, now evil and dark, rivals Teren's, and so the struggle for power escalates with entirely new levels of treachery.

ABOUT THE CHARACTERS

KANDIDE

Age:	19 (in human years)
Height:	5'5"
Eyes:	Purple-blue
Hair:	Gold and platinum
Hobbies:	Archery, aercaen, swimming
Heroes:	King Toeyad and myself, of course.
Favorite Book:	"I love them all."
Quote:	"What good is a Queen if she hides in her Castle?"

JAKE

Age:	27 (in human years)
Height:	5'11"
Eyes:	Green
Hair:	Black
Hobbies:	Archery, swimming, reading, and dancing
Heroes:	King Toeyad, Selena, Trace, Ari
Favorite Book:	Book Two: *Kandide: The Lady's Revenge*
Quote:	"Imperfects are equal by law, but not everyone accepts us."

PRINCESS TARA

Age:	17 (in human years)
Height:	5'4"
Eyes:	Green
Hair:	Auburn
Hobbies:	Healing, saving forest animals, and keeping her brother and sister out of trouble.
Heroes:	Selena, Queen Tiyana.
Favorite Book:	Book Three: *Kandide: The Masks of Deception*
Quote:	"Egan, you're brilliant."

LADY ARON

Age:	*None of your business!*
Height:	5'6"
Eyes:	Amber and blue
Hair:	Flaming
Hobbies:	Archery, politics, and spells
Heroes:	Me. Who else?
Favorite Book:	Book Two: *Kandide: The Lady's Revenge*
Quote:	"The problem with integrity is that I don't play by those rules."

PRINCE TEREN

Age:	14 (in human years)
Height:	5'4"
Eyes:	Yellow-brown
Hair:	Sandy blond
Hobbies:	Spell-making, pranks, wizardry, aercaen
Heroes:	Merlin, Viviana, and most other wizards.
Favorite Book:	Book Two: *Kandide: The Lady's Revenge*
Quote:	"What's patience got to do with anything?"

LEANNE

Age:	21 (in human years)
Height:	5'3"
Eyes:	Brown
Hair:	Dark brown
Hobbies:	Healing, dancing, singing
Heroes:	Selena, Jake, Trust, Ari.
Favorite Book:	Book One: *Kandide: The Secret of the Mists*
Quote:	"We won't know until we try."

TIYANA

Age:	49 (in human years)
Height:	5'5"
Eyes:	Purple-blue
Hair:	Auburn
Hobbies:	Painting, hiking, and poetry
Heroes:	King Toeyad.
Favorite Book:	Book Three: *Kandide: The Masks of Deception*
Quote:	"We all wear masks of deception. Some for good, some for bad."

EGAN

Age:	6 (in human years)
Height:	4'9"
Eyes:	Blue
Hair:	Honey brown
Hobbies:	Swimming and reading
Heroes:	Jake, Selena, Lord Aron
Favorite Book:	Book One: *Kandide: The Secret of the Mists*
Quote:	"No matter what she's done, she's still my mother."

GARGLAN

Age:	37 (in human years)
Height:	5' (to his horns)
Eyes:	Red
Hair:	Brown and black patches
Hobbies:	Eating Fée
Heroes:	Me
Favorite Book:	Book Four: (Maybe we win in that one)
Quote:	"Grrrr... Hisssss!"

SELENA

Age:	49 (in human years)
Height:	5'5"
Eyes:	Purple-blue
Hair:	Auburn
Hobbies:	Helping Imperfects, growing grapes
Heroes:	Jake, King Toeyad, Ari, Leanne
Favorite Book:	Book One: *Kandide: The Secret of the Mists*
Quote:	"We don't judge here, even if the handicap is ignorance or prejudice."

GENERAL KANDOUR

Age:	65 (in human years)
Height:	5'11"
Eyes:	Brown
Hair:	Salt & pepper
Hobbies:	Raiding villages
Heroes:	Myself
Favorite Book:	Book Two: *Kandide: The Lady's Revenge*
Quote:	"Listen to their screams. It's like a medley of macabre."

LORD MYWERK

Age:	57 (in human years)
Height:	5'11"
Eyes:	Brown
Hair:	Dark auburn
Hobbies:	Magic and Chessaé
Heroes:	Merlin, Viviana
Favorite Book:	Book Three: *Kandide: The Masks of Deception*
Quote:	"As in life, you must stay focused on the solution. Not the problem."

LORD ARON

Age:	50 (in human years)
Height:	5'10"
Eyes:	Brown
Hair:	Black
Hobbies:	Archery and entomology
Heroes:	King Toeyad, Egan, Queen Tiyana
Favorite Book:	Book One: *Kandide: The Secret of the Mists*
Quote:	"This isn't over, Firenza."

ANILE THE ASSASSIN

Age:	57 (in human years)
Height:	5'10"
Eyes:	Brown
Hair:	Black
Hobbies:	Collecting ears
Heroes:	General Kandour
Favorite Book:	Book Three: *Kandide: The Masks of Deception*
Quote:	"Or in some home for the nearly dead."

TRACE

Age:	50 (in human years)
Height:	5'10"
Eyes:	Brown
Hair:	Black
Hobbies:	Inventing strange contraptions
Heroes:	Jake, Selena, Leanne
Favorite Book:	Book Three: *Kandide: The Masks of Deception*
Quote:	"I would rather die than turn the Château over to that maniacal traitor."

ALIN

Age:	6 (in human years)
Height:	4'9"
Eyes:	Blue
Hair:	Honey brown
Hobbies:	Magic, archery, and reading
Heroes:	Lady and Lord Aron
Favorite Book:	Book Two: *Kandide: The Lady's Revenge*
Quote:	"Prince Teren's not the only one with the Talent.

CYNDARA

Age:	29 (in human years)
Height:	5'6"
Eyes:	Golden
Hair:	Black
Hobbies:	Spells, Chessaé, cooking
Heroes:	Lord Mywerk, Leanne
Favorite Book:	Book Three: *Kandide: The Masks of Deception*
Quote:	"Hope is for fools."

ADRIANA

Age:	14 (in human years)
Height:	5'2"
Eyes:	Golden brown
Hair:	Black
Hobbies:	Magic and reading
Heroes:	Viviana and Centrod
Favorite Book:	Book Two: *Kandide: The Lady's Revenge*
Quote:	"Don't you know the secret of a labyrinth?"

VIVIANA

Age:	46 (in human years)
Height:	5'6"
Eyes:	Brown
Hair:	Black
Hobbies:	Magic and spells
Heroes:	The Faery Vivian, Merlin, Centrod
Favorite Book:	Book Three: *Kandide: The Masks of Deception*
Quote:	"Until you are free from relying on your magic, you cannot control its power."

LADY BATONY

Age:	68 (in human years)
Height:	5'6"
Eyes:	Hazel
Hair:	Auburn
Hobbies:	Music, storytelling
Heroes:	My mother
Favorite Book:	Book Two: *Kandide: The Lady's Revenge*
Quote:	"When I was a young girl..."

LORD ROSSI

Age:	47 (in human years)
Height:	5'10"
Eyes:	Brown
Hair:	Brown
Hobbies:	History, philosophy, politics
Heroes:	King Toeyad, Queen Tiyana.
Favorite Book:	Book Two: *Kandide: The Lady's Revenge*
Quote:	"In the world of royal politics, heart rarely matters."

GENERAL MINTZ

Age:	67 (in human years)
Height:	5'11"
Eyes:	Brown
Hair:	Silver
Hobbies:	Dancing, poetry, military history
Heroes:	King Toeyad, Queen Tiyana.
Favorite Book:	Book Three: *Kandide: The Masks of Deception*
Quote:	"Revenge is the most corrosive of all emotions."

MATARI

Age:	96 (in human years)
Height:	5'10"
Eyes:	Brown
Hair:	Silver
Hobbies:	Military history, storytelling, fiddle playing
Heroes:	Selena, King Toeyad, Queen Tiyana.
Favorite Book:	Book Three: *Kandide: The Masks of Deception*
Quote:	"Revenge is the most corrosive of all emotions."

RECIPES
OF
CALABIYAU

FAVORITES OF EGAN,
TARA, AND JAKE

Rosemary Swirl Soup

This tasty vegan beet and potato soup is Egan's favorite. Calabiyau's Castle chefs make it with a touch of rosemary and swirls of rich creamy coconut milk. The results are, as Egan says, "Soooo good!"

Perfect for for any meal, it's also quick and easy to make.

Ingredients

3 medium organic potatoes

5 medium organic beets

1 organic sweet onion

2 tablespoons extra virgin organic olive oil

1 teaspoon rosemary

½ teaspoon garlic powder

½ teaspoon salt

1 ½ cups organic vegetable broth

1 cup extra thick creamy coconut milk

Directions

Peel and quarter the beets and potatoes. Boil until soft. While they are cooking, chop the onion and lightly sauté it in a saucepan with the olive oil, rosemary, garlic, and salt until the pieces becomes translucent.

Place the beets, potatoes, onions, and vegetable broth in a blender or food processor. Blend until smooth. Pour the mixture back into a saucepan and simmer. Remove from the heat and swirl ¾ cup of the extra thick coconut milk into the soup.

SERVING

Dish the soup into bowls. Add a dollop of the remaining coconut milk in the center, or using a knife blade, draw it into a heart or other shape. Serve as a starter or as a main course with a salad.

LEANNE'S WILD 4-BERRY PECAN CRUST TART

This wonderful vegan desert is a favorite at the Château. The pie-sized tasty tarts dissappear as soon as Margay makes them.

INGREDIENTS - FILLING

1 cup organic blueberries

1 cup organic blackberries

1 cup organic raspberries

1 cup organic cranberries

¼ cup organic sugar

¼ cup cornstarch

INGREDIENTS - CRUST

2½ cups pecans

½ cup melted coconut oil

¼ teaspoon ground cinnamon

¼ cup coconut flour

¼ cup brown sugar

DIRECTIONS

Preheat oven to 375°F. Grind the pecans in a food processor until fine. Add the coconut flour, cinnamon, and brown sugar. Blend thoroughly. Fold in the melted coconut oil. Mix until the ingredients are crumbly. If the mixture is too dry, add 1 to 2 tablespoons of water. Press into a 9 inch glass pie dish, leaving one third of the mixture for the top crust.

Gently toss the berries with the sugar and cornstarch, then place into the pie crust. Spoon the remaining pecan crumble on top of the berry mixture, pressing around the edges. Bake for approx. 40 minutes or until the berries are bubbling and the crust is golden brown.

SERVING

Serve warm with a scoop or two of vegan vanilla ice cream.

Leanne and the children of the Château love to gather around the large fireplace in the Main Hall, eat 4-Berry Pecan Crust Tarts, and tell funny stories.

*Wild Four-Berry
Pecan Crust Tart*

LADY CAROL'S MAGICAL SALAD

Tara's favorite lunch is a vegan delight. The chefs make Lady Carol's amazing recipe for her almost every day. It is full of nutritious and tasty fruits, nuts, and vegetables. And every bite is a magical adventure. Tara loves it with a cup of hot mint or ginger tea.

INGREDIENTS

½ cup organic greens – spinach, kale, arugula
1 organic celery stalk
3 organic broccoli florets
3 organic cauliflower florets
3 organic white mushrooms
1 organic beet
Shredded vegan mozzarella cheese
8 organic raspberries
¼ cup organic blueberries
6 organic blackberries
3 artichoke hearts
3 black olives (pitted)
3 cornichon pickles
1 hearts of palm
1 avocado
¼ cup chopped walnuts
¼ cup pine nuts

DRESSING

Organic olive oil
Balsamic vinegar

DIRECTIONS

Cut greens, celery, mushrooms, broccoli, cauliflower, heart of palm, avocado, cornichon pickles, artichoke hearts, olives, and beets into bite-sized pieces. Toss lightly. Add berries, chopped walnuts, and top with shredded vegan mozzarella cheese and pine nuts.

SERVING

Toss with balsamic vinegar and olive oil. Enjoy with mint tea.

LADY CAROL'S MAGICAL SALAD

CONTINUE THE FUN...

Games, Shopping, Music

Stories that continue the Adventure

More great Recipes

Contests

Teachers' Guides

Downloadable Artwork

Talk to Diana

And so much more at:

WWW.KANDIDE.COM

ABOUT THE AUTHOR

DIANA S. ZIMMERMAN

Like her novels, Diana's role in the performing arts as well as in the business world transcends the ordinary. She has been a performer, writer, and businesswoman since the age of eight, when she invested all of her resources into a small magic trick.

With a capital outlay of forty-seven cents, Diana parlayed her investment into a spectacular 25-year career as "America's Foremost Lady Magician."

She continues to be a highly respected teacher, lecturer, writer, and mentor in the world of magic. Diana sponsors a teenage magician's group—an organization she founded with the help of the legendary actor, Cary Grant, at Hollywood's famous Magic Castle. Magic superstars such as David Copperfield, Criss Angel, Lance Burton, and Collins Key, among others, have performed illusions invented by Diana.

Her transition into the corporate world saw the creation of CMS Communications Intl., a marketing communications agency whose clients include many of the Fortune 500. She is the CEO of CMS, and is considered to be an expert on Branding and Competitive Positioning. Diana is a much sought-after consultant and lecturer in both fields.

She has authored eight books—three novels, one coloring book, two business books, and two biographies. Diana is an avid collector of faery art. Some of her pieces date back to the 1700s. She is also vegan and a passionate animal rights activist.

MORE BRAVESHIP BOOKS